Stardogs

DAVE FREER

DEDICATION

This book is dedicated to the memory of the Old English Sheepdogs who have been the loves of my life, and whose loyalty is the original inspiration for Stardogs.

CONTENTS

Author's notes:

The Future History, and notes on the Empire, Denaari Homeworld, and the major protagonist groups are contained in the appendices at the end of the book. My thanks go to many people who read, advised, proofread and offered support for this book. Any errors are mine, not theirs. My especial thanks as usual go to Barbara, and, of course, to the dog at my feet, the nose touching my forearm, the loving eyes looking at me through the fringe.

PROLOGUE
BEGINNINGS AND BEGINNINGS

Everyone, everything, is from somewhere. To see into their future you must look back to their past. For the root, though hidden, is what gives rise to the plant.

Introduction to the third Veda of Kali-dewa and all the Saints.

Every story has many beginnings. Where does anything start? Well, you might say that this story began forty-three thousand years ago with a wild pack and a savage, brutal hunt. It was before the beginning of recorded human history. Before the rise and fall of two star-spanning empires. Before microscopic things destroyed not one but two sentient species. A time when the great packs used to roam freely across the empty spaces…

The feral pack hunted one of their own with a terrible, ferocious intensity. The old one, great, gaunt and silvered, struggled desperately to reach the distant rocks. Perhaps they would offer refuge, perhaps a place to stand against the younger males who wanted to pull him down and kill him. He gave his all to the flight.

Yet despite this, the pack were gaining. The faster young males ripped cruelly at his exposed flanks. He tried to turn, baring

1

his huge, chipped and yellowing fangs. He was too slow. Even a few months back it would have been different. The younger ones with their sharp new teeth closed in. Briefly, all too briefly, he managed to hold them at bay.

They weren't dogs. Nor even wolves. Not even remotely related. Yet, because of convergent evolution, very like them in some ways. They did not roam the empty plains of Earth, but the depths of deep space. Here, on Earth, evolution has filled every niche under the heavens. Inevitably, somewhere, around a distant star, she didn't stop when she got to the heavens.

The Alien sample-ship got there at last. It was too late to save the old pack leader. Despite knowing this the Denaari nest-minder pilot aimed at the squabbling, tearing beasts, trying to drive them off.

The pack scattered. In space they could neither snarl nor yelp, so in this way they differed from wild-dogs. Instead they bared fangs and circled. It was dangerous place to be, for the huge walrus-like tusky teeth of the space-dogs were not only used for pack hierarchy duels and mating fights. They could also rip chunks off asteroids as mineral sources. One bite from one of creatures could shatter the fragile chitin-silicate-metal shell of the little craft. Besides, flying something with metals in it into this situation was like riding a steak into a crocodile tank. If just one of the dogs swooped in and wrapped itself around the unarmed craft, then its belly cilia would cold-weld onto it. In a few minutes it could electrochemically leach out of the tasty hull-metals. The silica-metallo-chitin bonds would part. The ship would be gone in puff of disintegrating dust and space-lost air.

However, the feral space-dogs were alarmed too by this sudden alien intrusion in their realm. They showed no real sign of fight, and when the ship darted at one that came too close, they instead jetted away. The pack gradually drifted off toward the clump of asteroids that the old one had been trying to reach.

They left the dead creature hanging like a shredded blanket in the void.

The Denaari could not cry. Instead the eight emotionally traumatised nest-minders on the sample-ship chewed their wing tips and moaned softly as they huddling together. Proximity to the ferocity and cruelty of the killing hurt.

The two egg-layers, less emotionally sensitive, had already donned protective gear and gone out to see whether they could recover some of the creature's cells intact.

Later, in the together-hanging of roost, the ship matriarch reassured her still-distraught nest-minder mates. She promised that the creatures they would breed from the reservoir of cells now held in *in vitro* storage units down in the hold of the tiny ship, would be gentle. They would be creatures that the nest-minders would love. The smaller nest-minders gibbered doubtfully. She enfolded them in her wings.

They quieted, but she knew she must make good her promise. Should the nest-minders decide that she was callous, they would withhold their warmth from her gene-line. Still, the alien matriarch pondered, it was worth the risk. With the space-dog genetic material she could create something of immense value. The creatures were perfectly equipped for life in deep space. They had excellent bifocal visual imaging, with eyes that resembled oil-lens telescopes, but with better and more precise control. Their gravity-detecting organo-metallic nerve-net was complex and hypersensitive. They even had some small amount of wormhole surfing capacity. The genes could be teased, changed and manipulated. The result would allow her species to reach out their wing-claws to the stars.

●●C●●●

Step forward forty-two thousand years.

The vast, gentle Stardogs, who could leap the impossible distances between stars with the ease that a Jacana does the seemingly improbable trot across floating lily pads, had given the Denaari the stars. But now... the adored Denaari were gone. The Stardogs were lonely.

Some still cruised the routes between the now empty star systems. Systems their masters had colonized and later fled from in their panic. Yet, they were forever forbidden to go back to the distant Solar system that had spawned them and which was the only place they could breed.

Sometimes one would even return to visit a boring G0 type star in the vicinity of Sirius. The masters had had a field station there.

Then, after thousands of years, there was a ship...

●●C●●●

The planet the masters had visited here had never been a potential colony. It was too wet and too high G, to be worth it. But it had a sentient alien species on it. The Denaari had been observing this species. *Homo sapiens* had not been space-traveling at that time, but, as the nest-minders always said, it was

3

better to withdraw warmth from the egg, than the new hatched chick. The Stardogs rarely visited this system. Without their beloved masters the Stardogs preferred hotter suns, with far more sweet ultraviolet to bathe their back-cilia in, or systems more cluttered with tasty Lanthanide-rich fragments. Still, it had been one of the last posts abandoned, so still they came, once every half century or so. Lonely. Miserable.

Then they would drift away again, star-surfing back to the once crowded inner Denaari worlds. Only this time... The Stardog who came, planning on drifting the asteroid belt for something tasty... saw a bright-metal asteroid. An asteroid under power. Joy stirred and leaped along with her hopes. Along the far edge of the Stardog, the chemical reactions for rarely used flatulent rocketry began. With the consummate precision achieved by having several billion nerve inputs feedback-looped through half a million nerve nodes, the ten kilometer diameter bearskin rug accelerated toward the Mars-exploration vessel *EU Gloria Mundi*. Maybe if the Stardog had encountered the *US Ronald Reagan* instead, the future might have been very different. As it was the EU and their friends to delight in reducing the US and its allies to second-class powers. The US was subsumed into the world and then galaxy spanning Empire that this chance incident caused. Her people — or at least those that dreamed of freedom — moved or were transported out to the colony worlds like New Texas. Their dreams of liberty were suppressed, but not destroyed.

●●●つ●●

People and their pets tend to resemble each other. Usually in outlook, but often even physically. This is particularly true when the bond is close. Joan Cheng, the life support engineer of the EU sponsored Mars-explorer, had kept and adored a St. Bernard. A big, lugubrious-eyed, slightly overweight St. Bernard bitch called Matilda, who was terrified of thunder and quite a lot of other things. It said quite a lot about Joan. And right now she was lonely and miserable to the absolute core of her being. She had gone from the heights of happiness to the depths of despair. A week ago her cup had been overflowing. She, a deaf, too bright, Eurasian girl, had won a place on the long-delayed Mars exploration voyage. Yes... she had two PhD's, but studying had meant escape from the misery of a home where cultures had clashed and used her as their pawn. She'd never thought she'd get accepted... Then, she'd been in love. She had been deliriously happy, the happiness transforming her normally stolid face.

Captain Johannes 'Hans' DeMari Wienan. Handsome. Blond. Smooth talking. Captain of the vessel. He was a political appointee, true, but he was a rising man in the European Parliament. And he, in one of the few private spots on a crowded ship, had introduced her to sex. It had provided that physical contact she'd desperately needed for so long.

Looking back now, she was sure it hadn't been love. Not from Hans, the idol of thousands of girls, Earth-side. Just incidental lust. He'd popped into her hydroponics room on a routine inspection, or perhaps seeking the one place on the ship that you didn't have to share with three others. They were forced close by the high-racked narrow corridor between the plant-racks. As she had tried to step past him, terribly aware of his presence, his hand had brushed across her breast. Or maybe she'd brushed her breast across his hand... Anyway, her eager response had been electric and unplanned. She'd been ashamed, embarrassed. He'd been aroused. And he'd known exactly what to do. It had been a heady couple of weeks. A secret couple of weeks... but not secret enough in that tight community. They all thought that because she was deaf they could say what they liked.

She could lip-read.

The heat had got to politically sensitive Hans too. He'd avoided her, suddenly and without explanation. At first she'd rationalized his behavior... still believed he loved her. A catty exchange with the girl from the reactor room changed that. It was a cruel, barbed interchange, between a jealous ex-conquest, and an emotionally insecure deaf girl. Joan didn't know how loudly she was shouting. Half of the solar system must have heard her, never mind the fifty thousand cubic feet of the ship. The inevitable *letter*, on a ship whose living space you could cross in a sauntering two minutes, had come, appearing mysteriously on her tiny desk. Her tears had obscured the stupid, mundane, noncommittal words with which he'd buried their pyrotechnic physical relationship. *"I hope we can still remain friends..."* How do you say that to someone whose life you've just ruined?

Then, when it seemed that the blackness could get no deeper, in the routine two-hourly radio coms with earth had come the news that her Matilda was dead. Just that. You don't waste off-planet radio coms with details of unimportant irrelevancies like ill pets.

She stared into the void in the bleakness that precedes suicide. Her eyes were cried dry now. Looking out at the too clear unblinking stars she tried to face the question: How do you kill yourself when your death will mean that 23 other people must die, slowly and cruelly, as the fragile life support system fails?

She couldn't hear the alarm bell. She was so absorbed in her relentless peering into space that she didn't see the panicky flashing of the warning lights. Condition red lights. All she saw was that the emptiness outside her tiny view-port was full of an eye, a huge beer-brown soft eye. Deeper than oceans. Full of care. And she could feel the love, the unquestioning love of a lost dog who has found its most important person.

People who don't know dogs are often frightened by really big dogs. This merely displays their ignorance. When you're breeding animals the size of a small cart horse you'd better selectively breed for gentleness. For real trouble, medium-sized dogs-German Shepherds, Dobermans — that sort of thing — are more dangerous, and for sheer-nasty mindedness the little snappers take the lead. A Pekinese is infinitely more likely to bite you than a St. Bernard is. Owners of crocodile-jawed bull-terriers can actually describe the monstrous beasts as 'soppy old things, really' with perfect accuracy. Toddlers can take sticky- fingered liberties with walk-underable Great Danes that would have a Toy Pom in snarling apoplexy. The toddler's greatest danger is either being knocked over by accident, or being licked to death. Of course, you don't threaten the big dog's owner, or the owner's territory, unless you're tired of life. The only thing that could possibly be more dangerous is to hurt the dog. Then the besotted *owner* will probably kill you.

Those in the control room of the *Gloria Mundi* didn't know much about big dogs. They were frightened. Frantic messages to Ground Control with a twenty minute delay weren't going to help, and the *Gloria Mundi* carried no weapons.

Joan Cheng, however, knew a big soppy dog when she saw one. The panicking crew failed to notice an airlock being cycled, as they tried to move and assemble a geological-laser, which the Stardog would have found rather pleasant. The first the crew knew of it was when someone caught sight of the tiny white-suited figure actually climbing up between the Stardog's eyes.

At first they thought it to be some suicidal, brave hero. It was only when someone thought to switch into the suit radio frequency that they heard her say in flat, nasal, yet adoring tones "You beautiful, gorgeous girl. Oh, you beautiful, beautiful girl," as she lovingly stroked the filaments. If the ship had been further off they would have been able to see the ten mile long creature ripple and squirm with pleasure. The control room began frantically signaling to her. She ignored the LED display frenetically flashing across the top of her suit's vision plate.

Telepathy is little understood, and both the League and the Empire have long quashed any research into this area. Evidence of its occurrence existed long before humans encountered Stardogs, however. The evidence was fragmentary, the manifestations of the phenomenon diverse. The one common thread in all the scattered bits of information about the subject, is that it is inevitably tied to emotional states. Many dog owners will swear their pets are telepathic. Well, Stardogs are. They were bred that way.

Stardogs aren't very intelligent, but their diffuse minds have billions of gigabytes of storage and processing ability. Human telepathic output was different from that of the Denaari nest minders, but not so different that the Stardog could not understand that it was getting the love it had missed so badly. Communication had begun. Image to image at first. The adored new master wanted to go to that red planet - it would oblige. Well, not that red planet, but a similar one. The Denaari star routes imprinted in her hadn't included the nearby red planet, but there was one in the vicinity of Centaurus that was similar, at least in color.

The terrified crew of the *Gloria Mundi* found their ship enfolded in the outer mantle of the Stardog. Seated between the huge eyes, Joan Cheng rode the starswirl and became the first human to ever experience the mind jarring beauty and terror of wormhole surf. She wasn't frightened out of her wits, for the simple reason that the Stardog wasn't. Fortunately it was not too far, as distances in theta-space go. Her suit-tanks and suit insulation held out, although she was cold when they arrived. The red planet below them was indeed like Mars, in color, if not in potential for human habitability. This desert world had a humanly breathable atmosphere. It also had extensive ruins, of such size that they were even visible from space. The Stardog wriggled in pleasure at her amazement. It was much *better* than the other red planet, wasn't it? The old masters had liked this world very much. They used to bring the Stardogs such delicious little mineral tit-bits up from the gravity well...would she? Pleeeze?

●●●◕◕◕

Hans Wienan looked down on the alien world and was filled, not with wonderment and delight as were his fellows, but with chagrin. Why couldn't this have happened a week ago when he'd had the dummy under his thumb? Here was the key to ultimate power. He had to grasp it. He turned on one of the ooh ing and ah ing crew. He selected a slight Indian girl, with whom the dummy had a vague friendship. "Go out there. Get her to come in. She'll freeze if she stays out there."

The girl looked at him with the faint disdainful curl to her lip which was, eventually, in another story, to get her killed. "Why should you care?" She turned away to the viewports again.

He grabbed her roughly by the shoulder. Turned her to face him, and snarled quietly into her frightened eyes. "Because, you fool, I'll bet she is the only one who can control the creature. So, if she dies out there, we all die here. No way of getting home. Do you understand that?"

She nodded, silenced and frightened by the tiger that had slipped out from behind his normally smooth mask.

"Good. Now go." He thrust her away.

Shaken, she turned and went to the suit-locker.

The captain walked over to the ship's doctor and escorted that individual to his cubbyhole office.

ᐰᐰCᗡᐰᐰ

From the Stardog's back again, Joan looked regretfully back at the world they were leaving. She would have liked to go down there. To explore those ruins with her new friend. Sadly it could not be. For a Stardog to enter the gravity well was a one-way trip, the beloved one had explained, and anyway the doctor was in such pain... The poor man was grey-faced and writhing. She'd come back once she'd got Dr Da Silva home, she promised herself.

She had no idea that, back on Earth, the Stardog's whisking away of the *Gloria Mundi* had already saved many lives. A thousand petty conflicts and greed-wars stalled as the news raced around the globe. Humanity stood united in fear, vengeful, and ready to strike, when the Stardog popped out of theta-space to another drop-point much closer to Earth, released the spaceship and began drifting away toward the Trojan point. The Stardog needed a rest. It must feed for a while on the unfiltered sunlight of space. Two interstellar crossings in such short order had taxed its energy reserves... Also, after surf, there was always a certain amount of nerve-net damage to be repaired.

Joan had been so busy with concerns for the welfare of others, that she'd yet to turn a thought to herself, when the space suited figure came jetting over from the *Gloria Mundi.* Given a choice of *Homo sapiens*'s thirty billion people Hans Wienan was still the one she least wanted to see. She studiously ignored the voice-text printout appearing along the upper margin of her suit vision-plate.

When he was face to face she could no longer ignore him. He knew how well she could lip-read. "Come in, Joan. I need you."

"Go to hell, Hans. Leave me alone. You're upsetting my Stardog." Indeed the huge creature rippled, agitated.

It gave him the lever he needed. "Back on Earthside they're in panic. There are enough nukes being loaded onto launch-rockets right now to blow this alien monster of yours into component atoms. Stop being stupid. Come in, co-operate, and I'll see that no harm comes to it."

No other argument could have swayed her. She didn't realize that she was handing control of interstellar travel to one man. She didn't realize that she had just set the standard by which Hans Wienan's descendants would continue to control the Stardog riders... by threatening the well-being of their Stardogs. At first the methods were crude, such as a timed H-bomb attached to the beasts. As the Space Exploration and Development Control League, (later simply known as the Wienan League) took firmer control, this became refined. Each interstellar ship was fitted with special quarters for the rider and his or her League escort. The ships also had a torpedo tube aimed at the silicate life-form. Research on material taken from the filaments of the Stardog had produced a nerve toxin which would work on the great beasts. Painfully and terminally.

In the mean while Hans began the search for more emo-telepaths. He found them too. Often they were also suffering from a disability. And if not... he found it enhanced their receptivity if they were given one.

Some people will do anything for power. Others will do their bidding for money.

●●●つ●●

Joan Cheng spent the rest of her life incommunicado, except for one brief escape. There was an accident. One of those stupid things caused by driving too fast in London's thin slurry-rain. The driver, angry, got out. And failed to press central locking behind him. "You stupid bast..."

The man from the other car happened to be an amateur champion middle-heavyweight boxer. His car was only four hours old, and something he'd been saving for, for three years, so he could be forgiven for flattening Joan's driver. The security men on either side of her surged out of the car. One didn't even close his door. She was already around the corner before they noticed she'd gone.

The rain and the half-light of dusk favored her. But she wasn't even sure which city she was in. Scared and without any form of plan she ran blindly. Then, out of the gloom loomed the neon RSPCA sign. Joan had always been a loyal supporter of the organization — it was their shelter that her dog had come from. It was natural for her to turn to them with her troubles. The officer at the desk had his feet on it and a cup of instant soup in hand. He had a nice smile.

"Evening Ma'am. What can I do to help you?" He'd leapt up, rather embarrassed by being caught with his feet up. Like most of the population of earth who had access to TV, he'd seen acres of footage about the *Gloria Mundi* and many pictures of the crew, when the ship had abruptly disappeared. After the ship's return he'd seen acres of Hans Wienan, but none of the other crew members. He had an excellent memory for faces however. "I say, aren't you one of the crew of the spaceship that met those alien monsters?"

Her frightened face crumpled. She lip-read the words, but did not hear the admiring tone. "They're not MONSTERS!" she shouted. "They're gentle, wonderful animals. And they're being abused terribly. And you don't even CARE!" she sobbed.

"I...I am sorry. I don't really know anything about it. Look... tell me."

She needed no more invitation. She poured out the story of threats to the Stardogs, of Hans Wienan's hand-picked scientists' deliberate attempts to cause pain to the huge creatures. If they could hurt the Stardogs, they could use some kind of whip or spur to direct the beasts, instead of relying on Joan and the few like her that Hans had located to coax the dogs to fly between the stars.

She was still talking when seven suave men arrived. "Good evening Sir." The leader of the party produced an embossed plastic card. It identified him as James Johnstone, London Sector Chief of European Union Security. "This woman has escaped from our High Security Unit. She's... a danger to the public. Has she said much to you?"

The RSPCA officer thought fast, warned by the fear in her eyes. "No. She only just got here, you know. She was gabbling about star-travel and missing her dog. I thought she was deranged or something. I was trying to calm her down so I could 'phone the police. What was she on about?"

The security agent smiled, "Confidentially, Sir, she's as nutty as a fruit-cake. But..." he tapped his nose and winked, "highly placed relatives, you know."

They led Joan away. As soon as they were out of sight the officer immediately 'phoned his superior and passed on the gist of what she had said to him. That worthy might have taken no further notice if the desk-officer had not been coolly, clinically and effectively assassinated less than an hour later.

Thus the RSPCA became aware that the Space Exploration and Development Control League, the darling of governments and the opener of the starways to the human race, were actually conducting terrible and painful experiments on the Stardogs, attempting to find ways of controlling the beasts without the use of emo-telepathic riders. They also learned that Stardogs were not the alien and unfeeling sheets of silica they were being portrayed as, but sensitive and gentle creatures. Typically, Joan Cheng had not complained of her lot, nor of that of the other emotionally sensitive telepath riders Hans Wienan's minions had recruited. That the undercover RSPCA agents had to discover for themselves.

It was soon forcibly borne upon the good people of this and allied animal rights groups, that overt protest was terminal, and that public sympathy was heavily against them. The militant and lunatic fringe groups of animal rights activists and almost irreparably damaged public faith in them. They were - outside of the work with pets and shelter issues, lacking in credibility or popular support.

But they did not abandon Stardogs or their riders. They were forced to move this project underground, but it went on, slowly, carefully. It was to take centuries.

Of Joan Cheng's fate, little more is known, except that she disappeared in deep space with a Stardog. Perhaps she did finally escape.

●●●❍❍❍

This story rises from these deep roots. Parts of the story surfaced nearly 500 years later when man had colonized the whole of the corpse of the Denaari Empire, except the Denaari-Motherworld, a place to which the Stardogs could not, would not, return. It was a period of relative stability, but also of increasing hardship for the great mass of humanity.

CHAPTER 1
RIDERS AND NUMBER THREE'S

"Given the right conditions any human can become dangerous. After all, you can hammer in nails with a banana, if you dip the banana into liquid nitrogen first."

Obliterating a Prince: Nicola Para-Machiavelli

The little girl crawled, shivering, toward the only source of warmth in the shed next to the building. It was just below zero in here, yet the child was only wearing soiled undergarments. She was still bleeding from the lash-wounds on her back. The chained sled-dogs were huge and hungry. The child gave a brief frightened gasp of fear at the sight of the dark gleaming eyes in the fur mountain. The dogs growled, and then abruptly were stilled.

For no obvious reason she seemed reassured, and crawled forward. The dog and the bitch called her forward with anxious little whines. If it had not been for the chains they would have pulled her in. The bitch growled at her mate who was trying to sniff the child, and began to lick the wounds clean. Soon the girl was asleep, her thin arms wrapped around the bitch's neck. This child, who had cried herself to sleep most of her remembered life, slept now with a smile on her gaunt-boned face.

In the confines of a city, buildings go upwards, because there is no room to grow sideways. New technology must be evolved to allow them to do so. In the open spaces of the country buildings spread out. Methods of building remain the same generation after generation. In a similar fashion, now that the discovery of the Stardogs had freed mankind from the confines of Earth, and given them the vastness of the old Denaari Empire, social and technological evolution had stopped too. In some places it went backwards.

Here, on Prala 4, it had gone a long way backwards. Prala 4 had a high water-content for a Denaari world, but it was bitterly cold: the water was frozen; the air dry most of the time. What little human settlement there was ringed the equator, where water in liquid form could sometimes be found.

This hidden building was two thousand miles north of that. Even for Prala 4 what happened here was socially unacceptable. It was just as well that even the summer-time hunters didn't venture that far north.

In the warm observation room the white-coated Chief Psychologist looked through the double-glazed one-way glass at the sleeping child. She nodded in satisfaction. "We've got one."

"I'll bring her in then," said her assistant. He stood a hulking 6' 4" and his odor was thick and rank. It was he who administered the abuse. He enjoyed his work. He headed for the door.

She snorted. In this task you curbed all feelings. But she could not entirely curb her dislike for this... animal. "If you don't take a trank-gun with you those dogs'll kill you, you fool. She's an emotional telepath, and she has bonded with them."

The big man shrugged. "I'm not scared of dogs. But I don't want 'em hurting the merchandise."

He successfully tranked the two dogs. Although the bigger male managed to snap the chain in his efforts to reach the man, the tranquilliser was fairly fast and powerful. However, what he was unprepared for was the child's furious berserker attack on him. It was not desperation or fear. This man had attacked her friends, her loved ones. Hurt them. While she could, she would defend them with her life, while there was breath in her small body. The Chief Psychologist was obliged to send another two men out to rescue her thug and tranquillize the child too.

They brought the child whose name had once been Celine in. In to warmth and food. And hell. Pain. And remorseless, endless conditioning. Electroshock, and taped repetition. Over and over and over again.

"Those damned dogs are loose again." The thug was scared of them now.

"That's the third time this week. Can't you confine them properly?" The hidden facility's heavy door had been designed by the imperial labs to withstand armour-piercing weapons. It still vibrated with the furious impact of two 150 pound dogs flinging themselves remorselessly at it.

"They keep breaking their chains. Pulled the staple clean out of the wood last time."

The chief psychologist pursed her grim little mouth. "Shoot them then. She's drawing strength from their presence anyway."

"But they're expensive…"

"I said: shoot them. Do you dare question me?"

∞∞∞

The child was shut deep inside that secure building. She couldn't have heard a thing. Yet she screamed. A terrible, heartbroken tearing scream. The rare and valuble resource that the Emperor's security chief had personally ordered them to find and train lay in fetal ball and wept.

"Get up. Get up off the floor and stop crying or I'll send Hans in here."

But Celine didn't even seem to hear this dreadful threat. She wept on with racking, shuddering sobs. For days the chief psychologist was afraid she would die, and they would have to start all over again. But the regimen of conditioning and electroshock had continued. And somehow the shell of the child survived.

By the time the little girl was seven, she was ready. Celine was gone. The new name they gave her was Una. She was conditioned to respond to a complex sequence of hand-signals, to reply "Fudge" and then, if the number '662' was given in response to this, to become a zombie-slave obeying the trigger-man to the death.

After this she was given to a very harsh pair of Imperial Security agents, who set up 'home' with their 'daughter' on another planet. The agent-minders put her carefully in the way of the League recruiters. It was a job. When they'd done it with this child, they went and did it again. Twenty-three times.

The League recruiters....

Liton Bergersson's life story was typical of many of the riderfolk. Born on a tough outworld, he'd lost his father young. He could dimly remember the roundness of him. And the big hands throwing him up into the air. And the warmth of the laughter. Then his father, his rock, had been drowned in flash flood, while trying to rescue a friend. His pretty mother had remarried a very different kind of man. Allen Khama had been all spareness and angles. Not one of them was soft. Liton's mother was his second wife. He had certain expectations of a wife and of the boy. When these were not fulfilled he had a bull-whip. Liton's gentle mother had not flourished under this treatment. She died in childbirth less than a year later.

Allen Khama was a wealthy man. He found himself a third wife more in his own mold. She was never physically cruel to the boy, but her weapons of degradation and the erosion of his fragile ego were subtle and continuous. A slight child in the midst of robust half-brothers who reflected their new mother's attitudes, he developed a stutter, and numbered the big Zebu cattle on the station as his only friends. In a way being found by the Wienan League recruiters had almost been a relief. He'd been eight at the time, a typical age for recruitment. Too young to realize that he ought to run and run fast.

He remembered the last bellowing of the big Zebu bulls still. He had been surgically deafened soon after that and then entered the solitary hell that was riderschool. These schools were in remote areas. But he still wondered about the citizens who walked past the barred windows. How did they justify ignoring these places? It wasn't all bleakness however. There were books. And then there had been the glorious meeting with his Stardog. Lit was the first to admit he was besotted with Shahjah. The big beast was old, though. Starskipping was no longer a thing of ease or joy to her, but an effort. An effort she made happily for him. Something he was terrified of her doing.

It was no use him telling of his fears to the pampered League executioner that rode with them. The League cared only for the effective carrying of loads. So Liton was as obstructionist and stupid as he could be. It discouraged their use of Shahjah, to some extent.

Then there were the other riders. Communication between riders was actively made difficult. But the League was too mean to provide individual bathing facilities for the riders. So it was that Lit found himself lip reading a message from an older rider, on his first embarrassed naked encounter in the showers. It had shocked him rigid. It was not an indecent proposal. The man was offering to get a message to any kin, should he so desire. There had been no one in his case. The big Zebu's he'd known and loved would have been slaughtered by now. But despite the League's best effort to isolate the riders there *was* contact with outside. And a slow conspiracy to shake off the cruel hand of the League festered. But they had to be slow and careful. Otherwise the Stardogs would suffer.

It had been many years since that first contact in the cold showers. Lit was a star-browned fifty year-old man now. He himself had passed the contact on to several other scared newcomers. At the moment the compound was nearly empty. A few riders, and one newling. A thin, haunted looking girl called Una, with hazel eyes too big for her gaunt face. She was a symbol of the underlying problems that the League had with finding new riderfolk. Lit had been twenty when he came into service. She was seventeen. Older riders had told him that the riders used to begin work at twenty-five. The girl would be lifting out with one of them to go to the Stardog that waited for her. There'd be some nasty little League escort of course, and she would be anaesthetized. But at least they would be taking her from the awfulness of riderschool to meet the friend who would make it all bearable.

CHAPTER 2
STATIONERS

There is always something above you. God, or at least a space station.

From the collected sayings of Saint Sugahata the reviled.

Life on frontiers tends to be rough, true. But each of the worlds on which the frontiers existed had a tiny enclave of high-technology civilization orbiting above them. The stations had been built in the hey-day of Colonial expansionism. Because the Stardogs and the barges they carried could not make planetary landings they provided an essential stepping stone between planets and space. Yet to maintain and sustain a self- contained environment supporting a few thousand people needed skilled personnel. The people up here saw the world differently from their land-based compatriots. Down there, if one had a strong back one could survive. Here, a sharp, trained mind was needed, because if you did something wrong it wouldn't just be you who died.

Also, it would have taken a fool not to see that the well-being of the Stardogs and the future of the space stations was inextricably linked. Without the Stardogs man would take years to traverse even the shortest of stellar distances, and the stations would die. Besides, there was something beautiful and majestic about the beasts. By the year 2504 ISPCA membership on all of the 380 stations in the Empire was near universal.

That didn't mean to say it sat easily with everyone. "I don't want to go." It was said sullenly, with all the unhappiness and confusion that the divorce was feeding to the fifteen year-old boy. "I'm too old for ISPCA Youth. It's *boring*. Stupid games and endless 'be kind to our furry friends' crap."

"I don't want to hear you using language like that again, Juan! In front of Betty too. I'm ashamed of you!"

The slight fifteen year-old looked at his pretty blond twenty-three year old step-mother-to-be with resentment she didn't deserve. She understood him, and even liked the boy better than his present behavior deserved. Also, she felt faintly guilty. Hal and she *did* use the two hour Youth sessions to catch up on some bottled-up passion. And unlike Juan Biacasta's father, she wasn't twenty-five years removed from the confusion of being a teenager. She attempted to jolly him out of his rebellion. "But you like furry creatures, Juan. Why, I bet you've got Ratty in your shirt right now."

Juan blushed fierily, his olive skin darkening. She always did this to him, with her soft curves and soft voice. He'd had rather detailed fantasies about her, before he'd found out she was actually sleeping with his *father*. Now he was torn three ways, loyalty to his mother, jealousy of his father, and guilt at his own fantasies. "His name is Rat, not *Ratty*."

He stormed off, ignoring his father's demand that he come and apologize. He couldn't go that far. One couldn't in the 17 square yards of apartment. Of course, his father, as chief docking controller, was entitled to more, but with his political ambitions he wouldn't take any more than the minimum. Juan's own five square yard cubicle was supposedly sound-proofed. But that didn't mean that even through the headphones of his comp-unit he couldn't hear his father's angry voice.

Not even the drama he'd Hack-patched into (restricted access, no four to twenty-one) could hold his attention. His eyes drifted from the screen to the various hanging models suspended from the ceiling. The Denaari barge. The *Gloria Mundi*. An Imperial Chi fighter. A troop-lander. They should come down. None of his friends had kids' stuff like this in their cubes any more. Somehow he never got around to it. The models stayed, symbols of happier times when his parents had kept the disintegration of their marriage from him. He clicked comp access off. Went out.

"I'm going," he said sourly to his father, before the man could get a word out edgeways. "But I'm not going to namby-pamby Youth. I'm going to go and see Mother."

Even as he walked off down the accessway Juan knew it would be a waste of time. He'd said it to hurt his father more than anything else. She wouldn't be in her new 6.5 square yards of singles apartment. She'd still be in the electronics-lab, peering through a microscope at a circuit. She'd talk to him, sure. But half her mind would still be with her work. He flicked on to the slideway going to low-g. He'd go and mooch around the ball-courts instead. He wouldn't mind a game, but he didn't have his racquet or kit, and anyway Rat couldn't be relied on to stay in his locker.

He was frustrated and angry. He didn't realize that uncertainty about his return time, and the emotional tensions he'd stirred, had left his father and his father's girl-friend just as frustrated. Possibly, if he had known he would perhaps have chosen a better time for that silly revengeful practical joke with a tube of superglue from his mother's lab. She'd brought it for him to fix the piece of *Gloria* he'd broken off by accident the day before the terminal argument.

The glue had been the final item that had brought the disintegration of his parents' relationship to an open quarrel. It had led to her abrupt departure, and to Betty's too sudden appearance. The memory of the glue brought up the idea. He'd like to stick the old man's mouth shut so he'd stop carping... Of course he wouldn't actually do something like that, but false teeth...

Which is why the next morning Juan's father's roar of rage was through clenched teeth. "That's it! That is final. You're not going to Illuria station."

Juan stopped laughing. "You can't. You promised!"

"You're too irresponsible and childish to go. I'm sorry, but you've brought this on yourself. If..."

"I will go. You can't stop me." The boy stormed back into his cubicle. He sat there angrily on the fold-bed, staring at the forest-scenes on the picture-wall without seeing them. His father *could* stop him. Travel between stations was mind bogglingly expensive. The stationers managed it with a sort of *Quid pro quo* with the League. Favors for favors. His father, as Docking Controller, had a lot of leverage. He'd used it for this passage for his son to the cousins at Illuria. Officially, to the Station, the boy was going to learn Astral Navigation, a speciality of the college on Illuria Station, just as Amritsar Station had a reputation for micro-circuitry.

His father gummed angrily as he attempted to lever his teeth apart with a knife. Damn the League. On Kambar Station the bio-research crowd had achieved some truly brilliant results with cloned tooth-buds... But Kambar was something like a hundred and ninety League-ordained jumps away, even if its star was visible from here, and wasn't actually far as the Stardogs *could* have flown. Unfortunately, you could ship microcircuits but not tooth-buds.

Hal Biacasta knew he'd shot himself in the foot with this outburst. The boy was a little young to go, and perhaps he wasn't ideally suited for Nav. His results were good enough, in fact, they were exceptional. Not for the first time Hal wondered if the boy hadn't damn well finagled the comp-testing system. Juan's heart didn't seem to be in Nav., but at that age a boy's heart was seldom in anything but getting into a girl's pants, as he remembered it. Juan didn't appear to be any better at that than he'd been. Well, it had seemed a good idea to get the boy away for a bit, to give his son, as well as himself and Betty a bit of breathing space. That was the problem in a nutshell. The stations were really too small. But there was certainly no Imperial money for expansion, and no stationer ever volunteered to go down to the uncivilized worlds below. No stationer would ever want to.

He was wrong. His son, for example, thought of those rough, brawling worlds in pretty vid-image colored terms. But Juan was not studying the vid-images of the parks on old Earth now. Instead he was staring at the Denaari-barge model, an idea beginning in his rebellious head. Presently he got up and took the model down, and studied it more carefully. It was a perfect scale replica.

CHAPTER 3
THE GOTHA EMPIRE

"The Empire is like a cancer. Should it stop growing,
it will die. Peace and stability are the ultimate
enemies of imperialism."

From the collected sayings of Saint Sugahata the reviled.

The People's Empire of Gotha stretched across light-years. The mind-maps of the great Stardogs had taken men to 432 planets. The Empire held sway over all of them, even if only tenuously on a few like Arunachal. And of course many of the Denaari worlds had been virtually uninhabitable... But even so, the new Emperor, Turabi II, ruled absolute over 300 billion people.

Such power is beyond human understanding. Let us turn instead to a weeping girl who had hidden herself deep in the shrubbery of the vast enclosed imperial gardens of Phillipia, the seat of the Empire. She was nineteen. She had survived just about as many assassination attempts as she had years. This, the last one, an hour and a half ago, had cost her the life of her mother-figure as well as her father and step-mother.

She couldn't have cared less about her father and step-mother, even if their death had put that horrible little toad, her sixteen year old step-brother Turabi, on the Diamond Throne. The Princess Royal wept instead, bitterly, inconsolably for her peasant-born ex-nurserymaid, who had mothered her, raised her, and finally shielded her beloved charge with her own body. Flecks of Lea's blood stained her dress. The Princess knew that they were still out there, looking for her. Right now, she almost didn't care if they found her.

Princess Shari buried her face in the fur of a small dog of dubious parentage. The dog, with canine understanding, allowed this, despite the fact that he was a Dog-of-Immense-Dignity, who believed that cuddling should only be permitted at times and places of its own choosing. The dog growled abruptly. The delicate pale green curtain of hanging Sambar-lilies parted.

Shari looked up. For a moment she thought it was her brother's crony, Selim Puk. The man had the same almond eyes and dark hair, and moved with same catlike deadly grace. But this man was smaller. And the eyes were a softer brown. "I suppose you've come to kill me," she said calmly.

In his hands the thin garrote-wire gleamed, confirming the truth of this. But he was startled. Hers was not the first life the high-priest of Kali-Dewa had sent him to harvest back into the great cycle. There had been many. But this was the first time he had been greeted thus. "You do not beg or plead?" This was an honorable thing indeed. Surely her rebirth would be a great one.

She shrugged, unafraid now that it had come. "Why? It wouldn't make any difference. You've killed everyone I have ever loved. First Senn. Now my Lea." She scratched the base of the dog's ears. "I only have Otto here left. You won't hurt him, will you?" She gave a tiny sigh, and hugged the mongrel, who turned to lick her nose. "I wonder what will become of him. He was only half-weaned when I found him. I don't think he knows *how* to look after himself." The dog, reassured by the calm tones, jumped off her lap and went to sniff the boots of the killer. Without thinking the man put a hand down to pet it.

"I have killed none of these people, lady. I will not harm your dog. I give my word that I shall find it a suitable home."

She looked faintly surprised, but patted her thigh, calling Otto back to her. "Thank you. I didn't expect that from one of Selim's hatchet-men."

"I am no one's hatchet-man, lady. I am the holy executioner of the Kali-Dewa." He stepped forward, unwinding the garrote.

"How depressing. You're going to kill me for this 'Kali-Dewa' and I don't even know who he is. I thought you were too pleasant to be one of my late father's or my brother's pet murderers."

She made no move to resist as he skilfully dropped the loop of braided steel wire around her slim white neck. "You are a person of great honor, even if you do not know that the Dewa is always female. Where possible we are instructed to allow the victim a last prayer for their souls to ensure rebirth closer to the Dewa. I grant you this time to make your peace with the Goddess."

His victim sighed. "I've no one to pray for except Otto. Lea and Senn are dead. Kill me if you're going to. I'm so tired of running and being scared all the time."

The wire slackened slightly. "You are supposed to pray for yourself, for forgiveness."

"Why?"

The holy executioner was definitely at a loss now. "Because... well, because of your tyrannical rule of my people, and persecution of the holy church. You are the Duchess of Arunachal, after all."

His victim began to laugh helplessly. Eventually, interspersed with little hiccups of hysterical laughter, she explained to the puzzled killer, "I'm hiding in the garden from my brother's assassins. I haven't a friend in the world besides my dog. I might be an Imperial Princess to you, but believe me, I couldn't tyrannize anybody. I don't think I could even order lunch now. I'm the titular head of seventeen planets, and patron of dozens of organizations. You don't really think that really means anything do you? You don't think I'm allowed to actually do anything, do you? I don't even know where half the places are, never mind anything about them!"

"That is a sin itself. You should have found out, done something, gone to your dominions," said the executioner doubtfully, as the dog sprang off her lap.

She shrugged. "So kill me for it. I haven't even been able to get out of the palace to save myself, never mind visit my so-called dominions."

By this stage the holy executioner had forgotten the garrote in his hands. The dog barked and he almost throttled the Princess instinctively. But Otto was barking at someone outside the shrubbery.

"That's her damned dog, yapping. The girl must be in there

somewhere. Selim said we were to finish off the girl and that damn dog of hers." The voices were close. The girl ignored the garrote, and grabbed the dog who had pressed against her knees. The holy executioner stared in puzzlement as she turned away from the voices and held it her arms. Abruptly he realised that she was trying to shelter the dog from the bullets she expected. Yet, by the fierce look in her eyes she had been prepared to attack the newcomers barehanded to defend the dog, had she not been certain that the animal too would be killed.

It was a moment of epiphany. The executioner dropped his garotte, and, secure in the knowledge that he stood in the presence of a light-incarnation of the Kali-Dewa herself, went forth.

A single, small Aranachali man armed with two ancient fourteen-inch knives should really have been no match for two of Selim Puk's professional killers. The men were top-graduate assassins trained for two years by the Imperial Security Service.

It was actually no match at all. The Dagger of the Goddess had begun his training when he could barely walk. He had twenty years training to their two. His bloodline too had been honed for many, many generations to this purpose.

She waited. No bullets came. Instead the silence grew. She turned around, unable to wait any longer.

The slight, non-descript man who had held a garrote around her throat, stood there patiently. He was calmly tracing a cross in blood on a long zig-zag bladed knife. Even through the thin film of blood the blade gleamed with endless silky oyster fold patterns. "May they be reborn among the eaters of Denaar-filth." He wiped the blade carefully on a scrap of cloth which had once been an imperial trooper's insignia of rank, and slid the blade into its hidden sheath.

He bowed to her. "Your life has been called into the hands of the Kali-Dewa by the high priest on Arunachal, and I am one who is sworn to give it to her for judgment. Yet I see that your work in this incarnation is yet to be done. Accordingly, I must keep your soul within this body until the words of the High Priest Suttulej become truth, and you become indeed the Scourge of Arunachal and the bane of the Holy Church."

"And if I never do?" she asked with just a ghost of a smile.

He considered the question with gravity. "I shall have to guard you all your life and wait until your last breath. Then I shall part it from you with the holy blade, so that my oath may be fulfilled."

She shook her head. "You can't just do that. It's not that easy. I can't suddenly just have an extra servant or something, you know. Imperial Security will take you, torture you, and then... kill you."

"I am already officially part of your retinue, Princess. Or at least the man I have replaced...was." He allowed himself the shadow of a smile too. "He was also an assassin, and already part of your Imperial Security."

"You'll be killed," she said. "Everyone close to me is."

He shrugged. "I will surely be reborn closer to the Dewa. Shall we go, Princess? You will be safer in a more public place."

"What is your name? I can't just call you ... assassin."

"I have replaced a man called Amadeo Cerros, so that is what you should call me. I was given to the church as a newborn. I have never had an actual name. My title, by which I called, would be difficult for you to pronounce. It simply means 'Dagger of the Goddess' among my people," he said casually. Otto had jumped up against him, and he petted the dog as he spoke.

She reached a decision. "Otto likes you. Let's go then, if we can. Perhaps you can get us out of here."

"Is that all you desire, Princess?" Something about the way he asked indicated that he was certain he could get her past the superb security net that enclosed the palace.

She paused. Her brow wrinkled and she seemed to look elsewhere, on a far vision. She gave a tiny sniff. Eventually she said quietly, "No. Right now, what I *really* want is to destroy the entire Empire." She gave a small laugh. "Just me, one girl against the most powerful Empire in history." She raised her chin, quite unaware that she looked like her great grandfather Vespasian. The charismatic Vespasian who had led his troops from certain defeat to victory at Alresa. "I'd still like to bring the whole rotten structure down, and see the loyal people I loved avenged. No," she corrected herself, "Not avenged. My Lea didn't believe in that. Just... to see it couldn't ever happen again." She looked him in the eye, "Should I add independence for your Arunchal to the impossible wish-list?"

He bowed. "It is written, Princess, that nothing is impossible in God's time. We will not be able to do these things right now, of course, but they are noble goals. I pledge myself to them." He led her out of the shrubbery. "I agree, they will be easier to achieve from within, than from the outside. I will teach you the Arunachal Thuggee way of fighting, which is to use your enemy's strength against him."

It wasn't quite what she'd meant.

❦❦❦❦❦❦

Some two miles away, in another arm of the sprawling palace, a nervous but triumphant young Emperor held council with his new Security Chief, Selim Puk. "It's over then, Selim? It's all done?"

The almond-eyed man allowed himself a small smile, showing even white teeth. "Almost all... my Emperor."

The plump blond boy-man swelled like a turkey, revelling in the new title "I *am* Emperor now, at last, but I still keep looking for my father every time somebody says it, Selim! But tell me now, what do you mean 'almost all'?"

The Security chief shrugged his willowy shoulders. "A few of your father's old adherents in security are still being hunted down. Your parents' assassins have of course been killed... by a jailer who was too incensed by their crime to allow them to live. He will still have to face trial, but I will arrange his 'suicide'. Oh, somebody botched the elimination of your step-sister. The group I sent must have run into the remains of your father's old crew. I've another assassin in place, one of her servants..."

"Let her live. The silly cow is too scared to do or say anything. Besides, it's too late now. Another killing will look like a purge. We can always deal with her later," said Turabi, magnanimous in his moment of triumph.

The Security Chief nodded. "A wise decision. One fitting of an Emperor." He smiled slyly, "We can even lean on her to corroborate your story. And she's no real danger to you. She can't rule of course, being a woman, and being sterile she can't produce any heirs as rival claimants to the throne."

"You mean the bitch can't breed, Selim?"

He nodded. "Your father had her tested when she was thirteen. I've seen the records. She was totally infertile. It was why he let her live."

The boy-Emperor snorted, worldly wise. "Her mother must have been damn close to it too. Only one child in five years. And a girl at that. No wonder the old man had her done away with. Well, you just keep a watch Shari. She may be no danger to me, but I don't like her. One step out of line..." he drew a finger across his throat.

Selim Puk nodded. "Of course. As I said, I've a man in place already. I'll see to it that she is surrounded by my agents."

But men can be replaced. Records too can also be replaced, especially when your father-figure and bodyguard had been a highly skilled security agent himself. It helps too if you have a loyal and willing mother-figure-nursemaid who was sterile.

●●●⊃●●

The Princess Shari had not expected God's time to last nearly twenty years.

She hadn't even expected to live half that long. But she had not expected the dagger of the Goddess Kali-dewa either, or for him to present her with the list of organizations and societies she was supposed to be patron of. And her official, embossed writing paper, retrieved from a forgotten drawer. He had been very methodical in searching her quarters. He was just as methodical in plotting her future.

"I don't know who they are, Deo."

He shrugged "The letters will bear the Imperial seal, Princess."

"But I don't know anything about those organizations and societies. And to honest I don't think I want to."

The briefest of smiles flickered across his impassive countenance. It was the tiger-smile... "You will write as a bored but dutiful Princess. Some will ask for money, some will merely borrow your presence. Your presence outside of this... trap. And money you will have to give too. You can draw from your estates. We will build lines of communication for future use."

He was right. Days later she leafed through the pile of replies. "Money. They all want money. Or me. Do you know what you have done to me, Deo?" She held up an elegantly curlicue-flourished letter. "Post Post-Modernist Neo-Gothic Opera. Oh joy!" He winced, sympathetically. "A gala event. They would like me to attend."

"I can obtain some earplugs for you," said her assassin. "The coiffeuse will contrive suitable hairstyle to hide them, Princess. Consider yourself avenged. I shall have no such luxury."

"Well, this one is interesting. The Disabled Veterans League want me to open a center on Carab."

"You will refuse. Politely. They are worthy of being cultivated."

"Deo, I thought I wanted *out* of this trap," she said, plaintively.

"The Emperor would refuse to allow you to go, my Princess. So you will say that with the death of your father so recent you do care to travel far from your brother's protective hand. In year or two he will send you to something that he does not dare attend himself."

"I don't know that I can wait that long. Or that I'll be allowed to live that long."

"The hand of Dewa is over you, Princess. And I watch over you too. Now, what other invitations are there?"

"Just this Gala-fund-raiser for the Imperial Society for the Prevention of Cruelty to Animals."

"Ah. Well, I think you should attend that, Princess. The ISPCA are not likely to be perceived as subversive. They stay out of politics and look after deserted and injured domestic animals, and run adoption shelters for them."

Which shows how wrong perceptions can be. The ISPCA, which rapidly became her favorite charity, was subversive in the extreme, plotting open revolution, in fact. At first they had attempted to use her as a stalking horse, but she had gradually penetrated their innermost councils, and after five years she was in it up to her elegant neck. Still, she had become a public figure, and thus far harder to dispose of.

••••••

Time, and the fact that she apparently supported him, had dulled Turabi's suspicions, if not his dislike. She was also being useful, and giving the Imperial rule a frothy and acceptable face. He permitted her first off-planet venture, and in time became accustomed to the fact that she spent less than six months of any year in her dingy apartments in the old part of the Imperial Palace, and the rest of her time star-hopping on the elderly imperial barge, engaged in fund-raising for her three pet charities. Turabi didn't like her popularity, or the entourage she had acquired, but he tolerated it.

He did not notice how she avoided virtually all engagements on Phillipia, and how she attempted to maintain a low profile here. Off-world she was much better known than she was in the Imperial capital. The emperor did not travel. He did not dare. He sat, like a fat spider and pulled the strings in the web of his empire, hidden from all but a few thousand of his people. His step-sister on the other hand flitted to even the most irrelevant of outposts, and was personally known by millions. The Emperor taxed. She gave. He would have had her killed if he had realized this. And her death would surely have sparked rebellion.

As it happened Turabi decided to have her eliminated because of a clumsy attempt at flattery at an Imperial Levee. Here, The Archduke of Tzar had bowed low on his being introduced to the Emperor. "I am delighted to meet Your

Magnificence at last" he simpered, "I've met your charming royal daughter so often. My people are besotted with her." He had actually met Shari once, and had no idea that a great many of his people were in fact very attached to her.

The fat, dissipated Turabi had not like that at all. He wasn't happy that his despised elder sister should be taken for his daughter either. In a later consultation with Selim Puk it was decided that she had to go. Selim, as usual, had several nasty plots brewing. The security chief saw a suitable opportunity to dispose of several birds with one stone, as it were.

●●●●●●

"But, Your Highness," said the rather florid-faced elderly man, peering at the list she'd handed him, "they're all backwater planets, again." He shook his head, despairing, "We'd make twice as much money on any one of the Inner worlds!"

She smiled at him, graciously. She'd discovered that her smile was one of her most powerful weapons. "I know, Sir Syrian. But it is important that the people of the smaller places should feel involved too. Some things are more important than money." It was a difficult concept for the former advertising executive, drafted out of retirement into the service of the cash-strapped ISPCA, to accept. At least two others of her audience also didn't agree with her, but neither of them was going to voice their opinions. The handsome Viscount Martin Brettan wasn't going to say anything because his slender stipend depended on staying in the Princess's good books. The footman who was attempting to surreptitiously read the list that Syrian Brynant was fuming over wouldn't say anything either. Footmen didn't.

Syrian Brynant hadn't received a knighthood for lack of effort. "Well, Your Highness, what about a gala departure event here? I could raise..."

"Absolutely out of the question." Her voice was arctic.

On the rare occasions Shari snapped like that you could forget further questioning. The fund-raising campaign manager bowed, defeated. "Very well, Princess." He turned to go.

"Sir Syrian. Do you mind leaving the second copy of that itinerary with us?" Shari's voice was all urbanity again. "I think some of us would like to peruse it." She smiled at the froglike, glasses-magnified eyes of the dumpy, oddly made-up woman in the corner. Inwardly Shari seethed in irritation at the clumsy footman-spy. Best to make it easy for the fool. It was, she supposed, some comfort that she was still being spied on by idiots and not competent men. But it was all so futile. The itinerary would be going to Imperial security anyway. And if he was a Wienan League spy, they'd be getting her itinerary as well as her politely-worded-but-brooking-no-refusal request for a Stardog for the imperial barge. The itinerary would cause their usual rash of protests and suggested changes, which she would, as usual, ignore.

Lady Tanzo Adendorff's badly pinned bun bobbed like a buoy in wind squall with her eager nodding. "Oh yes... I'd love to! I like to get my reading done first, you know." Tanzo agreed wholeheartedly with the Princess that some things were more important than money. Well, one thing anyway. Xeno-archaeology. Money was only worth having if it could transport you to Denaari sites. But interstellar travel was ruinously expensive, and Imperial interest in archaeological research-funding was non-existent. As part of the Princess's retinue she at least could sponge free transport to worlds far beyond her modest means. The odd-looking woman was no fool. In return she did what was expected of her, to deflect the intelligentsia from the princess at social gatherings. It was boring, but a small price to pay.

Selim Puk had ensured that the Princess was never quite alone. The bodyguards were, of course, his men. The major domo, Amadeo Cerros, was also, of course, his original plant. The man had also been approached by Wienan League agents and, on Selim's instructions, passed on certain edited information. Baroness Tanzo he had considered and rejected. He had a generous budget, but really, money spent on watching Princess Shari was wasted. He wished, however, that he could have recruited the Princess's other foil.

Unfortunately, the stunningly beautiful and amply curvaceous Demoiselle Caro Leyven had two kinds of armor against his wiles.

Firstly, she was the scion of a wealthy merchant house. Her grandfather had bought his title, and then trebled the family fortune, which was still very much intact. Caro had never needed money and found it of no interest. Selim couldn't buy her.

Secondly, she was just too dim for blackmail, even if he could find or fake something she'd prefer to remain hidden. She'd blurt it out to the first man who smiled at her, and with the effect this woman had on heterosexual males, his blackmailing agent would end up dead. She had no interest in the itinerary. Wherever they went there would be men to be nice to her. She had no idea why her dear Princess had asked her to join the royal retinue. But it didn't matter, did it?

There was one other within the dingy audience-room, with its half-century out of date wall-paper, that cared even less about where they were going. Otto III, possessor of one of the most impressive moustaches in all of the empire, (despite, or possibly because of his dubious ancestry), didn't care where the princess went, as long as he went along. He was loyal beyond any possibility of corruption. He also occasionally had fleas, which if you are the animal-shelter-chosen companion of a Princess, meant baths. Otto didn't mind what his Princess did, or where she went, as long as he was there, and there were no baths.

Standing behind Tanzo Adendorff the footman had managed to make a careful study of the list at last. Phillipia - Abelard - Barhain II - Samburia - Amritsar - New Sahara - Nekrat - Erzulie - New Australia - Prala III - Bretonia - Mali V and then back to Phillipia. Arrival and departure times. He memorized them carefully, not realising how obvious he was being. Still, spotting a spy is one thing. But it is sometimes difficult to tell just for whom the spy may be working.

eec3ee

Prince Jarian stared in horror at the dead man — not because death horrified him, but because it was his own bodyguard. The strangers who had shot the bodyguard, it appeared, had saved his life. And now he was here, without as much as a pistol and entirely without any form of defense, should they want him dead. He'd never seen either man before, and although they'd killed Naylin in the act of turning his weapon on his master, Prince Jarian, neither had put their guns away. Jarian wondered if he was going to be next. "Wh... who are you?" he stuttered.

"The only friends you have in the world, Prince Jarian," said one of the men sardonically, "Or, should I say, Jarian. Seeing as the Emperor has stripped you of all of your titles and ordered you an unobtrusive death. Selim Puk traced the toxin seller... and found you were the only buyer. You should have tried something less exotic."

Jarian's pale eyes darted around the room. He wanted to run. He HAD to run. He should killed the supplier. But his older brother relied on the fool for recreational chemicals, and the dealer was a little too careful. "Friends?" he quavered clining to the last straw.

"The Wienan League have reasons to want to keep you alive," said the other man. "No one else does."

Jarian knew why. He knew they'd want a puppet-pretender if they took action against his father. The Emperor Turabi knew that too. He'd kill any son that tried an alliance with the League. But what choice did he have?

"You'll have to get me out of here."

The self-admitted League agent nodded. "And off-world. On Phillipia they'll find and kill you, sooner or later. Not even in the league Dacha would you be safe. But we have hidden facilities elsewhere. We have the perfect vessel to get you out on too. The Princess Royal's barge. They'll be searching elsewhere very diligently."

"Shari... " he detested his aunt. "She is with the League?" That information could be traded, perhaps for his life.

The league man smiled nastily, obviously guessing his mind. "No. She is above suspicion and search, that's all. We have someone in her retinue. Viscount Brettan and one of the stewards will see to your welfare, once we have you aboard."

CHAPTER 4
THE WIENAN LEAGUE

A vine, should it be unpruned, yet given access to water and fertilizer in unlimited quantities will produce poor and watery fruit. The Wienan League is such a vine.

The Upanishad of the Gardener-Dewa Celine

The descendants of the nine powerful political families who had formed the Council of the Space Exploration and Development Control League lived in the kind of sybaritic luxury that even their wealthy ancestors could never have dreamed of. The hereditary councillors of what now openly called itself the Wienan League, skimmed the cream off the interstellar Empire they'd created. For the Empire itself had begun as a puppet, a means by which the Wienan League could repress their former puppet, the Council of Planets.

The new puppet too had begun to become uppity in the last hundred years or so. The League now politely requested audiences with the emperor. A mere 120 years ago they'd sent the man peremonitary orders, which were obeyed with alacrity. Now... the League didn't like this diminution of its power. The

Wienan Oligarchy planned to replace the present ruling house with yet another puppet. But the League remained small, controlling a slowly decreasing pool of Stardogs, and the Empire was vast. And even with their declining numbers of Stardogs the League had been obliged to accept some loyal outsiders into their ranks. Offspring of their own were just too few these days.

The core of power remained with the hereditary-Wienans however. One child of this bloodline was Johannes Wienan XXIII. He could never rise to be League Chairman, because his father had foolishly married outside the League, but he was still a powerful young man in the year 2505. Well, he was not powerful in the physical sense anyway. He was already, at twenty, unfit and rather plump. The power came from his birth, and from his Great Aunt Mariet. She was Chairman of the League Board, and when she summonsed him, even though he was in the middle of a luxurious bath, he responded with commendable alacrity.

"She wants me?" He fumbled for the switch of the mechanical massager. A skilled masseuse-slave would have done a better job, but the antique gadget was a symbol of Wienan wealth and power. People were cheap, machines expensive.

His neat-featured brunette slave switched the device off for him, without allowing the least sign of her disdain to show in her face or her voice. "Yes sir. But only at seventeen thirty. You have nearly half an hour."

"Well, even so, I can't hang about, Lila. Get a move on, girl. Hand me that towel, and go and get my formal clothes ready," he said hastily, surging naked out of the bath.

She handed him the large fluffy towel. He made no attempt to hide the fact the massage had aroused him "Yes master," she said calmly, hiding her relief that there would be no time for sex.

●●●3●●

Twenty seven minutes later, at exactly 17h29, he tapped politely on the open door of the audience chamber. Mariet Wienan looked at him with narrowed eyes from under her carefully manicured eyebrows. She raised one eyebrow. Then without giving him the least acknowledgement, she looked at the large ornamental clock on the far wall. It read 17h37.

He advanced, smiling confidently, ignoring the clock. He had been trained to manipulate people himself. After all, that was truly the core profession of the Wienans. He knew the enormous value of initiating any verbal contact with the other party being apologetic, defensive and fighting off the back foot. He made an exquisite bow. "Good afternoon, Great-Aunt. How may I serve?"

Slowly she turned to look at him, wintry approval showing in her pale blue eyes. "Very good, young man. Your tutors reported that despite your laziness you show considerable promise. They also say it is time you were posted. I agree. Eh, Jan-Pieter, what do you think?"

Johannes's heart fell to his to his boots. Wienan's weren't posted out until they were twenty-three or four. What was he going to get? Some horrible back-planet sector? He shivered slightly. His second cousin, Jan Pieter Wienan XVII, who sat statue-still in his wing-backed wheelchair was far more frightening than Great Aunt Mariet's little clock parlor-trick could ever be. The little old man with his twisted body, and scalpel-sharp but equally twisted mind, headed Wienan League Intelligence. At the Wienan League's orders ordinary people died. At Jan-Pieter's orders even League members died. Perhaps Jan-Pieter had some nasty plan for him. He just hoped it wasn't involved in that supposedly super-secret Stardog cloning program out on the rim. Those who went there never came back.

He was relieved at the old man's cracked, dry reply when it finally came. "He'll do. He's enough of a fop to consort with royalty, without being a complete idiot. Besides, that pretty mother of his was some sort of relative of the Emperor's, wasn't she?"

"I won't have that slut mentioned in my presence," snapped the Chairman, sudden anger and loathing in her voice.

Johannes realized with surprise that Jan-Pieter had done it on purpose to goad her. "I use what I can, Mariet. I use what I can," the old man said calmly. "And we need to put a stop to this business. Now, shall I take him away and brief him, or do you want to sit in on it?"

She scowled at him. "Take him away, Jan-Pieter. You've spoilt my day as it is."

Jan-Pieter shrugged a twisted shoulder at her. "Very well. I'll handle it from here. Come, little cousin, follow me." The ancient servos in the motorized wheelchair whined as he rolled away. Johannes found himself hastily bowing and then scurrying after the wheelchair. As he reached the door his aunt's voice reached after him. "And Johannes, don't *you* come back with some out league trollop. I had enough of that from your father."

Johannes bowed and ran.

Jan-Pieter's quarters were stark, without the everything-covered-in-fur luxury typical of League rooms. As Johannes stepped through the portal into the feared rooms he felt his hair rise. Static crackled off his feet. He looked at them in alarm. "You should wear rubber-soled shoes," said the spy master grimly. "Don't worry about it. It's just a device of mine to ruin radio transmission out of my quarters. I have to make these things myself. Decent artificers are hard to come by these days." He sat back in his chair. "Mariet's forever moaning about it, but we can't go on suppressing the sciences and still expect them to flourish, but only produce what we want. Now, your assignment. It is an awkward but simple one. Do you want a drink or something before I start? You'll have to help yourself. I won't have slaves in here."

Hastily, Johannes shook his head. "Very well. Sit." Johannes sat on the only chair. It was not upholstered for comfort. But then Jan-Pieter cared little for his own comfort, and nothing at all for the comfort of others. His attempts at solicitude made Johannes rightfully suspicious, especially when he continued with "I apologize for raking up the coals about your mother. But I wanted you out of there. Your great-aunt is not strictly dispassionate as far as you're concerned. She had designs on your father."

Johannes's jaw fell open and he hastily caught it. He was stunned, not by the revelations, for inbreeding if not actual incest were the rule rather than the exception in the League, but by Jan-Pieter's apology. First being offered a drink, then a seat, then an *apology*. Whatever it was that was planned for him must be dire. "It's quite all right sir. I barely remember my mother. I've never really thought about her." It was true. He had avoided thinking about her, but her face still recurred in occasional nightmare-dreams.

"Hmm. Well, I'm not here to talk about history. We've a job for you, young man." The rictus of a smile twisted the spy master's face. "We want you to do what the League has spent five hundred years preventing." He flicked a switch. The lights went out and the head and shoulders of a rabbity looking man appeared on the far wall. The man's hair was greying and he had a weak, indeterminate chin. It was the face of a hungry man, yet despite this there was a gentleness and a softness about the eyes. Even before he noticed the coarse tunic the fellow was wearing, Johannes knew that this was a rider, one of the League's cattle. "Liton Bergesson. You must make this man rebel."

The young Wienan's jaw fell open again. "But.... "

"Not outright rebellion. Just refusal to do a stellar-jump. It should be easy enough. Afterwards, but before he makes contact with any other rider, I will have him disposed of," said Jan-Pieter matter-of-factly.

"But, but," stuttered Johannes, "What about the Stardog? Do I kill it?"

"No. They're a diminishing resource. We simply can't afford it. Not even," he flicked the switch again and the image of the rider disappeared and a woman's face appeared in its place, "for her."

The face that now appeared on the wall-screen was one Johannes recognized. The woman however could never be described as beautiful. Her nose was too big for starters, and those grey eyes too steely. With her mouth set in a hard line and her determined chin slightly tilted she looked imperious. It was an unusual pose for the princess Royal. Shari normally took care not to look like a potential threat to her brother. "We're doing what an Imperial wants?" Johannes was now distinctly puzzled.

●●C϶●●

Jan-Pieter snorted. This fool would never understand the simplest of the complex plots he maneuvered the League's interests through. "No. We're putting a stop to her movements." He flicked the lights on again. "We don't actually know just what she's up to. But it *is* something. Every off world trip she cuts at least two isolation sectors. She's using her charity work as an excuse, and the ISPCA as a useful front. Personally, I don't give a damn what she's up to, *but* as an unpleasant side-effect for us, she's moving riders. We don't want contact between the different sectors. That's why the trade routes were set up like that, to keep the riders isolated, to remove any possibility of conspiracy. We, of course, keep the princess's riders apart in the compounds, but the space-station facilities are limited. We can't refuse the Princess directly, because that would be an affront to the Emperor." The fact obviously irritated him.

"But", the head of Wienan security smiled, shark-like, "if the *riders* refuse to take their Stardogs through a jump... well, we'll have an excellent reason to make her highness follow normal trade routes. We have chosen this fellow because he's ripe to rebel, as much as these weaklings ever are." He pointed to a slim dossier sitting on the table. "Psycoprofile. Study it. You'll be expected to prevent the fifth jump, cross-sector from New Sahara to Nekrat. I'm including a Leaguesman carefully chosen to resemble the rider's late stepfather. We'll also put a spare rider on board in case Bergersson goes beyond control."

●●C϶●●

Johannes knew this to be typical Jan-Pieter planning: every contingency catered for. It was why the Wienan spy-master beat his Imperial counterpart so often, despite Selim Puk's vast resources.

Uncertainly, Johannes stood up and took the dossier. He didn't dare ask questions. Anyway, he was still too stunned to think straight.

"Close the door as you leave," Jan-Pieter said in dismissal, turning his chair away.

Later, in his soft-lit luxurious chambers, Johannes Wienan peered disconsolately at the dossier, as the servant set before him a desert of dried black figs marinated to plumpness in Silenius seven-star brandy, stuffed with dark chocolate and almond-slivers, then oven-baked with just a delicate touch of sage, and finally capped with whipped cream decorated with chocolate curls. The Smyrna figs came all the way from Earth. The tiny wasps which fertilized figs had not been successfully introduced to any other colony world. These, the best, came from Greece, at fabulous expense.

He'd toyed with the previous courses, not giving them the kind of attention that the efforts of the perfectionist martinet in his kitchen deserved. He sighed and took a spoonful of the desert. Then pushed it away. The brunette slave looked apprehensively at him, and the storm signals coming.

"Some coffee, Lila. The dark-roast Jamaican," he snapped. "And tell the chef I don't want to see this muck again." Three weeks ago he'd described it as exquisite, the perfect ending to a magnificent meal. She left hastily, happy to do the table-servant's job, as it got her out of the room. When he was in this sort of mood, which was fortunately rarely, he hit people. It would be sex tonight, and it would be rough, but at least what she had to report would hurt both him and the damned League far more.

That night, as Johannes snored, she inspected the bruises on her buttocks and breasts in the bathroom. Then she washed herself, scrubbing the sore places, trying to scrub even the memory away. As usual, it was the shame that got to her the most. Knowing that her body had responded, against her wishes. Stepping out of the shower unit, she left the water trickling and splashing. Then she took down the shower-rail and shook out a tiny comm unit. She turned on the hand-basin tap. Knowing that she could not be overheard above the water-noise, and that the narrow-beam transmitter would encode her message before sending it out in a microsecond-long blip, she carefully related all the details of her master's mission.

In his chambers Jan-Pieter smiled his twisted shark's grin of satisfaction as he put aside the headphones. He'd modified her transmitter himself. Now, a few small alterations to the content of the message, and he would send it out. Mariet had a soft spot for the boy. But he had to go. Johannes would have done well to remember that the plots of the spy master were as multi layered as onions.

The Emperor had a thin web of agents controlling and reporting from four hundred and thirty two worlds. The agents' reports had to travel through space. Guild controlled space. It had been most amusing to make this transit the point at which their information was neatly filched. Or even filched and replaced, slightly altered. The League was happy to let the vast clumsy mechanism of the Emperor's secret police do most of the legwork. It was happy to supply a few clumsy idiots to provide the Empire's counter-espionage men with employment.

There was a lot of garbage that they were quite cheerful about letting the Emperor's spies have. However, Jan-Pieter was sure the clone-project had not been penetrated. Unlike the Emperor's own mechanical-starship project. Jan-Pieter snorted. The League kept a careful watch on technicians. Those whom it couldn't absorb, and who were also reasonably competent, it had killed or corrupted. Technology stood at a lower base now than it had in the mid-twentieth century, when building a starship was a fool's dream.

Not that the starship idea wasn't tempting. It offered a way to break away from the limits of Denaari-worlds. To choose their own planets. The Denaari had preferred dry, cool low gravity worlds, with thin air. Some of those on which they'd left extensive traces of settlement were too bleak for serious human colonization. Earth herself had almost certainly been a hardship post with a bare minimum of staff, possibly just there to study the natives. The Stardogs were far more common around the dry, bleak worlds than the occasional Earth-visiting Stardog had been. Still, it was to the worlds the Denaari once populated, and those worlds only, that the Stardogs would go to.

Jan-Pieter stopped musing and took off the headphones. Well. Perhaps it would be a pity to kill off young Johannes, but it couldn't be helped. Unlike his second-cousin Mariet, who sat on the league throne at the moment, Jan-Pieter had no desire to keep the League for the Wienan-bloodline. His own line ended with himself. All Jan-Pieter wanted was power. The idea of his own mortality had never crossed his mind.

He stood up, not without difficulty, and walked from his office slowly across to his chamber. There would be no one in his bed. Jan-Pieter had no real interest in sex, taking his pleasure from his power.

The window was open. Across the predawn silence someone in the rider-compound below started to sing. The sound drifted upwards, full of sadness. The haunting words were full of deep emotions, sung in the loud, tuneless fashion of the deaf. Or, in this case, of the deafened. With irritation Jan-Pieter snapped the tower window shut. If there was one group of people that he totally despised it was those spineless riders. Useless dummies. Well, if the clone-project succeeded they could dispense with them.

He had to admit that at the moment they were a problem. Less good candidates every year, it seemed. Yet the population of the Empire was increasing. You'd think there'd be more soppy dummies. There seemed to be a pattern now of fewer coming from the central worlds, and more from remote frontier worlds and backwaters. These had never been good recruiting grounds in the past. Pioneer families tended to take care of their offspring. He wondered, not for the first time, if sterilizing riders had been a good idea. Had the resource been mined dry? Were they systematically stripping the human population of Stardog rider genes, when they ought to breed the revolting little creatures? But it had been tried in the past. The riders simply refused to co-operate. They would rather die than give up their young to the League. It had caused the death of two Stardogs, too precious to be wasted, as well as the League guards and the Riders and their offspring. If the riders realized the League intent they refused to even allow a chance of conception.

And there were disquieting signs that, despite the League's efforts, some form of organization or at least communication must exist between the riders. Yet a spy, one who was capable of emotional bonding with a Stardog, had yet to be found.

Artificially breeding riders seemed to be the answer. But, as the Stardog cloning-project had revealed, the supply of competent bio-techs was limited. Between the Empire and the League, the sciences at Universities had been quietly strangled, especially in the fields that could pose a threat to either. The League had the best they could recruit for the avenues they wanted pursued, but still it seemed that research was not very successful as a unidirectional thing. There was a need for supporting disciplines.

●●●◌◌◌

Back in his apartment Johannes Wienan stirred uneasily in his sleep. The girl had slipped quietly back into the bed. In less than a week he would be riding the shuttle up to the space-station. Then on, across the open spaces between the stars. He would be carrying the deadly silicon life form nerve-toxin, attached to a heart-monitor. A dead-man switch that had never been needed in the last five hundred years.

Lila still did not know if he was going to take her with him. She hated him, but at least he wasn't depraved like some of the other Wienans. She was a debt-slave, her contract sold to pay off her father's debts. The contract still had seven years to run. Then she would be free, and with the money earned by her second job, independent. But seven years could be a long time to survive in this place.

CHAPTER 5
THE YAK

"In the well-ordered garden it is always the weeds that grow fastest. So too in an ordered society, it is the weeds that grow with astonishing rapidity. You can either spend all your energies pulling up weeds, or you can learn to use them."

The Upanishad of the Gardener-Dewa Celine.

Sam Teovan was five years old when the new-born Princess Shari was wrapped in the softest of coverlets with its border delicately embroidered in gold thread and carried to her jeweled cot for the first time. He had been wrapped in old newspapers and destined to be thrust into a bin behind a dingy night-club when he'd been born. It hadn't quite happened, and he'd received the food and warmth he craved from the mother who'd been nearly desperate enough to kill him. But he did have something in common with the Princess. At four and a half she'd abruptly lost her mother, and so had he. But while she had been taken from her palatial apartments and a small army of servants and handed over to a peasant-nursemaid with a solitary, crippled, too-old security man to obey the forms of giving her a bodyguard, he had had to flee to the dumps. She'd at least gone on living in the palace, if under far less opulent conditions. You could get killed for being an out-of-favor Princess in the palace, but children in the dumps seldom lived past a few weeks. For Sam it had been a stark choice of the dumps or being sold to the paedophile market. The preternaturally sharp child had known that the dumps, grim though they were, were the better option. Sam always knew the best option.

The Imperial city boasted of having the largest of many things, buildings, baths, subways. It also had the largest dump in human space. Nobody boasted about this, not even the scarecrow people who lived their entire, usually short, lives in the fifty hectare gradually infilling valley. It is said that you could find anything in the dumps, from lost jewels to tetanus or poisoned food. Somehow Sam always knew how to avoid the latter.

The Princess had gone from being an item to be pampered without fondness to gradually becoming the utter darling of two people who loved her unstintingly and eventually gave their lives willingly for her. Sam Teovan had gone from a loving but hopelessly drug-enslaved foolish mother, whom he had tried to save with all his too-old-for-four but too-young-to-understand ability, to the dumps. Here he had never again allowed himself to get close to anyone, not even the others of dump-urchin gang he'd run with, and eventually come to lead. Most of those who came here that young just died, but not Sam. He made the right choices, joined the right gang. To the gang he became a near-sacred oracle. When the Muti-men prowled at night, looking for body-parts for their foul trade, his lot were always elsewhere. Gang-fight traps somehow failed on Teovan's bunch. He was also infallible about poison.

Then, late in the afternoon, just before the police death squads had moved in, he had told them to come with him into the city. They'd balked. The dumps were home, their life, their turf. He walked away from them, away from leadership and the power that had cost him the razor-slash across the cheek to win. He didn't want to go either. But somehow he knew that to stay was to die.

Sam had gone from being a dump-picker to being a mugger and a second-story man, sleeping and living in the dank alleys of the poor, half-warehouse part of town. The scrawny wire-tough boy grew to be a scrawny wire-tough man working independently in the back streets of an area where you didn't even pick a pocket without permission and a cut to the organization. The Yak.

Humanity's diaspora into space had brought about a terrible fusion of some of the various aspects of organised crime. These hybrids, particularly the Corsican-Japanese-Russian blend, had grown explosively. The last hundred years or so, as the Empire became more stable, and gradually more corrupt, had been particularly good to them.

Of course various families contested for turf. Only Teovan could have found the one fence that was secretly working for another family in Caranzia-Heiki territory. The man was thus prepared to buy Sam's wares, which no loyal Caranzia-Heiki would have. Somehow, Sam's instincts had drawn him to visit the fence on the day that the Sakhalin-Carrisi family planned to move on their rivals. The moment he walked into the pawn-broker's shop he knew something was wrong. It had taken him seconds to spot the two hidden men with automatic rifles. Behind him Salvatore Caranzio-Heiki walked in. He had only one bodyguard with him. This was the heart of his own turf, and he was secure in it. Sam took one brief look at the beefy head of the Caranzio-Heiki Family and knew what was coming. His instincts told him where the choice between life and death lay.

A wealthy businessman had, some ten years ago, disposed of his partner and his unfaithful wife one dark night. He'd used an antique .22 target pistol, and a cunningly made silencer. Afterwards he'd put the weapon, and several boxes of ammunition, into a plastic bag, driven thirty miles and tossed the bag into a passing dumpster. Sam Teovan had unearthed it. After that his gang had always been able to feast on roast rat when nothing else offered. Sam didn't miss. Stationary targets, like the two waiting men, were just about too easy.

Afterwards, the meaty Caranzia-Heiki had slipped his own weapon back into his shoulder holster. His bodyguard had absorbed the whippet blast that the fence had directed at him. He looked at the sprawled bodies of the ambush team, and at the scrawny, stunted man with the .22 still in his hand. "Roll up their left sleeves, boy," he said to Sam, his gravel-crusher voice unperturbed.

Sam Teovan did, exposing intricate tattoos.

"Ah. Carrisi. The bastards will pay a deep price for this shit. Now, let's see your arm, boy."

Sam pulled up the ragged sleeve. A few scars showed, but no blue and red tattoo. Sal Caranzia-Heiki frowned. "You not with the Families, boy?"

Sam shook his head warily. "No, San."

Salvatore took a look at the two hit-men, each with a neat hole exactly mid-forehead. He took a ring off his pinky finger. "You are now. You know where the Salomar Hotel is?"

Sam nodded. Drunks from the place were soft targets.

"You go to the desk. You give Gio this ring. You tell him Sal says to give you a room, food, an' get you some decent clothes. And have a bath. You smell like you haven't had one for months." Actually, Sam couldn't remember ever having had one.

Sam looked briefly at the heavy ornate gold ring the man pressed into his hand. Briefly he thought of what it would fetch, and then knew with absolute certainty that selling this particular item would be terminal.

●●●⊃●●

Sam Teovan's upward progress within the family was meteoritic. He was a major factor in the rise of the Caranzia-Heiki family to supremacy on Phillipia, and to enormous power elsewhere. He was also a major factor in the demise of the Sakhalin-Carrisi family. Sam's operations never went wrong. Salvatore always said he was fanatically loyal to the Caranzia-Heiki because they had taken him in, given him the family he needed. But it must be remembered that Sam Teovan knew instinctively which were bad options. Perhaps the alternative to loyalty to Sal was worse.

He sat in on the big meeting and was part of the plan. At least he didn't say anything against it. But when he left his mouth was dry and his head full of a distant thunder. He was one of the privileged few who rode in Sal's own groundcar. When they were clear of the carefully chosen neutral site Sal relaxed. "Well, Sam? What you think, huh?"

Sam shook his head. "If we can do it San, it's good. The fuckin' League have had their foot on our necks for too long. But I don't like that *Caporegime* from the Dakada-clan."

His master's eyes narrowed. He knew of Sam's instincts and used them. "We need the bastards. This thing's too big for one family. The Dakada's smuggling connections are important in this thing too, *paisan*. But afterwards.... " he drew a thick finger across his throat. He put a big hand on Sam's slight, wiry shoulder. "Sam. This one I want you to take." And Sam once again had that feeling which had driven him to save this man's life. His own life, he knew, stood at a cross-road. And none of the choices felt good.

The next meeting was held in one of the clubs in the red-light district. The Green Door was not a Heiki place, but the family who owned it were old and trusted allies. Salvatore was at ease here. Sam was not. Prostitution was the norm in his world. Even so, this place gave him the creeps. It dealt explicitly in boys, drugs and pain. In the Imperial city, there was a niche market for almost any form of vice, and the Yak serviced all those niches.

Sam moved around the back room like a stepping razor, eyes never truly still, hand close to the infamous .22. He watched that almond-eyed Dakada bastard in particular. That willowy individual was smoothly at ease however. He was the one who got the game of cards started while they waited. Sam didn't play, but although he couldn't swear to it, he thought the man cheated… with the intent to lose? Sam couldn't figure it out. Eventually the one they waited for came.

He was a footman. A man in Imperial service, even if he had carefully shed his livery. That morning he had been waiting on Princess Shari. His unpleasant tastes led him to frequent places like the Green Door. Indeed, these depraved tastes had left him putty in the hands of the Yak, who had pandered to him… and then enmeshed him.

The cauliflower-eared waiter pushed him through the hidden doorway of the sound-screened back room. "He got caught up in watching the floorshow, boss." A thin scream came down the passage. "He'd still be there if I hadn't hurried him along." The disdain in the waiter's voice was unmistakable.

"Thanks… Sergio." The waiter left, closing the soundproof door behind him.

The footman bowed servilely. His lips were wet and his eyes a little bright and wide from what he'd seen out there. "I… I thought it was best not to be too obvious coming in here. I was just lingering in the common-room awhile until I thought I could come here unobtrusively."

His excuse was greeted with silence. The kind of silence that is far more frightening than words. "I… I've got the itinerary. Dates, times… everything you wanted." The footman was sweating freely now.

Salvatore stood up, dwarfing the footman. He held out his hand. "Where is it, *Eta*?"

"It's all in my head, Sir. I can't leave the Imperial compound with a list like that! Selim Puk's men would find it for sure!" The almond eyed card player put his cards face down with a slight smile. "But, honest, I've got it all memorized. Just give me some paper..."

Salvatore looked at him, cocking his big bullet head slightly. "Don't fuck about with me, mister." He turned away, to the elegantly underdressed girl who had been serving drinks. "Bring pretty boy here some paper and a pen. And then scram, honey." She left as fast as her stiletto heels could carry her. Once she'd returned with the paper and pen she again made a rapid exit. She'd been working in this house for two years now. She had a pretty good idea what might happen in that room, and she wanted no part of it.

With slightly shaking hands the footman wrote out the Princess's itinerary. If he got out of here alive he turn over a new leaf... Then he thought of the reward he'd been promised. He licked his lips again.

Salvatore took the list to the others at the table. The Dakada smuggler got up and looked at it. "It checks. Well, we can get your men the berths. Their stuff will have to come on at the Barhain II stopover. We own that shift of customs."

"Well, Sam?"

The small man nodded. "Fine by me, San."

"And your men, Georgio?"

"Blower Yu and Turk Osman. I'm giving you my best, Sal. I'll have to pull them off somet'ing else, but like you say, if we can pull this one off..."

The bald, ultraviolet-dried elderly man who had said nothing so far allowed his straight-line mouth to twitch into the semblance of a smile that didn't extend as far as his eyes. He was from the asteroid miner's union, and crucial to their plans. He was also wary. "We'll be there, Carranzio-Heiki. We'll have a ship waiting when they pop out of surf. Your boys'll have maybe twenty minutes to get control, dump the barge and get us to jump instead. Maybe two hundred years ago, before the League set up their sector system, the dogs used to jump New Sahara - Caladar IV all the time. In all the rocks in the Caldahar System we can disappear for as long as need be."

Sal flicked a glance to Sam. The Union man had said too much in front of that footman. Well, he was about past being useful anyway.

The spy shifted his weight from foot to foot. "Well... I've done it. Now, my money, and... and that boy, er, Mr Carranzio, Sir?" He licked his lips again, greed and other unpleasant desires overcoming his fear.

"Sam'll sort you out."

A week later they fished his body out of the sewers. His face, teeth and hands had been carefully mutilated. Sometimes the Yak didn't like their victims being quickly identifiable.

⦿⦿⦿⦿⦿⦿

The Emperor sat, fat and impassive, and listened to his willowy, almond-eyed security chief.

Selim Puk smiled cruelly. "They've taken it hook, line and sinker, my liege.

"The Yak are implicated beyond doubt?"

"Absolutely. I have names, dates, places. I lost a witness, unfortunately. That fool footman heard too much from Wright...the asteroid miner's man. But we can do without a footman. One of the others will crack, when they see I know everything."

"It is one of your better plots, Selim. At one stroke we discredit the League, dispose of Shari and give me reason to crack down on the Yak, hard. They've been getting above themselves."

"And, if all goes according to plan, we have a Stardog of our own, beyond League control."

"Yes. But that depends on the agents in place. How do you rate this Brettan?"

"Greedy, my Liege. Greedy, aging and impatient."

"And he is definitely not in League pay?" The fat-folds around the emperor's eyes crinkled.

"Definitely not. He has a deep grudge, a deep and a real one. If it were not for the League he would be a wealthy man. A very wealthy man. His older sister married a Leaguesman. One of Wienan's, no less. She had a falling out with them, and tried to run away, with her child, more the fool her."

"Stupid. They might have let her get away, but not with a half-Wienan child," said Turabi, with the clinical assessment of a master of dynastic elimination.

Selim Puk snorted. "Jan-Pieter was brutally thorough, as usual. The young Viscount was in the Imperial Space Navy at the time, on a long patrol, which is why he didn't get taken out too. The family purge was most thorough otherwise, and the purge of their assets left our Viscount literally destitute when he came home. Anyway, I've had him sent for. He should be here any minute now." On cue there was a knock at the heavy door.

"Enter."

Captain Viscount Martin Brettan's nerves shrieked as he passed the bodyguards. He hoped it didn't show. An audience with Selim Puk and the Blob didn't happen every day, even if he was some sort of distant cousin to the Blob. You could afford to turn into a lard-lump like that if you were the Emperor. If you were just a pretty-boy beefcake like himself on a thin spy's salary you had to work out in the gym every day to keep being pretty. He knelt. It was not a mistake despite the fact that this was not a formal reception. The Blob liked to be reminded of his power, even now, nearly twenty years after he had seized it. "My Lord Emperor. How may I serve you?"

The Emperor was well enough pleased by the fawning to be gracious. The fat face nearly creased to a smile. Graciousness of course didn't extend as far as offering the man a seat. "We need your services, Viscount Brettan. We are sure Selim has already briefed you."

The handsome aristocrat nodded warily. He wondered if he dared question why he had received such rapid promotion in the schemes of the Empire. "Yes Sire. Of course I'm willing, Sire... but why me?"

"A modest man, eh Selim?" said the Emperor.

"It is a useful trait, my Liege. Captain, you're being used for this because you are an agent in place. Moving new men in would cause suspicion. The major-domo is of course also an agent, but he also spies for the League. He does this with our consent... but it reduces the degree to which he trustable. As for the two bodyguards... Hayley is a good executioner, but he doesn't have the brains we require for this. Albeer is loyal, but just hasn't displayed the right attitude for this aspect of security work. Squeamish. He was dumped there, I'm afraid. Anyway, any or all of them may be corrupted by the League. But you'll have a team among the crew of the barge. Good, safe, clean men. You be able to deal with the Yak easily enough. There are only four of them. I sat in on their planning," said Selim Puk.

"But don't fail us, Brettan. If you bring us a Stardog, we'll make good again all that the League robbed you of... but don't fail us." It was said so mildly that if anyone other than the Blob had said it, it wouldn't have been a threat.

Martin Brettan knew it for what it was. His face paled slightly. "I won't fail you, my Emperor."

"Good. You are dismissed, Brettan," said the Emperor.

The Viscount bowed and turned. As he walked away he heard the Emperor say to the head of security. "Selim, that problem with that son of mine. A possible solution has..." The heavy nail-studded door of the private audience chamber closed behind the Princess's escort. Rivulets of sweat touched the stiff fabric of his tunic as his tense shoulders began to relax. He walked past the last of the hawk-eyed guards. He'd have given a great deal to have heard which of the Emperor's sons was in for the chop this time. A lot of people would have given a great deal of money to know who *not* to position themselves behind. With five of the seven sons still surviving the dynastic battle was hotting up. Martin Brettan suspected Prince Vartan would be next to go. There were rumours about certain expensive and hopelessly addictive drugs drifting around, hooked to that young man's name.

●●●⊃●●

The Viscount was wrong. A drug problem meant that Vartan could be manipulated, true. But the Emperor was more concerned by a subtle and nearly successful attempt on the life of his own Imperial person. Prince Jarian had to go. Young Jarian was only sixteen, but then, by that age, he, Turabi, had already eliminated his own brother and his father and mother.

●●●⊃●●

Sam Teovan had the meeting and training session with the wine-nosed old toff patsy himself. He didn't like him. The fellow was too old and too damn soft. But Sam's instincts held that the old fart wouldn't chicken out on them. Not while they had all that black on the old boy's son. Still, the man was a weak link. Sam resolved to put no faith in him. The man's purpose really had been as a double-check on all the other information. It might be useful to have a man on the inside, yes. But Sam had more trust in professionals like Blower and Turk. They had a good rep, those two. Georgio was really giving the boss his best, to prove his faith.

But the whole thing still felt... bad. And he had no way he could back out.

CHAPTER 6
JOURNEY

*Our journeys have many dimensions, physical,
mental, spiritual. The physical journey to the
expected may lead us to unplanned destinations in
the other dimensions. Always be wary about the
water in these places.*

**From a tomb-epitaph in the churchyard of our Lady of
Chatterjee, in the grounds of the Thuggee training-
madrassa on Arunchal.**

It was cold in the rider-compound in the early mornings. Looking
up from the raked gravel of the exercise ground you could see the
mullioned windows of the League Grand-Dacha. They shared the
same outer perimeter wall. There the similarity ended. The ornate
Neo-Ottoman design of the Grand-Dacha on Phillipia was used as
a model by schools of architecture. The irreverent claimed it to be
the finest example of bad taste that money could buy. The rider-
compound was a prison. Built of un-plastered cinderblocks the
architecture compared well to East-German slave-labor camps.
But the architectural students who came to see the Grand-Dacha

were quite skilled at ignoring the compound. Besides, compared to the vastness of the Grand-Dacha, it was tiny.

Liton stood along with the other fifteen inmates of the compound out on the exercise-ground and shivered and waited. Somebody would be leaving today. So, as usual, they'd all been left to stand, waiting. The morning porridge would be congealed and cold in their wooden bowls when they were allowed to go. That was a matter of no concern to the compound guards. It was only the riders' time, and to the compound guards, the time of the 2300-odd riders whose on-planet lives they ruled was irrelevant.

Once there had been far more riders than Stardogs. Once there had been 3762 Stardogs. Now there were less than 2500... the exact number was a well-kept League secret. And now there were too few riders... Even here at the center of the Empire there were only fifteen riders in the compound and not in use. Rest periods, for both dogs and riders, seemed to be getting shorter and shorter.

In a few minutes... or a few hours, depending on when the League men arrived, some of them would be sent out again, told to leave at a moment's notice. It didn't really matter. Riders had no possessions to pack. And in space they were back with their dogs. Here, on-planet, they were only half alive, surviving poor food and punishing gravity-acclimatization and bone-structure maintenance exercises until they went to space again.

The inner steel door of the compound slid open. Even the machine-gun armed guards in the watchtowers saluted the two men in the maroon uniform of League officers who entered. The sector system, the ban on communication, the jails, the locked cabins on shipboard, the guards, were part of the Wienan paranoia, and their total failure to understand the psychology of their rider-chattels. Leaguesmen would have taken to violence and escape, but not the riders... Riders hated Leaguesmen, but the level of empathy needed to communicate with Stardogs precluded the easy hurting of others. And killing would destroy the killer. Besides... the League held their Stardogs hostage. The Stardogs were not mistreated, but they could be.

The two Leaguesmen wore identical uniforms, but that was all they had in common. Liton recognised the shorter blond man as a pureblood-Wienan. His facial lines had been cursed and hated by thousands and thousands of riders for more than four centuries. Yet, it was when the aging rider looked at the other leaguesman that his blood ran cold. The angular face with its harsh planes and deep-set cold intolerant eyes was something out of his childhood. Something terrible. A face he'd tried desperately hard to forget, but that still recurred in his nightmares, time and again. He shivered now with something more than just the cold. He prayed hard that he would go with the Wienan.

The two Leaguesmen walked forward. To his relief Liton saw the young Wienan point to him. Then, to his horror, he saw the other man go to the slight young girl. The new one. The Leaguesman smiled. A cold, hungry, feral smile full of teeth and unpleasant intent. He beckoned, his hand like a talon.

The gaunt girl started, as she realized it was she who was being summonsed. She took an involuntary step backwards. The Leaguesman licked his thin lips, relishing her obvious fear. He beckoned again. She stood frozen. The fleshy compound guard who had been bringing their shackles stormed towards her. She shied and whimpered, holding up her thin arms to ward off the expected blow.

"I,I,I will go with him inst,t,tead," stuttered Liton, knowing it was futile. He could see others in the courtyard volunteering too.

The guard and the angular League man ignored him, and the others. The Wienan's hand wove in rapid handspeech however "Behave yourselves, or we'll have your dogs whipped." Most of the riders could lip-read to some extent, but it had long ago been decided to isolate the riders as much as possible. Therefore League agents used an ancient code of hand-signs, not known outside of the League.

The other riders in the courtyard were stilled. She would be tranquillized soon and going to her own Stardog. After that they would never hurt her again. They didn't physically abuse riders once they had actually bonded with a Stardog. The dogs simply wouldn't tolerate it. But in the exercise yard the hatred for the Wienan was so thick in the air you could taste it.

Liton and the girl were shackled and guard-escorted to the waiting groundcar. It was a long, elegant-looking vehicle, with real gold trim gleaming amid the polished maroon paint work. The League men were bowed into their seats by a chauffeur who held the door for them. In the less-well-upholstered seat behind them sat a girl who was plainly a servant. She didn't even look at the riders, but sat rigid, staring straight ahead.

The riders were shoved into a bare expanded-mesh compartment at the back. Stowed like luggage they began their journey to the waiting shuttle-craft. The vehicle stuttered and burped and smoked, belying its elegant appearance.

The new girl wept quietly in the corner of the baggage compartment, repulsing Liton's efforts to comfort her, hiding her face in her hands. So the older rider thought about Shahjah instead. The too-thin frightened girl looked up from her crying. Plainly he was projecting the love and happiness. Her red-rimmed eyes showed disbelief, and just the faintest trace of hope. He smiled at her. She looked warily at him, and then allowed a weak, unaccustomed smile to touch her lips too. But his own mind was full of confused emotions. He was going back to his beloved. But they would make him fly his darling between the stars, and Shahjah was too old... too old...

The groundcar bumped across to the shuttle. Soon the riders were struggling up the steps in their hobbling shackles. It was a relief to reach their places in the acceleration seats next to the open door. Usually this was the signal for the shuttle to lift, as the other less important passengers would have been waiting for the League-man. But now they sat, waiting. The shuttle was empty of other passengers, except for seven liveried servants, obviously also destined for the waiting ship.

Then through the doorway Lit saw an ornately gilded flyer land. Two men in blue and gold, the Imperial colors, leapt out, unfolded the stairs and held the door open. The party that emerged looked like odd exotic butterflies against the stark dun colors of the landing field. They sauntered slowly across the intervening space, giving the two riders, who were openly staring, ample time to study them.

There were the blue and gold-uniformed two, who walked the outside edges of the party with wary, catlike tread, eyes roving, hands never that far from side-arms. Between them walked a handsome gentleman with a lady on his arm. He wore an elegantly tailored blue-black Imperial Space-navy uniform ribboned with gold braid. She wore a gem-glistening tiara, perched in a carefully curled elegant nest of grey hair. Her coiffeuse secretly despaired about the color. He'd never been asked to tint hair grey before. Her clothes were the height of current fashion, in metallic-finish amber and chartreuse.

But her face could have come off an old coin. One of the ones that showed the Emperor Vespasia. The high, wide cheekbones and the aquiline nose were not pretty-pretty. Neither was the determined chin. Or the wide, sensual mouth. She looked every inch of an Imperial Princess. Liton had never seen her, or even a picture of her, but he decided that it *could* only possibly be the sister of the Emperor himself. He gaped. Looking at her, Liton decided that the clothes had simply failed to measure up to the person. The shapely curvaceous creature behind her, with her honey-blond hair and happy smile suited the frilly clothes. But the Princess, he thought, would have looked more at home in armor.

There were three other members to the party. Beside the elegant strawberry-blond trotted a short, frumpish lady with glasses perched on the end of her nose and several extraneous parcels, who managed to make the current fashions look like bizarre add-ons. Behind them all walked an unobtrusive man in unornamented grey. And in front of the party walked, or rather sniffed, a small, fluffy dog. It was for the benefit of the dog that the party sauntered. When the dog had finally relieved itself, the party entered the waiting shuttle. Knowing that to sit was to die, the entire crew stood up.

The Princess smiled. She smiled right to the eyes. It altered her face, taking it from the cold, powerful Imperial to the warm human. By definition, the aristocracy do not ever say that they are sorry. Whatever goes wrong is your fault, not theirs. She waved to all of them, and broke the rules. "My apologies to you all. Otto," she pointed to the tail-wagging dog surveying them, "you understand, is prone to having little accidents, if he does not, er 'go' before lift-off. As he insists on sitting on my lap, I try to make sure he has the opportunity before we leave. Please sit. As I assume you will be my Crew for this tour, I want you to know that I don't believe in protocol in flight. I will enjoy meeting all of you soon." Her manners were legendary, even in the underclasses. It was a shock to discover the legend understated the truth.

She took her seat, and Otto took his with a bound. Lit wished he could have heard her voice, not just lip-read. But his mind was full of questions. Why was he, one of the more obstreperous of riders, being used to ferry the Imperial Princess? Why had the League decided to use an old Stardog like his Shahjah? Why was there a new, inexperienced Leaguesman going along? The thoughts jostled in his head as the gravscoops began to thrust the shuttle upward. His fellow rider-to-be, however, had no such thoughts. She was simply staring at the brown eyes of the princess's fluff-ball. Her face ran the gamut of expressions from fear to a desperate yearning.

At the space station the Imperial party was split off from them, piped aboard with full military honors by the Imperial Military Unit stationed there to guard the missile stockpile that each station held for the Empire. With a handful of nuclear missiles hanging overhead, insurrection became unthinkable, except on a very minor scale. Space station duty, with its cramped quarters and non-existent recreational facilities, was an Imperial trooper's idea of purgatory. The troopers weren't even allowed to fraternize with the civilian stationers, to prevent any possibility of infiltration. It would appear that this suited the stationers very well.

The League also maintained quarters on each station. These were not as sybaritic as those of the planetside Dachas, but the wastefulness of both space and resources were still apparently a source of envy and immense irritation to the stationers. The League also kept a six by eight foot cell for riders, with four tiers of narrow bunks, a basin and a sluice. Liton looked forward to it. It was the one place that riders could meet and pass messages, other than in the communal showers in the compounds. This was better than the showers, for it was known that station-cells were totally and utterly spy-proof. The cell, being part of the station's climate control, was warm and pleasant, also unlike the compound showers. Also, the stationers fed them, and the food was always good.

Besides, here in space, he was closer to Shahjah. She was out there, coming closer, aware that was back from the gravity-well. Soon they would ride on her back like fleas, bouncing between stars. Liton settled onto the bunk. It was narrow but upholstered to a degree of comfort he was unused to. Well, they were secure and safe for a few hours at least. He began to relax.

Then the apparently solid wall opposite him split aside. A stationer stepped into the rider's little island of security. The woman made a sign. The sign of the moon. The new moon. The symbol of rebellion. Frozen and frightened the older rider watched. The girl on the lower bunk didn't. She screamed, or Liton assumed she must have because the stationer put her hands to her ears, before hastily putting her finger to her lips.

The stationer reached for Liton. Despite the sign, and all it implied, the rider flinched. Then she placed something in his ear. He clawed frantically at the ear. The thing was burrowing into his head! "...on't panic."

The rider nearly fainted. He heard her. HE HEARD HER!

"What...?" his own voice sounded strange, fuzzy... but audible.

"It is a bone-induction hearing-aid. Please help me with the girl."

The girl rider was lying in a fetal ball on the couch, eyes closed.

"Fainted," said the stationer. "Probably easier." She slipped the device into the ear of the girl. "I hope she doesn't take too long to come around. I'd rather talk to both of you at once."

"Is this the revolution come at last? Will my Stardog be safe?"

●●C ●●

Station tech Karson smiled reasurringly at the poor little rider. "You riders all ask the same questions." She shook her head and sighed, "No, I'm afraid this isn't the revolution. You know that isn't intended to be a bang, but a whimper when it does finally come. Nobody knows the date, for obvious reasons, but it must be a number of years off yet. Probably not in your lifetime, I'm afraid," she lied. She knew the empire's computed infall was less than ten years off, but there was no point in telling this poor man. "And, yes, hopefully your Stardog will be safe, after this." She handed him a small glass vial. "I'm afraid you'll have to hide it in your rectum. It won't show on scan. Break the container onto the filaments, or if possible apply it directly onto the skin of your Stardog."

"What is it?" the rider asked warily.

"Toxin antidote. The animal will be safe against the League rider's toxin capsule after that," explained Karson.

The look on the rider's face was worth many lifetimes of struggle. The new-rider girl stirred and groaned. Gently Liton took her hand. "She's a friend. Really."

"I'm scared. Don't hurt me again. Please." Then the girl-rider clapped her hand to her ear. The one the device had been put into. A wild, hunted look darted across her eyes. "This is a dream... isn't it?" she asked plaintively, her thin voice on the edge of panic.

Karson stifled the fury that boiled in her. Few stationers or even ordinary planet-people had seen what the League had done to these poor people. Her anger would simply frighten the girl. "Calm down. No one's going to hurt you. It is not a dream, child. But we're not going to hurt you. It is just a hearing aid."

"Take it away. Please take it away. I'm so scared. Please..." she shivered.

The stationer looked at her, puzzled. This was not the usual reaction. The riders were afraid, yes, but delighted to hear. "We can take it out if you like. But I've got an on-off switch for you to put onto one of your teeth. Don't you want to be able to hear again?"

In answer the girl looked fearfully at the door. "No. They'll find it. They'll hurt us. You must go! They might come any minute now." She clawed at her ear.

The stationer smiled reassuringly at her, habitual creases forming in her face. "Relax, child. The door won't open, even if they should come to it. It is stuck... apparently. Actually, the central computer is locking it. They'll have to call station personnel to unstick it. By that time I'll be gone, and everything will be absolutely normal. The hearing aid is designed to pass undetected by everything but dissection and examination under a microscope. We're a long way ahead of the League in technology. You can, indeed you must, turn it off most of the time. It is hard to pretend deafness, especially in the way you speak, so the hearing aids are only for emergencies. Besides, isn't it nice to know you have friends?"

"It is." Liton looked at the little glass vial. "But, if you are so far ahead of the League, then why are we still captives? Why have we not had the antidote before?"

"You're still captives because you riders don't want any risk to your Stardogs, and the antidote is very difficult to manufacture. We have... a small number of places... which can do it. Getting the stuff across sectors and distributed has been incredibly difficult. We can't take the slightest chance on a load being intercepted, even by accident. Making the stuff is the devil, but any halfway competent League Chemist could tell them what it is. You see, there are a number of different potential poisons the League could use, and if the antidote is discovered the League could simply change poisons, and we'd be back to square one, eh?"

The rider nodded in wholehearted agreement. "What else can we do?" he said helplessly.

"What you can do on this particular trip, which is one of the main reasons we've made this contact, is to watch the Princess and her party. We're sure the League has something plotted. It is... absolutely vital to the cause, to the survival of the Stardogs, that they fail."

●●●ɔɘɘ

Liton blinked in surprise. "Yes, but... we won't even see them again. Riders are kept isolated from passengers. We might see her in the shuttle, but not otherwise."

"On the Royal Barge you will not be isolated. You will be right there on the Nav. Deck, with the party. We don't expect you to be able to do anything, but information, any information, may help. Listen in to conversations that the Leaguesmen are making, if possible." Suddenly she cocked her head slightly, obviously listening to something they couldn't hear. "Comp informs me that the Leaguesmen are leaving their quarters on their way here. I have just three minutes to show you how to operate the tooth-mounted on-off units. Please open your mouth.

When the door opened to admit the Leaguesmen the room showed no signs of any visible disturbance. Liton had a disturbed rectum and a severely disturbed mind, however. He was rider, true. But that didn't mean he couldn't put two and two together. The only reason he could come up with for the Princess Royal's journeys being so important was that the antidote courier must be part of her party. It was brilliant. Of course they wouldn't be searched. The Princess's trip must provide the New Moon with perfect opportunities. No wonder they didn't want her stopped.

❄❄❄❄❄❄

The Denaari ships had been found nearly fifty years after the League had first begun systematically mapping the Stardog ranges. New Sahara had been the Denaari idea of a fine colonial world, which is to say a vegetationless, cold, dry hell. In the trojan-point between the planet and the small moon, the explorer ship had found two drifting Denaari hulks. The ships were small, much smaller than the League lighters and cargo barges. They appeared to be in perfect preservation, except that the airlocks had been left cycled open. One of the two had been presented with much fanfare by the League Chairman to the Imperial house. That Emperor had seen fit to have the vessel refitted as his royal barge. It had been a hundred years since the craft had last been used by a scion of the royal house, before Shari. Her brother, in a spirit of unpleasantness, had offered it to her for her fund-raising campaigns.

It was one of his many attempts at odiousness which had backfired due to his own ignorance. He disliked leaving the palace; and space, where the hand of the League would be around him was simply not to be considered. He'd never been up there and never seen the Denaari craft, but the idea of the tiny, alien designed ship frightened him, arousing claustrophobic feelings. Apparently, because of space constraints, the ship's only lounge was also the navigation deck. It had vast forward windows, actual thin transparent stuff, not just the safe, switch-off-able viewscreens of human-built ships. Through this the starswirl chaos of wormhole surf was not only visible but unavoidable. In addition there was actual physical contact with those revolting space-monsters too. It was the sort of gift he'd enjoyed giving her. He was suitably nastily gratified by her tepid but unavoidably polite response.

Actually, she loved it. Unlike the deep-space vessels of the League, lumpy things built out here where gravity and streamlining had no dictates, the old Denaari craft was externally cat-sleek. The make over had tacked secure cabins into the interior. However everything, roof height included, had originally been suitable for Denaari sized passengers. It had been impractical to change the height of the ceilings. Thus, while all other ships plying human space had standard 7 foot ceilings, the roof in the Imperial barge came in at just under twelve feet. The rooms were of suitable Imperial dimensions. The ship, now fitted for twenty-three humans, would, in cubic footage, have carried more than ninety people in League container-ship space.

The stardeck, on which one could watch the endless panorama of gravity-shifted light was her favourite place. Etching by space-dust and micrometeor impacts had made human ships resort to small and replaceable external lenses and interior view-screens. But the windows of the Denaari-barge had some miracle of crystallographic engineering about them. Even after centuries in space the huge windows were not opaqued by micrometeor scarring. Indeed you could watch the scars happen... and heal.

The Stationers had the ship ready. That was unusual. There was usually a suitably arranged delay so that she could spend several extra hours on station. And judge yet another guinea-pig show! Her lip twitched at the thought. One day perhaps she could reveal that they were *not* her favorite animal. Otto II had nearly caused a major incident by chasing one.

But among those who were to be her crew the stationers had identified at least four recognized League agents. Killers... and then there had been Syrian.

Of course the efficient Syrian Brynant had been waiting at the Space-Station. Fussing about like a mother-hen. She'd known that he'd soon start to pester her with a slew of high-profile functions he wanted her to attend, at the expense of several back-country visits. As usual the thought of the pointless argument irritated her. She'd sighed to herself, in annoyance... if he wasn't a faithful old retainer... But that was the way her brother treated those who were loyal to him. She was damned if she'd be tarred with the same brush. So she'd greeted him with every sign of pleasure. "Dear Sir Syrian. A delight to see you again. I trust you have organized everything with your usual efficiency?"

He bowed low. "Yes, your highness. Everything is perfectly in hand." His voice seemed slightly strained, but he led her forward to introduce her to the station commander. That worthy greeted her with the perfunctory politeness that the egalitarian Station-folk customarily accorded any of the hereditary title-holders of the empire. The only vaguely unusual public deed was his request to take a holo-pix of Otto III. That request was unlikely to attract much attention from his Imperial masters.

For the first time ever Syrian hadn't tried to alter her on-planet schedules! Normally, he tried desperately to shuffle her itinerary. This time... he hadn't. Something must be wrong. So the Stationers had hurried things along to try to upset any assassin's timetables. She was really upset by the Station folk too... Usually, they were so carefully aloof, even when there were no Imperial officials present. Now, suddenly, the corridors were full of people who had fawned about and wanted to touch her, or touch her clothing, or touch Otto III, even when there were Imperial or League witnesses. Plainly, they didn't expect her to come back. And Otto hadn't liked being pawed by all and sundry.

Even if she was heading into danger... she was relieved to be back in the ship. Maybe she was being sentimental, but the imperial barge had a warmth about it that was missing from the League ships. Somehow she felt that it was a place which had been loved, once. It would be a good place to face whatever was coming. And at least while they were in surf it would be safe to relax for a while. The League would never move while she was in surf. It might disturb the Stardog.

The stubby tugs pushed the barge away from the space station, and off into space. The Stardog was on its way and would intercept them there. Shari watched from the stardeck. She'd seen it several thousand times now, but never tired of it. This time the poignant knowledge that this might be her last trip, made the sighting of the indrifting Stardog, with its filament-mat gleaming like a filigree of silver wires against the blackness of space, even more rich and rare. As if to reward her this beast was the most gloriously silvered she'd ever seen.

Gradually the rest of the retinue came up to join her. Last

came the Guildsmen and the poor rider, looking like a dog that had just been whipped for no reason he could understand. If only she could tell him… She ignored him, acted as if he simply wasn't there. Accepted the Leaguesmen's bow coolly, and turned away from them and the rider.

Actually, she was watching them, particularly the rider, in the reflection of the highly polished bar that some long-dead emperor had had fitted to cover the inscrutable Denaari instruments. The odd-shaped alien couches had also been ripped out and replaced. In their place they had fitted comfortable, velvet-upholstered loungers for the Emperor's guests to enjoy watching the star-swirl. She wished the pompous ass had been less fond of Lapis-Lazuli inlays in the mirror-polished surface of the bar. She loved watching the riders while they discovered the difference between Denaari and human ships. The bar gave her a way of doing so without being obvious.

●●●○●●

Juan Biacasta studied the model of the Denarii barge again. Carefully he opened the small airlock in the tail-section. It was something he'd found by accident, and he was sure that most people had no idea existed on the centuries old ship. He'd checked it in every online resource he'd been able to find. The Denaari engine-room airlock had been welded shut when they converted the ship to the royal barge. Of course no-one would be able to access the Princess royal's ship while it was in port. No one would be allowed into the docking area. Well, no-one who did not have his father's access codes. And the main airlock would be well guarded.

Which was why he would not go near it. In fact he wouldn't even be at dock level. The airlock was underneath, out of sight. He could be waiting in the refuel area. That was such high security… once you were in, and if you were good at hacking…

CHAPTER 7
FLEAS

As wanton flies to boys are we to the Gods. We sport
with them, bringing ourselves to their attention, and
they kill us. It is wiser to leave them strictly alone.

From the collected sayings of Saint Sugahata the Reviled.

The League-watcher had an ornately carved throne in the front of the cockpit. The rider was accorded a low plastic chair at the League-watcher's feet.

Liton looked around cautiously. Since he had been brought forward from the riders' cabin in which he had been locked before the barge had left the space station, he hadn't dared raise his eyes. Now he risked a glance. The royal party sat about the foredeck, talking cheerfully while watching the tugs pull them toward the sun-grazing Stardogs. The cockpit was plainly a familiar locale for the royals, who treated the stunning space-view with the disregard that one accords to the everyday.

Shahjah knew he was coming. She was already jetting slowly away from the other dogs towards them. His heart leapt as it always did when he beheld his beloved. He didn't understand how people could possibly say that all Stardogs looked alike. She was larger than most, and she also was more silvered. To an uninformed person that was beautiful. To the rider it was tragic. She was silvered because many of her filaments had lost their ability to absorb and transport light. She was getting very old... Still, he could already feel her love, and suddenly the room full of rich and powerful people no longer frightened him. He had stopped being a half-person. And they had stopped being of anything but trivial importance.

Several members of the Imperial party had greeted the Wienan League Watcher. They ignored the rider, which was hardly surprising. He would have been alarmed to be greeted people by such as these. The girl rider was missing, doubtless tranquillized and locked up, but her League escort was already there. He stood on the far side of the cockpit, an uneasily held drink in hand, looking uncomfortable. Liton avoided his eyes and stared out into the blackness once again, watching Shahjah.

He was startled to find himself being tapped on the shoulder by a stocky lady who wore ultra fashionable garments with total disregard for their appropriateness to coloring or figure. She also had a terrifyingly white face behind the glasses. Apparently she had got as far as putting on a make-up foundation, but had been distracted into looking up a few peripheral matters and forgotten to proceed. "I say, do you hear me?"

Liton stood up hastily. Bobbed his head servilely. Of course he hadn't heard her. He was in a quandary. Riders were forbidden to speak to Non-League people. In Human built ships their quarters were segregated and the situation had never arisen in his previous experience. On the other hand not to reply would be construed as an insult.

"He is deaf, M'lady." The Wienan smoothly interposed. This young soft man did not look at all out of place here, sipping a cocktail from a tall glass.

"Yes, I'd heard you did that to them, but it had slipped my mind." The scholar suddenly peered over the edge of her glasses at Johannes. It was an alarming sight, and he started back slightly. She continued. "I have some questions to ask. Use your sign-language to pass them on to him."

The young Leaguesman was at something of a loss. He cast an anguished eye across at his League colleague. "I cannot ask him about certain matters. They are League secrets, you understand..."

The dumpy woman snorted. "I'm not interested in the League.

You are recent and transient history. I want find out what he has learnt from his Stardog about the Denaari. It's a line of research that has never been pursued."

It shocked obviously shocked the young Leaguesman to have the League described like that. His fellow Leaguesman also stood open mouthed, and nearly dropped his drink.

Liton smiled at her, however. A trusting, disarming smile. It was one of the reasons the League kept riders from the general populace, apparently. She didn't even notice. "I lip-read quite well, my Lady," he said. Shahjah was near. He was brave. He didn't even stutter. "If you speak slowly." He carefully turned so that he could not see the Leaguesman. The only way for the Leaguesman to interrupt the conversation now would be to rudely step in front of the Princess's companion.

The woman, absorbed in her questioning, did not even notice his actions. "What does your Stardog remember about the Denaari?" she asked. The rest of the group's conversations had died away, leaving this centre-stage.

Liton shrugged. This was safe to answer. "The Stardogs remember them. The Stardogs are not clever, you understand, Ma'am. But they don't forget. They loved them. They were very lonely until we came."

"Hmm. So how long ago did these loved ones leave?" the woman asked.

"About three thousand five hundred of their years back," Liton replied drawing the knowledge from Shahjah.

The little woman flushed with excitement even through the plaster of make-up foundation. "Excellent! That'll give Hargreaves something to put in his pipe and smoke." Her head bobbed forward in an oddly predatory movement, "But wait! *Their* years. What are their years? Do they measure time accurately?"

Liton nodded, quite entranced by interest. "Very accurately M'lady. They need to, to navigate. And they have perfect memories. They're just... not very clever. Their year is longer than Phillipia, and shorter than Nekrat. It is hard to explain. They use solar-revolutions to measure years. They don't understand days and nights."

But his answer had her rivetted. "The Denaari motherworld! It must be the orbital period of the motherworld! Do they know on which world they were made?"

He shook his head. "Shahjah, my Stardog, was born, not made."

She shook her head dismissively. "Silbersohn and Ohnasha proved that that is impossible. The Stardogs were plainly the product of a species far in advance of ours in genetic engineering. The gene structure...."

He was angered. He shared to some imperfect extent Shahjah's memories. He remembered her birth. "No!" he burst out. The way she straightened and pulled away he knew he had spoken too loudly. "No. She was born. She could also have pups of her own!"

The strange glasses-magnified eyes bored into him. "Where are the pups, then? Why are there none now? And where is their home-world?"

"Lady Tanzo. Leave off grilling the menial. We need you for a fourth for bridge." There was no ignoring a summons from Princess Shari.

With an, "I'll speak to you later," the dumpy little matron turned away and left the rider. He was relieved. He had no answers to give her.

A rough hand took him by the shoulder, turned him from the window. He found himself facing not one, but two angry Leaguesmen. The angular man signed furiously, his hands clumsy with haste and anger. "Your dog be whipped. Food rations be cut. Your dog ..."

"If you don't mind, Leaguesman Kadar, I shall handle this," said the Wienan. Liton could not hear the tone, but he could feel the hauteur. "This is my rider. I shall deal with him."

Johannes Wienan faced Liton again. His hands flickered, as he signed with more skill than the angular man, "Your Stardog is old...you say. Do not endanger her by speaking to the woman again. That is all. Sit until it is time for you to go out." Somehow he had far more power to frighten than the angular man. Liton huddled down on the hard plastic seat.

"Leaguesmen." It was the handsome officer in the midnight blue uniform. He looked across the crumpled rider as if Liton was not there. "Her Majesty has decided she would like to play Vingt-et-un. You are summonsed." The rider was left sitting staring into space again, a picture of abject misery.

●●●○○○

Very little of Shari's attention was focused on the game. But she continued her cheerful, non-business chatter with her card-playing companions without having to devote much of her mind to it. Her companions scarcely saw ever Shari being serious, except

67

in planning her trips in her role as Patron of the Society. Her companions were always similar. A pretty bit of brainless fluff; a handsome male escort, usually a relatively low-ranking officer-gentleman of some sort, a useful ladies-man; and a bluestocking to get the brainy ones off her back. Each carefully selected for filling a social niche. Each chosen to run interference for her.

After the last trip Dame Olga m'Themba had been obliged, because of her worsening arthritis, to give up travelling with the Princess. Shari had asked Tanzo to join them in her place. Shari wondered about the wisdom of that now. Tanzo was a brilliant scholar, but unlike Dame Olga, she was very narrowly focused on the Denaari. And Tanzo rushed in where angels feared to tread. Still, she had been a good foil for Shari. The Leaguesmen now regarded Tanzo with grave suspicion, and the obviously bored Princess with some approval. By the way the hypocritical, thin, bony one was peering down Carol Leyven's cleavage, he was becoming more distracted by her other foil too. Still, those Leaguesmen were going to keep a close eye on that poor foolish rider from now on.

She had to admit, however that Tanzo's questions had fascinated her. Lack of Stardogs was a major factor limiting interplanetary trade. Although a shortage of riders too was hampering the League. That plan had rather backfired on the Society. They'd hoped by helping potential recruits, getting them into their foster-home system, and away from the League, would serve to reduce the increasing work-load being put on the Stardogs. Well, it had improved Society's membership quite dramatically in the last fifty years...

The great silver fur shawl drifted up to them. It slid into place around and under the barge, as the tugs disengaged. She loved watching this, and watching the working of that centuries-old Denaari system. It would fail one day, and all the passengers of the barge would be sucked to a horrible, explosive death. But in the meanwhile...

There were the strange sucking and grinding noises. The slow hiss. Then the section of floor-plate slid aside. She thought that it went very much against what the little rider had said about the creatures being born, not made. The physical structure on the back of the neck was too contrived. Nature would surely not have designed a space-tight animal-to-metal interface. She risked stealing a direct glance at the rider. This was always the best bit, when they realised they could actually physically touch their beloved.

When it was over she threw her hand in. "Gentlemen, Ladies." she yawned artistically. "It's has been a long day. Forgive me, but I need my sleep." The game she'd got up, folded. They straggled off down the passage, the Viscount, as usual, gallantly offering her his arm. When they arrived at her suite she dismissed him, and called out to the Countess, who was flirtatiously running her fingers up the young Leaguesman's arm. "My dear Lady Caro, won't you come and help me with these nail-Icons? My stupid maids have not as yet learned how to get them off in one piece, and of course you always know how to do these things."

Naturally, the Countess was delighted. That was the thing about dear brainless Caro. She really *was* delighted. She parted from the young leaguesman without any signs of distress. Out of the corner of her eye the Princess noticed that he too was unperturbed, but the ungentlemanly older leaguesman who had rudely avoided giving Tanzo his arm, was plainly pleased.

Once the bodyguards had checked the room, and removed themselves to their outer enclave, she sat in front of the huge mirrors at her dressing table. The maids temporarily dismissed, Shari and the Countess enjoyed a comfortable, private tete-a-tete. Caro Leyven's slim, delicate fingers carefully teased loose the tissue-thin illuminated pictures painted onto mica-sections which the ladies of fashion wore on their nails. "Cutting a dash with that young Leaguesman, Lady Caro?"

The honey-blond countess shrugged. "He's nice. But men always are."

Shari lifted an eyebrow. Her fashion-conscious companions insisted they were too thick and too dark, but she could bring herself to have them removed. "Not the older one. He won't pay you any attention."

The Countess twitched her full lips. "Oh? We'll see."

The Princess said no more. There was no need.

●●●○○○

Liton sat. Somewhat uncomfortably. He longed to go and suit up, to go out to Shahjah. But that too-clever Wienan had said to wait, so wait he did. He watched the floor-plate before him slide away with something akin to horror. If it had not been for the Stardogs obvious happiness he would have run. A moment later he was down on Shahjah's dark skin. Actually touching it flesh to flesh. It was cool, but far from the temperature of space. He would have frozen onto *that* on contact. And there was none of the filament fur that coated the dogs. The how-what-why questions Shahjah answered for him into his own mind, even before he had finished thinking them. This part of her was normally covered yes, but it had lips that could part and seal around the outer lip of the cockpit. The underside of the cockpit had heating panels which then warmed the skin-surface until the panel opened. The old ones had liked to touch the dogs. It was nice to feel him there, much better than the usual way humans rode. Now, if he would just scratch the nodes up on the top edge...

The tugs had cast loose. Shahjah began accelerating the drift. Using existing V and tiny compensations of lateral thrust to drop in to the G point. The web of complex nerve endings on the fringes of the Stardog's mantle made it able to detect the smallest of variations in gravity. The total flexibility of the mantle made the response of the Stardogs gas-flare emissions amazingly precise. Mechanical spacecraft were capable of greater acceleration, but they came nowhere near the manoeuvrability and efficiency of Stardogs.

Liton began imaging the steps to the Abelard Solar System. He had excellent photographs and a detailed knowledge of all 432 worlds, or at least how they looked from space. Excellent visual memory was a rider's most essential requirement, even more than a close tie with his or her Stardog. Otherwise the animals would take you leapfrogging all over the place, as they had in the early days of exploration. It was a typical piece of League logic. They taught you 432 and allowed you to use perhaps twenty for the rest of your life. Abelard was a familiar enough destination. But he wished he knew where they were going after that.

Then they broke into the mind-jarring reality of surf. Like riding the tumbling cascade of a broken wave, it was another arena in which the biologically adapted Stardog beat any mechanical competitor to smithereens. The dogs had huge, multi-sectored brains, with a very different synapse transmission system to carbon-lifeforms. Most of the brain-space was simple reaction-feedback loops. All of this was needed to survive the ever changing nature of *between*. To outsiders, the Stardogs' transition between here and elsewhere was miraculously easy. To the riders it was simply miraculous. It was a buffety ride this time. Shahjah was struggling to keep up. Over the years there had been gradual irreparable damage to some of her nerve nets. Now each time they went through surf was an agony of fear for Liton. He was not afraid for himself. He was afraid that *she* might not make it. And now, for the first time, he was afraid for their cargo. He was involved in something far bigger than himself, or even Shahjah.

They made it. Step one. Another seven steps out to the rim. Liton stretched out on the soft ridges of rugose hide, exhausted. At least his Stardog could rest now. It would be at least a day before they were in position to surf onward. After a few minutes the Leaguesman prodded him to his feet, and he had to leave his contact with Shahjah and head for his small cell.

●●●ↄ●●

"I get the feeling there is something odd going on. What do you think?" Johannes asked as he sunk back onto the soft cushions of his bed, to allow Lila to pull his boots off.

She actually stopped what she was doing. "You are asking me, Sir?" There was no way she could keep the surprise out of her voice.

He was surprised himself. "Sure. Why not? You're human aren't you?"

"It is the first time in eight years my master has ever noticed *that!*" she said, tartly. Instantly she was contrite. "I am sorry master. I'm a debt-slave. It is not my place to have opinions."

He shrugged and stood up, and raised his arms so that she could take off his tunic. "I know you are not stupid. It just never occurred to me to ask you questions before. You don't have to answer me. I just wish I could consult Jan-Pieter 19."

That sent a shiver through her. But then, Jan-Pieter's name was enough to make most people shiver.

●●●ↄ●●

Four days later they arrived in the Abelard system. Dumped V on a tangential to the G points. Swung in towards the dun and pale blue of Abelard 2 and the familiar metal wheel of its Space-Station. Soon Liton knew he would be heading into the strip-search of League-Customs. But the vial he had been passed had carefully been broken open and rubbed into a fold of Shahjah's rugose skin. He had much on his mind. They would be off-ship for a week, then they would cross League-sectors. In the rider-compound below he would ask for messages to be taken across. It was a rare opportunity.

●●●ↄ●●

Shari had spent her whole life knowing that the time was coming when either her brother or somebody else would decide to have her killed, and that not all Deo's ingenuity could stop the assassins once her fate had truly been decided. But one can only

71

stay terrified for so long, and then you become increasingly blasé about living on the edge. At least, you could either become nonchalant about it, or lose your wits, and she still had all of hers. The small dog on her lap sat up and licked her nose. She hugged him. He might spoil her make-up, but at least he would never betray her. She reached into her purse for a small compact. A brass-band reception awaited her landing. She'd go through this last trip like an Imperial Princess, dammit. Give them all something to remember.

It was only back at the ship, after the week's tour of the bleak planet's high and low spots, ranging from a visit to the ISPCA's camel-shelter, to the Lord Lieutenants Bun-fight, that she realized she might have been overdoing it. It was Caro Leyven who brought it home to her. She was taking off the nail-icons the Princess had worn for the crowded farewell. In this privacy protocol was largely ignored. "Shari, are you... well... in love? You seemed so... alive this last while."

Shari smiled, trying to ignore the droplet in the corner of her eye. "How could I get any man's attention for long with you around, my dear?"

Caro Leyven was not intelligent. But she was tenacious and loyal. "You've taken at least two men away from my court at the last function alone. You normally keep yourself aloof. Please be careful, my dear Princess," she said quietly. She gave a small sniff. "You know what that... brother of yours is like." She turned away, sobbed, "I couldn't *bear* it if you were killed."

"We shall do our best to see that doesn't happen, M'lady." The grey-clad Deo had entered the dressing-room so silently that neither of them had heard him. It was hard to find any trace of expression on that poker-face. But there could have been approval.

Later that evening, when the countess had been comforted and had gone off to stalk her usual evening prey, they talked further. "The League must plan to do it on the ship before we go in, or probably just after we come out of, surf, Deo. And it must be with small arms, poison, or knives. Surely, Sirian wouldn't come along on the ship with us if they were going to kill me by destroying it." She spoke quietly. Deo had mopped the area. There were no wired or transmitting bugs. Thanks to Station-technology they were some long jumps ahead of those who wished to spy on them.

The factotum permitted himself the smallest of smiles. Shook his head. "We don't even know who got to the Sirian, or with what. We cannot second-guess the unknown, my Princess. We also know the steward, one of the cooks and one of the engineers are not *known* League agents anyway. The steward does not know how to serve drinks very well."

She raised an enquiring eyebrow. "Staff security falls under my dear brother's Counter-intelligence. Does he connive with the League in this? Surely the League men could hardly get in without Selim Puk being aware? Has Turabi decided to do away with me after all?"

Deo shrugged. "It would not surprise me if Selim should use new men as red herrings. The attempt could just as easily come from your bodyguards. And, after all we are in space. The League controls that. Perhaps even Selim Puk has been out-maneuvered."

She sighed. "I'm even sleeping in that damned uncomfortable jacket the Stationers made for me. But I'm willing to bet it will be after the next hop."

Deo nodded. "I will be watching."

She smiled through her nervousness. Scratched Otto's ears. "Where would I be without you, Deo?"

It was the Factotum's turn to smile. Properly now, to the eyes. It changed his face, and she quite understood why the nondescript man never permitted himself to do it in public. "You flatter me unduly, Your Highness. But Otto and I shall do our best. I think we can probably rely on your human fluffy companion too."

"That surprised me. I didn't think she had enough brain to understand what was going on."

The factotum made a wry face. "I was deceived, too. But you create loyalty, my Princess." He stood up. "Good night, your highness. I will be sleeping across your door."

She knew that he meant it. Deo had done just that since the day he had come to kill her. He had quietly taken control of the servant body. And even as the head of her servant household he still slept on a thin, plaited grass mattress across her doorway. He preferred the door to be open.

❦❦❦❦❦❦

Liton lay on his hard pallet, staring at the ceiling. There was not much else to stare at in his tiny cell. Two more short jumps, and then the big one across the sectors to New Sahara. Shahjah was holding up well, so far. She said the old ones' barge was easier to manage than the human-built ones. But he would not

73

have been a good rider if he hadn't worried.

The metal walls of the cell ran up to fit flush against the old hull, where they had been roughly welded on. The original hull-metal was swirled with oil-on-water patterns, which gave his imagination plenty of scope. Shahjah's memories of the old ones' barge had been from the outside. He wished she could tell him how the inside had looked. If the finish on the hull-metal was anything to judge by it had probably been far more beautiful than the empire's rehash had been. There was a click from the locked door-latch. He started. The Wienan couldn't think Shahjah was ready to fly yet?

Another click. And then a series of three more. The door opened. The dumpy figure of Lady Tanzo stood there, silhouetted by the passage light. She stepped in and swung the heavy door closed behind her. "Hello, rider. They wouldn't let me talk to you, outside, so I've come here." She moved her mouth slowly and deliberately.

"Go away. They'll hurt Shahjah!" he said fearfully.

She sat down on his bed. "Your Leaguesman is busy with his servant. The other Leaguesman is with Countess Leyven. They won't know I've been here. Answer my questions then I'll go away. Her hands wove clumsily in sign language.

His eyes nearly popped out. "You are a League spy!"

She snorted. "Don't be silly. Spies are young and pretty. Your sign language is a League secret now, all right, but it was public knowledge back in the twentieth century. I just looked it up. I've had eleven days to learn and practice. All I want is to know about the Denaari. Then I'll go away and leave you in peace."

He pointed at the door. "The Wienans' say their locks cannot be picked. They tell us this often. Go away."

A small smile came to her pinched mouth. "So you believe them, because they have told you often enough." She held up a piece of wire. "I can show you how to do it with this."

"You are a spy! No one else would know how to do that kind of thing!"

She shook her head. "I'm a historian who has had to support her research with theft." She stood up again, and walked over to the door and re-locked it with the piece of wire. "It's easy, see."

He was unable to resist. "Show me, then I will try and tell you what Shahjah remembers."

Her eyes narrowed and her head came forward in her characteristic bob, as she focused on his face. "There is no point in your escaping now. You'd just give both of us away."

He shook his head. "No. I cannot leave Shahjah anyway. But when I get back to the compound I will show the other riders. They have been left to die when the Leaguesmen have abandoned ship before."

She grimaced. Nodded. "Understandable that you should want to learn. All right. Take the pick. I'll try to guide your hand. There are just two levers. It is a very simple lock, really."

Tanzo was an amazingly good and patient teacher. After an hour he could, given ten minutes, do what she could achieve in ten seconds. Finally, they sat down on his bed again. "Now. I checked the orbit-periods. Nekrat 375. 24 days. Phillipia orbit takes 375.19 days. Of the remaining four hundred and thirty there are none between them.

Liton shook his head. "The motherworld is forbidden to the Stardogs."

She bit her lip. Peered at him. "Why?"

He was silent for a while. Then he spoke slowly. "The old ones forbade it. The sickness…. was carried by the Stardogs."

"Quarantine! Of course! Probably too late. It always is," she said, shaking her head. "But that was over three thousand years ago. Why haven't they gone back?"

He shrugged. "The old ones said not to. They do not disobey"

"That's a long time to stay loyal. But surely the Denaari plague is over now? Surely they must go back to their old masters?" she wheedled.

He shook his head. "They want to. But they cannot disobey. I don't understand, but Shahjah can't choose to disobey."

She pursed her lips. "Imprinting from when they were made."

Once more he shook his head. "No! They were not made. But they cannot have pups unless they go back. The Stardogs are all old. They will all start to die soon. My Shahjah is one of the oldest. But they cannot live much longer than four thousand years anyway. They usually only lived about two hundred years. The same as their rider-friends.

She stood up. Sighed. "It's like that bloody welded shut drive-chamber. Did you know this ship has engines? But they didn't understand how they worked… so they welded the accesses shut. The League and the Empire don't want to know. They're still scared of the Denaari. And they don't want to admit that they're nothing more than a bunch of maggots feeding on the corpse of an alien Empire." She struck her small fist into her palm in frustration. Then pushed her glasses back along her nose. "Well, thank you, rider. You've at least told me more than I knew before. I'll stop by and bring you a spare pick, when I am sure it is safe." She went out and locked the door quietly behind her.

CHAPTER 8
COLD IRON

There is a crucial timing in all things. Affecting the course of human affairs is very like blacksmithing. To weld iron it must be at the right temperature when it is drawn from the forge. Too hot and it will twist, or even melt. Yet, if you strike iron when it is too cold it will not weld, and can even shatter... The successful revolutionary must manipulate these times, striking when he is ready and forcing enemies to strike when they are not.

Nicola Para-Machiavelli: Obliterating a Prince.

Abelard. Bahrain II. Samburia. Amritsar... the royal journey continued. So did the Princess, conducting her last grand tour in the grand manner. She found herself unable to return to the distances in which she had formerly carefully isolated herself. She drank of life like a backsliding alcoholic at a free wine tasting. And she spoke to her audiences from the heart, with a fierce fire she'd never before allowed to burn in public. When she spoke to the Imperial Legion Meeting on Samburia about the need for real and adequate reward for disabled veterans she found tears streaming down her face. And afterwards the cheering mass of ex-soldiers had carried her on their shoulders to the waiting transport.

It was heady stuff. Heady and dangerous. It made one feel invulnerable. She wasn't. At Amritsar Station signs of the mass hysteria she was generating were visible. For the first time ever the missile-guard legionnaires had to be deployed to keep back the cheering crowds. About the only stationer who didn't disobey instructions to come and bid her farewell and watch her departure was Juan Biacasta. He was, none the less much closer to the Princess than most of the cheering stationers. He'd been there for hours, having got to his position ages before the crowds.

⚫⚫⚫ ⊃⊃⊃

Sam Teovan was faced with a bloody choice. Go against his instincts and deal with whatever trap was waiting. Or fail to go through with it and be killed by his waiting associates. He chose the third option. It... felt better. Not good, but better.

He was a bar-steward. At least it was something he knew a little about. Unlike his two companions. Niccolo 'Blower' Yu was part of the kitchen staff. Blower could cook up explosives. Camo Osman was supposed to be in charge of the ship's maintenance and plumbing. Well, he could field strip and re-engineer firearms. But anyone asking him to repair a toilet was pushing their luck. And they had the toff. Not that he'd be much good.

There was supposed to be a Syndicate operated miner-ship on standby when they came into the New Sahara system. They were supposed to strike three minutes insystem. Well... it would do no harm to come out of surf in control of the ship. Then if there was something unwanted waiting... they could slip right back where those without Stardogs could not follow.

In a way it was a pity that the League was so impenetrable. If what Stardogs did in wormhole-surf had been public knowledge, Sam might have understood the folly of what they were going to attempt. The very idea had never occurred to either of the devious minds of Selim Puk or Jan-Pieter Wienan. It was totally insane.

⚫⚫⚫ ⊃⊃⊃

The starswirl was at its height. It was something she never got tired of. But the poor rider was sweating. She wished she could at least say something, and tell him what she was doing. The star-barge would be coming to New Sahara and whatever was planned for her in a few hours. She would have liked, just once, to be open about the way she felt. But her secret agenda was too big for that. Hopefully it could still go on without her at its head. After all the ISPCA had worked toward liberating the Stardogs and the riders since the tearful Joan Cheng had approached the distant parent organisation, back before there was an Empire.

ΘΘΘϽϽϽ

The Leaguesmen, the Imperial party, the rider, they were all there. Without a hint of warning the light social banter was ripped into silent shards. The Yakuza thugs suddenly pushed the bewildered-looking rider-newling, and Johannes's terrified debt-servant into the cockpit. They brandished fire-arms that should never have been able to ooze past League customs.

Teovan had his trademark antique .22 pistol. Camo carried a light machine-gun, and Blower a wicked looking whippet. The way he held it you could see he felt little more than disdain for something that only killed one person at a time. In the other hand he held a trigger-transmitter. Its red light winked. That device he held with great care.

"Nobody move," Teovan said, as others might say 'Good morning'. The bodyguards were seriously off-sides. On the window side of their charge. The short stocky one, furthest off, realised his hands were invisible to the three. But as his hand touched the butt of his issue pistol, he felt the muzzle of another weapon pressed to his ribs. Syrian Byrnant said, "Don't," very quietly.

"Raise your hands slowly and carefully." Everyone responded. Everyone, but the rider. His hands were gently caressing the nodes of the Stardog, trying to calm the beast who was riding a wild *between* wave, and coping with an emotional storm.

"You!" Camo stepped over and prodded Liton with the barrel of the LMG. "Hand's up!"

Liton had been genuinely unaware of the hi-jacking attempt. All he had known was that powerful emotions were upsetting Shahjah. The jab with the gunbarrel made him fall sideways. He looked up into the bared teeth of the huge Yak killer. And started with fright. Johannes found himself grabbing the barrel of the machine-rifle. "You madman! we're in Surf. In theta-space! And you never threaten a rider in the presence of their dog!"

The warning came too late. Despite the fact that riding the gravs in surf took all her mental and physical ability, Shahjah suddenly twisted and rippled like a mad thing. Chaos erupted and they were all flung about like rag dolls.

In the falling writhe of bodies Sirian Brynant lost his grip on his firearm. The shorter bodyguard managed to draw his while falling. And in its thunder Sirian realised that being a good campaign-manager hadn't taught him to kill. He could die without training, however.

Johannes Wienan clung desperately to Camo's weapon, as they cartwheeled. But the soft leaguesman was no match for the strength of the thug. Somehow the Yakuza had found his feet. Despite all the young Leaguesman could do in a few seconds the muzzle of that thing would be pressed into his abdomen. Then, abruptly, the strong hands went slack. The Yak fell, a thrown eighteen-inch *Kukri* sticking out of his neck. It had severed his spine.

Shari's second bodyguard had tried to take on Teovan. And died before he could even draw his weapon.

Blower saw it all going wrong. Saw his friend Camo, his protector and companion of many years, dead, in a fight with the little Leaguesman. He dropped the bomb-trigger. This had to be personal. He raised the whippet in both hands. It was a cut down .410 over-under, loaded with solid slugs. Took aim. Fired.

But it had taken a split second to do that. Not enough time for the shocked Leaguesman to do anything. But enough time for Liton to dive in front of him. At that range the solid slug went right through the rider's chest, through his spine, and struck against the Leaguesman's arm. Too late the surviving bodyguard staggered to his feet and shot Blower, before the little explosives man could squeeze the second trigger. Like Teovan, who had rolled toward the shelter of the cocktail cabinet, the stocky bodyguard was an excellent shot.

Shari had been shocked by the speed of it all. Now she realised that she at least was protected by her Station-made bullet-proof garment. "Behind me!" she screamed, and tried to pull Tanzo and Caro behind her not very substantial form. Her yell drew fire. It also elicited the wrong reaction from the previously shocked-into-immobility Countess. She flung herself like a shield in front of Shari, knocking the Princess down. And took the bullet that Sam Teovan had intended for the Princess's brain.

Teovan had forgotten about the other rider-girl and the debt-servant. The rider-girl was just screaming in a foetal ball. But Lila had armed herself with a fallen bottle of a very rare liqueur. It was made from hand-picked wild black cherries and had flakes of real gold suspended in its syrupy 130o proof liquid. She hit him over the head with such force that the heavy handblown glass broke. He fell like a polled ox. She barely beat the leaping Deo, another *Kukri* in hand, to him.

In the meanwhile the cataclysmic ride through the chaos of *between* continued. Deo, his poker face transformed into a flame-eyed killing mask, pulled Teovan to his feet with one hand. The Yakuza man's head rolled and lolled. The *Kukri* came up, the weird light of red-shifted stars twisting and leaping in the flame-pattern of the ancient steel.

"DEO! Come help me!" Shari's voice was full of fear.

Looking at those killer eyes you would have thought nothing could have stopped the unobtrusive servant-turned-killing-machine from first cutting his victim's throat. But at her call he dropped Teovan and ran to her. She was trying to rip open the fallen Countess's elegant blouse top, and being defeated by the clumsiness of her fingers and her fear. He solved the problem with a slash of the *Kukri,* exposing Caro Leyven's two largest assets. The bullet had struck one of these difficult-to-miss targets, from the side. The .22 entry wound was small. There was little blood here. But the exit wound... the bullet must have struck a rib and skied along that... The exit path was a long, bloody ragged tear, that was beginning to bleed copiously. Shari saw the wound, bit her lip and closed her eyes. The tears welled out from under the lids.

Her servant took her by both shoulders and squeezed. "Enough, my Princess. Your silly brave friend will not die."

She opened her eyes. Almost smiled. "Thank you Deo. I... thought she'd got herself killed for me."

"She will live to prattle on, my Princess. She was lucky. The wound there bleeds already because it is a surface wound. Make a pad of material and apply pressure to it, to stop the bleeding. Don't press too hard. She may have a broken rib. I must see to other things now."

She nodded, grateful to be told what to do. You could prepare for your whole lifetime, but it was not the same as experience. At least her personal assassin had the experience.

Others, in the aftermath of the brief violence, had begun to react. The angular Leaguesman ignored his wounded compatriot and picked up the alternately sobbing and screaming rider-to-be. He shook her furiously so that her head snapped about. It seemed to be making little difference. Lila had picked up Teovan's gun. She stood over him, gun in one hand, a bottleneck full of jagged glass knives in the other. The surviving bodyguard had pulled himself to his feet, and, seeing that the situation was reasonably safe, had set about first making sure that Sirian Brynant was disarmed, and then seeing what first-aid he could render.

Tanzo Adendorff did not react fast. But she was not prone to panic either. She found her fallen glasses. Perched them on her nose and surveyed the scene. Then she went to the sprawled rider. There was still life in the limp body. Without knowing quite why she did it, she managed to drag the slight man onto the Stardog's exposed skin.

She sat there with his head in her lap, as his lifeblood pumped onto the grey rugose skin beneath them. She had no idea what to do, but in actuality it made no difference. There was nothing that could be done. The rider opened those innocent eyes of his briefly. And somehow, above his own pain, he smiled at her. He tried to say something. It could have been 'mother'. Emotion-wells twenty-five years undisturbed in the dry mind of an impoverished and single-minded scholar were opened and overflowed. She wept as he died.

Only Captain Viscount Martin Brettan, and the dead, had not moved. His eyes were cold, calculating. He considered the situation. He knew his mission remained the same. But not now. First the Stardog must be saved. And that meant the rider. There were various possibilities. Well, he would try the least compromising first.

As Deo went to the younger Leaguesman's assistance, Martin Brettan stepped across to the other and removed the sobbing, screaming girl from his bony hands. Pushed the startled man aside and took a bottle from the clasps in the cocktail counter. Firmly pushed it against her lips, and, as she opened her mouth to scream again poured neat hundred year-old Cognac down her throat. She gasped, gurgled and spluttered. A detached part of his mind reflected that it was an awesome waste of very good liquor.

A quick glance satisfied him that the enraged Leaguesman behind her could not see his hands. He risked the hand-signal for 'calm'. She was wide-eyed and shaking, but at least she'd stopped screaming. "It's dying!" she said in a small, frightened, flat voice.

He turned. "Here, you fool Leaguesman. Tell her what to do with that damned hand wiggling of yours. Frighten her again and I'll beat you to pulp. She says the beast is dying."

With an icy glare the Leaguesman took the girl's elbow. But the Viscount noticed his grip was gentle, as he led her across to the exposed piece of Stardog-skin. The leaguesman also attempted no threats when he signed to her. He simply gave instructions. The still occasionally sobbing girl sat down, her short, bitten-nailed fingers gently touching the hide.

"Princess Shari." The surviving bodyguard bowed before her, as she and Otto fussed over Caro's wound. She looked up. Fended Otto's anxious nose from the Countess's face. "What is it, Albeer?"

"Your Highness, the pris... Sir Sirian is calling for you. He is dying, your Highness."

"Oh. I... I don't want to leave the countess. I suppose I'd better. Will you come and hold this pad for me, please."

The bodyguard looked confused. "I should go with you, your Highness. He was one of the conspirators."

A flash of her old imperiousness returned. "Sirian! He faints at the sight of blood. *I* can deal with *him*. Now, come and hold this pad. You've got to be gentle because Deo says she may have broken a rib. But you've got to press hard enough to stop the bleeding. Tch. Don't be afraid of her breasts. They won't bite you, man."

She walked across, followed by Otto, to where her former Campaign-manager lay.

He looked feebly up at her as she knelt beside him. His normally slightly florid face was drained and yellow-white. His lips were beginning to turn blue. He reached up a weak hand. She took it. "Forgive me, Princess." She squeezed the hand. He fought for breath. "They... promised me there'd be no... killing."

"Why, Sirian?"

He shook his head weakly. "My son... They took photographs... Said they'd expose him...."

She squeezed his hand again. "You silly old man. You should have come to me. I'd have fixed it."

His face was twisted in pain, but it seemed to lighten. He did not reply, but squeezed her hand weakly. Then his grip went slack, and she knew there was no point in staying any longer. The starswirl outside the cockpit did not seem so red any more. Or was that just the burning behind her eyes?

She went back to where Caro lay, just in time to be there when she opened her eyes. "Just lie still, dear. You are going to be all right."

The countess blinked, trying to focus. "I was shot." Shari sighed to herself as she reached down to fend off Otto. Caro

Leyven might be loyal, but she did tend to state the obvious. Usually twice.

"Yes. You decided to... to save my life." The Princess smiled, and stroked her forehead. "Now Lieutenant Albeer can stop admiring your... endowments, and leave me to hold the pad against your wound." She turned to the bodyguard, and said with a smile that he found thanks enough, "Thank you. If it is not too much trouble, Lieutenant, will you find me some cushions and something to cover Countess Leyven with?" He scrambled hastily to his feet, nodding and saluting.

Shari shook her head at his departing back. "Really Caro. How could you expose yourself to that poor man? He lost about three pounds in sweat holding that pad."

It drew a weak chuckle from the war-wounded. "Ow. That hurts. Please don't make me laugh, Princess."

Shari smiled. "I'm just glad you still *can* laugh, dear. I though you had killed yourself for me. You made both Otto and me very anxious."

One of those relative lulls of silence settled over the cockpit. Martin Brettan was busy tying up the still groggy Teovan. Deo was splinting the arm of the younger leaguesman. The girl rider sat up. "It's no use!" She suddenly announced in her too loud deaf-person voice. The statement was full of unbearable pain. "The Stardog is grieving and dying... it can't spare enough to talk to me."

The realization of what that meant spread like melting jelly across the cockpit. Only Otto did not pull back into himself. Instead, the little dog left Shari's side, and walked across to the rider-girl and lifted her forearm with his insistent nose. It took her a few moments to work out what was happening. Then she looked down, and with an inarticulate cry took the small dog into her arms. She buried her gaunt face in its fur.

The Leaguesman was shocked into forgetting that his League had deafened the riderfolk. "Hey, you! Girl! Leave that dog alone!" When he realized that she wasn't going to hear him he stepped forward either to hit her or to strike at Otto. Sharp white teeth were bared from under the moustache and a menacing growl totally out of proportion to the size of the dog, warned him off. Otto was a small dog, not bred for gentle behavior. Well, his actual breed was not identifiable. But he had nothing against biting this particular human if it came near him.

"Don't bite him unless you *have* to, Otto. He'd probably give you food poisoning." The Princess's voice would have cut glass.

"Leaguesman Kadar. I suggest you remember who that dog belongs to. Touch him at your peril. And I don't just mean that he'll bite you."

The affronted Leaguesman drew himself up sharply, his jaw thrust forward. His eyes bulged. His thin lipped mouth worked. He was plainly full of barely contained invective. Finally he burst out. "You! You dare to threaten the League?"

She snorted. "I dare. What are you going to do about it? Kill the dying beast we are riding on?"

"But the League made you! The League made the Empire!" Spittle sprayed.

"To the Empire's discredit. We aren't going to get out of this mess. So I can *finally* tell you exactly what I think of you. You League scum ought be destroyed, and destroyed utterly. You'll be a befoulment in hell."

The debt-slave clapped. The snarling Leaguesman turned on her, looking for a softer target, perhaps. He didn't find it. She stepped closer, brandishing the broken bottle-neck full of razor-shards of glass under his nose, smiling with a trace of insanity.

And the red-shifted stars…changed. Blurred toward normality. "We're out!" screamed someone, their voice shrill with relief. But all Shari felt right then was regret.

ᴔᴔᴔ

The eyes of Agent-Supervisor Leaguesman Kadar Shilo almost glowed with savage pleasure. He looked out of the cockpit dome eagerly. The League lighter ought to be ready and waiting. He'd just go and get the transmitter in his cabin going. They'd be aboard in fifteen minutes. It would be regrettable that those wicked Yakuza had killed the Princess and her whole entourage. It was going to be even more regrettable when they revealed that the Emperor's own espionage head was implicated. He smiled savagely and scanned the darkness ahead.

ᴔᴔᴔ

Even his blurred vision couldn't hide the emptiness of space. No minership! So that side had come adrift too. Sam Teovan wasn't surprised.

ᴔᴔᴔ

The Viscount was surreptitiously watching the forward viewpanels too. He had to dispose of the League fool and kill her, and take control. But things had gone badly awry with the Yakuza side of Selim Puk's plan. The bomb threat should have been sufficient to disarm the Leaguesman. They hadn't even got as far as that, before their stupid plot had come adrift. Also... was the Stardog really dying? The Emperor wasn't going to thank him for a dead lump of silicates.

ᏅᏅᏟᏗᏗᏗ

Johannes Wienan cradled his splinted arm and looked out of the window panels. Shook his head. No!!!!

He was one of the few modern Wienan's with any real grasp of Astronomy. Most preferred to leave that to the lower life-forms, the riders. Besides, who needed it? The dog did all the real navigating, and it was never to any place new, after all. But the young Wienan had been fascinated by the deep-space pics of different star-systems. And before they'd left Imperium he'd had a refresher look at the systems they'd be visiting.

He shook his head again. His voice was strained and high-pitched when it finally came out. "This isn't the New Sahara system!"

The riders were trained to expertise at system visualisation. The girl rider, Una, had looked up when he had spoken. He signed hastily to her. She studied the growing planet with care. Eventually she announced, "It is not an Empire world." There was a stolid toneless quality to her voice which made it utterly believable. It distracted the Leaguesman's attention from the fact that she'd reacted to his speaking.

Deo had walked over to the instrument panel set in the arm of the League-watcher's throne. "And we are not slowing down either."

CHAPTER 9
H.E.

It is said that it is better to light a single candle than to curse the darkness. But it is still better to tell the electrician that if the lights aren't on in ten minutes you're going to shove that damned lighted candle up his butt.

From the collected sayings of Saint Sugahata the Reviled.

Leaguesman Kadar was the first to recover. "Impossible!" He leaned threateningly toward the rider. "You're lying. And if you've brought us out at the wrong world I will teach you the meaning of punishment!"

But she had deactivated hearing-aid, and was locked in her silent world again. She just stared out of the viewpanels. The world they were heading towards was still distant. They had many hours to fall towards its amber and white surface.

Johannes Wienan was sore, and he was of the kind whom pain makes irritable. "Leaguesman Kadar. You have no authority here. You are merely a passenger on this ship. Conduct yourself accordingly."

"No authority! You... spoiled young pipsqueak! I'm an agent-supervisor in the security section. I am here on Jan-Pieter the nineteenth's personal orders."

Johannes felt the cold sinking to his gut. As usual his devious uncle had been playing both ends against the middle. He probably had strings attached to middle too, to make sure it did just as he wanted. But he wasn't going to back down. "My authority, *over this ship*, is vested in me by the Wienan Leaguemaster herself. Challenge my authority and I'll have you put off the ship. Right here. Can you breathe space, *Agent-supervisor?*"

"Enough." Shari had put on her imperial dignity again. "You are arguing about nothing. We are in a system beyond the Empire. We have no means of return. Unless the Stardog recovers we'll be aboard the lifecraft in a few hours. Stop your bickering. Leaguesman Wienan, I suggest that someone accompanies you in search of medical supplies. Leaguesman Shilo. You will go to your stateroom and remain there until you are fetched. Lieutenant Albeer will accompany you and lock you in."

"Lock me in! You dare..."

"Shut up, Leaguesman." The Viscount snapped. So this was his opposite number. Incompetent fool, letting his temper betray him like that. "Her Imperial Highness has given you your orders. Move."

Kadar showed his yellow teeth. "We're beyond the Empire... she says. Outside her authority."

Martin Brettan administered a careless backhander across the Leaguesman's mouth. "You're not beyond my hand. Next bit of cheek from you and I'll go through with the other Leaguesman's suggestion, and toss you out of an airlock. Now, move. I'll take him down, your Highness."

"Thank you Viscount. We will meet here again I think in... twenty minutes."

The handsome and muscular Captain hustled him away down the passage to the main body of the barge.

"Well, Leaguesman Wienan, what are you waiting for? I want the passage clear to take the Countess to her room."

He bit his lip. Looked down the passage. "Your Highness. Be careful with that man. He is one of my uncle's assassins. I can only think he was put on board to kill you."

She raised an eyebrow. "And you weren't party to this, Leaguesman?"

He flushed. "No. I... I was supposed to make the rider refuse to continue crossing trade sectors. I knew nothing of this."

"Honesty from the League of lies! You knew nothing of the plan to kill the rider?" It was Deo's seldom heard voice. Accusing. Oddly deep.

Wienan looked confused. The man was a menial — yet speaking thus? "No. I'd never be so stupid as to try something in flight…"

"Then why was the new-rider not tranquillised?" The grey-clad man's eyes bored into his.

"But…but I saw Kadar give her the injection myself, before we came up here… We stopped on the way. And Kadar's face when she was pushed in. He… can't have known."

Deo nodded. "Truth, Princess. I saw the Leaguesman's face too. There is another conspirator."

She sighed. "Surprise me, Deo. Well, get along with you, Leaguesman."

He bobbed his head. Turned to his servant, "Come on, Lila."

"Go to hell." To emphasise her point she cocked the pistol and raised it. "Before the bank took our farm, I used to shoot whistler-ducks with one of these. Keep away from me."

Johannes Wienan's jaw fell open. "But…"

"Just go, Leaguesman," said Shari, tiredly.

He went.

The debt-slave girl bowed low to the Princess "Your Highness, I am an agent of the Imperial Intelligence Service. I am at your service. Don't trust those Leaguesmen, Princess."

Shari raised her eyes to heaven. How could she point out to this child that Imperial Intelligence was also probably plotting to kill her? "I'm sure Lieutenant Albeer will appreciate your help. I believe," she said, with an enquiring tilt of her head, "that he is also in the IIS?" He nodded, reddening slightly. He seemed about to say something, but she turned her attention instead to her wounded companion. "Caro, do you think you can walk, or shall I find a nice man to carry you?"

The countess smiled. It was almost her old, easy smile. "I'm fine. The nice man sounds, well… nice, but I'll manage without one, I suppose."

Deo and the bodyguard helped her to her feet. The Princess offered her arm. Shari looked at the ruins of the cockpit. "Deo?" she began.

"I shall remain here, Your Highness. I will see to it."

She knew that by the time she came back, there would be no

bodies, and probably no blood. Deo was terrifyingly efficient.

When she, the countess, Albeer and her newest bodyguard had left, followed by Otto, who would comfort someone while his mistress was there, but would not allow her to leave without him, the ubiquitous servingman turned to the rider and to Lady Tanzo. He bowed respectfully. "Lady. I shall have to take the dead rider's body. Would you not comfort the living instead?"

For a minute the stocky little woman just stared myopically at him. Then she spoke, her voice unaccustomedly sad. "You know, he died trying to tell me where we were going to. He thought it would make me happy. I didn't understand at first. But I do now." She looked at the heavy wavy-bladed knife he was retrieving from the neck of the fallen Camo. "Does the Princess Shari know that she has one of the Kali Ghurka as her servant?"

Deo paused, in the act of retrieving his knife. "The lady is well informed. What does the Lady Tanzo know about the Kali Ghurka?"

She shrugged, showing no sign of fear. "I know you're a fanatical sect from Arunchal. The product of Earthgov's dumping of a mutinous Ghurka regiment, a bizarre Hindu religious group and a ministering order of Catholic Nuns together on an isolated planet. The ruins on Arunchal are very unusual. I wanted to do some research work there. I was warned to keep out of your way at all costs."

Deo almost smiled. "The holy ones would have called for your death for the description of the origins of the Holy Church of the Kali-Dewa. Never-the-less, the Princess knows who I am, Lady. There is no further need for you to advertise it. Please take the rider girl away. I will put your rider in a place of respect, fitting for a brave man. Then I must dispose of the trash."

Tanzo helped Una to her feet. "Including that one, I trust." She pointed to the bound and gagged Sam Teovan.

Deo looked at the blade of his knife. Only a man with no further use for his thumb would test the edge in the ordinary way. "Yes. Goodbye, Lady."

When she had gone, Deo, who had picked up the weapons of the fallen with obvious professionalism, walked over to the wide-eyed Teovan. Deo's face was, as usual, expressionless. The *Kukri* edge just touched the gag that the Viscount had tied with surprising professionalism. The material fell aside. "You will tell me who you are, who you are from, and how you came to here."

Sam Teovan's famous instincts told him that to lie was to die.

Deo's next statement confirmed this. "I have been trained to tell the truth from falsehood. Speak only the absolute truth."

"You won't kill me? I can make you rich." He really didn't think it would work. But it was worth a try.

He was answered by a cold stare and no change in expression. It was more terrifying than a threat. Instinct said 'start talking, and start talking fast'. "I'm a Caporegime of the Yakuza-Syndicate."

Deo nodded. "True. Who assisted you? The Empire or the League?"

Teovan shook his head. "No one. No one knew. It was Sal. Salvatore Caranzia-Heiki. He's a Big Capo back on Phillipia. It was all Sal and a couple of other big guys' idea. They set it all up. It was supposed to be a sure thing."

"The League knew. You never got those weapons through without them knowing."

"Hey, that was Kaparov, the Dakada smuggling boss. He organized that stuff."

"League, probably. Jan-Pieter's sort of trick to run smuggling past his own customs. Who got you onto the staff? Who recruited Sirian?"

"I dunno. Sal. Sal and that tall, thin Dakada guy."

"A tall, thin man. Very graceful as he moves. High pitched voice. Slightly slanted eyes?" asked Deo impassively.

"Yeah… I don't know his name…"

"He would not have used his own anyway. That was Selim Puk. The Emperor's Security chief. Once his chief assassin," said Deo with finality.

"You mean it was all a set-up? I'll kill bloody Sal…"

"He was almost certainly set-up himself. And you will not kill him. You are about to die. It is the custom among my people to give the victim, if possible, an opportunity for a last prayer. Do not waste it by pleading." The blade of *Kukri* was set against his throat.

Sam's little piggy eyes widened. He looked into Deo's unblinking brown eyes. His dry mouth struggled for words. "The bomb."

The knife was pulled back slightly. "The bomb?"

"Yeah, look. Blower, the dead guy over there, set a bomb. That's what he did see. He was our explosives man. There's the trigger-box on the floor."

"He was killed before he could use that," Deo said, looking at the transmitter.

"Yeah. But we was supposed to scram off this boat. Use the bomb threat to get the toxin off the Leaguesman, rendezvous with our ship, an' leave this one. Take the Stardog and the Princess for ransom, and dispose of the evidence. Blower put a timer in his bomb. Easiest way, he said. Lemme out, and I'll show you where it is."

Deo shook his head. "We will just abandon ship earlier than previously planned."

Sam snorted. "I nearly bust myself laughing when I heard you all talking about that. You think we'd leave the boats in working order?"

Deo looked at him, long and hard. At last he said, "You have earned yourself a temporary respite. Where is the bomb?"

Sam shook his head. "I'll show you, if you promise not to kill me, and to let me loose." He was instinctively sure this man could be trusted to honor his word. Which gave him, Sam Teovan, a serious advantage over the sap.

He didn't even see the grey-clad man's hands move. Deo was holding the top half of his ear pinna in front of him. "Do not attempt to bargain with me. You live. If the bomb destroys the craft... you die. Show me where it is."

Sam could feel blood trickling down his cheek and neck. But he was no soft touch. "Look at the trigger-transmitter. It'll have a timer on the display-screen."

It was Deo's turn to shake his head. He picked up the transmitter, deliberately not looking at it, and held it in front of Sam. Liquid crystal seconds flickered away. "Show me."

Unwilling, but frightened, Sam led off down the passage.

●●C Ɐ●●

Changes, deep changes, were occurring in the tissues of the Stardog itself. Some cells were developing a gel cushioning. Nutrient, and indeed life, was being sucked from others. The beast was preparing to close the great circle. The intelligent part of its brain had shut down. Gone to roam free in the stardark, with its dead master. Only the almost mechanical reflex sections of the brain functioned.

●●C Ɐ●●

"So, there is a bomb on board. And the lifecrafts are sabotaged. Well! A day in the life of the average Princess," said Shari calmly. Having waited for the inevitable death with no way of escape, she was now almost light-headed. For the first time since she was nine, she realized that her future was at last uncertain. The chances of survival were poor, but at least she didn't know that she would be killed. "Take us to the bomb, murderer." She said to Deo, "This one and his companions killed the rest of the crew. Martin found their bodies. Tied up and shot, execution style."

Teovan looked blankly at her. "We didn't! We tied…"

"Shut up. You nauseate me. Show us the bomb." Her voice was cutting.

With a prod from Deo, he turned and led them down into the bowels of the ship, to a passage along the one flank. "You'll have to shoot the lock," he said sullenly. "Blower turfed the key into the recycler-system. He reckoned it left us in a better bargaining position if the bomb was out of reach. Besides all the keys were numbered, an' he didn't want you to know where the explosives were."

The Princess sighed. "Well. Can we fix the lifecraft?"

"Why?" Martin Brettan already had drawn the heavy calibre automatic from his belt, and was pointing it at the door.

Shari shrugged, "Because you'll never break that door down. These cabins were built for royalty, assassination scared royalty."

Teovan stared at her face, reading truth there. "The life-craft seals are wrecked. Unfixable. The pieces are in space behind us somewhere. "

She looked at the LCD seconds flicking away, flashing the remaining three minutes. "I am going back to my cabin. To prepare myself to die like a Princess. Deo, come with me… please."

The sound of a nervously cleared throat echoed in the sudden silence. "Er. I believe I may be able to help." Tanzo came forward, a silver bright section of thin wire in her stubby fingers. She put the wire into the lock and began feeling "I heard the noise, she said, "and Una and I came to see what was happening." She smiled kindly at the frozen-faced girl next to her. "Ah. One tumbler." She pulled the wire out and began modifying it. Reinserted it. Another click.

Teovan stared, fascinated. These royal parasites were not supposed to be very proficient lock-pickers. He was no door-tickler himself, but he'd seen enough other practitioners at work to know that she was good. When the kidnapping had been set up, he'd understood they'd have to take on two bodyguards and a bunch of nancy-pants sycophants, who couldn't even clean their own teeth.

The Yak, it seemed, had been badly misled.

The door swung open. Inside was a selection of cooking pots with Blower's 'soup' in them. It appeared Blower had found his position in the kitchen useful after all. The one in the gold and black fancy uniform was first into the room. He might not have known much about lock-picking, but he plainly knew explosives and detonator circuits. He carefully lifted up the entire battery and timer, and the small vial hanging in the 'soup', to which they were wired.

Without ceremony he handed them to Deo. "Dump these. You've still got 130 seconds." Deo hurried away. The Viscount smiled, "I wonder, Lady Tanzo, if we could prevail on you to lock this room again... with your rare skills." The look she gave him would have damaged scorpions, but she complied.

The Viscount turned to Sam Teovan. Teovan knew the man intended to kill him. "Well, murderer? Any more nice little surprises you have for us?"

Sam Teovan kept his mouth closed. He knew that to open it was to sentence himself to death. At all costs he must avoid being taken away from the view of the rest of the survivors. The Viscount smiled at him, catlike. All good even teeth. "I'll just take this one and lock him up somewhere safe, shall I?"

Sam's numbed brain scrambled for a way out. But the necessity was taken from him by a sideways buffet, followed by a terrible wrench that sprawled all of them like skittles down the passage. "What in hell!"

"Did we hit something?" Another lesser buffet struck them.

"We'll have to go up to the cockpit and see." The group battled its way up the passages. On the way they met with Deo and also with the younger Leaguesman, looking green and attempting to shield his broken arm.

"Was that the detonator?" asked the Viscount. "Did you cycle it?"

Deo shook his head as, like a veteran seaman he navigated the swaying passage to cockpit. "No, M'lord. This is something else, M'lord."

In the cockpit it was apparent what else it was. They were under attack.

"They look like Stardogs." The Leaguesman's voice was incredulous. Stardogs didn't attack other Stardogs.

"Much smaller," someone commented. But yet the broken-umbrella shapes were very Stardog like, just perhaps a twentieth of the size. Ripping at the flanks of the huge beast that carried them.

"We must stop them! They're ripping our beast apart!" Tanzo shouted, anger filling her.

The Viscount raised a sardonic eyebrow, despite having to hold on to a stanchion to stay upright. "How, Lady lock-picker? Go out there and beat them off with sticks?"

"Perhaps the rider can communicate?"

The girl shook herself. "No. They're horrible. Horrible. Just hunger." She seemed to sink into herself again.

"We'll feed them then." The leaguesman spoke between gritted teeth. He risked his broken arm to hold up the toxin-canister with his good hand. "Here. It's disconnected. Cycle it. If it'll kill Stardogs, it should kill these brutes. They're ingesting the gobbets they rip off. I just hope they'll eat each other too."

Without a word Deo took the canister of nerve toxin and swayed hastily back into the passage. A few moments later the deadly canister had been spat out into space. The lead proto-dog was too intent on its attack to see the bait, but it was taken by one of the smaller followers. The others stopped to attack the dying. The toxin was plainly concentrated enough to continue to kill.

Shari looked at the young Leaguesman as the flight path steadied. At the sobbing rider-girl. "Well Leaguesman. This is the first time your kind has been in space without a threat to keep the riderfolk in place. You'd better hope that they don't want revenge as badly as you think they do."

Deo returned, as unobtrusively as usual. "I'm sorry your highness. The bomb-scare prevented me finishing the clean up here. If you would be so kind…"

Shari pointed at the expanding planet before them. "It seems pointless, doesn't it, Deo. In another hour we'll hit that atmosphere, and burn."

The viscount looked out. Memories of the idealistic young man joining the Imperial Space Navy, the paint on his glory dreams still wet-surfaced. He had not always been the perfect consort, twisted into the plots and greed of Empire. No. In those days he'd been a starry-eyed dreamer, learning the depths and distances of deep space… without Stardog distance-cheating. The perspective of space that navigating interplanetary craft lent told him they had less time than that. Suddenly, the maneuvering and scheming, the deaths, the smirching of the soul of the last fifteen years seemed so wasted. He could have been happy…

CHAPTER 10
PLANETFALL

"See how I fly!" said the lordly eagle to the brick. "I
soar! I glide! I bank! I spiral! I rise! And you, common
clay? What can you do but sit?" To which the brick
replied. "I can fly down pretty well, maybe even
better than you. And sooner or later both of us must
fall."

From the parable of the Sergeant-Major, The Gospel
according to St. Gopal.

Deo took Teovan to the lifecraft, to make him point out just what
had been sabotaged. Not being one to waste time or labor, Deo
had carried one corpse and loaded the other onto his prisoner.
They came back a few minutes later. The grey-clad man plucked
fastidiously at some fluff stuck to his sleeve. "I am afraid, Your
Highness, that the lifecraft are completely beyond repair."

"We may not be in dire straits yet." The Leaguesman was
studying the limited bank of instruments. With the Stardogs and
tugs doing the navigating, instruments were considered to be
unnecessary on interstellar craft. The original extensive panels of

alien readout had been covered by the cocktail unit. Simply cutting it out blindly had been too full of disaster-potential. So, in the fashion of the empire, they had simply been hidden, and ignored. It was like the system that maintained the barge's 0.92 gravity, without the inconvenience of inertial spin. Ignored. But still functioning.

The leaguesman, with rusty math, attempted to calculate the changes in vector. A few yards away, hidden beneath panels of Terran walnut inlaid with dark Aldera jacnithwood, data screens plotted the tangents and showed that the Stardog was in fact aiming for a spiral near-orbit pattern. But the alien data screens with their insect screeds of numbers wouldn't have made much sense anyway. The folk in the cockpit would not have known that, besides Leaguesman Kadar's increasingly frantic signalling, other calls too were flickering across space toward a control centre on the world below.

Below on the edge of a sand sea, from the vast bulk of a grey-stone pyramid structure, a reply, not just a guide-path, was beamed upwards for the first time in more than three thousand years. A challenge. A warning. A demand for something beyond the mere automatic responses of the ship above.

The only thing that happened was that the panel allowing the rider contact with the Stardog's skin slid slowly closed and sealed again with a small hiss.

***

In a luxurious cabin somewhere toward the aft end of the vessel another passenger stirred. Hunger had pulled him from sleep. Hunger was something he had never experienced before. What had happened to that damned steward? He was several *hours* late. He would have the fellow flogged to within an inch of his life! Then he realized that he would not. He no longer had the power to have anyone punished. He was dependent on the steward, at least until the League agents could spirit him into hiding.

Fear nibbled at him, and he bit anxiously at his knuckle. Had his father's agents discovered the steward? Prince Jarian felt the gnawings of terror, and they savaged his vitals more strongly than the hunger that had nearly driven him out into the corridors. He knew he'd get no help from that supercilious bag of an aunt. Besides, she was surrounded by his father's spies and hatchet men. He would stay for a bit longer in this room. This refuge. This prison. It was lucky he'd got wind of the plans for his assassination. Lucky the League-agent had been able to get him off-world, and onto the one ship that would not be searched. He went and lay down again, and attempted to displace the pangs of hunger with his favorite daydreams of revenge.

●●●●●●

In the welded-off drive chamber Juan went again to pound at the doors. There was no response again. At least the ship had stopped bucketing about. And the…shots he'd heard? What was happening out there?

An odd noise came from the alien machinery behind him. He turned. Parts of the dull and silent assemblage were glowing. A set of globes had begun to spin, trickling slow fat blue sparks down into huge cables. The boy shivered, and pressed himself against the obdurate door. A small pink nose stuck itself out of the boy's shirt and whiffled about.

●●●●●●

Scraps of paper lay about as the Leaguesman and the Viscount frantically attempted to calculate what the changes in vector would do to the barge's course. Deo, methodical as always, had carried the rider's body away, before returning with a bucket and cloth, and clearing up the signs of the fight. He waived attempts to assist, seeming to find security in the performance of mundane tasks. Thus the others were left to peer out of the windows, which is why they were able to see the separation. The dying Stardog, having delivered its cargo, peeled away from the imperial barge. Its last thrust pushed the ancient craft downward, into an inward spiral, before the Stardog began the last internal changes that would send it on its final journey.

They also saw the apparently solid hull crack to allow stubby wings to push out. "The Denaari craft were obviously intended to be able to land," said Tanzo calmly. "It still seems to be functioning. I hope the Imperial re-fitters didn't mess about too much."

The relief eased barriers. Smiles spread like ink. Relaxation flowed into the set of shoulders. The Viscount was the first to recover his poise. "Acceleration couches. The refit crews didn't intend this craft for atmospheric work. We need to make some kind of plan."

A few moments later the streamlined craft shrugged off the tick-like human-built life-craft. But there was nobody in the cockpit to see that.

●●●●●●

98

It ought to have been obvious. There had been no orbital stations around the Denaari colony worlds. Of course their craft must all have had planetary landing capability. As they drew into the magnetosphere, long quiescent systems awoke. The ship's near total hibernation was over. The metallo-silicate-chitin creature flexed, checking awakening motor and neural circuits. The Denaari, after all, had used genes as humans used welding tools.

Something was wrong! The roost chamber was full of dead steel clutter! The hold area was intended for that! The cabins, which the refit crew had fitted into what had been the Denaari roost, cracked and bent as the ship-beast struggled to achieve the conformational changes required for landing its frail-winged Denaari passengers. The doorframe of the chamber in which Prince Jarian was hiding twisted. The lock cracked and shattered. The doors of the rooms in which Teovan and Kadar were imprisoned, survived. The walls split instead. The drive chamber's doors, leading as they did out of the hold, were not affected.

"What's happening!? Is the ship breaking up?" Shari came running out of Caro Leyven's chamber, where she and both her new and old bodyguards had been attempting to turn the well-used mattress into some kind of landing couch for the girl. A piece of metal shrapnel from an exploding stanchion screamed past her, and Lieutenant Albeer's dive brought her down.

Deo came staggering up the corridor. "Princess! To the kitchen quarters! Quickly! The ceiling appears to be coming down here."

Getting to her feet she turned back to the chamber she'd run from. "No! Others can bring her! Come." He attempted to hustle her down the corridor.

She shook free of him. "No Deo! Not without her!"

"I'm coming Princess. Go!" Pale and swaying Caro had obviously made it from the couch. Hastily the Lieutenant, who had also found his feet, scooped her off her feet and ran with her. The others were also in the corridor by now and joined the frantic rush toward the kitchen quarters.

"What about the prisoners?" Deo nodded and headed back up the corridor, now that his greatest concern was attended to. He was nearly bowled over by the terrified Kadar. He found the bound Teovan squirming his way determinedly down the passage. Sam Teovan knew where the safest place on this ship was, and he was getting there. A slash from Deo's *Kukri* freed his legs and hands.

Together they fled, the grey-clad servant helping the numb-footed Yak to run.

A section of steel pipe fell, spraying water. It struck Deo just behind the ear. He staggered. Without knowing why he did it, but knowing he must, the wiry Yak grabbed him and half-dragged, half-carried his stunned rescuer down to the kitchens.

Prince Jarian lay, frozen in terror, looking at the now swinging open door. They'd blown the door! Surely any minute now the assassins would bundle in through it, shooting? He whimpered. Then, grabbing the heavily quilted duvet around himself he rolled off the bed and under it. The ceiling split with a thunderous crack. Oblivion seized the heir to the Imperial throne rolled in his duvet, and cowering under his bed. But Prince Jarian didn't know that his older brother's latest experiment with a combination of hallucinogens had ended abruptly off a balcony at the Imperial palace. A sixth floor balcony. Thinking himself to be merely second in line for the diamond throne, Jarian felt quite entitled to faint as the ancient Denaari ship entered the exosphere of the planet.

●●●つ●●

In the ground-control pyramid far below, the tracking-systems followed the incoming ship. To the west a second object was detected, heading for the usual crash-down site in the pupping-grounds. Stardog.

The logic circuits of ground-control's enormous organo-computer flicked over the incoming data. The only non-instinctive inbuilt response coming out of the incoming ship had been a stream of pure gibberish, and not even on the usual hailing frequencies. It was strange to hear the automated signal responses coming out of a ship again after all these centuries. There'd been the others. The ones the in-surf dying Stardogs had brought in the past, but they'd all come in too fast, without the control that this craft had displayed. There had also been none of the recognition signals that this craft had given. The others had, inevitably, burnt on re-entry, which made following the ancient orders unnecessary. This one, however, was following a perfect entry trajectory, and was slowing. Well, the directives hastily given so long ago were clear: Destroy; incinerate regardless, rather than allow the contagion to spread. It had been a wise order, if late.

Deep within the pyramid relays clicked. The missiles slid gently onto the launch ramps. The explosive matter in the warheads was 1.8 centuries past replacement date, but that couldn't be helped. Computing the standard infall pattern of Imm class personal craft was too precise to allow any possibility of a miss, and the impact would destroy the craft even if the explosives failed to vaporise it. The computer calculated the areas of highest probability of debris outfall and sent off appropriate warnings to the various regional civil defense command centers. Sections of rock slid aside and the eight missiles roared out of the launch ports. The symbols and measurement of time used were alien, but calculations showed impact in minus four minutes and twenty-three seconds.

ⴲⴲⲥⴲⴲⲥ

Even in the lower ionosphere the difficulties that the metal junk inside her was causing to the ship-beast began to affect her. She'd been unable to reach the optimal descent shape and heat-dispersal configuration ideal for an Imm craft. It was also affecting her flight path and speed. The creature did her level best to compensate despite having to arrange special conduits of coolants for that piece of her integument. The Denaari had genetically engineered a high degree of safety in all their creations. As the Stardogs had instinctive death-in-surf-return-home patterns imprinted into their complex nervous systems, so too the ship-beasts had enormous capability to protect their cargoes from potential disasters. Enormous capability... but not enough to survive the impact of the eight missiles that were streaking inexorably towards her.

The poor shape configuration caused untoward vibration as the ship dropped into the stratosphere. It was causing the ship's small mind enormous distress. Despite her best efforts the ship would undershoot the perfect landing at Ground-Control's landing area... Calculating the effect of the higher air density in the troposphere she would land nearly 3 miles short. The landing area was perfectly flat for nearly 600 square miles, but the ship's brain was a perfectionist by Denaari-improved nature. She organized slight changes in her braking configuration allowing a little more speed despite the vibration... Yet they were still nearly thirty yards from perfect position when they reached the point at which ground control had predicted impact.

The missiles were one minute and forty two seconds underway when the minuscule difference between the predicted and actual flight-speed of the incoming ship was noted by Ground-Control. A second salvo of missiles, ones with guidance systems this time, was launched with all possible haste. There was no help for it. The second salvo impact would be just inside the troposphere, and within 120 miles of Ground-Control itself.

The ship-beast that the human explorers had found abandoned off the planet they called New Sahara was one which had been bred specially for the mission to the Sil, the aliens who had struck back so hard at the Denaari, whose nano-mech plague was then destroying the Denaari. The ships had been sent in a last desperate attempt to negotiate, but the plague's mech-viruses had got to the crew first. It was thus a very unusual Imm class ship. It was one of the two Imm ships imprinted with evasive action patterns. The near miss in the stratosphere activated these circuits in the ship's brain. She dropped like a stone.

The humans clinging to one another, and to the mattress they'd piled into the sous-cook's bedchamber, screamed. In the drive chamber Juan heard them faintly as he slid wildly across the floor. He caught himself on a strut, before he landed in the heart of one of the strange alien devices. He clung desperately onto it, only to be knocked loose by his own kit-bag. Fortunately, the craft was now banking the other way, and he rolled across the floor and into what could have been an alien acceleration couch, except that it hung against the wall. It *definitely* hadn't been there earlier. Something hit the ship with a hammer-blow, and Juan found himself bounced against the huge alien wall-hung recliner.

And, as it had been bred to do, it swallowed him.

Fortunately his face was sticking out of the gel-matrix, or he would have suffocated. As it was he just screamed. And screamed. He was, understandably, terrified. But, of all the humans on the crippled but gamely struggling ship-beast, he was also undoubtedly the safest during the wild maneuvers that followed. The gel did allow slow movements, but he was still too panicked to work this out.

Then a second missile finally struck home. The ship summersaulted. Died.

The chair, which was also an ejector escape pod, responded. A transparent lid snapped across the pod, and the ship-fabric parted to allow Juan and the pod clear of the ship. Looking down as he hurtled away, the boy could see the stricken craft, which must have been ten yards from achieving a successful emergency landing, roll and half bury itself into a huge-sand dune. The escape pod flung him a good thousand yards away from what it considered a danger-zone, before drifting in to a thistle-down landing.

For the first few seconds he just lay there, too scared to move. Then the transparent lid of the ejector-pod seat snapped back. Juan was the first human to breathe and smell the unmixed air of the Denaari Homeworld.

It stank.

He struggled furiously. It was no use. He was still stuck. Stuck in an alien device, on an alien world, on the wrong side of a low black ridge of what looked like volcanic glass. On the other side there was a crashed ship. There might be other survivors. There might even be help. He shouted. His voice echoed thinly down the valley. There was no other response.

●●●○●●

On the other side of the ridge, in the imperial barge which had proved to be no barge but a planetary lander and a brave creature too, there was silence. Then a low groan.

"Can you get off me?" a plaintive female voice said in the darkness.

"I'm sorry."

"Ow! My arm!"

"Sorry, Leaguesman"

"Grr!"

"There, Otto. It's all right, babykin."

Then there was light. The ubiquitous Deo had produced a small glow-stick. The makeshift crashcouch arrangement of mattresses and straps had failed to remain in one piece. It was just as well. They would all have been hanging from the ceiling otherwise. Now the only problem was that the upside-down doorway was nearly six feet up the wall.

They all seemed to be alive. Alive and sore with several bloody noses and some concussion or dead faints, but alive. The ship definitely wasn't. You weren't aware of the ship's life-noises until they stopped. Now, the normally ever present murmur of the air-cyclers was stilled. The space-wise Martin Brettan knew claustrophobic fear. The air- lock... could it be cycled manually? If this was a Denaari world surely the air would be breathable? If they could even get to the lock. The access-way had been between the forward chambers and the cockpit. They must have at least several hours of air in here, but the still air already felt... dead.

"Well I suppose I'd better go and scout. We'll need to find a way out of here," he said keeping his voice even, not without effort. "Can I take the light?"

"We'll need it to treat the injured. You can explore later." Shari's voice had an edge to it. She'd been more upset than she should have been over the injury to that menial of hers. For the first time Martin wondered about the silent, near-invisible factotum's position in the Princess's life. Was the man her bed-warmer? Despite the dire situation a twinge of jealousy stirred in him. He carefully cultivated rumors about his own success in this field, but they were entirely baseless, despite his best efforts. It made him less than his usual urbane self in reply.

"Unless we can get out of here, seeing to the wounded will be a waste of effort. In case you hadn't noticed the air-cyclers have stopped, Princess."

Kadar, nursing his bruised and bloody beak snorted. "A rescue ship will be underway to us already. You can't crash-land on an Empire world without being spotted."

Something in the Viscount snapped. "You purblind fool! This isn't an Empire world! You can stop deceiving yourself! And if those breakneck maneuvers on the way in weren't evasive action, then I'm a Dutchman's Aunt. Anyone coming to find us isn't coming to *rescue* us!"

Kadar staggered to his feet. Even in the sickly light of the glow-stick his face was red and contorted with anger. "This is an ISS trick! You..."

Several hands, including Lila's, pulled him down. She held Teovan's .22 under his nose. "The air will last a lot longer if I blow your brains out."

"Enough bickering!" Shari assumed command without even having to raise her voice. "Let us quickly give some first aid where it is necessary. Then you can take the light and go and see if you can find a way out, Viscount."

"He's not going without me. I don't trust..."

"Shut up, Kadar," said Shari.

Deo, who, having given the glow-stick to Caro Leyven to hold, had been quietly checking the status of the injured while this went on, spoke up "Princess, Lieutenant Albeer appears concussed but is breathing well. Lady Tanzo and the rider appear to be reviving. There are torches in the maintenance workshop. I shall go and fetch them."

"No, Deo! You're on the sick-list yourself. Viscount Brettan can go." There was no hiding the concern in her voice.

He shook his head, a brief involuntary spasm of pain from this action crossing his usually impassive face. "The Viscount would not know where to look, Princess. I am perfectly all right." The slight stagger as he stood up belied his words.

"No! You can hardly stand!" she protested, catching at his torn grey sleeve, pulling him down. The Kali-Ghurka holy assassins are trained to an incredible degree of toughness from an early age. They are taught how to block pain while in combat. But Deo was no longer feeling as young as he had been then... and blocking the pain didn't prevent the dizziness and the nausea. His shaking legs were glad to stop being stood on, even if his mind was still willing.

"Hell. I'll go." Sam Teovan stood up. "I know where the torches are. Or were."

"I'll go with you." The distrust in Martin Brettan's voice was palpable.

"Sure. As long as he does too." Sam pointed a thumb at the lean Leaguesman. "And as long as you two hold off fighting. Now, how about letting me get up on your shoulders, and I'll try and open this door?"

The three and the light disappeared. Deo's aching head found the darkness welcome, but he wished he'd looked around with better focused eyes while he could see. He was going to need a clear place to vomit shortly. Very shortly.

eecɔɑɕ

Navigating the passages of the crashed upside-down ship was difficult. Besides the doors, the un anchored debris which one stumbled across was something of a hazard. Teovan, in the lead, tripped over something soft. It was a body. One of the chambermaids. Tied. Gagged. And shot neatly through the head, from behind. Sam knew that Blower had doped the coffee. He'd helped to tie them up. But somebody else had shot them. As Blower had said, there was no need, really. When the ship blew those still on it would be component atoms.

Sam walked on. He made no comment. But the small of his back was very cold. The maintenance workshop door was fortunately open. Teovan mantled it with ease. His skills as a second-story man gave him a serious advantage over the meaty Brettan when it came to climbing things. He filed the information away for future reference and reached his hand up for the glow-stick. He had a few seconds to spot, grab and secrete a chisel while the heavily-built Viscount struggled to pull himself up and over.

Five minutes later they were back with the rest of the party with five functioning headlights, and a more buoyant state of mind. When the Viscount pulled up on the door-sill and looked in to the upside-down room he saw and heard the Princess's factotum retching in a corner. The Princess was holding his head and patting his back. He shook his head and the light-beam in surprise. That was really no way for royalty to behave.

A minute or two later they and the welcome lights were being helped back into the room. "There are cutting-torches. If this thing is built at all like Imperial fighters it'll mean a double skin, but at least we can get through it." The Viscount was distinctly more cheerful, now that his spaceman's fear of slow suffocation was eased.

"A big if." Tanzo Adendorff was awake again. "As things proved, the ship wasn't a bit like human craft. And of course nobody ever bothered to find out how or from what the Denaari manufactured anything. One of my colleagues held the Denaari were much more primitive than humans, because their buildings, some of which still stand after three millennia, mind you, are irregular."

"Spare me the history lesson, Lady Adendorff," said the Viscount tersely. "I think I'll take a party forward with three of the lights to see if we can reach the airlock. I'd like to take all the able-bodied people. We may need some brute force to get through the forward section."

"Deo stays. I'll go. Caro, Leaguesman Wienan, Tanzo and that young girl had better stay. The Lieutenant is still unconscious. Miss... Lila is it? Will you come too?" asked Shari.

The debt-slave smiled at the aristocrat, surprised at hearing that the Princess knew her name. She stood up and slipped the .22 into her waist-band. "Lila Tandy Macrae at your service, your Highness." She gave a small curtsey and suddenly felt remarkably stupid.

The Princess smiled at her. "Well the first piece of service you can offer me is to give me a leg-up. These clothes are hopeless for climbing." She moved across to the doorway, arms reaching for the sill.

"Una and I will come too," announced Tanzo Adendorff, getting to her feet. "Nothing wrong with either of us, and who knows, the Viscount might need my lock-picking skills, even if he doesn't need my advice on the Denaari."

Passage through the forward section of the ship was difficult but not impossible. It wasn't so much brute force that was needed as squirm-ability. And care. The ripped metal edges were dangerously sharp. One couldn't move fast, and the large Viscount who was supposedly leading this expedition was the person who found the going most difficult. Thus it was that the whole party were right there with him, rather than him being a safe distance ahead when they heard the weak cry for help. Too late the Viscount remembered the other task that the imperial agents who were supposed to be his team were meant to have done.

"It must be one of the servants that those murderers didn't kill!" said Shari. "Poor soul. We must get to him."

Sam Teovan started. All the servants had been put into a room together, near the kitchen. And they'd all been thoroughly and efficiently gagged. He moved forward toward the door from which the cry had come. "Not you." The Viscount pulled him back roughly. "I'll go."

But Martin Brettan was unable to fit through the narrow gap that was all that remained of the doorway. The leaguesman's debt-slave tried. She was able to wriggle through and into the room beyond. A few minutes later she pushed someone out of the gap to blink in the torchlight.

Shari looked at the weak, spoiled plump face and sighed. "Jarian. What a co-incidence. What a happy family reunion. Did Daddy send you along for a bit of murder practice? Let's kill Auntie, eh?"

Prince Jarian was affronted, even if he was scared and confused. The old bag never treated him with respect. He *hated* her. But obviously she couldn't know about his falling out with his father. "Aunt Shari." He was damned if he'd accord her her title either. "Where are we? What happened?"

She shook her head at him, grimacing. "Come down, you idiot. Later, if we can get out of here, I shall take great pleasure in explaining it to you."

Part of the corridor ahead was impassable, but by detouring through two shattered cabins they reached the airlock. It didn't respond at all to Martin Brettan's hasty jab at the power switch. Staring at it in the torchlight the Viscount found a small flanged wheel set into the very center of the lock-door. He tried to turn it. It wouldn't budge.

"All Denaari threading is anti-clockwise. Hargreaves suggests that this implied that they had sinistral dominant brains," said Tanzo dryly. "I suggest you try turning the other way."

He did. The inner lock door slowly swung open. It was just as well. They could have burned away with cutting-torches at the outer hull of the Imm class vessel for a week without even getting it warm.

The Viscount stepped into the lock. It was not a wide space, although Denaari tall, and thus only Shari stepped in beside him. The lock behind them had to be closed before the outer lock would budge. So once the door behind them was closed and sealed, Martin Brettan spun the second manual lock-screw. The door groaned open about eight inches. A cascade of fine, faintly warm sand rushed in as it did. Within seconds it was already up around their knees.

"Close it!" she screamed at him.

The outer door began to close, and the sand cascade slowed. But then, with a horrible grinding noise the door.... stuck. Sand poured in steadily through the egg-timer crack. "I can't." He tried harder, exerting every ounce of his beefy muscle. The door closed perhaps a tenth of an inch more. Sand still filtered in through the crack. "Unless we can close this door the inner one won't open," he said through clenched teeth, still straining. The trickling sand fell inexorably.

¤¤¤Ɔ¤¤

The sun was hot. It looked to be about mid-afternoon. Juan had given up shouting. Obviously nobody was coming. Either nobody had lived through the crash, or nobody cared, or nobody had heard him. Anyway, he was hoarse. And very thirsty. And no longer quite so alone. Above him, drifting in a slow twist were some birds. Big birds, for all that they were high up. They were getting lower, however. Sooner or later they'd come and pick his eyes out and he wasn't going to be able to do anything other than scream. He wished anyone or anything else familiar and friendly was here. A small tear escaped. What had happened to Rat? Poor Rat.

As if on cue a pink nose whiffled into his face. And then wriggled into the gel that had safely transported it here and down into Juan's shirt. How?

The stuff allowed him to move enough to breathe! So.... small movements.... Gently, slowly the arm he'd strained and struggled so to free earlier was lifted. It came free of the gel with a plop. Two minutes later he was sitting on the barren earth of the Denaari mother-world in front of the escape pod, laughing hysterically, stroking Rat.

CHAPTER 11
CASTAWAYS

There are many myths of a first man and woman.
None of them have Eve saying to Adam, "I wouldn't
have you if you were the last man on earth." This
does not mean it could not have happened, just that
no ancestors will relate this tale.

The Veda of Holy Matrimony

Shari dug around the seal. The sand-gap in the door seal was a mere inch and a half. But airlocks are logically designed to only allow one door to open when the other is air-tight. The stuff was so fine and so dry it wouldn't pile. Despite her digging Martin couldn't move the door another hundredth of an inch. He sat down on the sand-surface. Measured carefully with his thumb. Looked at his elegant chronometer. Looked for something to mark the wall with, and settled for spittle.

"What are you doing?"

"Seeing how fast it is coming in. It looks like about a cubic foot every… say three minutes. We must have about 20 cubic feet left in all. We're going to drown in sand in less than an hour."

"We must be able to do something, surely?"

"With what? We've the clothes we stand in."

"And that pistol you were brandishing earlier. Shoot the lock."

He shook his head, looking grim in the torch-light. "Ricochet. There is nowhere to hide in here."

"Well, let's use our clothes. Off with them, Viscount. We can at least stop more sand coming in that crack."

He shrugged and began to take off his jacket. "We either drown in sand, or suffocate for lack of air."

"We also pound on the inner door. Perhaps they can get us out."

He shrugged again, putting the torch on top of his jacket. "I'll keep my pistol. It won't make much of a chock in that crack, and we might want it when the sand gets neck high."

"Very well. Turn your back please."

"Why?"

"Because I am taking all my clothes off. You can start pounding on the inner door."

He turned away with a snort, and began thumping the inner door. Here she was, about to die a slow unpleasant death and she worried about modesty. She was, probably, as legend had it, a bloody hermaphrodite. She hadn't turned away while he stripped, had she?

Shari might have allowed questions of morality to influence her. But her real aim was to avoid revealing to him the stationer-made bullet-proof jacket, the needle gun and the stiletto Deo had taught her to use. She might be going to die. But then, she might not. And as Deo had repeatedly said it was better to die with aces still in your sleeve than to reveal them prematurely. She'd noted the Viscount's very professional shoulder holster with care. She'd always had her suspicions about the man. She wondered whom he'd worked for. Not that it made much difference now, one way or the other.

●●C ϽΘΘ

The cutting torch hadn't made any impression at all. Sam, the only person who had known how to use it, kicked the obdurate door. "You'd think the bastards would put another fuckin' emergency release somewhere!"

"Surely if there was it would be on the door? Or near the door?" Lila shone her torch anxiously at door area.

Tanzo slapped her forehead. "Of course. A wingspan." She pushed Sam out of the way, and stood against the door, carefully lining her fingers up with the odd flanged wheel. "Put your fingers on the wall here where my right shoulder is. Watch out. It is a bit warm from that torch"

The Leaguesman complied "What are…"

"Shut-up. I'm calculating." She measured again, from that point. "Now… about where my elbow is. Look up. About three yards. Shine the torch there. Anything?"

"There's a pair of holes. Little ones. Too small for fingers."

"Excellent!" she fished in a pocket. Emerged with her lock-pick. "Come Leaguesman. You're the tallest. The Denaari used claw-holes for things they didn't want bumped by accident. Pick me up, man."

The Leaguesman gaped at her, but failed to move. Sam pushed him aside. Squatted down. "On my shoulders, lady-lock-tickler."

He lifted her without any visible effort. It was not an alien lock to challenge her, but just two simple switches. They just wouldn't stay down. "Lila, turn that wheel while I push these down." With the safety interlock successfully interrupted, the inner airlock door opened with a cascade of sand and two naked people and a small dog.

●●●✸●●

Shari had recovered her blouse top and a shiny jacket thing that Lila assumed must be a support garment for the very rich. The sand-gaps had been plugged with strips of blanket from a ruined bedchamber. "So… how do we get out?"

"Can we dig? I mean, is it far to the surface?" asked Tanzo.

"Heaven knows. Surely it can't be. The sand is warm. But as for digging… well the faster you dig the stuff out the more it pours in."

"Stabilise it," said Lila professionally.

The others looked her in surprise. "Er… do you know how?" Viscount Brettan had recovered his trousers. He had magnificent muscles, she thought.

"PVA in water, is what my dad used. But I don't suppose we have any paint."

"Didn't see any in the maintenance workshop." Sam Teovan kicked the fine sand. "Look, if the top is close, if we just open the outside door, some sand will come in, but we'll be able to get out." The idea felt good.

"Maybe. If outside is close enough."

"So push a pole up and see where the sand stops."

"And how will you know that, Yak?"

"When the pushing gets easy suddenly."

Shari stood up. "I'm going to go back to the others. They must be very anxious by now. Perhaps they'll have some ideas."

Someone cleared their throat back in the darkness. "There's no need, Princess. I have just come up to see what was happening. The Lieutenant is awake now." Deo stepped out of the darkness with a piece of water pipe. "Perhaps this, with a U bend on? It would be like a harpoon. Possible to push forward, but not draw back unless the end was into the open air. It would also act as a snorkel..." He toppled forward, and the ridergirl, who happened to be nearest, was obliged to catch him or be squashed.

By the time the factotum surfaced again, his 'snorkel' was out in the sulfur-tainted air of Denaar. His head was pillowed on the Princess's bare thighs and he wondered, briefly, whether this was one of those disturbing dreams he occasionally had now that his supply of the sexuality-suppressing drugs the Arunchal assassins used had run out. He stirred. She leaned over him. "We have to move you, Deo. They're going to try opening the outer airlock now."

He started to sit up. "Stay down. We'll move you. Martin. Lila. Give me a hand, please."

From further down the accessway Deo heard the grating of the airlock being forced further open. More sand spilled into the accessway. "Bring it in. Make more space for it to fall," someone shouted. And then there was light. A shaft of dusty sunlight.

Somebody was scrambling out. Briefly cutting off the sunlight. Slithering, scrabbling and swearing. "Like being in a bloody ant-lion hole." The Yak. He slithered back down bringing more sand with him. His tough face was grim. He picked up a handful of sand and let it trickle between his thick, stubby fingers. "There's a bugger of a lot of this stuff out there, and sod all else."

"Nice of you to come back to tell us," said Shari sardonically.

A grin split the tough face. "I thought of doing a runner. But there isn't much to run to out there. Just blooming sand. I'm a city boy, see. Don't know much about sand."

"You'll speak with respect to your betters, scum," said Viscount Martin Brettan, aiming a kick at him.

The Yak dodged easily. The Viscount stepped after him.

"Stop it." Shari barely had to raise her voice. "Martin. You. Whatsit. Sam. We're stuck here. Probably forever. What happened in the past is past. We're going to have to live together, and rely on each other to stay alive. That is if we can stay alive where there is nothing but sand. And among the useless things we have our titles are going to be the most meaningless and useless. I for one, intend to drop mine. Call me Shari."

The entire group was silenced. Shocked beyond speech. Hereditary power was the core of the Gotha Empire's being. The idea was as alien as the world they now stood on. The princess had already extrapolated a castaway future. She'd also realized the potential of shock in maintaining her fragile control over the group. The statement provoked the response she'd required... and more. Viscount Brettan and Prince Jarian looked at her as if they'd abruptly awoken to find a snake on their chests.

Deo sat up. His deep voice was oddly calm. "To me, you will remain Princess Shari. But you are right, Princess. To survive we will have to set aside our differences and work together. Is there nothing outside but sand?"

"Big rock ridge over that way. And lots of sand."

Tanzo sighed. "No buildings?"

"Just black rock and sand, Lady lock-tickler."

The little scholar looked aggrieved. "I would have thought we'd land at some historical civilization site."

"It was a rather forced landing, Tanzo. I don't imagine sand and more sand was the Denaari's idea of a holiday resort."

The dumpy woman shook her head. "You're wrong, you know, Prin... Shari. The most heavily settled Denaari worlds are virtually bare of vegetation. Too dry. This place is probably like that."

Shari thought of New Sahara. Of Gobi V. Shuddered. "Water discipline is going to have to be our priority then. Fortunately, we have the ship and all the materials on it."

●●C⊃●●

On the other side of the ridge Juan didn't have the advantage of a ship from which to garner the wherewithal of survival. He had a serious thirst problem and all he had was an alien escape pod. It also looked like he wasn't going to have that for very long.

He'd finally gotten over his hysteria, and started a brief exploration of his environment, trying to work out the easiest way up the razor-backed ridge. He had to get over it... there would surely be other survivors? He could join them in finding the way to the nearest settlement. Also surely the stationers would have tracked the descent of the ship. Rescue craft must surely be on the way already. He must think of some way of signaling to them or he could be left alone out here. The idea terrified him. Perhaps something from the escape pod could be used as a mirror. He looked back at the pod. It was dissolving.

He turned and ran back.

The pod wasn't dissolving under its own steam. It was being assisted by a myriad of little spitbug-starfish-like creatures. Frantically he tried to brush some aside. The spittle burned his hand and he hastily rubbed it off on the sand. It still burned. He spat on it. That seemed to help. He worked his mouth trying to make more spittle in its dryness.

The creatures' digestive enzymes were actually totally ineffectual at breaking down carbon-based lifeforms, but they functioned best in a low pH environment. Anyway the creatures had been designed to clear up dead scrap and to recycle the nutrients and minerals therein. The Denaari would have been horrified at the idea of their garbage cleaning system attacking something living, but Juan didn't know this. He backed off a good ten yards, still spitting on this hand. It wasn't that bad really. It had just burned the cuts and scratches he'd acquired. He stood and watched as the escape pod was digested, ready to turn and run. As the chair crumbled, the starfish-spitbugs began blowing larger bubbles which fused into little gasbags. The creatures began drifting away down-valley as the last remnants of the escape pod fell into de-mineralized dust.

Juan stared. It couldn't have taken more than fifteen minutes. And it was all gone. Every bit of it, except that sort of circlet left in the dust. Cautiously he went for a closer look. The thing shone, even dusty like that. It was... a sort of crown. Using a splinter of glassy rock he drew it closer to him, and then knocked the dust off it. It gleamed silver-gold in the afternoon sun. It would do for a mirror. Pulling his sleeve down to cover his hand Juan picked it up. It was surprisingly heavy. Well, he would just have to carry it, and be careful he didn't drop it.

He didn't know it then, but it wouldn't really have mattered if he'd pounded it with a rock. A Denaari mnemonic crown was designed to withstand whatever fate overtook its wearer, and carry back the precious life memories and emotions to its nest-mates and roost. With the mission that the owner of this crown had been on, it was designed to survive a point-impact of up to eighty tons per square inch. Diamond was soft and brittle by comparison. But Juan didn't know this and handled it with care. It was a damned nuisance as he tried to find a way up the virtually impassable ridge. He often found he needed two hands. If he slid it up his arm, it wouldn't stay slid. His shirt kept coming untucked when he put it inside it. Besides, Rat didn't seem to like it.

The awkward crown was one of the reasons Juan gave up trying to climb the ridge. The other was that the sun was distinctly lower now and as little as he might like the idea of spending the night out here, he liked the idea of a night stuck on a little ledge up there even less. From the height he had gained he could see up-valley. There was a little saddle a few miles further up. Surely that must be easier to cross. So he climbed down from the ridge, managing not to drop the crown.

It was as well that he didn't drop it. It wouldn't have broken, but he might have lost it. And it was probably worth at least twenty times what the Gotha Emperor's grandiose seventeen pounds of platinum and rare gemstones was. There were, after all, only forty-one other mnemonic crowns as yet missing from the Denaari memory vaults. When the Denaari wings had spread over 433 planets there had been nearly two billion crowns scattered across the outworlds. All but the last forty two had been gathered in, sent back to Denaar, the crowns full of memories and the love of the dead and dying crowding desperately needed minerals and materials, and even the living off the ships. The remaining crowns, the crowns of those heroes who had stayed to the last, had been recovered by their keening and grieving small servants. The loyal echinate-creatures had loaded the last crowns onto the messenger ships, before following their beloved masters, even into death. The idea that inanimate things could carry this mysterious constantly mutating non-living plague never occurred to them, as it never occurred to their masters. The many-armed Sil, who had destroyed all life but themselves on their mudball-heavy-metal world, had had a similar problem with the Denaari-introduced viruses.

Walking up the valley Juan would have cheerfully traded the crown, even if he had known its worth, for a drink. He'd have given two of them for some human company, but all he had was that distant skein of birds, now high up again. He wished they'd piss off. Juan was a teenager, so he wasn't a great believer in older and wiser heads. But, right now, he secretly admitted to himself, what he really wanted was his Dad or Mum, or even his step-mother-to-be. This had to be all their fault!

●●●●●●

"Birds!"

"Probably not. Probably some local creature," said Tanzo

Lila squinted into the late afternoon sun. "Birds. Condor-harpies. You can even see the markings on their wings."

"But they're native to New Texas!" said Tanzo, whose knowledge was expansive, even if xenoarchaelogy did color it.

"The Denaari might have brought them here," said Brettan.

"What for? They're disgusting horrible things!" Lila was surprised at the depth of her feelings. But seeing them had brought it all to the surface again. She could remember those terrible toothed beaks tearing into the cows, and the way the cattle's eyes had rolled as the Condor-harpies talon-poison paralysed their muscles. It been the flock of Condor-harpies that had been the last straw for the farm, after the drought.

"They're carbon-based lifeforms. They eat meat. Therefore there must be meat for them to eat. Therefore we too can find food. Or we can eat them," said Deo gravely. He had refused to stay back in the ship, and appeared to be keeping up well. Shari still watched him anxiously.

Lila felt herself retching at the thought of eating Condor-harpy. She turned away, unable to speak.

"Well, I'm blowed if I'll eat something like that. I'd sooner dine on one of you lot," Sam Teovan surprised her by bursting out. Lila found herself looking at the wiry scar-faced man with approval for the first time. Sam had surprised himself too. The hit on Oz had been a failure in that their target had already fled into the outback. By the time Sam and the local contact had tracked the man down the runner had already fallen victim to Condor-harpies. They'd killed the paralysed man who had had his eyes and part of his liver ripped out by the birds. But if the man had been able to speak he would have begged them to do it. The memory frightened Sam in other ways too. In the city he was as at home as a rat. Out there, well, nature had nearly killed him a couple of times.

"Be sure you'll be first on the menu, Yak, if we get to that," Martin Brettan said grimly.

Shari sighed. They were still bickering, instead of exploring as they'd set out to do. Couldn't they see they had to unite to survive? She'd try for a change of subject. "Isn't that a cave over there?"

"Could be, Princess. Could be. You got sharp eyes. Let's go and have look." Sam gave her his lop-sided grin, and set off.

"I still think we should kill that bloody Yak scum," Martin

Brettan muttered. He was surprised when the angular Leaguesman next to him agreed vehemently.

The cave was about a quarter of a mile from where the ship lay half imbedded in the slip-face of a huge sand-dune. As caves go this one would have rated a Neolithic minus 10. It was stony and shallow, and the roof had, in the past, parted with huge shards. Several hanging pieces still looked unstable, as if a shout might bring them down. The wind off the sand blew straight into it. "It'll do for a start. I think we should carry as much stuff up here as we can tonight," said Shari.

"Tonight!" Johannes Wienan looked at the unappealing overhang.

"Tonight. It might as well be as soon as possible. We are going to have to live here. That dune is eventually going to swallow the ship. We might as well get as much out as we can while we can still get in through the lock. Of course the injured come out first. Then water. Then food. Tools. Warm things."

"But we can't live out here!" Kadar stared at the cave.

"Where else?" said Deo.

Tanzo nudged the frightened looking rider-girl. Then, with a particularly nasty smile she bowed to the leaguesmen, and in hand-speech said, "Welcome to your new Dacha, lords."

Kadar snarled at her, seeing another spy.

Johannes didn't. Instead his eyes narrowed, noticing those who laughed. The Princess. The Viscount. His rebellious debt-slave. Even the Princess's factotum permitted himself a flicker of a smile. The rider had just looked, as usual, scared. But that was five people who knew the League's supposedly secret way of communicating with the riders. Warily, he filed the information for future reference.

"We can construct sleds, if …Sam, can cut some of the cabin walls for us," Deo, ever practical, said, turning toward the ship and beginning to walk back.

"Remember, once that gas is finished we've nothing more to cut metal with," Martin Brettan said grimly.

"True. And no fuel for a forge either."

●●●↺↺↺

Johannes ached. He had literally never worked so hard in his life before. His eyes had nearly popped out of his head when he had been pulled to his feet from where he'd been sitting on the sand, and told to stop slacking and carry. "But the servants…" The man who had pulled him to his feet looked into his eyes. Suddenly

Johannes Wienan was very, very frightened of the Princess's factotum. "The Princess has already explained that those who do not work, do not eat... or drink."

"But my arm..."

"We have made up some packs while you sat idle. I will load you. And see that you do not dawdle."

Johannes soon had reason to wish he'd kept his mouth shut and just chosen to carry things he could manage with one hand. The packs were heavier than anything he'd ever lifted. Then they'd made him join in pulling the loaded sheet-metal sleigh across the sand.

His arm was swollen. He was stiff in every muscle he knew he had, and a few more. The only person who seemed to have taken it worse than himself was that young Prince. Jarian. Turabi's third son. Why had he been on board the ship? Whatever the reason had been, the Princess had been taking it out on the boy. She'd slapped him when he'd refused to carry a pack. He'd cried. She'd slapped him again. And he'd picked up the pack. Funny, she'd been the one that was all for giving up ranks and titles, but she still gave the orders. And nearly everybody still called *her* 'Princess'.

The moons were up and shining silver on the wreck of the spaceship. Johannes shivered. It was going to be cold out here tonight. The Princess stood up, and began handing out mugs. Johannes saw his debt-slave attempt to stand up and take over from her, and be told firmly to sit. Deo followed with slices of bread. Not very large slices from one of the five loaves they'd found in the kitchen. There'd been less food than they'd hoped. The ship carried very little more than it required for each hop, taking on fresh supplies at each space-station.

Johannes didn't approve of the mugs. Robust china, intended for the kitchen-staff, they'd survived. The fine porcelain hadn't. He tasted. Water. Plain water. There'd been ample wine. They'd poured it out to make water bottles! They'd said that water would be more important than wine. Despite the lecture the dumpy woman had given him about alcohol's diuretic effects, Johannes could never agree with that statement.

It was just plain bread too. He was damned if he'd eat this! Without meaning to, he took a bite, and discovered that hunger is indeed the finest sauce.

He'd drunk the water. Eaten every last crumb of that inadequate piece of bread. He was still both thirsty and hungry. Prince Jarian had asked, no, demanded, more. He'd got a flea in his ear from the Princess, with support from her sycophantic cabal. Carefully Johannes noted them. That dumpy little Duchess. The Countess with the large breasts. The factotum. Well, he would, he was her servant. The surviving bodyguard. And Johannes's own rebellious debt-slave. If he ever got back to where the rule of Imperial law held, that girl was going to suffer.

Johannes shook his head. He wasn't going to tolerate this. He wasn't a pack-mule and he needed better food. And he wasn't going to put up with any more abuse either. Well, on that one his fellow Leaguesman and he were in agreement. But what other allies did he have? And what weapons could they muster?

The Prince, certainly. But the boy didn't look very tough, and probably didn't have a gun. Mind you, you never could tell with someone like that. And perhaps, as he was nearer to the throne than his Aunt, Imperial loyalties could be called on. The bodyguard? It was worth considering. Then there was the Viscount. The thought of Martin Brettan's face on seeing a bottle of the magnificent 2437 vintage Chateau Lafitte poured out almost brought a smile to the plump, tired Leaguesman's face. Yes. The Viscount was supposed to be Shari's consort, but he was definitely unhappy and ripe for a rearrangement of the hierarchy. He was armed and he knew how to use the weapon.

Then there was the Yak. Yes. At the moment the Yak seemed to be basking in the light of the Princess's favor. She'd definitely warmed to him after he dragged her factotum in, half-concussed. Huh. The Yak had probably hit him. The man would work for whoever offered him the best deal, Johannes was sure.

He fell asleep at this point, leaving the rider-girl right out of his equation.

●●C つ●●

Martin Brettan was not making that mistake. It was nice to know he had a hole-card. But the Viscount had thought further into the equation than the young Leaguesman. This was not just about food and drink. This was about survival. And offspring. He, Martin Brettan, was going to come out top of the power hierarchy and the reproductive hierarchy. And if he couldn't get there by charm he'd make sure he'd get there by force. None of these others were in his league. He waited until Shari got up and walked outside, and then followed her.

"The stars are almost familiar, aren't they? I can make a pretty reasonable guess at where we are... Not that it'll do us or our children any good." He put an arm around her waist.

She pushed his arm away and turned the full force of her disconcerting stare on him. In the moonlight he could see her face was expressionless. He knew her well enough to know her danger signals. "Our children?" her voice was just as flat as her expression.

"We're not going to get back you know. We'll live and die here. You're beyond the Emperor's hand here. There is no reason why we shouldn't..."

She stepped away from him. "Except one. Nothing personal Martin, but I wouldn't have you if you were the last man on Earth."

His nostrils flared. "You prefer your low-born paramour, do you? Well, Shari, *you* should remember this isn't Earth, or the Empire either."

"Paramour! How melodramatic. Whom, pray?"

"Don't play with me, Shari. Remember you don't have a title, position and bodyguards to hide behind any more. I offered you a choice. But I'll take what I like when I want to. Neither you nor any of the others can stop me." He stepped towards her. Otto, hitherto silent, snarled at him.

Somebody cleared their throat in the darkness. "If we may be of assistance, Your Highness?" Lieutenant Albeer, appearing not at all as if he'd been concussed, but instead looking very dangerous, stepped out of the shadow.

The 'we' was not wasted on either the Martin Brettan or Shari. He knew it might be a bluff. But then, was this thickset man, whose heavy eyebrows formed a continuous band across his broad face, capable of bluff? Shari knew it meant that Deo simply waited her word.

"Thank you Lieutenant... Mark. Kindly escort this... person back to the cave. There are certain things a girl needs to do... alone."

The burly bodyguard's tenseness eased. "Certainly Princess. Come along, you."

Martin Brettan turned and stormed off back to the cave.

Shari waited until she was certain they were out of earshot. "Deo," she said quietly, speaking to the darkness, "I really do need... privacy."

"I will avert my eyes, Princess."

She sighed. Shook her head at the man in the darkness and squatted, blushing to herself.

CHAPTER 12
FAR SWEETER THAN WINE

*Desert xerophytes can survive in the ordinary warm
sun and frequent rain which makes soft green things
flourish. But take them to the desert and try them
with blistering hot days, bone- freezing nights and
water as a distant dream, and then the soft green
plants will die. The xerophytes will not. They will still
survive. Some will even flourish. Ordinary human
society hides many, many xerophytes.*

The Upanishad of the Gardener-Dewa Celine.

Juan stumbled, for perhaps the three-thousandth time. He had
never had to deal with anything but absolutely level corridors
before. He had never had to learn to watch where he put his feet
before. He was learning fast and hard now. The darkness hadn't
helped either. On the other side of the ridge the rising moons
made it quite bright. Here in the shadowed valley it was pitch-dark.
And *cold*. The thermo-controlled environment of the Space-station
had not prepared him for this. The station was always a
comfortable twenty-four degrees… He was dressed for a little

more than that because the controlled temperature on the royal barge was set for the comfort of gentlemen in jackets. But with the rapid coming of desert night the air temperature had plummeted. The breeze coming up the valley had been warm at first. Now it cut like a whip through his station-weave. Surely it must be going to snow any minute now? At least that would give him a drink.

The clear sky above him meant nothing to the boy. Perhaps the way the stars twinkled instead of burning cold and steady was an indicator of the coming snow. He stumbled on, grateful when the light of the first moon actually made it past the lip of the valley and down onto his rocky path. It also showed him that the saddle he'd been heading for, that he'd thought he'd reach in twenty minutes max, was still a long, long way off.

Eventually he just had to stop. He found a rock which offered some shelter from the horrible wind, and hunched down behind it, huddling his body around the warmth of Rat. He was exhausted and very, very thirsty. The rationed mug of water that Johannes had felt so mingy on the other side of the ridge would have been heaven to the boy.

Rat, in the fashion of rats, repaid Juan for the transport and warmth, by squirming out and dropping plumply to the ground, before setting off, nose to the ground into the tumble of rocks. Juan stared owlishly at his sole companion's departing white posterior for a moment. "Hey Ratty! Here, Rat!" Rat paid him no attention, but followed his whiffling pink nose. Juan had little choice but to crawl after him, through a groove so narrow that it pressed against his ribs. Juan thought cracks in the rock were cracks in the rock, but this one was in fact a water-worn chute. It led into a small rock-enclosed bay of sand and debris. Along the one edge of the bay under the wide overhang that kept the sun off, lay a deep rock-pool full of water, rippling away from the drinking rat in the moonlight.

Juan couldn't believe it. He touched it several times before he dared taste it. Then he drank until his sides ached. Then he turned to find Rat, to heap totally undeserved praise and affection on the animal's head.

Rat, having drunk his fill was contentedly nibbling at a seed he had found. There were plenty more still hanging from the dry stalks of cirrith-grass from Abelard that had hastily sprouted, grown, and seeded again just after the rain had come. The little desert ger-mice native to Tani V didn't come here. The cirrith-covered corner next to the tank had a resident diamond-back pseudosnake, who was, at the moment, still sleeping off its last meal. Anyway it was too cold to stir now.

The flavour of raw Cirrith seeds has been described as peanut-scented oily cotton waste, by the flattering. Even the ravenous Juan couldn't say they were delicious. But if Rat could eat them, surely they were edible? He chewed and swallowed the handful stoically. His belly was dutifully grateful, and he washed it down with more water from the pool, before venturing on some more. Actually, Cirrith is the source of about a third of Abelard's income, and is processed into a bewildering array of products from cattle-cake to sperm-whale oil substitute. And yes, you can live on it. Juan only knew that by the time he'd eaten three handfuls of the stuff he wasn't hungry any more, just incredibly tired. He managed to scrape together a few handfuls of cirrith-straw in a corner, and passed out on it, Rat once again cheerfully snuggled against his belly, the Denaari Mnemonic crown lying on the sand beside them. He slept well into the next day.

eecɔϑϑ

On the other side of the ridge the other crash-survivors awoke to the sound of collapsing metal.

"What the hell?" Mark Albeer was up, his gun in hand. So was the Viscount, but their weapons were not going to be of any use. The sound came from the wreck of the ship. Part of it had collapsed. As they ran towards it, the morning sunlight shone on streamers of drifting iridescent bubbles, homing in on the ship. The ship was being digested. The clattering was the human installed ironmongery falling. The little starfish-spitbugs were even burrowing into the sand, devouring the remnants of the ship.

"Back off. They're eating the engine section. The power unit, whatever it is, is bound to blow," shouted Martin Brettan.

They retreated, but other than the sound of more bits of falling steel from the human refit, nothing happened. The starfish-spitbugs began bubble-blowing and drifting away.

All that was left were human-refit debris in a half collapsed sand hole.

"Oh shit." The Leiutentant Albeer pointed.

It seemed a terribly inadequate thing to say, when the ship's water-reservoir was slowly draining onto the sand.

A frantic and largely unsuccessful effort to block the rip in the ship's cistern followed. Of the ten thousand litres it had contained, perhaps seventy remained in a corner. Afterwards the castaways found themselves picking through the leftover debris like a flock of dejected vultures. He was so dispirited by the loss of the water that Johannes almost kicked the radio unit from the ruins of his fellow leaguesman's cabin aside. Then, without any eagerness he bent and picked it up. It seemed to be still intact. Why had the Leaguesman had a radio-unit in his personal chambers? Even an agent-supervisor had no need of such a thing, surely?

"Hey! Leave that! It is mine!" Kadar stormed across toward Johannes. He attempted to snatch the radio unit away from him.

"Ow! My arm!"

"What are you two scuffling about?" Mark Albeer had, with frightening casualness, picked each of them up by the scruff of the neck.

"Let go of me, you... That is my radio-unit." Kadar kicked, his face red and his eyes popping.

"Radio-unit? Does it work?" The bodyguard asked as if he was not holding two people aloft.

"Don't know. I just found it. Let me down!" protested Johannes.

"Here Lila. Come check this out." Mark called to the girl who was digging out bottles.

She came over. He put the two men down but retained his grip on their tunic collars. "Give it to her, Leaguesman."

"I was going to... I wasn't trying to keep it to myself." Johannes was indignant.

"Yes," said Albeer, dryly. "And the devil hands out free ice-creams at the gates of hell. Do you know how it works, lassie?"

She nodded, finding herself flushing slightly. Lassie indeed.

"It's mine!" said Kadar, reaching for the unit.

"Shut up." He twitched the collar again.

She clicked the power switches. An LED came on. "Well, we've got power, but it probably needs an aerial."

"See if there is an extender at the back?"

There was. She unreeled the four yards of cable. "We'll have to try it at various angles, but let's see if we get anything." She spun the dials. Suddenly out of the crackling silence, an eerie sequence of rapid clicks and whistles came across the ether.

Most of the rest of the survivors had gathered around them by now.

"There is something out there."

"And we are the first humans to hear Denaari speech in more than three thousand years." Tanzo's voice was full of reverence.

"They don't speak such good Imperial, do they?" Sam Teovan

grinned crookedly. "And they're probably not going to be that pleased to see us, eh?"

"It is probably an automated signal," Shari said cooly.

"Yes. Welcome to Denaar. Now go away, or we'll blow you to smithereens," said Martin Brettan, deliberately without respect. "What I want to know is why you Leaguesmen had a unit like this on board the ship?"

"Ask Kadar. I had nothing to do with it," said Johannes sulkily.

But that man was listening in horror to the gibberish coming out of his radio. "It's what I heard in space," he said dazed. "I thought it was just some kind of Imperial scrambler... on the ship....

"And you didn't tell anyone, so we couldn't reply. What a nice man you are Kadar. Who were you trying to contact?" Shari's eyes burned at him.

He stuttered.

"The Emperor used the Yak. You were planning to blame the Imperial agents, weren't you? So whose agents were those who were killed?"

"Mine! You witch..." Mark Albeer slapped Kadar with an open hand, and Leagesman fell.

Martin Brettan noted the strength of the stocky man. Strong, but then was Albeer a master of martial arts and an expert in the use of sabre and pistol, as he was? The bodyguard was probably trained with firearms and also surely had had instruction in the basic hand-to-hand combat stuff.

●●●○○○

Martin Brettan was unaware that Shari was observing him as carefully as he was observing the bodyguard. The man had shown no reaction to the information that the people who had been shot on the ship were not Imperial agents, but League agents. Well... either he had known nothing of it all, or he'd been the one that killed them. But why?

Deo had not been in the crowd. He'd been watching someone else who wasn't attracted to the alien radio-broadcast. Prince Jarian ought to have taken sneaking lessons. He'd been painfully obvious trying to slip off to the remains of the cabin he'd been confined in. Deo followed like a ghost. He saw Jarian scrabble through the ruins of the wardrobe. He heard the boy's crow of delight when he found the small black case he'd been looking for. He watched as Jarian shoved it into his pudgy waistline and attempted to fluff out his doublet to make it less obvious. The

Prince headed back to the rest of the party. Deo drifted silently away towards the bare ground where the engine room had hung. There were two solitary bags lying there, and he wanted to investigate them.

The bags were stationer-made stuff. He cautiously opened one bag. It was full of badly packed stationer-style clothes. And in typical stationer fashion each garment was neatly labelled.

J. BIACASTA. AMRITSAR.
SECTOR V. CORRIDOR 29.
APARTMENT A17

He shook out the top coverall. Whoever J. Biacasta was or had been he was not very large. Male, by the cut of the garment, and small. He put it aside and bent to examine ovoid bits of something that wasn't the polished sand of Denaar. Ah. Rat droppings. Well, that was at least easier to understand than the presence of the clothes of either a small or a young stationer. He made his way back to the argument around the radio-unit.

"Look, we must go to the source of the signal, even if we don't signal back." Tanzo was flushed and vehement.

"They tried to kill us, Lady lock-tickler. You want to give them a second chance?"

"It was an automated defense system. Incoming ships carried a plague."

"After more than three thousand years? What sort of system would survive that?"

"Either a self-repairing one or one built to last. Our ship lasted that long."

"In deep space, yes, but in the atmosphere?"

"The Denaari built to last. The original colony building on Joshua has been restored three times. The Denaari buildings are still intact and they're in better condition than the restored colony buildings." Tanzo held stubbornly to her thesis.

"Our choice, as I see it, is a simple one. Either we stay here, and if we don't starve or die of thirst, we dwindle into a desert tribe of involuntary colonists, or," Shari paused, "We go hunting either live Denaari, or their civilisation's remains. Much as I dislike being a scavenger, it could give us a head start."

Sam grinned, "I'm with you, Princess Lady. I'm a city a boy, and even a dead and ruined city has got to be better than this."

"But which way do we go?" Caro looked at the dune-desert. "I mean, if we go out there we'll just get lost and die. People do, you know."

Deo spoke quietly. "The radio unit has a signal intensity meter on it. A little experimentation will give us direction."

The Viscount looked at him sharply. He might be the Princess's rent-boy, but he had a sharp mind. "With a bit of patience we can even work out distance. Good thinking, Watsisname."

It took several hours of patient pacing and considerable calculation to work out that they should go north over the ridge. The signal was coming from roughly two hundred miles off.

"Well, we should be there in four or five days", said Johannes, rubbing his hands together.

Lila looked at him with contempt. "We'll be lucky if we get there in four weeks."

"But it's only two hundred miles. Say if we walk four miles an hour, say for ten hours a day..."

He could read scorn in her eyes as she stared at his flabbiness. "On the flat with nothing to carry, and good food and water, *you* couldn't walk forty miles a day. Over that," she pointed at the scree and steep glassy krantzes above them, "you could take a day to cover one mile in the right direction."

"And we'll have to carry food and water. And we do not have enough," added Deo quietly looking up from his calculations. "At two pints per man per day for the twelve of us, we have, including all our bottled supply, less than eight days of water. Even rationed we don't have enough for the weeks it will take us."

"We'll just have to search for water."

"But if we fail to find any, we'll have even less," Johannes said.

"If we don't find water, we're dead anyway."

●●●⊃●●

Juan had enough water. Enough food for a while too, if you counted cirrith seeds. A direction was what he didn't have... or a way of reaching the water. For on the sand between him and it and any possible way out lay a fat New Oz diamondback, sunning itself and occasionally flicking its slim dark tongue across its glossy black-purple lips. The boy didn't dare move. He hardly dared breathe. Three yards away the snake lay fat and lazy and didn't move either, keeping an unblinking pseudo reptile eye focused coldly on this large invader to its domain. Actually the only reason the diamondback hadn't left was another fascinating smell

127

it was tasting with its flicking tongue. Warm, frightened rat.

Juan's tensed muscles were screaming. His legs were getting to the point where no matter what orders his frightened brain sent, they had to straighten.

His knee jerked. The diamondback hissed like an angry kettle and began to bunch itself up, to strike... or flee. Galvanized by fear the boy screamed and flung the Denaari Mnemonic crown at the creature with all his might. Juan was a better-than-average null-g ball player. It didn't help him much down here in the gravity well. He missed by miles. The snake, however, decided that discretion was the better part of valor, and, with a sinuous slither, left for less populated parts.

For minutes Juan just stood there gulping air like a water-dispossessed goldfish. Snakes had seemed pleasantly frightening and exciting on vid. You could *keep* them in real life! Finally, tentatively, he bent down and retrieved the crown. The odd-shaped thing hadn't been damaged at least. He held it between both hands and then, without thinking or intent, he put it on his head.

●●●●●●

"Did you hear that?" Sam Teovan paused, head twisted, listening.

"No. What?" Mark Albeer was hot, out of breath, and already beginning to be thirsty. He was regretting volunteering for this expedition. He didn't have the build for rock-climbing and this was rapidly what the attempt to cross the ridge had turned into. Looking back you could see the others picking through the remains of the ship's fittings.

"Sounded," pause, "like a," pause, "scream", panted the third expeditionary and the reason that the bodyguard had volunteered. Caro Leyven was even less well suited to climbing than himself. They'd had to wiggle up several cracks and she'd loudly cursed her breasts several times. Mark had expected to have to help her back to the cave after a short distance, but despite her obvious exhaustion and the sweat gluing her blouse to her body in interesting places, she hadn't complained.

Mark scanned and counted the people down in the valley below them. "All there. Nobody showing any signs of panic. Couple of them sitting down idling, mind you."

"It came from over the ridge." They were nearly at the crest now.

"Animal maybe? Something we could eat?"

"It sounded like a person to me." Sam looked doubtful.

"Well, let's listen for a few minutes."

But the only sound was that of Caro trying not to pant. After a while they went on. About ten minutes later they could see into the next valley. There was no sign of life. It was a narrow, steep sided valley. Beyond it lay yet another ridge, higher than the one they were on, and lipped with cliffs.

●●●つ●●

Down in between the tortured valley boulders the source of their scream lay in a fetal ball, clutching the thing on his head. He whimpered from time to time as alien images and emotions he could not understand plucked and teased at his consciousness. The images were alien and expressed in colors which the human eye is blind to. The emotions, the love and the unfettered sexuality of a Denaari five were beyond his ken too. But there was no escaping the terrible sadness and sheer misery of what had happened. He wanted to keen and chitter and chew his wing-tips.

When he'd put the crown onto his ill-suited cranium, he'd been a boy. When several hours later, he took it off and stood up, he was boy no longer. Part of him was a Denaari nest-minder. The crown lacked the ability of the Stardogs to reconfigure its output to human telempathic norms, but the recipient had been similar enough to comprehend the non-detail parts of the crown's content, the images and raw emotions, tastes, smells and gentle touches. Juan's head was full of tall towers bright with colors for which he had no words, of the spiral Denaari fives soaring in the sun-bright sky, of the feeling of wind beneath his own wings and of shaping and controlling it, of the taste and the scent of a rare spice which would kill humans instantly, so they could never know its wondrous and intense flavors. Worst, his head was full of the creeling and mewing of the beloved new hatchlings.

●●●つ●●

Lying down here in the thrall of the crown Juan had not seen or heard the noisy descent of the party from the ridge. They had failed to find water, although the bodyguard had realized that the debris he'd seen must be the product of flooding.

Later, back with the others, Mark held up his spoils. "It's wood."

The others examined it. The grey-black fragment was broken and abraded, but when cut with the bodyguard's pen-knife showed wood-grain. Tanzo squinted intensely at it. She scraped the black end of it. Sniffed the residue. Finally tasted it. "It's been burnt."

129

"There are other people here!" Kadar was jubilant

"Not necessarily," said the xeno-archaeologist. "There are natural fires, you know. And alien species also use fire. But at least there are plants somewhere upstream. If there are plants there is water."

They stared at the wood fragment as if it was a sacred relic.

"Well. I think first things first." Shari was as pragmatic as ever. "We must take ourselves to the source of this bit of wood. Can we get over that ridge the way you went? With a reasonable volume of supplies?"

Sam looked at the black ridge glowering in the afternoon sun. "You'd break your ass trying to get over 'fore dark. Best to wait for morning, or maybe look for an easier way."

They prepared packs. It was the right thing to do, even if the search for wood and water might be a vain one. Having a common purpose and direction to work in eased some of the underlying tensions. Still there was a near fight that evening about the water ration.

"I need more water than this! It's been hot out there dragging stuff around in the sun. The ones who went for a walk can have less."

"Shut up, Jarian," said Shari dismissively.

"I won't! What makes you in charge anyway, you old bag? I out-rank you. I'll give the orders! Give me some more water! Now!"

Nobody moved. Loyal oaths and common sense warred in Mark Albeer's breast. Surely the Viscount? No, not after last night's humiliation. Perhaps the Princess's factotum who had called him to that scene, and let him take the frontal role while he skulked? That man was outranked too.

A similar, if less well defined, argument was going on in Lila's head too. She was loyal to the Empire. It had taken her in, paid her, given her purpose through the degradation of being Johannes's body-slave. If it had been the League rising against the Princess she would have had no doubts.

Actually, Deo was merely coolly waiting. Any person who posed a direct threat to her would die, but in the meanwhile, let her foes be revealed.

"I could use more water too," said Johannes, declaring himself in, and unwittingly swaying Lila toward the Princess.

Kadar started to open his mouth.

"Oh stop it, you two." Tanzo stormed up to the Prince, and literally pushed him over. He sat, gaping at her. "We're all thirsty.

Nobody is getting any extra. And I don't care, Prince Jarian, if you do outrank me. I'll *sit* on you if I have to. The Princess, I mean, Shari, is doing a lot better than *you* could. As for *working,* why you're laziest person I've ever met. You were forever sitting down and slacking off when the rest of us were working. The only one who came anywhere near you was your equally lazy supporter."

"Well said! Oh, well said, Tanzo. I'll help you if you need me to," said Caro, clapping, surprising herself, and influencing a large bodyguard considerably.

The dumpy little woman looked slightly embarrassed.

"Yeah, Lady Lock-tickler. I reckon I'll also give you a hand if you need one," said Sam, having made his assessment of Deo's readiness to kill.

"Is anybody loyal to me?" asked Jarian in a half-whimper. "I'll have you all flayed..."

The Viscount squatted down next to Jarian and whispered in his ear. "Not now! Back down, or we'll be killed."

Jarian burst into angry, frustrated tears. "There. That sorted him out," said Martin Brettan with a disdainful twist of the lip. "We really cannot afford to bicker about things now."

"As for you Yak, if you call me 'Lady Lock-Tickler' again, I'll sit on *you*, never mind call for help," said Tanzo in a grim undervoice to the surviving hi-jacker.

Sam grinned his crooked grin at her. "Anytime, Lady Lock tickler. It could be fun. And I reckon I won't need no help."

The dumpy woman retreated in confusion, not knowing how to reply. First having to be grateful to that blond complete airhead she'd always despised, and now picking up, what, unless she was very much mistaken, were definite sexual signals from that wiry little Yak. Well, she reflected, in an economy of scarcity you couldn't choose your friends, and it did wonders for making one attractive to the opposite sex. It was something she had never found herself being before. Unconsciously she straightened her shoulders, and pushed her chest out a bit. The make-up she'd always turned into a disaster area was lost somewhere in the debris. She'd made no effort to find it, but now she wondered... Well, it was probably buried by now. And she'd always hated the muck. She'd just have to do without. She couldn't see her own face so she didn't realize what a wise decision this was.

eec๑ee

Concussion, the medical texts will tell you, can have many strange subsequent side-effects. Things like amnesia, black-outs, delirium, chronological distortion and character shifts have been widely reported. The blow to Deo's head had been more serious than those who worried about him realized. His bio-control training had helped to make the severity of the injury less serious... in appearance. He should have been in a hospital, under observation, on strict bed-rest. As it was, his own powers of observation were most obviously diminished. His normally preternatural sensitivity to sounds or movements, even when he was apparently asleep, just weren't at home tonight. He slept the deep, heavy sleep of the injured and exhausted. He didn't even hear the tiny clink of glass on glass, which would normally have stirred him instantly to watchful wakefulness.

Otto did. He growled softly. In the wan light of the two sinking moons shining into the cave he could see a person drawing the cork from the wine-bottle with his teeth. The growl did not even make his mistress stir. The dog stood up as water, their precious water gurgled down a throat. Otto barked loudly and angrily. The bottle was dropped with a terrible crash, and the sound of more breaking glass.

A headlight snapped on.

Prince Jarian was trapped in mid-flight. The light reflected off his wet mouth, face and shirt. Then the torch swung to focus on the pile of bottles. At least five were broken, the precious water trickling down into the sandy cave floor.

CHAPTER 13
FAITH

*The dynamics of a society are governed not by
politics or even power but by belief. And if you
believe, I've got a bridge to sell you. And faith isn't
the only thing that moves mountains.*

From the collected sayings of Saint Sugahata the Reviled

An amazing number of people buy bridges

**Scrawled in pencil in the margin of the original
manuscript, attributed to the sister of Sugahata, the
self-made multi-billionaire Dugra Schmitt.**

It was a scene of angry barking and ugly recriminations.

"It's that damned dog's fault! He gave me a fright!"

"It was the dog's fault that you were stealing water?" said
Tanzo.

"I just needed a tiny drink, that's all. I wasn't stealing. I
would've told you in the morning! Really!" Jarian whined.

"I will kill him." Had anyone looked in Deo's eyes they would have seen that his pupils were unevenly dilated. The man who normally moved with catlike grace lumbered clumsily to his feet. Jarian squealed in terror. Mark Albeer, himself still groggy from sleep, saw the scion of the Empire retreat whimpering towards his bedding. Deo advanced, hands slightly outstretched, his long fingers bent like claws, twitching convulsively. The bodyguard scrambled to defend the Prince. He didn't like the boy, but he was raised loyal. It wasn't his place to like or dislike. He believed in the boy's right to command, to take... even their precious water. He raised his hands, watchful. He didn't want to have to kill the Princess's servant. He should be able to incapacitate the fellow.

Deo came closer. Then he stepped right with blurring speed. He was so unsteady he nearly fell over, before beginning to strangle an unoffending piece of air, with brutal efficiency. When it was done he stared at the corpse he plainly saw at his feet. "An'tchai. It is done." He knelt and began to sing in a strange, keening fashion. The song was in Ghurkali, and would have been incomprehensible even if the singing was not so appalling. It was just as well the others couldn't understand. The re-enactment of the Dagger of the Goddess's first killing was unpleasant enough without the psalm from the Mass of blood. Tears trickled down the man's agonized face.

"What...?" Martin Brettan still held his pistol ready, as well as the light he had trapped Jarian in.

Mark Albeer shook his head. "The concussion, maybe? Back in basic we had a fellow who had a pole fall on him. Cracked his skull. He lost his memory. Also had fits as I remember. They had to bandage his hands and tie him to his bed."

"Shoot him!" said Jarian, his voice quavering. "He's not safe! He might strangle us all!"

Shari got up. "Well, I wish he'd started with you, you little toad. I'm putting him back to bed."

"Be careful. Leave him," said Brettan, watchfully.

She ignored this piece of sound advice. "Deo has been my loyal servant since the last Emperor died. I'm damned if I'll leave him like this." She walked over to him, and gently took the sobbing, singing man by the shoulder.

He looked up at her with unnaturally wide eyes. "Dewa. You will is done. Will his rebirth be closer to you?"

"At my right hand." She quoted from the words she had heard him use when forced to deal with her enemies.

A kind of peace came across the face of man in torment. "He

was dearer to me than a brother. Why must I follow this path, Goddess? Surely Sugahata was no servant of the Denaar' Demons?" The voice was querulous, and struggling between the tenor of a boy and the deep voice of the man who had served her.

She wondered how to answer this. Again she quoted one of his favourite sayings. "Like wanton flies are we to the Gods."

He laughed. It was a strange, melancholy sound. "It is written. It will remain no matter what the priests say and do. They can wash the land with blood. It will remain."

He allowed her to lead her to his blankets. He lay down, and his eyes closed. His breathing, ragged a few minutes before, gradually slowed and became regular.

Shari stood up. "He's asleep, I hope," she said quietly. She looked across at Prince Jarian, who had carefully climbed back into his blankets and was faking sleep with poor skill. "As for water *thieves*, I think we'll discuss that in the morning. I don't want to disturb Deo. If he should be woken up again…. He might not throttle ghosts. Otto."

The small dog looked up from her heels, and cocked his head. She led him to the pile of bottles, took off her cloak and put it on the ground beside them. She scooped the dog up and put it on the cloak, first administering a kiss. She patted the bottle-pile. "Guard." Then she went back to her own bedding. Otto, who always slept beside her, made no move from where he sat, watching, listening.

◐◖◖ ◗◗◗

Under his bed-clothes Jarian fingered the small black case he had secreted there, and thought of death. That dog first. He tucked the case into his waistband, despite the discomfort.

◐◖◖ ◗◗◗

Martin Brettan lay in his bedding and thought of his childhood and the perimeter patrol of the palatial estate where he had grown up. He remembered the Dobermans, and watching with his father a display put on by their handlers. "Guard!?" Who would have thought that the princess's lap-dog was anything but a lap-dog? Yet the animal had plainly been trained, and trained well. Well, it was no Doberman. A little dog like that surely wouldn't be nearly as alert. The Viscount didn't know much about dogs.

◐◖◖ ◗◗◗

The sun burned down from the pale sky. Juan was already up, gathering cirrith seeds. He wore the mnemonic-crown again. It balanced at a rather rakish angle on his odd-for-a-Denaari shaped head. It would not have occurred to a living Denaari to take off the crown while the crown still lived. It would have made the creature, which the Denaari had shaped into a memory repository, unhappy. The crown-beasts used body-heat as a source of energy. Juan didn't know that it was finding him a trifle too hot, and finding his thought output difficult to codify. All Juan knew, with the Denaari nest-minder part of his memories, was that the crown of the dead one must go back to the memory-vaults.

His new memories could picture the planet from space. He now had some idea of where he was. This was probably the edge of the Repapaa-clan's sheeter-herd grounds. The dune-fields would be the sand-fungus lands from which the Repapaa's justly famed delicacies were produced. Not more than twenty-five zefts flight across the dunes was the tall Roost-Repapaa. The equatorial lands were still sparely populated. The wing of fortune had surely sheltered him in landing him in such close proximity to help.

Then the human part of his mind attacked the confusing alien matter with logic. It didn't understand the image of the roost, even if it understood the concept of shared warmth, love and sex that were inextricably tied to it. But it did know that the Denaari were no more. Juan-human didn't know what world he was on, but no human-discovered world had been populated by the silica-bat creatures of his new memories. As for a mere twenty-five *zefts* that Juan-Denaari recalled, what was a *zeft*? The distance imaged might be easy to those who rode thermals and to whom the understanding of air-currents was as instinctive as breathing, but the crown-bearer had no wings, just very sore feet. Those dunes were as un-crossable as a sea. Sea? Ah! that rather toxic hydrogen-oxygen compound that the Juan-human required. The mnemonic crown bearer was indeed very alien. Well, Juan-human would be wise to use his sore feet to get out of the low-country and into the high-places. There would be H_2O precipitation there. They used it in the high-altitude terrace-paddies for growing some of the rarer crystalines. Besides, to a creature that didn't fly, a sheeter herd might be dangerous.

With no way of carrying water, and no idea what a sheeter might be, except that it was big, flat, and nearly mindless, Juan set off up-valley. It was still early, but already it was warm. He welcomed the breeze.

●●●꜀꜀꜀

The 'cave' was little more than a long overhang where the

sand-crusted wind off the dunes had eaten out a segment of softer rock. At its deepest it was barely three yards deep, with the roof perhaps four yards up at its highest point. It offered little real shelter from the elements. Yet... it was airless and stuffy. And, although Juan was already walking with painful feet up-valley in the bright sunlight with sweat dripping off the rim of the crown and running down into his eyes, in the cave it was dark and cold.

"We're shut in." Lila's torch-light wavered slightly as it shone on the white filamentous surface which totally sealed off the mouth of the cave.

"What is it?" demanded Johannes.

He got the sort of look this sort of idiotic question deserved. "How in the hell do you expect us to know, sonny-boy," said Sam, eyeing the fur wall warily.

"Look!" Caro pointed. A part of a metal sheet they'd used as a sled had been half pulled into the cave. Now only the inside half of it remained. Cilia from the bear-rug clung to it. Digesting.

"Gods! Shoot it! It'll eat us all!" yelled Lila almost hysterical, forgetting she had a weapon.

Martin Brettan's heavy automatic came out. He held steady, but shook his head. "I don't see that it'll do a damned thing to something big enough to block the cave. Still... better take cover behind that stuff in case it ricochets." He waited, and when they were ready, and Otto had been called off guard, he fired. The sound in the closed off cave was terrifyingly loud. After a few moments he walked closer. Peered into the circle of focused torchlight. "I hit it, but it's... it's like I never shot." He studied the fur without quite touching the waving cilia. "There's not even a mark." His voice too showed the edge of panic.

"Perhaps it will go away." Tanzo got up from behind the bags and rocks and peered at the cilia. She sounded more curious than alarmed. "It's a bit like Stardog belly cilia isn't it?"

Her pragmatism steadied them. "Maybe it will go away, as quietly as it came. How could something that big get here without us even noticing it?"

"How are we for air?"

"Enough for a good few hours yet."

Sam looked at the gently moving fur-clad wall. "It doesn't feel bad," he said slowly.

"You touched it?"

"No. I mean... it won't... harm us. It'll go away."

The lean Leaguesman snorted, irritated. "How could you

know? Stupid Yak bastard." He picked up a rock from the back of the cave, where, as it happened, sheeters couldn't normally reach. The fragment was pleasantly mineral rich, unlike the accessible material which generations of sheeters had already probed for minerals. Kadar flung it with all the might of his sinewy arms.

It struck the fur. The fur-wall indented with the force of the blow. Then the wall bounced back. The rock, however, stuck. Cilia clung hungrily to it.

"Brilliant. That has of course made the huge creature so sore it's bound to scamper away. Of course a rock flung by *you* would be more effective than a mere bullet." Shari hadn't slept much after the water-theft and Deo's strange fit, and her tiredness and worry were coming out in knife-edged words. Actually, she was more concerned by Deo's robotic obedience of her orders, on being woken from his unnaturally heavy sleep, than about the alien behemoth sealing off the cave. She had so desperately hoped he would be well when he woke up. You don't rely almost completely on someone for nearly twenty years and then find it easy to suddenly have them reliant on you. She was nervous, worried... and resentful. The last emotion upset her, and she felt guilty about it, but that didn't make the resentment go away.

Tanzo was so absorbed in studying the cilia and the rock that she failed to take in the sarcasm. "Actually I would guess that rather than driving off the creature, Leaguesman Kadar has just fed it. It'll probably stay longer."

The little rider-girl shivered and began to sob, huddling in on herself. Otto went across to her and began licking her conveniently placed face. She enfolded the small fur-ball in her arms. For some reason this seemed to incense the older harsh faced Leaguesman. He'd stood glowering, tight-lipped while Shari's sarcasm had slashed at him. He'd smouldered at Tanzo's comment. Now he exploded and rushed at the wide-eyed Una. "Leave it alone you useless little slut-slave! LEAVE IT, I say!" He kicked out at her. His fists were balled and he bent to strike. The frightened girl dived away. She rolled, with her arms still around the dog, toward the rippling cilia of the fur-wall.

"NO!" Screamed Shari, frozen, seeing the rage-crazed man kick Una, with the dog in her arms, toward the hungry cilia.

Deo leaped. His "KIIIIHAI!!" strike-scream tore at the fur wall as the wavy blade in his hand slashed at it ahead of the rolling girl and dog. It parted like tissue paper. A sheeter is, after all, rarely more than a quarter inch thick. Heat and light smote in at them as the girl and dog rolled straight through the slash. Then, within a second, before the surprised people had a chance to react the slash began to knit.

The Dagger of the Goddess, shook his smoke-filled head. What had he done? Why was he here? Everything swam confusingly about his mind. Why did he have the holy dagger in hand? What was it about a woman and a dog? He couldn't remember. He shook his head again. It hurt. The dagger was not supposed to be used for lesser purposes than human blood. He fed it, traced the cross in red, and cleaned it on the insignia he had cut from the sleeve of the commander of the Imperial garrison on Arunchal. Strange. There were other rusty brown marks on the patch he had cut only yesterday. He looked in puzzlement at the people in the ill-lit cave as he put the blade away.

"Well. At least we can get out and we know we won't suffocate," said the dumpy woman with glasses. "Quick thinking, Deo." She seemed to be talking to him. Then the Dewa appeared at his side, and took him to sit down. He was grateful. His muscles hurt.

They could hear Otto barking. Then the dog came running back into their midst, flinging himself at Shari. The far corner of the cave was now exposed as the sheeter continued its flatworm progress across the sun-side of the rocky ridge. Soon they were able to scramble out. Down the length of the ridge were a score or more sheetlike black creatures, moving slowly down-valley, their thin bodies clinging and taking on the contours of the rugged terrain beneath them. They appeared to have no interest whatsoever in the small motile bits that had just emerged from under the rear mantle of one of their number. Even that creature simply went on moving steadily and smoothly with the pack, as if nothing had ever happened.

Una was huddled in a foetal ball in the sunlight. Tanzo hastily went to comfort her. Sam stepped over to the tall Leaguesman who was looking decidedly wary. "Listen good, shit-for-brains," he said quietly, "Do something stupid like that again and you're going to get killed, see."

The Leaguesman was too cowed by the sequence of events to do more than stare uneasily at him.

Shari clapped her hands, calling their attention. "Hear me, everybody. I spent a lot of last night thinking. This incident this morning just reinforces it all. We need to talk. We need to decide on how our group can work together. We need to decide who will lead us, and what the ground-rules are. We're a small group, and we have a limited amount of resources. We can't hope to survive unless we do this."

"The structure of command was set out clearly in Coda de Gotha five centuries ago," said Prince Jarian stiffly.

Shari took a deep breath. "Jarian. Besides the fact that I personally would rather take my chances on my own than take orders from you, do you think you have the experience to lead us? I think this is the first time you've been off Phillipia, if not the first time you've been outside the palace." She shook her head. "You might know more about murder and intrigue than the rest of us, but that won't help us in dealing with those creatures. No. I'm afraid you'll temporarily have to suspend your rank, as I've done. If, as I suspect, we stay here forever, Jarian, the Coda de Gotha will never mean anything again. No. Let's all agree on someone."

His plump-petulant face crumpled. "It's not fair. You sterile old hag, you always spoil everything!"

Shari showed her teeth. "I'm not sterile. Old for childbearing maybe, but not too old."

"Hah! That's what you think! Grandfather had you tested! You're as barren as... as this place!" he snarled, spitefully pleased.

Shock wrote itself over Viscount Brettan's face. She noticed it. So... he'd been *that* ambitious, even then? But surely he'd realized that a child would be killed, preferably even before it could be born, along with its father and mother?

She smiled pure malice at both of them. "Yes. The Emperor had to be deceived, didn't he? Otherwise I'd have been killed, wouldn't I? When, if, my child is born, I'll call him Senn, if it is a boy, or Lea, if it's a girl. In honor of the two brave people, my childhood bodyguard and my nurse-maid, who fooled even the Emperor for me, and kept me alive."

It was very sweet indeed to watch the parade of expressions across their faces. Shari noted that her supposed sterility had been no secret to the Guildsmen. "Now that we've dealt with that little aside, perhaps we can get back to discussing leadership," she said crisply.

Leaguesman Kadar grimaced. "What basis will we use to choose a leader? The League has steered human affairs for time out of mind. I suppose you would have us reject that too."

Sam burst out, suddenly agitated. "We need to get away from here." Nobody paid him any attention. The various parties were too intent on how to lay claim to the power they saw as theirs by right.

"Given the circumstances, I think we should consider individuals and their abilities rather than groups or histories," commented Tanzo dryly.

The horizon rippled, and then the ground shook itself like a wet dog. People tumbled and fell to the ground as if they were marionettes whose strings had just been scythed. "RUN!" screamed Sam. "Away from the cliff!"

"Albeer. Carry that rider," Shari yelled. "Brettan. Lila. With me! Fetch the water! Go on, the rest of you, run!" She pushed Deo, who had staggered confusedly to his feet, in the direction of the sand-flat in front of the dune. She and the two she'd nominated ran into the cave amid the groaning of rocks, grabbed packs, and more by luck than judgment managed to run clear before a huge slab of roof-rock came down. They pelted down-slope with new scree-fragments and pill-bug rolled sheeters bouncing around them. When they were nearly at the group on the sand-flat an aftershock breakdanced the ground beneath them, and they had to fall. Above them the ridge itself seemed to sway. Shari fought her way to her knees. The ground still quaked. "Keep going! Crawl!!"

They fought their way to the middle of the sandflat, where Sam was trying to hold the group. He'd had to resort to knocking the Prince down, threatening Johannes with his chisel, and shaking the screaming Caro. "We've got to keep away from that dune too, you crazy woman!"

He was quite right. The huge dune was slipping, flattening, and cascading with wild plumes of excited dust swirling about it. That was nothing to what was happening to the ridge. Small rocks had fallen. Now the big ones, the office block sized ones were coming loose with a slow grinding, and then falling with ground-shaking thunder. The group, amid the giant beach-balled sheeters, watched as the perpetual tectonic renewal of the Denaar-motherworld's resources occurred. They were on the edge of a particularly stable and ancient plate. Most of this world could not be described as stable. The creatures who had evolved here needed it that way. Their food sources were sunlight and raw minerals. Raw surface minerals. Any form of mining would have been a non-survival evolutionary strategy. Mobility, particularly flight, was a distinctly advantageous trait.

The ground drum-rolled, and those who had been foolish

enough to stand up fell over again.

●●C●●●

On the other side of the ridge, up-valley, Juan was wishing desperately that he too could fly. It was what Juan-Denaari would have done if he could, rising high, being careful of the turbulence these events always caused, riding the potentially unstable thermals away over to the less disturbed sand-fields. As it was he huddled beside a huge rock, which had vibrated like a gong and shifted alarmingly a few seconds ago. Juan-Denaari had been philosophical and unsurprised by the quake. They happened all the time. They had to. It was a pity, and a tragic major killer of nestlings, which is why they had to learn to fly so early.

Juan-human, on the other hand, had been stunned and shaken in every way by the seismic event. He cowered closer to the mega-ton boulder. A slab of rock guillotined past him. He balled himself still tighter, trying to make himself small. He wished with every fiber of his being that he could be elsewhere. The parts of him were divided as to where 'elsewhere' should be. One part wanted to be aloft, heading for the memory-repositories. The other part also wanted to be aloft. A lot further aloft. Outside this damnable atmosphere which wasn't controlled, away from ground that shook and quivered beneath your feet. It was bad enough that the ground wasn't corridor-flat, and hurt your feet, but this! He desperately wanted to be back in his own cubicle. Even his father chewing him out would be sweet.

The part that wasn't Juan-human seemed to think his going home feasible. After he'd returned the crown to the vaults, of course. The flood of bio-images nearly stunned the boy. So that was how it had worked!

●●C●●●

The gigantic beachballed sheeters unrolled. They eagerly undulated back toward the ridge on their millions of cilia pseudo-feet. They were keen to begin feeding again, on all the lovely new mineral traces that would be exposed. Even in their haste they weren't dangerously fast, just very big. The castaways had no trouble dodging them.

Mark Albeer scanned the rocky ridge carefully. "Well, the animals seem to think it's over. But I can't even see our cave now."

Sam grunted, rubbing his ribs where the Prince's flailing fist had caught him. "There's a new section of cliff where we got across the ridge yesterday. We'll have to try for another spot to cross."

The broad bodyguard nodded, being glad that it hadn't happened while they were up there. "We'd better see if any of our stuff survived first."

"We've got seven packs, at least." Martin Brettan had somehow managed three. The Viscount, his once elegant blue-black uniform torn, and his face bloody from a touch of a passing rock, didn't look like a lady's gentlemanly officer escort any more. He looked big and tough. And grim. Decidedly grim. "I'll come along with you. We'd better go careful among that new-fallen stuff."

"And the leadership race?" said Tanzo also getting to her feet, obviously intent on going along, but, as usual, tenacious.

"I think it resolved itself, back there. Who gave the orders when the crisis struck? Princess Shari. She's the only one who kept her head, and organized. My fleet commander couldn't have done it better," said Martin Brettan, still shocked enough to be absolutely honest. Besides, if things were hopeless, a part of his mind said, it would be better to have a scapegoat. He could take over, by force, if things panned out well.

"I agree. Does anyone have any other ideas?"

"I do," said Kadar softly. "But I don't suppose anyone will listen."

It appeared that nobody else did, or at least nobody was prepared to come out with them. They were all still too shaken up by the earthquake, and the potential loss of all that had not been rescued from the cave, to play politics now. Now they were like children, wanting someone else to provide direction.

Shari shrugged. This hadn't been quite how she'd intended it to come out. What she'd had in mind was using Martin Brettan as a stalking horse to enforce what would be unpopular orders. But right now they needed steering. Instinctively she turned toward Deo. But he was lost in a soft-crooning, wide-eyed trance. No use thinking he could help her now with his almost imperceptible eye-signals. She took a deep breath. "Well, my first comment is that it is a poor idea for all of you to go to the cave. Sam... you go and have a look."

He grinned his wry half-grin, without looking her in the eye. "Best if you lose the Yak, huh?" But he turned to obey.

She walked after him, and caught up with him once he was away from the rest. She took him by the shoulder. Turned him to face her. Looked him straight in the eye. Spoke quietly. "No. But I noticed you cried warning before anyone else. That's the third time I've noticed you've known of trouble *before* it happened. I think you're probably better at staying alive than the rest of us. If I'm right I'm going to use that. I'll use that to keep us all alive. It will improve your chances too, if more of us survive. I haven't forgotten that you saved Deo's life."

It was one of the few times in his life that Sam Teovan had been truly amazed. He looked at her expressionlessly for a moment. Then he nodded, slowly. "First time I work for a woman Capo. Bit of a shock, see. You a steppin' razor, lady. Your old man musta taught you real good."

"My father, God rot him, let my brothers practice their assassination skills on me. In a way that taught me, all right. It taught me the value of the loyalty that kept me alive. Now go, and be careful."

He bowed, with respect, as to a Yak Capo, and left at a dogtrot. Privately he admitted to himself, as he approached the cliffs, that she'd earned his respect already. And respect is major requirement for loyalty.

"What was that about, Princess?" Martin Brettan asked, his suspicions rising.

"Reassurance," she said offhandedly. "Now let's see what we've actually got in the packs we grabbed."

As they unpacked and counted stock Sam Teovan edged cautiously through the new-fallen boulders, and up towards the cave. It was still there, to his surprise. Had his survival instincts been wrong? A second look told him they hadn't. A huge slab had peeled off the ceiling. Anyone who had stayed in the cave would have been jam. The supplies they'd carried so laboriously from the wrecked ship lay under 70 tons of rock. Squashed flat.

CHAPTER 14
THE HOT BREATH

The long road to heaven is made of many small,
steep steps. So is the road to hell, the steps are just
shallower, wider and go the other way. So, when the
walking's easy, don't believe the road signs.

From the parable of the highland pot-mender, The Gospel according to St. Gopal.

The radio-unit had survived. It had been in one of the packs that had been snatched in haste. The decision that they must go through with the plan to go to the source of the radio-signals, or at least follow the next valley up to a possible water-supply seemed inevitable now. The few remains of the ship had vanished beneath the sand during the tremor, and there seemed little to be gained by remaining here. The rough packs were divided up, and they began to walk parallel to the ridge. Although nobody said it, nobody was keen to walk too close to it. After nearly two hours of plodding, the ridge simply grew higher and steeper, and walking in the endless soft sand just grew more exhausting, Shari realized that the searing heat and walking on the sand would kill them all just as certainly as a rock-fall. It would just take longer. She pointed to an outlier-boulder. "Let's rest in the shade a bit." Deo was worrying her particularly. He was... so robotic. Even the small water ration so eagerly consumed by the rest, after they'd collapsed in the small patch of shadow, had to be pushed towards his mouth. He hadn't savored it slowly or gulped it. Instead he had sniffed it, then tasted it, cautiously. And then he had poured a tiny libation of a few drops onto the ground with muttered Ghurkali words.

"He's wasting the water!" Jarian squalled.

"It's his ration."

"If he doesn't want it, I do!" Jarian reached for the cup.

●●●㋡㋡●

The Dagger of the Goddess knocked him down, but gently, before he could defile the sacrament that had arisen from a blend of alien nano-technology, twisted Catholicism and a murderous Hindi sect. The holy assassin's head was full of dust and shadows. Many times he had taken the sacrament in the rite of cleansing. He did not remember anyone daring to try and interrupt it. Remember? Why? It was actually happening... wasn't it? Or was it? He stared, confused, at the boy with blood on his lip and fear and murder in his pallid blue eyes. Almost, *almost* he knew the face. But it was gone, *ignis faatus*. Devil's work. Denaari demons sent to lead the believers from the true way. Turning away, he continued with the rite.

"What are we going to do about him? He's a dangerous man, you know," Tanzo asked quietly.

"He's off his head." Martin Brettan was himself puzzled by the strange behaviour of the man. He'd seen his dossier. Amadeo Cerros came from an unassuming background, with no strong religious overtones. What he was doing was distinctly odd. Also the dossier had rated his weapons skills as moderate, and noted that he had failed the unarmed combat module of his training. That didn't gel with what he'd seen.

Shari shook her head, and said with confidence she was far from feeling, "He'll be fine, I'm sure. He's just suffering from that knock on the head."

Martin Brettan shrugged. "You may have to make hard decisions about him, if he doesn't recover soon. A man like that could be dangerous to all of us, you know. No use putting past loyalties in front of our survival." He was still pointedly avoiding using her name.

Shari shrugged. "Tell that to our little Prince over there." She shook her head again, and then raised her voice. "We should adapt ourselves to the conditions in which we find ourselves, Ladies and Gentlemen. We'll rest in the heat of the day and move when it is cool. Also we must give up walking out here on the soft sand. It's too tiring. We'll have to risk walking on the rock."

"And hope it doesn't all fall on us," grumbled Johannes. But he said it very quietly.

Most of them slept. Shari worried instead. When the sun began to send spiky dragon-shadows off the ridge, they got up and walked on. On the rock. Soon they would have had no choice, for another shallow ridge rose up from the sand to their right and they found themselves in an ever-narrowing valley.

They'd crash-landed in the tropics of the Denaari-motherworld, a harsh area, always poorly populated because local geological stability meant mineral-nutrients were scarce. It meant that the party did not encounter any other native life-forms. There was no water in this valley so they did not encounter any of the zoo-biolab escapees from the colony worlds. It also meant that when they rounded a corner and found themselves in a bowl surrounded by vast cliffs, that night fell abruptly. The twin moons weren't up yet and the darkness was deep. The stars shone down from an alien heaven, innumerable and clear.

❄❄❄❄❄❄

"Look! That's the Salamander!" Lila pointed at the stars. "It's not quite the same as from New Texas..." She choked up, remembering a boy who'd taken her out into the soft night to show her the stars, and a great many other things. She hurt. It was just... the stars had suddenly been so familiar she could almost have been at home, without the passage of the intervening seven years of hell.

The star-formations meant a great deal to three other people. Martin Brettan, Johannes Wienan, and the girl who had been called Una Quail all knew now almost exactly where they were. How close to the Empire. The first two were intensely frustrated by it. The girl was just afraid. But then, she was usually afraid.

"Yes. I'm sure that as the Stardog flies we're near your homeworld. Unfortunately, we've no way of ever reaching it, as far as I can see. Right now, I'm more concerned about these cliffs. I don't see any possible way up them either. Point is, do we wait for daylight or start walking back now?" enquired the Viscount, frustration putting a snappy edge on his voice.

147

Several of the party groaned. Shari realized yet again that leadership was fraught with unpopular decisions. Yet... it had seemed a choice between riding the tiger or being eaten by it. "We might as well start back now. The ridge must be lower in the other direction."

"Then why did you bring us this way in the first place? You are supposed to be leading us." Shilo Kadar was tired, thirsty and irritable in the extreme.

"Very well, Leaguesman. You show us the way back down then," she said with careful evenness.

He snorted, and led off too fast in the darkness. Inevitably he fell down a small rock-slip. After that he was a lot more cautious.

ᗱᗱᑕᗐᗷᗷ

Eventually, when the last after-tremors had died away, Juan had resumed his walk. There was a spring in his step now. There was a way out of here. As he got hotter and thirstier his steps became less eager. He wondered about going back to the pool Rat had led him to. His mouth was terribly dry. It was late afternoon before he came to a place of choices. The valley forked. To the left lay a steep, narrow canyon. The other valley was wider, easier going and also lead, it seemed, directly in the direction he needed to go.

The space-born and reared boy didn't recognize the signs of water-erosion that were present on wall of the steep canyon. They were absent from the valley he chose. His valley was merely the byproduct of an intrusive dyke of volcanic rock, and a fold in the sedimentary stuff through which the canyon cut.

ᗱᗱᑕᗐᗷᗷ

It took the other party two days to reach this point. They had passed the hidden pool where Rat had found water without an inkling of it having once been there. The tremor had cracked the dolerite sill that had held the water in its impermeable grip. There was nothing there now.

Already, some of the members of the party had dropped into distinct roles. Lila and Sam walked a scouting prowl ahead. Already both had proved their worth, Sam in refusing to allow them to go into a narrow steep walled section of the lower valley. He'd insisted on climbing laboriously around that part, and despite the rash of protest, Shari had backed him up.

"Oh please, not out into the sun again!" Caro found the heat debilitating.

"I can't see why." Back at the rear of the party Kadar was

148

once again flexing his muscles.

"You'll do it because we have a leader." The big-framed Brettan was also finding the heat exhausting. Kadar's constant sniping was getting to him. "If you want to go on you'll have to go through me," he said, positioning himself across the valley. Nobody had tried it.

The detour took two hot, difficult clambering hours to skirt the narrow section of shady, even-floored valley that would have taken them ten minutes to walk.

When they'd got back to the valley floor a shouting-match had ensued. The noise alone had been enough to trigger a thunderous rock-slide into the section they'd avoided. The quarrel had stopped abruptly.

Lila had produced the first food the castaways had taken from the Denaari Motherworld. She could throw rocks with some skill. Some of the party had balked at raw snake, even if the creature was not a true reptile but merely pseudo-snake. Mark Albeer had then produced a number of small pieces of long-ago-flood debris he had been steadily and methodically collecting as they walked. Nothing big had washed down this far, but he had a good three double handfuls of fragments. They were dry and burned well, if rather fast. Half-cooked snake, Shari told herself as she ate her piece, carefully avoiding any sign of distaste, was still a big step up on raw snake.

When they walked on the next morning, she had them all looking for and gathering fragments of wood. There was no protest at this. It seemed she wasn't the only one who thought half-cooked snake was better than the alternative. Besides, the sight of those small flames had been deeply comforting at a primal level.

"You can see how the water has cut into the rock here. Look at those stones piled up on that bank there. They're rounded. Water comes down that canyon" said Lila.

"But the main valley's bigger. Surely that means more water?"

"I don't see any sign of it myself."

Shari sighed. She looked at Sam. He shook his head. Shrugged. "The canyon looks as steep as hell. Let's all search the next hundred yards or so of the main valley. If we find any water-borne debris then we'll go on up it."

They spread out in a long skirmish-line, Deo being positioned with a gentle push. She doubted he even understood what was happening. In the last day he seemed to have retreated deeper into a sort of melancholia. They pushed on up the wider valley, without finding any sign of anything which could have been carried there by a flood. A geologist would have found the change in the nature of the material on the valley floor obvious. The xeno-archaeologist had also trained herself to spot detail. "I don't think this is a water-cut valley," she said, peering at walls. "Everything is too angular."

Shari had managed to inconspicuously take up station next to the small Yak soldato. "What do you think, Teovan?" she asked quietly

He gave her the benefit of his wry grin. "This ain't the streets or the dumps, lady. What do I know? Both feel bad."

She took a deep breath. "All right. Back to the canyon."

As usual this produced a rash of protests from Kadar. Johannes, in whom the latent Wienan political strain was beginning to assert itself, said nothing. Kadar's other supporter, Prince Jarian, was oddly silent too. His eyes were narrowed, focused on the water bottle that protruded from the bodyguard's rough pack. It was a fairly distinctive bottle, with the apple-green glass deeply etched in a grape-vine pattern.

The rider-girl, who certainly never questioned or protested, also stared intensely at something. It wasn't the water bottle, but a clear footprint left in the fine ashy-dust on the section of sheet-rock in front of her. Another human had walked here, going up-valley, recently. Very recently. The wind had not even blurred the dust-edges. But as was her habit, she said nothing. Just turned and followed the rest of them, leaving her own even smaller footprints beside it, pointing back to the canyon.

Canyon was an inadequate descriptive term. Semi-vertical polished chute would have done better. For a leisurely scramble with a swim and a large supply of cold beverages at the end of it, the water-cut winding slash through the ruddy layers of aeolian rock would have been beautiful. Thirsty, hot, and knowing the canyon took them off at right angles to their destination the friable group found it another version of hell. The nature of the terrain split them into various fractions based on the clambering skills and determination of each person. Walking was made even more difficult by the newly fallen debris. In places there were huge new chocks across the valley that had to be climbed over or squeezed around or under.

Shari found herself chivvying tail-enders along and then trying to catch up with the front-runners to tell them to slow down. It was an exhausting and unrewarding pastime. Somewhere along the way on one of these jaunts the man she called Deo detached himself from the rest of them and disappeared. It was nearly twenty minutes before she realized he was missing.

There was only one possible place he could have left the party. She struggled back down. Jarian was keeping up well, she noticed. He was just behind Caro and the bodyguard, who, *just* per chance, was travelling at the same speed as the well-endowed Countess. The bodyguard should be careful, she thought. The lean leaguesman could easily try to murder him at this rate. Caro and the bodyguard had just climbed up a narrow crack at the side of a new chock-stone, and he was just reaching down to take the packs from the Prince when she reached them. The Emperor's eldest surviving son was struggling to lift Mark Albeer's pack. Shari noticed the apple-green bottle protruding from it. It didn't seem well stoppered.

"Better push that cork in a bit more." Her voice startled them. The bodyguard nearly dropped the pack on Jarian's head, as he attempted to stand hurriedly, years of habit reasserting themselves. "Er... Yes, your Highness. I don't know how it got like that. I'm sure it was much deeper in." He rammed the cork in to flush with the neck of the bottle with one of his big hands.

Shari had a good idea how it got like that. The man she was looking for had trained her in the minutiae of observation. There had been teeth-marks on the cork. So that was why the little skiver had caught up.

"You haven't seen Deo, have you?"

Caro shook her head. "Not since we left the big valley. He's not lost, is he?"

Shari bit her tongue and avoided raising her eyes to the narrow strip of pale-blue heaven far above. There was no doubt that the countess *meant* well.

"Only place he could have gone was into that cave we passed about three bends back," said Mark slowly. "Do you need some help, Princess?"

She shook her head. "I don't know. I don't think so right now. It didn't look deep. He's probably just asleep. He is confused and seems to want sleep a great deal. He never seemed to ever sleep... before. Well, if I have a problem I'll come and fetch someone."

"Don't you want a drink before you go, Aunt?"

There was a greasy sheen to the little Prince's eyes, as he

looked at her attempting to drip sincerity. So he had been stealing water, again. Little toad.

"No thank you. I will manage with my ration, the same as everyone else," she said evenly, trying to refuse him the satisfaction of letting him see how angry she was.

"Really, you should, Aunt Shari. You deserve it. Go on. Perhaps a bit for Otto? Good dog." The good dog growled at him.

The damned slimy little snake! Trying to suck up to her when he'd been stealing again! She shook her head, too angry to speak to him. Instead she said to the others "I've left my pack further up. I'll pick it up on my way back. I should be back within an hour."

A hundred yards or so back she passed Tanzo toiling along steadily, then Kadar, and finally Johannes. She wondered how he would manage the obstruction with his injured arm. Oh well, she could always help him on her way back up, she thought tiredly.

The cave was a narrow slit into the canyon wall. It breathed coolness into the hot mid-day air. She could quite understand why Deo might have gone into it. It was tempting to step inside and collapse for a few minutes herself. Instead she put on the head-torch she'd brought along from her pack, and stepped into the cave. "Deo!" Her voice echoed. It must be bigger than she'd guessed. She flicked the torch on. The yellow beam stretched into the darkness. It didn't shine on a back wall.

The cave was not wide, but it was deep. She walked on, following the faultline, downwards. There were occasional cracks and fissures off to the sides, but fortunately the floor was smooth and water polished and dusted with fine sand. It was easy to see Deo's footprints. Otto could have followed the man by scent, but instead stuck close at her heel. He did not like this place. That in itself was odd. At least one of Otto's varied ancestors was a terrier, and he was partial to holes normally.

Something soft brushed past her shoulder. She screamed. Otto barked furiously. Briefly, in the torchlight she caught a glimpse of something black, fluttering. "There Otto. It's only a bat. Just a bat." She was, of course, entirely wrong. There were bats here on the Denaari-motherworld. Like the others they were escapees from one of the biosphere-genepool-zoos that the Denaari had made for the off-world treasures they collected. But no bat would be stupid enough to come in here.

On she walked. The cave twisted and wound down to where the pressurized water had eaten away at the fault-breccia. She heard a distant groan. It was followed by a breeze from deeper in.

It carried a distinctly sulphurous-smell. And it was warm and damp. At first the cave had been cool…

"Deo!" she called yet again.

"Deo-o-o-o." Only the cave answered. Yet that must have been him groaning surely? But it had seemed such a huge distant sound. Well the echoes did strange things to noises. She pressed on into the stygian depths.

●●C ●●

The Dagger of the Goddess knew that he had arrived in hell. He had walked down an endless dark corridor. He had come out of the darkness and into a region of sickly green, glowing luminescence. He walked now amid the steams and smokes. He had seen demons flutter and cluster about these fumaroles. In front of him were a series of fissures from which the groans of the damned issued along with the fiend's reek of sulphur. The caverns of Hell sighed and thin screams echoed. Surely this was the place to which those who were denied even the lowest rebirth were sent.

The pressure in the cavern dropped abruptly, with a sound like a carillon of kisses. His head throbbed angrily again. Within his skull the nano-mech control centre sent out yet another hasty string of orders. The pressure change had been enough to start subdural bleeding yet again. Repair. Repair. The organism needed to be rested. But the damage to the brain was such that the nano-mech control over the organism was severely impaired. When the humans had been dumped on the Sil colony world nearly a thousand five hundred years ago, the last of the colony-born Sil were dying. The world that men called Arunchal lacked certain essential trace elements that the metal-rich Silur-homeworld had provided in abundance. The Sil grasp of biological matters had been rudimentary. The only species which survived on Silur were the Sil themselves. The Sil's energy and genius had instead gone into mechanisation, and then micro-mechanisation.

The Sil would not have chosen mountainous Arunchal as their first and only colony. They'd failed to beat lightspeed limitations, however. Arunchal's sun was the nearest to Silur. Its planet might not be ideal, but it was close.

Then had come contact with the Denaari. The Denaari who considered all life-forms as building-blocks. Whose ships and houses lived. The Sil considered non-Sil life as an incidental nuisance. Water and oil. And conflict was inevitable.

The Sil had struck first with missiles and a military honed by

153

endless Sil-on-Sil warfare. The captured Denaari vessel wasn't armed! On Silur a short triumphal war was foreseen.

The Denaari struck back with a weapon so small that it destroyed the might of the Silur military and their civilization without ever being seen. The unicellular creatures ate copper. Along with the mechanical core of their society, billions of Sil died, as machines failed. Space travel was of course worst hurt. The fledgling Sil colony on a Denaari discovered world was left isolated.

The Sil were wounded. Gravely wounded, but not destroyed. Anarchy and starvation took much of the home planet. Yet a technological core survived. Using other metals and synthetic molecular plastics they returned to strength. The Sil emerged after a dark century stronger and determined on revenge. They'd also learned from their enemies.

The self-replicating nano-mech plague which physically slashed Denaari nerve cables was as alien to the Denaari as the unicellular copper-eaters had been to the Sil. The Sil had also attempted to defend themselves. The nano-mech surgeons they had introduced to their own bodies were capable of repairing virtually any mechanical damage to the organisms. The colony on distant Arunchal was not forgotten either. They got nano-mech surgeons in the robot-rocket post.

Surgeons, even the best nano-mech surgeons, cannot deal with entire organisms poisoned by virus-released toxins. Silur died, even as the dying Denaari desperately sent out two specially made ships to sue for peace.

A thousand five hundred years later, when barely a hundred Sil still survived in hidden bunkers on Arunchal, the Nuns, Ghurkas and the Kali-cultists had been dumped virtually on top of them.

Rape. Murder. Anarchy.

Then the many-armed Sil had come forth and enforced peace. Their reasons are beyond knowing now, but perhaps they saw humanity as a weapon against their species' old foe. To the terrified and grateful humans they were Gods with Godlike powers. So to serve them they shaped a church from the disparate sects. The Sil honed it into a weapon against the Denaari. They provided their weapon with a supply of modified nano-surgeons.

No Denaari Stardog had brought more convicts or traders to Arunchal for two hundred years. The Sil numbers dwindled as they further sharpened their new weapon. Three years before the League-catalogue ship had arrived the last Sil had died. The religion-weapon was left in the ready hands of their priests, who in the fashion of humans, used it to their own ends.

And thus the Sil became extinct without discovering that their ancient foes were gone too. Now a modified nano-surgeon Sil unit had finally reached the heart of the Denaari empire. And the carrier-organism was out of control and badly injured. The surgeon worked tirelessly to repair it. That was what it had been built for. But a surgeon can also kill. This miniaturized marvel had been modified with that end in mind. But the nano-mech was a thousand light-years from the orders of the high temple on Arunchal. Tanzo would have given anything to visit that secret place. It was still functioning Sil bunker.

●●●ↄ●●

"Deo! Deo! Come away from there!" At first the dim light had alarmed her. She'd approached cautiously, Stationer-made needler drawn and ready. Otto was plainly frightened, his plume-tail pressed hard between his legs, and that made her wary too. Were the strange noises from some kind of machinery?

She'd looked into the steam-wreathed cavern very cautiously. The light came from some kind of bio-luminescent fungus-like growth which covered large leprous patches of the roof, walls and floor of the cave. Mineral encrusted spouts twisted gargoyle-like up from the floor. The roof, particularly the areas coated in the glowing fungus-stuff, dripped. Strange dark fluffy bat winged creatures chittered and squeaked and squalled and squealed as they scrabbled at the intermittently plopping mineralized mud-turrets. And the man she called Deo walked blindly toward a huge gaping hole, in the center of the cavern from which a deep groaning noise issued. He didn't seem to have heard her.

She had to run out there and stop him. She should have put the needler away first. He struck her forearm as she tried to grab him, training over-riding his confusion. The needler flew spinning and bouncing down into the hole. For a brief moment they wrestled on the very edge of the ant-lion steep pit. Fortunately, the surface was not muddy as it was in much of the rest of the cavern. The geyser had blasted this bit of rock clean. At the moment its regular eleven hourly pressure-blast of superheated steam was choked by dislodged rocks from the recent seismic event. When hot water and steam finally did escape this time it was going to be a big one.

"Dugra?" His grip weakened. His eyes were wide with shock. "I... didn't know it was you." He swallowed convulsively. "I had to kill him. I didn't want to. I swear. I tried to hold back. My hands... I never truly believed... but the Goddess... she took control of my hands. I swear it... my love." The words trailed off brokenly. He bent his head, bowed by the enormity of it. He'd told her once that she looked very like... someone he'd once known.

Then he straightened, pulling himself together. "Kill me!" he demanded. "Kill me now. What I did was beyond forgiveness. My life is forfeit."

"But I do forgive you. And I wasn't going to kill you, believe me. I came here to rescue you. Now come away from this place!"

"You refused to kill me. You said I must live with the worst of punishments. Myself. Do you now forgive me?" He teetered on the brink.

"Yes! Now come away, do. Away from this pit-edge, back up the tunnel and out of here. This place is dangerous. Now come. Please," she said, keeping her voice calm.

"No."

She stamped her foot. "Come away. Now. I order you!"

He shook his head. "I have arrived in hell. I have come here rightfully. I tried to disobey my Goddess. I betrayed you. I killed Sugahata. Go. Leave me. You were right. I cannot forgive me. Go. Go now. See, the demons come for me."

Indeed, the bat winged furry things were rising in huge flocks from their steaming feeding-places, and were heading towards them. "I'm not going without you."

"Dugra! You must go!" They could see the eyeless shovel-snouts of the lead creatures now. They looked like winged, broad-bladed spears, trailing fur. Otto began to bark hysterically. Training took over again and the assassin began reaching for his knives.

The flocks joined into a single black mass. And flew on straight over them, heading for the tunnel in single-minded flight. Self-consciously Deo blooded his knives, before putting them away. "Why... Dewa? Why? Why have I been spared?"

She saw the potential. Whatever that blow on the head had done, she couldn't get to him with logic. He was wandering through a maze of past deeds and guilt. His concussed brain was obviously superimposing his past onto the canvas of here and now. Perhaps she could use this. She struck a regal pose.

"Because your work is not yet done. Follow the demons." He

nodded, and turned away from the pit obediently, and began to stride determinedly after the fumarole-pseudobats. She had to jog to keep up. Behind them the cracks in the cavern floor began to issue supersonic screaming whistles as the pressure below built. Otto stopped, whined and pawed frantically at his ears. She picked him up and then ran on up the passage after Deo. Her headlight shone on a solid mass of fleeing pseudobats.

There was a terrible cracking sound behind them. A minor vent, subjected to pressure as never before, shattered a piece of obstructing rock to screaming shrapnel. Steam howled out, billowing up the passage. It was hot, but nothing compared to the flesh-melting temperature of the superheated steam that was oozing the seventy ton rock-cork out of the main vent.

CHAPTER 15
TOXIC WASTE

Fear the open wrath of Princes. But be truly terrified
if one begins to act with kindness and consideration.

Nicola Para-Machiavelli: Obliterating a Prince.

Thirst had eventually turned him back. Juan decided that he had no choice but to go back to his pool. The Denaari memories suggested that it could be an immense distance, even to a flier, to the snow-caps in the mountains. Down here he couldn't even see them, though he knew that the thermals there were treacherous and difficult to ride.

The snake... Distance lent courage. He could throw rocks at that damn snake. Drat. His tongue seemed to filling more than its fair share of his mouth. He plodded back down the valley. The walk seemed endless, and he kept staring at the ridgeline, trying to spot landmarks. He would have done better to look at the ground. He crossed the trail of the others several times without noticing.

Eventually found the place again. The snake wasn't there. Neither, to his horror, was the water. The sand it had leaked into was hardly even damp any more. He crawled out of the rocks despondent, despairing.

He stayed on his knees, lacking even the will to get to his feet. For a while he just stared at the tracks he'd crawled onto. He was station born and bred, but those could surely only be human boot and shoe-marks. Surely these must be the other survivors of the crash. Surely, surely they must have water?

He was too thirsty and desperate to think logically. He just set about following tracks, like a very inept Apache, sometimes unknowingly even following his own trail. He passed the canyon. If it had not been for Una's definite footprint beside his on the rock-sheet, he'd have followed his own tracks back up the dry valley. But he saw the print, like a message to him personally, and looked back to the narrow canyon and knew where they'd gone. Why? It was away from the Memory Vaults, away from the Stardog Imprinting Centre.

It was so steep and he was so exhausted that he nearly gave up. At least, being slight, he had no difficulty squeezing through the gaps that had given Martin Brettan and Mark Albeer such trouble. The crown and Rat were awkward in some of the tighter wriggles, but he couldn't take Rat out of his shirt. He also wouldn't have dreamed of taking off the crown. Denaari-Juan knew that was simply inconceivable.

He was flagging, reaching the point of give-up-and-collapse, when he reached the slit-entrance to the cave into which Shari had followed Deo. A puff of hot steam curled out, wafting and eddying before him. For an instant he just stood there, looking at it. Then slightly delirious imagination took over. A vid-fantasy about dragons, fire-breathing hungry dragons, was woven into his perceptions of reality. Adrenalin kicked in and Juan-human ran and scrambled while Juan-Denaari tried to comprehend which of the creatures of his native world could be described as dragons. Nothing quite matched, although there were a few creatures that came remarkably close.

●●●ↄↄↄ

Behind them more pseudobats, perhaps from a further chamber, came hurtling up the passage. Shari and Deo found themselves enclosed and bowled along in the flying frantic mass. They had no choice of where they went, it was merely a supreme effort to keep on their feet. They were forced up a steep and awkward slope, into a different branch of the vent-cave system.

Then Otto wriggled free. He was lost somewhere in the moments of chaos that followed. Trying to turn, Shari found herself shoved forward by the sheer weight of pseudobats. Then she was falling, sliding tumbling down a long slope. She was almost unaware of it. For the air was filled and then overfilled with the roar of the big geyser finally blowing its cork-stone. The air boomed with the pressure wave. And the noise went on and on. This cave was isolated from the main fault vent, but even so the heat would have been enough for severe burns had the man, woman and dog not been insulated by the mass of pseudobats whose asbestos filament fur effectively sheltered them all.

Then the shovelnosed pseudobats began unfurling their wings, chirruping to their fellows and shaking their entwined filaments free of each other, quite incidentally freeing the two humans and the dog from a gordian tangle, and dropping them into the water. The pseudobats began heading for roosts. The pressure-cooker on the fault-line would release several more blasts of decreasing volume before that cave breathed pressure in again and it was safe to go and feed. In the meanwhile it was time to roost, mate, squabble, and feed nestlings.

They left the humans and the dog to their own devices on this cave floor, in the shallow drip pool into which they'd fallen. Even now, condensing steam was beginning to drip off the roof and replenish it. The water did slowly seep away to recirculate in the geyser system that the canyon floods topped up. Shari didn't know or care about this. All she was aware of was a persistent nose pushing at her face. As yet Otto couldn't hear either, but his nose was not affected. The head-torch was lost somewhere in the tumble down into this place. She was aware of cold, of wetness, darkness, Otto, and a silence which was turning into a distant ringing in her ears. Holding a cupped hand to her nose she sniffed. Of course the nearly pure distilled water condensing on the roof ridges of the cave had virtually no odor. She tasted it. Water. Her dehydrated body would allow no other thought but to drink.

The pool was only a few inches deep... but if Deo had fallen face down into it? You could drown in an inch of water, if you were unconscious.

She began feeling frantically about. Something she touched squirmed away. She was aware of having screamed even if the sound seemed to be incredibly distant. She steeled herself and forced herself to go on. Deo was only a few yards off. He was unconscious, but fortunately lay half on his back, propped up on his pack. She managed to pick him up. He hung limp and heavy in her arms. Now what was she to do? She walked. The water grew deeper. She almost dropped her burden by stumbling into a hole. She turned, staggering now, and headed the other way. She was rewarded by shallows and then damp rock, and a place to put her burden down before she dropped him.

Sitting next to the unconscious man inside whose head the nano-mech devices laboured frantically, she wrapped her arms around her wet dog and sobbed. She had no idea where she was or how to get out. Anyway, even if she could find it, the slope she remembered falling down had been long and steep... She could never carry him back up that. She wished desperately that Deo would come to. Even if he was still in his confused state, at least she wouldn't have to carry him. At least she wouldn't be alone.

θθ૯ᴐθθ

In the pia mater teams of mechsurgeon-slave units, the size of dust motes, communicated with the nano-mech surgeon unit. The pinhead sized unit itself, with its nano technology brain, sat far from the proximal damage site down near the brainstem. The surgeon unit concurred with the slave-units' diagnosis however. At all costs the carrier organism must be rested. At least eight hours and the carrier might have a reasonable chance of recovery.

θθ૯ᴐθθ

Otto snuffled, burrowing himself into a more comfortable position on her lap. He was content. He was, after all, with the person he loved most. He'd had a good drink. Now, a nice dinner and life would be sweet. He certainly didn't feel trapped. To him the way out was nasally obvious.

θθ૯ᴐθθ

The roar was deafening even to the waiting party about a mile and half further up the canyon. To Juan, barely five hundred yards off, and luckily virtually under a huge newly-fallen boulder, it was terrifying. Without thought the boy squirmed into a dark crack and then rolled himself into a catatonic ball.

"What the hell?" Hot steamy air rushed up the canyon. A few rocks tumbled from the canyon rim, unheard above the geyser's throaty bellow.

"Princess Shari! My God! Do you think they're all right?!" asked Caro staring at the column of steam now visible in the strip of sky.

"What was that? A bomb?!" Sam looked back, horrified. He hadn't even felt the danger. Was he losing his touch?

"Geyser, maybe. We saw them on Taa'maz last trip I did with

her Highness. I've never seen such a cloud of steam, though. If they were too close to it they'll be cooked, I'm afraid," said Martin Brettan grimly.

"Well, I'm going back down to see if I can find them. I should have gone with her." Mark Albeer stood up. Guilt and worry shadowed the stocky bodyguard's voice.

"I'll come with you." Caro swayed to her feet.

"Me too." Three others stood up.

"No, stay, all of you. Remember what she said about all going to the cave. It could still be dangerous. I'll go alone."

The small Yak pulled himself to his feet. "Then I should go. Or at least the two of us, in case one gets into trouble."

Captain Viscount Martin Brettan assumed command smoothly. "All right. Do that. Don't take any chances. Sit down the rest of you. We'll wait."

Johannes was not sure how or why he'd got to his feet in the first place. He sat down quickly hoping no one had noticed. His arm throbbed and itched.

The bodyguard and the wiry Yak made their way hastily downwards, clambering over the rock that Juan was still cowering under, passing Shari's pack, and to the steam-streaming cave mouth. The place was still furnace hot. Mark wanted to venture into it.

"No. Come away! The thing's going to blow again. Run!"

Something about Sam's voice prevented the bodyguard even questioning him. They were nearly the other side of Juan's hiding place when another blast of steam roared out of the fault-cave. It was nothing like as fierce as the first one but it still left the two of them cowering behind a rock edge, wide-eyed and silent.

They didn't go back to the cave. No one could live through that. Each, without consulting the other, began to walk slowly back up the canyon.

It was coming to Shari's pack that broke the silence. "I suppose we'd better take it." Mark Albeer was clearly reluctant.

"Yep."

Neither of them made any move to pick up the pack. "I should have gone with her."

The Yak shrugged. "Then you'd be dead too."

"I was supposed to be her bodyguard, dammit."

To his surprise, Sam Teovan felt a stirring of sympathy. What did he have in common with a bullet-stopper? Nothing. But he felt guilty too. She'd trusted him. If he, Teovan, had gone along with her, as opposed to the bullet-stopper, he could have warned her. "Look, she was a good Capo. I wouldn'ta thought a woman could be. But like my ol' Capo say 'Dead is dead, an' we mus' go on'. We gotta go back. The others will think we been cooked too."

Mark Albeer sighed and shouldered the pack. "I was supposed to let her get killed, you know. I'd been told to step aside in the firefight that was planned for your crowd. I wasn't... I wasn't even getting any sleep. I was so bloody glad you Yak struck early."

Teovan paused mid-step. He grabbed the bodyguard. "WHAT?"

"I was supposed to step aside and let Hayley, my fellow bodyguard, shoot her. Shoot her myself if he failed."

"But you were her fuckin' bullet-stopper, man! How the hell..."

"Orders. Orders from the Emperor himself. Now let go of me. I didn't do it. I didn't know if I *could* do it. I'm just bloody glad I never needed to."

Sam took a deep breath. "Man... Forget it. She's dead."

"Caro, I mean, the Countess... How in the hell am I going to tell her?"

Sam shrugged. He avoided saying 'nice tits but nothing upstairs'. His instinct told him that that could get him killed. "Maybe she'll just be glad you didn't cook too," he said dryly.

In some ways Mark Albeer was very young. A ready blush betrayed him.

They met the entire party coming to look for them a few hundred yards further on.

⦿⦿⦿⦿⦿⦿

In the psuedobat-cave Shari held her hands over her ears, and doubled over Otto who was sensibly hiding his head in her midriff. Her hearing had just about returned to normal after the first blast. In a way the steamy gust that found its way in here was welcome. She was cold and wet, and between geyser-blasts the cave chilled off rapidly. It was why the drip-pool, from which she had so gratefully drunk, existed. Her thirst being slaked Shari felt she'd settle for not shivering herself to death. If only she'd brought her pack. She could have wrapped something around her ears and maybe even found some dry clothes to put on. Also Deo should have a blanket over him... He had his pack with him! As the geyser blast-noise died away she began feeling for his pack. In the dark it was difficult to find the opening. She took the pack off his back. It was a struggle but at least he'd be able to lie more comfortably. He groaned slightly, but remained on his side. The pack was no easier to get into now it was off. Oh for a light! She remembered the lumitube Deo had produced when they were trapped in the dark of the crashed ship. He must still have that!

She knew he wore a bandolier under his tunic. He'd produced weapons from it on occasion. Now she felt under his jacket. He was colder than she was. For a moment she was terrified that he was dead. But he wasn't that cold, and yes, she could feel a pulse, fast and soft, but there. It was awkward to get in to his tunic at the neck. She went down to the waist and lifted it. Her fingers touched a narrow belt as she did this. The fingers explored. His body stirred beneath her hand. She flushed pulling back... If he were to wake up now! He lay still. After a few moments she went on, telling herself not to be so stupid. All the same she felt a bit depraved with her hands inside an unconscious man's trousers, and, in the back of her mind, just a little curious.

A piece of silky cloth. A handle... The lumitube. She pulled it out, and bent it to activate the device. In the pale light she could see that in lifting the tunic she'd exposed not one but two bandoliers, carrying a pharmacopoeia of small bottles, four flat-pak grenades, an assortment of tools and electronic instruments, several slim-bladed knives, spikes, tiny cases and a piece of narrow tubing. And two more lumitubes. How like Deo! "Better to die with cards in reserve than to show your entire hand too soon, Princess". He must have said it a thousand times. The memory tightened her throat, made her eyes burn. She pulled his tunic down, and, using the lumitube opened his pack without difficulty.

The blanket wasn't wet, unlike most of the rest of the pack. Gently, ever so gently, she rolled him in it. A pair of trousers and another grey tunic were the total contribution she could find for her own warmth. The food he'd been carrying had unfortunately got wet. It could only improve the five day old pastry of the *boeuf et poivre en croute*. She felt faintly guilty as she and Otto shared most of it, but comforted herself that it would have gone bad anyway. In the distance the geyser roared to life again, its regular cycle disturbed by the rock-choking.

Dry clothes and food helped, even if wearing trousers felt very odd. She'd have given anything for dry footwear... Deo still felt cold. The geyser had been silent awhile. She wondered whether she should risk trying to find her way out now, and bring the others to help her with Deo. She'd decided on this, after all, she had a light now, when the geyser told her to stay put. She would have to wait it out. She did, getting colder. Eventually she took off her wet shoes and burrowed under Deo's blanket. She felt a bit self-conscious about it, but he still seemed to be colder than she was. At least Otto provided a patch of warmth in the crook of her knees.

●●○○●●

It was dark in the canyon, much darker than it had been in the open valley. The darkness was appropriate to the bleak spirits of the party. In the blackness Caro had come to take shelter in his arms. Mark Albeer had often dreamed of holding her. Now the actuality was clouded by her grief and his guilt. They didn't know that they'd been observed by the lean leaguesman, who certainly felt no remorse about the death of Shari and her servant. His feelings meant no good for Albeer or the quietly sobbing girl he held, however. The group were still too shocked to do more than doss down for the night where they were. Several of them spent the better part of the night thinking and planning.

Viscount Brettan started the ball rolling the next morning, before they'd even had their ration of water or food. The bottle, an apple-green one with a grape-vine pattern from Mark Albeer's pack, stood waiting on the rock slab. "I'm afraid now that the Princess is no longer with us, and we'll miss her sadly," he said sententiously, "we need a new leader."

There was a wary silence.

Then Caro burst out. "It's too soon, Martin. I just can't bear it. She's hardly... hardly gone and you're scheming for her place. "She turned away sobbing. Mark and Tanzo went to comfort her. Prince Jarian poured a mug of water from the apple green bottle, and took it to her. It was such an uncharacteristic gesture that it nearly startled the Countess out of her tears.

"Here," he said awkwardly. "I'm very sorry she's dead."

"You! YOU! You hated her!" exclaimed Caro.

"I didn't know her. I was starting to realize just how... good she was. I wish I'd had more time..." The prince swallowed convulsively, and turned back to the others. "Viscount Brettan," he said thickly, "I think we need to eat and drink first. I... I know we need someone to take decisions, but let's all eat and drink first, before we discuss it. Personally I think you're the right person, but, later, eh?"

"No, let's settle it now," said Kadar viciously, fumbling at his belt.

Lila tapped the barrel of the .22 pistol in her hand against the rock and smiled at him, all teeth and no humor. Whatever Kadar had been planning died stillborn. The others all said "Shut up, Kadar," with various degrees of force, except for Johannes, who said that a drink first was what was really called for.

So they drank. The reformed Jarian took each person their ration. He didn't take one for himself. "I stole water, that first night. I... I owe it to my late aunt to make up for it. I'll go without," he said, looking longingly at the bottle.

Johannes, trained in the same arts, found his performance poor. The rest of the audience were not so discerning, however. Perhaps they wrote off his voice tones to inexperience at remorse. "Don't be silly, Jarian. Shari didn't expect you to do that. At least have a little." Tanzo's tone showed that she at least was impressed.

Jarian hung his head. "No. Not this time. I need... to make amends, somehow."

So he sat out while the others drank. Nobody tried that hard to make him drink.

After they'd finished Martin Brettan stood up, and cleared his throat. "I don't want to seem callous, but we really do need to choose a new leader for this party. On the basis of experience I think that I had better take it on. I don't expect to do as well as the Princess..."

"Actually, I am your new Master," interrupted Prince Jarian, his voice was so changed it was hardly recognizable. Gone was the put-upon whine they'd all become so accustomed to that they hardly noticed it any more. Now his voice was ugly with triumph. "You all live or die at my pleasure."

"He should've drunk that water. He's finally flipped," said Sam, beginning to gather his gear.

Jarian held up a small bottle. "You've all just drunk water containing ectipain. Do know what that means, Yak scum? I've a good mind to let you die for that."

By the sudden silence most of the audience knew exactly what ectipain was. Faces became white and drawn. Jarian, too self-centred to understand other people, did not realize how close he stood to death. "What is it?" whispered Caro to Mark Albeer.

"Ectipain? It's what they call the 'slave drug'. If the victim doesn't get the antidote regularly the nervous system starts to disintegrate. It is so incredibly painful that most victims try to kill themselves, but as they lose control of their hands and feet first... It takes up to a day before the heart and lungs are affected. The brain is always the last to go," he whispered back, hands clenching and unclenching.

Martin Brettan had both thought and moved fast. He seized the prince, holding him in *Qua Teng* position, which is *not* comfortable. It was unnecessary. The flabby little princeling was no match for the gym-honed muscles of the big Viscount anyway.

Jarian squalled. Instinctively, Mark Albeer stepped forward. "I wouldn't," said Brettan coldly. "For starters I'd break the little poisoner's neck before you could get here. Secondly, for his attempt to poison his own father, the Emperor has struck away his titles, disinherited him and put him under a death sentence. You owe him no loyalty."

Mark Albeer stopped dead in his tracks. "I... it was just my training. He's just poisoned C...us. I don't want to save him."

"Right. Which is why I want him searched. I want that antidote. Not you, Albeer. That bottle came out of your pack, and you just moved to defend him. You, um, Macrae...Lila. Put the gun away and search him."

"It won't do you any good," spluttered the ex-Prince angrily. "Let go of me. You'll suffer for this. Especially you, Viscount. It is all a lie, bodyguard. Force him to let go of meeee!!" he ended with a squeal as Martin Brettan tightened his grip.

The burly Viscount snorted. "I heard it from Selim Puk himself, ten minutes before we left the palace. How do you think you managed to get onto the ship, little cock-o'-the whoop? Did you think we didn't know about you?"

Lila searched. She searched with most awesome thoroughness. Under his testicles she found a tiny vial. She held it up. "I thought I was going to have to search his anus," she said with distaste.

"That's what you all need now. I've hidden the rest," said Jarian. "And I won't tell you where."

"Oh yes, you will," said Kadar, coming forward, a thin-bladed knife in his hand. "Let me, Viscount. I am an *expert* at this sort of thing. He'll talk. He'll be glad to." The Leaguesman had an evil glitter in his eyes.

But Jarian had anticipated this, although without the possibility of being in pain. He'd imagined it rather as a triumphal showdown with them uttering threats, rather than someone stalking in on him with the morning sunlight shining off their knife-blade. "It'll do you no good," he squeaked. "I can last longer than you can survive without the antidote. And I promise you, the ones who touched me are going to be left to suffer."

Kadar Shilo didn't seem to have heard. He stepped forward, moving the knife slowly before his victim's eyes. They all watched, hypnotized. Suddenly a look of unease crossed the lean man's features. He paused. Put a hand to his stomach.

"See! It's starting already, Leaguesman," said Jarian, his moment of terror turning to triumph. "Put the knife away. I'll treat you well. I'm going to need someone to administer punishment. Especially to you, Brettan."

Kadar had dropped the knife. He doubled over, and was clutching his stomach. "Oh Gods! What have you done to us!" He lay down and groaned.

Even the Viscount was shaken. He let go of Jarian. "Here, Kadar. You'd better take one of these pills from this vial. Oooh! I think we'd all better!" There were eleven tiny violet tablets in the vial. So, he'd been anticipating Shari and the manservant as well. Despite the cramps Viscount Brettan made sure he held onto the vial with the two extra tablets in it.

The antidote tablets might have stopped them dying, but the tablets barely lessened the violent stomach cramps, and the cataclysmic effect on the lower gut. All of the party fled into the surrounding rocks, leaving Jarian, their new overlord, to help himself to a generous drink and the best breakfast he'd seen for days. He enjoyed it in a leisurely fashion. Then he went to see why his new subjects had not returned.

Ectipain was supposed to give the first twinges to the extremities in about three hours. Whatever this batch had been corrupted with had certainly had a violently laxative and emetic effect. He found them all passed out in various places between the rocks amidst the evidence of this.

Shaking them had no noticeable effect, so Jarian went back to the makeshift camp and had another drink and second breakfast. Then he had a leisurely walk back down-valley and collected some more of the tiny tablets from one of his stashes. He had a bad moment when he couldn't find the spot, but, on a second try, he located it. He counted out nine tablets. The antidote wouldn't be needed again for three days and then not for 21 days. The antidote doses became further and further apart, which was very convenient. Eventually, after five years or so, the body developed a resistance to the original Ectipain. Well, when that came up he'd have to make a new plan.

He began walking back up the valley. He was so deep in cruel and pleasant daydreams that he failed to hear Juan's delirious mumblings as he clambered past the huge rock the boy lay under. Instead Jarian went back to enjoy the peaceful sleep of the unjust.

It was late afternoon when his future subjects began dragging themselves bemusedly back into the makeshift camp. No one attempted to question his authority as he gave orders. It was very gratifying. Kadar showed great vigor in the whipping he gave to the Viscount, and was rewarded by an extra water-ration. The Leaguesman fawned at the new power in the land. The Viscount, reading the nature of both his assailant and Jarian, had screamed suitably. Actually he could and had borne worse punishment with gritted teeth and silence. But he knew stoicism would have caused worse aggression. So he screamed, and schemed. He couldn't quite bring himself to beg.

Evening came and Jarian's new subjects were allowed their water-ration, something their dehydrated bodies badly needed. Their lord and master sat in princely splendor and drank from his personal bottle, as he watched them share out the meagre food-ration he'd allowed them. He eyed the women. It had been a while... who should it be tonight? It was a pity his Aunt had managed to escape him. Rumor had it she'd never slept with a man, and he'd have enjoyed humiliating her. She'd never treated him as if he *were* a man. He'd like to have shown her. And killed that damn dog of hers.

●●C ⊃●●

Shari stirred. She was deliciously warm and comfortable. Except for one arm. It was trapped by something heavy and warm. She tried to move it. The something warm stirred against her. In her half-asleep state she found herself rubbing up against him... She sat up abruptly, realizing just where she was, and what she'd been doing. Otto, who had been rudely awakened and turfed from his warm nest, grumbled.

Deo rolled slightly, as if seeking her. His face, unguarded in what was either unconsciousness or a very deep sleep, looked so much younger than usual in the wan lumitube light. He looked terribly vulnerable and weak. She reached out a cautious hand. At least he felt warm now. If only there was something more she could do...? Perhaps in all those identical little bottles there would be something she could give him? He seemed to have an entire pharmacy with him. Maybe there would be something she recognized.

Cautiously she peeled away the blanket. Lifted his tunic. The first two bottles were labelled, the labels neatly printed in Deo's minuscule hand. The third bottle had no label, but there was a piece of paper inside it. She opened it and fished it out. It was also in Deo's hand, but the writing was a hasty scrawl. She struggled to make it out. Then, with infinite care, she replaced the paper, put the bottle back, and shuddered. With the other hand she pulled his tunic down, and the blanket over him.

How could he use such filth? She tore a strip of cloth from her damp skirt and cleaned the hand that had touched the paper with extreme care. Then she walked away and found a cranny in the cave wall to drop the scrap of cloth into. For a long time she sat in the darkness, sparing the lumitube, staring at nothing.

The cave had never been silent, with pseudobat noises in the distance and the drip-drip-drip from the roof. But now there was a new sound, a whirring sound. Otto edged against her leg and barked. Hastily she bent the lumitube and activated it.

The air was streaming with flickering fur-trailing bat-shapes, ducking past the low roof of the drip-pool and then beating their way upward against the near wall. There they and the roof were lost in the darkness.

For a minute Shari panicked. The last time the shovel-nosed creatures had fled, the geyser had erupted. But after a moment she realized that this was no wild and desperate flight. Instead it had a hum-drum Monday-morning commute feel about it. She shushed Otto, who had made several hopeful predatory leaps into the air, now that he could see what made the noise.

So, up that wall was the way out. She walked across to it, splashing into the shallow pool. It was steep, but not unclimbable. She looked back. Deo was sitting up, looking into the light.

CHAPTER 16
RETURNS

Be wary about rooting out dead plants. It may just have been winter.

The Upanishad of the Gardener-Dewa Celine.

The living we can part ourselves from. But our dead are always with us.

From the Liturgy for the passage of all souls: Memorium for the dead.

The capabilities of the mind of the rat are generally overestimated by the animals' adherents. Yes, they are capable of a degree of feral sharpness, but, generally speaking, the thinking of fat and pampered long-domesticated creatures like Rat doesn't go much beyond dinner, warmth and comfort, and occasional problems with constipation. Now Rat was having to deal with his master, who had always provided, being unresponsive to numerous suggestive nosings. Juan just moaned and muttered. Eventually Rat had had to gnaw his own way into the zippered pocket full of cirrith-seed. The high oil content could at least be broken down to provide some water. The pocket made a reasonable nest, even if he wished Juan would stop tossing and turning so much.

OOCOOO

It was the afternoon of the next day before Juan returned briefly to semi-lucidity: Crown-induced semi-lucidity: Denaari-Juan only, left in confused control of an alien body that would not, could not, fly. He was not aided by Human-Juan, who was still muttering and wrestling in the confused realms of adolescent reality, which is bad enough without added delirium. Despite this, the body of the boy with a crown emerged from its hole and began crawling upstream. Parts of his mind wandered further afield and would occasionally try to make his body attempt null g-ball or low-g acrobatics, and address long diatribes to his father...

Rat accepted movement as part of his norm. He didn't know that the tiny transmitter-chip which was part of every station-pet's life was causing all sorts of upset with the Sector civil defense bio-computer unit. When the micro-transmitter started to move yet again, now heading into security zone, the biocomputer stopped vacillating and opened ancient transmission relays.

OOCOOO

The cave-wall cliff was climbable. It was persuading Deo that he wanted to climb it that was difficult. At least he seemed more lucid and coherent now that he had slept. His recollection even of yesterday was hazy, but at least he seemed prepared to deal with today. He seemed prepared to deal with it in a typical Deo fashion: suspiciously and cautiously. If she had not been so hurt and angered by what she'd found in his collection of drugs and potions, if she had not been so anxious to get out into the sunlight again, she would have been glad that he was no longer so robotic. As it was, it was a pain that he wouldn't just take orders. Eventually she had to resort to entering his confused world to tell him what to do. It seemed she was the Dewa again. She was not sure who she had sent him to kill this time.

Then there was Otto. He was not designed for rock-climbing. And he was not very keen on being stowed in Deo's makeshift pack, which Shari had appropriated. The man showed no signs of being aware that he'd carried it before. Then the lumitube had begun to die. She had to ask Deo for another one. This he produced with a faint look of puzzlement, as if his hands knew what to do without his mind understanding it. At length, after a last drink and making sure that all the water-bottles were full, they climbed.

Shari realised how lucky they'd been to fall into the mass of the bat-creatures. It was a long way, especially with a heavy pack and a small dog that kept threatening to wriggle out of it. She was afraid that the pseudo-bats would come back. The fall without the furry creatures as flying cushions would probably kill them. But they reached the top, and then managed the short scramble to the niche into the main passage. Although all she wanted to do was run for the outside, Shari paused for long enough to mark the little cave-crack she'd come out of. Then, pushing Deo occasionally, and with Otto scampering eagerly ahead, she hastened up the tunnel and towards the outside. The cave was breathing in now, warm, dry late afternoon air. Soon they were out in the canyon. Never had daylight looked so beautiful.

Otto barked excitedly and Shari couldn't restrain a yell of pure delight. Deo looked alarmed and confused. They began walking up the canyon in the deep late afternoon shadows. The rest of the party must be far ahead by now. She wondered, briefly, if they'd have left her pack.

●●●ᴐᴈᴈ

Blood seeped sluggishly from Juan's abraded knees and palms. He just kept going. Even the failing light and the night-cooling didn't stop his slow, mechanical progress. The canyon walls kept him going in roughly the same direction. Upwards. Towards where the last of a precious supply of wood-fragments was being burned to gratify the new Lord and Master.

●●●ᴐᴈᴈ

He looked at the women with an unpleasant hunger in his eyes. He was too insensitive to realize that they were aware of his lascivious gaze. He was too confident of his power over their life and death to understand that to ordinary mortals there are some things which are more important than mere life and death.

As the first moon began to rise over the canyon rim he'd reached his decision. The girl. The ridergirl. She looked so scared and vulnerable, that just looking at her aroused him. As a prince of the blood any number of aristocratic ladies and a few men, in case his preferences should run that way, had pursued him since puberty. They'd shown him that courtiers were merely courtesans by another name. They bored him, and, he always secretly suspected they despised him, despite the flattery they heaped on his efforts. His preference ran instead to the young and weak. To servants and chambermaids who might have wished to say him nay.

The others could wait. They were all his. But tonight he'd take the scared-looking one. He pointed a lazy finger at her. In the dying firelight she looked even more helpless than usual. "Una. Ridergirl. Come. I'll have you for a bed-warmer tonight." He giggled. "The rest of you women will have to wait for the pleasure of my royal pleasure."

The ridergirl stared at him as if he was a snake and she a rabbit. It excited him. Suddenly he registered an incongruity. She'd jumped when he spoke. But she was deaf...

He had no more time to ponder this. Tanzo Adendorff was advancing on him, a rock clumsily held in her upraised hands.

"Keep away! You won't get the antidote next time! I warn you!" He retreated.

"So what, you... filth. She's just a *child*. And you'll be dead."

"Kadar! Wienan... Albeer... Yak, even you, Brettan. STOP HER! Or else..."

The two leaguesmen attempted to grab Tanzo. With hysterical strength the small woman flung both of them away, although she lost her rock. Then Martin Brettan added his bulk to the fight. He grabbed her from behind and held her struggling in his arms. "Let me go!" she screamed.

He put a big hand over her mouth, and turned her away from the frightened Jarian. He whispered harshly into her ear. "We get the next antidote in three days' time, you silly bitch. Then we've got twenty days to make the little bastard talk. I promise once we've got those antidote tablets out of him, I won't stop you killing him. We've just got to 'shut up and put up' for the next three days. The girl won't die from it."

She bit him.

He hit her with calculated force and she slumped in his arms. A quick glance showed him that Albeer was up and heading in to the fray. The fool hadn't even drawn a weapon. The Yak had disappeared. That farmer girl bodyslave had drawn her weapon however. She held it rock-steady, a bead drawn on Jarian.

"Prince Jarian." She might as well have said 'dogturd'. "Tell them to leave her alone. Do it. Or I'll shoot your balls off."

"She's er... fainted," said Martin Brettan warily. "She'll be fine in a minute or two, I'm sure. All the same, these highly-strung types." He put her down gently.

"She'd better be. Listen...Prince. *I'll* sleep with you, if you've got to try to prove you're a man. Just leave the kid alone, see."

"I don't want you," said Jarian, sullenly. Anything less

appealing than this virago who despised him, was hard to imagine.

Tanzo sat up and groaned. "What hit me?"

"You're going to be punished. I'll have you flayed and then leave you to die!" Jarian picked on a softer victim, or at least one that was unarmed.

Deliberately the Viscount stepped into Lila's line of fire, obscuring the Prince. "Your Highness. You may need this woman," he said slowly and calmly. "We're on the Denaari homeworld, heading for a Denaari radio beacon. She is an acknowledged expert on the Denaari."

"Hah! The Denaari! They're extinct."

Tanzo tried to stand up, and then decided to remain sitting. "You wouldn't even know what they looked like, you....excreta brain."

In the shadows behind Jarian the small Yak grinned despite the situation. 'Excreta brain'! She aroused in his feral mind gentle emotions which had been dormant since his mother died. He regarded the rider-girl as a non-entity, a flank you didn't have to watch. The little turd was welcome to her. He suspected her bed-arts were restricted to weeping. He had to admire the way the lady lock-tickler had risen to defend her chick though. That was why he'd moved to cut the little prick's throat, despite himself. He'd have to teach the lock-tickler to swear, if they got through the next few minutes alive.

"Of course I do, you... you old cow! They always looked the same in the pictures, with those stupid helmets and batwings. Well, show me one and I'll believe you need to live. Go on. Show me one. Otherwise you're going to *die*."

Tanzo looked up, her eyes still blurry. And smiled. Her rather prim little mouth stretched wider than it ever stretched before. She pointed. And never was the word "There!" more triumphal.

What she was pointing to was a moon-shadow on the canyon wall. The two sharp -edged rocks between which Juan's crown-bearing head was silhouetted, made good wings. It drew all eyes.

The tiny fire had died to glowing embers. The canyon floor was dark, and the moonlight very bright. The shadow-play Denaari was real enough to make Sam drop his chisel. "Well fuck me!"

The appearance of an alien and the sudden knowledge that the Yak had been behind him set Jarian screaming. He wasn't alone. But he was the only one screaming "Kill it! Kill it!" And he was the only one who decided to run.

Originally, they'd stopped to wait for Shari in a small bowl amidst a tumble of boulders. Ahead was a water-worn cliff, which had given Sam and Lila pause, and allowed the rest to catch up with them. Here, where the canyon-floor widened, Juan's crawling progress had finally led him astray. He'd crawled out of the main channel, up an old rock-slip, and was now forty feet above the other castaways. He'd actually been there for quite some minutes before Tanzo had noticed his shadow.

He'd heard the entire confrontation, but, as it was in an alien language, it hadn't meant much to him. Now it occurred to him in the sudden silence as the Princeling fled and several guns pointed at his shadow, that he could call for help. Only his mouth was dry. Dry and too full of tongue. Also it was only Juan-Denaari who was home. His attempt at a 'nestling-in-distress' call did little to reassure the people below. All it did was call attention to his actual position.

But Tanzo, although unsteady on her feet, was already struggling eagerly towards him. Sam had retrieved his chisel and rushed to support her. She accepted his arm without even noticing who he was. "Up the rock-slide!" Her voice was full of an intense eagerness that somehow made the little Yak's heart sink.

As they battled up the slope the alien visitation managed a second whistle-croak. The previously immobile group began taking cover. With a despairing croak the boy nearly toppled over the edge, before Sam and Tanzo could reach him.

●●●つ●●

Jarian ran. The shadow-Denaari had been upstream. So had the suddenly revealed Yak. So the princeling had run downstream. Down toward where Shari, Deo and Otto were struggling upwards in the dark, wishing that the moonlight they could see shining on the canyon walls would get to them.

Shari could swear she'd heard voices. But surely they must be miles away by now? She'd definitely smelled woodsmoke on the down-valley breeze. Good! That must mean they'd found food. Probably snake again. But she was hungry enough for even that to have appeal. It wasn't so bad, really. Just the idea of it that was rather repulsive. Her pack had gone, not to her surprise. But with it had gone the prospects of a meal, and her stomach was grumbling.

They climbed up the obstructing chock-boulder that Juan had managed to wriggle under. At the top they were bathed in moonlight. Otto began to bark furiously. Prince Jarian, who hadn't had the breath to scream for some time, managed a hysterical, terrified squeak before toppling over in a dead faint.

When he came to, his head was cradled in Shari's lap. His eyes bulged wide with terror but he remained conscious to hear her acerbic commands. "Stop it. Stop it right now. What's wrong?"

"You're, you're... *alive*?"

"So it would appear. And we've found water, although getting it is no fun."

A way began to open in Jarian's weasel brain. They at least had water! "Thank God I found you. I just escaped. The Denaari came. They've killed everybody. For God's sake don't go up-valley. We must flee."

"What happened? Sit up and tell me, boy. How far up valley were you?"

"Oh aunt, I'm so glad to have found you. The Denaari attacked us just after nightfall. I managed to kill one and escape."

That was one lie too many. "Yes, a likely story. Did you steal the water again?"

"No! Truly! You never believe me. I saw the Denaari myself."

"And then you probably ran like a rabbit. Come on Deo. I think we'd better get ourselves up there. And I think we'd better take this one with us."

He'd listened to the entire conversation in silence. He'd become accustomed to being called 'Deo' although he did not understand why. "This one is lying about some of what he says. He has a look about him of the one who dares to claim he rules the Church." For centuries the Holy Church had ensured that Imperial control over Arunchal was barely nominal, and a death sentence to any who tried to extend Imperial writ more than ten miles outside the Imperial fortress enclaves. Even in these areas, death was frequent, sudden and often inexplicable. But for centuries the dagger-hands of the Church had kept it so, confining themselves to the planet. Now, he had heard, they planned to strike offworld. Against the head on the coins. He'd seen one of those, once. Possession of one was considered heresy, and punished accordingly.

The Dagger of the Goddess was confused, living partially in a world he'd left twenty years before. Still, part of him knew that the whining boy-man had not lied about the Denaari. Deep within his skull the nano-surgeon unit also registered it. Denaari: the carrier species name for the ancient enemy. It had been programmed for this eventuality.

Shari reached her decision. "We'll go up, but cautiously. Come on... you."

Jarian ground his teeth and considered his options. God, he hated her.

"Up. Make a sound that betrays and I will kill. Lead the way." The grip of the Dagger of the Goddess's hand on his shoulder was like a steel vice. Jarian found he had no options. He had fallen down enough things while running away earlier. He was lucky he hadn't broken his neck. Besides, he was scared his aunt might catch him, and was truly terrified that her manservant might catch him first. And even if he got away he'd be on his own, without water or food. He felt in his pocket. The pill-vial was still there. Perhaps...

●●C⊃●●

They'd carried Juan down, set his back against soft things and given him water. At first he'd tried to fight off the water before Denaari-Juan realised that this was what the alien body needed so desperately. They'd loosened his clothing, cleaned his wounded knees and raw palms as well as possible, covered him with a soft blanket, and gently given him more water in small doses. But he would not let them take off the crown. So they just left it there, burning a hole in Tanzo's curiosity.

She'd been bitterly disappointed to find that her Denaari was as human as she was. But she'd been kind and caring. Only the most suspicious of nature would have thought it just because she wanted to grill the boy about where he'd found the crown. There was however, no doubting the sincerity of the mothering he got from her slight, big-eyed and shy sidekick: The girl whose near-shaved ridercrop was turning into a head of short, soft curls. Something about the delirious boy liberated mothering instincts in her.

Between the boulders Shari, Deo, Otto and a very unwilling Jarian crept closer. They could hear voices. Human and recognizable voices. Arguing.

"We'll have to go and look for him."

"And what do we do if, when we find him? We can't let him go on this way. He's drunk so much of the water and eaten the best of the food..."

"It's only another two days. After we've got the next dose we'll torture it out of him. We've got days in hand then," said Brettan

"We can't let him go on. The women aren't safe," said Mark Albeer, ponderously.

"And death is better, eh. Come on. We can settle it if we can find him," said Brettan.

"Better in the morning. We can't see properly and we'd probably break our necks," Johannes said, nervously.

"By morning he could be out in the main valley again, going God knows where. We've got to find him."

●●●つ●●

Behind the rocks Shari turned on the quaking Jarian. "Well, so much for your story of the Denaari having killed all of them. But they seem to want you back. I must say I think the better of several of them, risking their necks in the dark to find you. Been stealing things again, have you? I must admit I didn't think you had the courage to molest a woman who could fight back, though. Or are they talking about somebody else? I haven't heard the Yak, but I didn't think that was likely of him."

"Obrigato, Princess-Capo," Teovan spoke from the shadows. "I see you brought the eta back. That's good."

"Hello Sam. What are you doing hiding out here in the dark?"

The small man stepped out of the shadows. They could see he was smiling his crooked smile in the moonlight. "Keeping a look-out, I guess. I just had a feeling... Besides, with that one," he jerked a thumb at the cringing Jarian, "you can't be too careful."

"It's a lie," said Jarian, sullenly. "They're anti-royalists, dearest Aunt. Not to be trusted. Especially this criminal."

Shari noticed that Otto had peacefully gone and greeted the Yak, who had patted him in a startled sort of way. "Well, I'll just have to abdicate. Lead on. Let's make them happy that they don't have to go out into the night looking for my suddenly affectionate nephew."

"Don't believe a word of what they're going to tell you," said Jarian desperately, as she pushed him forward.

●●●つ●●

One could have called it a gargantuan computer... In that the nano circuits were grown and not made according to internally evolved designs, it was also a biological creature. But, because of its access to the crown vaults it was something more, both the memory and the conscience of the Denaari. It was busy, as it had been for the last 3000 years, cataloguing. It had received a massive input which had strained its already overstretched indexing facility. It still had a couple of centuries' worth of work to go. The interruption from some puny-brained back-country civil defense unit, with nothing better to do than sit about all day and direct its maintenance units to scratch its excretory orifice, was not welcome.

Security zone Delat: It reviewed: A bio-zoo unit that had reported irreparable cataclysmic damage, and requested materials and assistance- a screed of numbers followed: 2023 years seven days and four hours and twenty-two minutes seventeen seconds and 11 microseconds ago; a geosynch-line anchorage point that hadn't had any reported traffic for - another screed of numbers: about 3006 years, nineteen days and twenty-five hours and three minutes, and a tracking-eye unit that hadn't reported for... five days seven hours and three minutes... It had sent a long data string then... to Ground Control.

The huge bio-computer was not equipped to sigh. Nor did it have the capacity to psychoanalyze itself, to discover that it was suffering from both guilt and depression. It didn't want to deal with yet another non-situation. The travel-speed of the transmission picked up by Sector Delat civil defence bio-computer unit would, at present rates, reach the ruined bio-zoo in approximately 119 days. And that was the nearest of the items in the Security zone. Wow! Panic! The message sent back to Sector Delat civil defence bio-computer unit could roughly be translated as 'piss off and leave me alone'. However, in a minor flicker of conscience, a low-priority message was sent to Ground Control, requesting more input about the tracking-eye's datastring.

000000

It was right that the people should greet the Dewa with such delight and adulation. It was not right that they should come within such close proximity to her. Unease stirred. He screwed up his eyes, trying desperately to make sense of it all. Why did he feel that he must defend her? The Dewa's incarnations were part of the Kali-Dewa. Beyond harming by mere mortals. His head. Oh, his head. Why was he here? Was this some kind of purgatory, where the light-Dewa led in a re-creation of his past deeds giving him the chance to atone, to do things right so he might be reborn instead of going into the pit?

He had seen the pit, and the demons. He remembered it cloudily. He also remembered waking with her warm beside him. She had led him out. But he had betrayed her. Not with his hands, but with his heart. The Dewa knew this, as she knew all things. He had rebelled against killing Sugahata. He had allowed Dugra to escape, deliberately delaying the attack. Why then?

He puzzled at it angrily, fiercely raising his blood pressure in a way which severely distressed the nano-mech surgeon within him. Then a verse out of the second Veda came to him, redeemed him. 'The pathways in the mind of God are myriad and beyond the following of mortals.' It would do. There must be reason but it was not his to question. It allowed him to focus again on this bizarre half world mixture of memories and the alien place through which the Dewa guided him.

"He gave you all Ectipain! How?" Shari eyes pierced the huddled Jarian. Both Sam and the Viscount watched Jarian. They were making sure he didn't run away again.

"In a water-bottle that came out of your bodyguard's pack," said the Viscount shortly. Shari realised it was the bottle Jarian had attempted to offer both her and Otto a drink out of. Albeer could have co-operated... but not if it meant poisoning Caro. The poor boy was obviously smitten. Unfortunate for him, if hardly surprising. Caro loved men and left them. "He didn't drink any. Made excuses about being too upset by your death and his guilt at stealing water before. He's hidden the antidote somewhere. He reckoned it made him Lord and Master of us."

"Those fuckin' stomach cramps made damn sure we wasn't in a hurry to argue with the eta about it. He's still got most of us by the balls." Sam grimaced feeling his stomach at the memory of the pains. A flicker of expression darted across Deo's face.

"Yes. I'm afraid we need those pills before the day after tomorrow. Anyway, ectipain cramps or not, when he decided on... um... taking that rider-girl for a bedfellow, Lady Tanzo snapped. Went for him with a rock."

"I haven't forgotten that you hit me," said Tanzo coolly from where she was administering a small mouthful of water to the boy in the Denaari crown while the rider-girl gently held his head.

Brettan shrugged. "I was doing my best for all of us."

Tanzo snorted and opened her mouth for a blistering retort.

"Enough." Shari was in a poor mood for bickering. "Jarian. I want those pills. Or I'll feed *you* Ectipain. That'll send you running for the antidote."

"He poured the rest of the bottle out. We don't have any more of the stuff."

"That is a problem *I* can solve... very quickly, believe me." Somehow there was no way that you could have doubted her. "The antidote, Jarian. Now."

Sulkily Jarian drew out the vial with its carefully counted tablets. Popped the lid. "I'll have it like that, thank you," said Shari, reaching out a hand.

Instead Jarian put a tablet into his mouth, and scattered the rest into the darkness. He swallowed as both Sam and Martin Brettan grabbed him.

"Stand still all of you. Get a torch here. We must find those tablets." Shari snapped.

But they could only find five of the violet tablets. And Jarian, having laughed and told his witch of an aunt she could give him ectipain now if she wanted to, passed out beyond waking.

Shari took charge of the pills, in the grim knowledge that four people would have to die now, and that she would have to choose.

She struggled to sleep for the rest of that night.

CHAPTER 17
TO THE RUINS OF EDEN, PLUS SNAKES, VARIOUS.

The enemy of liberty is not totalitarianism. It is bureaucracy. To destroy a prince utterly, add to his records, endlessly. The development of an effective computer filing and retrieval system may spell the death of revolutionaries as surely as a firing-squad. Fortunately, such systems as there are, were designed by humans and are run by bureaucrats.

Nicola Para-Machiavelli: Obliterating a Prince

Jarian had woken refreshed from his night's slumber. He found his movement was restricted. Somebody had mummified him with a blanket and a length of rope. He squalled protests before he thought about it. Had he been slightly sharper first thing in the morning he might have pretended to still be passed out. It could have been more pleasant.

"Ah, my *dear* little nephew is awake." Shari didn't look as if she'd seen much sleep. There were dark rings below her eyes. And she hadn't bothered to do any repairs to her hair. She looked very like the witch he'd accused her of being. A very bad tempered witch. "Well, Prince Jarian. Oh I forgot. Jarian. I gather you're not even a Prince any more. Do you still support the order of command being dictated by the Coda de Gotha? Because I am telling you that you're going to show us where you hid those antidote tablets."

Jarian smiled at her. A nasty smile. She frightened him, but he held all the aces. "Certainly. On certain conditions."

"I want those Ectipain antidote tablets, Jarian."

"Untie me and we'll talk about it." He could see the softness now. He was sure she wouldn't be prepared to torture him. Then Deo stepped forward. Jarian's smile faded. There was something very frightening about that man.

Deo bowed respectfully to her. "As you know, Dewa. I carry antidote tablets."

Shari was so relieved she could have kissed him, right then and there. All those bottle he carried! She'd only read the lables of the first three. But it was hardly surprising, considering...

Jarian's self-satisfied world fell apart as the man held out a tiny bottle, virtually identical to those in his poisons case, except that this one's label was neatly handwritten, not printed.

He was still thirsty when he showed them his stash, and after a little more persuasion the second hidden bottle. Shari allowed no expression to betray her feelings but her heart sank seeing those bottles. There was no way that there were enough doses for nine people for five years. Not even with Deo's meagre supply added.

"Do I get a drink now?" moaned Jarian. "I've given you the pills."

Shari raised her eyebrows. "Yes. You can drink your fill, while you fetch the water. You're going to work for it, though."

They'd brought all the empty bottles down with them. Now Shari had to grit her teeth and brave the geyser-hole again, to lead five of them down to the water. Jarian had been wrong about one thing. Someone who could face this a second time wasn't soft. And she had been prepared to torture him... herself. She wouldn't have asked someone else to do it, but for the others she would have tortured him... and, by doing so, hurt herself. But her pain threshold was far higher than his.

They emerged unscathed, laden with water, ten minutes before the next blow happened. They had water, they had antidote tablets for the foreseeable future. They were running low on food, and so Shari decided that they'd do better to carry the boy with the Denaari crown, and move on. It was frightening to leave the water, but they could come back. She could see no future, except death by slow starvation, in staying.

◉◉◉つ◉◉

One can speed up computer transmission times to near lightspeed. If one is prepared to cheat a bit, and muck around with space/time and interdimensionality one can even exceed that, although the consequences are... well, cataclysmic. But all known attempts to speed up bureaucracy have only resulted in it dropping into a still lower gear. When computers (even bio-computers) take over bureaucracy, this slow-down effect is cubed. While circuits in the Ground-control pyramid played with daily weather predictions for ships that never came, and would be destroyed if they did, the request for more data on the input from the tracking-eye in security zone waited in a holding circuit. The Biocomputer in Ground-control was under-utilised, and could have dealt with this scrap of a request easily, but that is bureaucracy for you. Certain things transcend species.

Sector Delat civil defense bio-computer unit sulked. It had only tried to help when it had told central about the transmissions. Now it was damned if it was going to alert Central again, to be abused in that fashion. Even if the rate of travel of the transmission from Rat's chip had speeded up by several orders of magnitude. Civil defense had been a new notion to the Denaari, who had never had internecine fights worse than the occasional mating battle. War had been a concept they'd struggled to master, even when the Sil attacked them. The sector Delat civil defense biocomputer kept tracking, however.

◉◉◉つ◉◉

The boy was a puzzle. Where had he come from? He was wearing stationer clothes, or what was left of them. He had that Denaari relic, though. How had he got here? Was there another ship? And could they go the way he had come.... was there a way out of here?

Tanzo and Una had tended him all night. Mostly it had been Una, as Tanzo had fallen asleep mid sentence and Una would never have dreamed of waking her. An errant fact picked up somewhere in Tanzo's voracious reading had been the need for isotonic fluids in cases of dehydration. The boy had been given their best effort: sugar, of which they had plenty, a generous pinch of salt, of which they had little, stirred into the water they poured slowly into him. An intravenous drip would have been far more effective, but... Anyway he was mostly conscious now, although

185

he slept a great deal, even while carried. They had no poles for a stretcher, so Mark Albeer had hoisted the boy onto his back, and they'd tied him in place with a blanket. He still talked a form of clicky, squeaky gibberish when he was awake, and refused to part with the crown. Any attempt to remove it, even when he was asleep, would have him clutching frantically at it.

Juan-human was still subsurface and even Juan-Denaari wasn't doing too well. But the boy was mending, and the crown-beast itself was doing much better. It was managing to configure human thoughtwaves quite well now. It could replay human thoughts and images perfectly. It could even probably get some Denaari thoughts to its new host, in a form it could understand, at least at a level much less coarse than its earlier image flood. The chaos inside Juan's head still existed, of course. Large parts of his brain, hitherto unused, thought like a Denaari. Or as much like a Denaari as an alien could.

It was nearly evening of the next day, when Juan's latest bearer had laid him down, that the royal barge castaways learned that he did know human tongue after all. Una had given him more of the home made isotonic brew, and he had helped her to control it instead of choking and spluttering on it. Then Rat had decided he needed a drink too. The previous night he'd appeared and been stroked and given water and a scrap of bread by Una. She hadn't, of course, said anything. She never did.

This time Sam saw Rat too. "Dinner!" By the way he said it you knew it was not intended as a joke.

Juan managed to put a protective if battered hand over the animal. "Rat," he said weakly.

"He said 'Rat'. He spoke!" Una was alight with excitement and pleasure.

"I know it's a rat. I reckon most of you folk don't know that rat is good eating," said Sam. "Especially a big fat one like that."

"Oh! But this one is his pet. His friend! You can't eat it," said Una firmly.

The little thing was actually taking up a defensive stance in front of the boy. Sam was amused, despite himself. Then something struck him. "You're supposed to be deaf, girl. How did you know what he said? How did you know what I said for that matter? The lock tickler always talks to you in sign-language."

Now the girl looked frightened. "I lip-read. Not too well," she said after a small pause, her soft voice full of terror. She'd had to think desperately to find that answer.

Sam grinned his lop-sided grin at her. "Well, keep it under your hat, kid. Useful trick." He winked at her and went off to inform Tanzo and Shari that the boy was coming right, could talk sense, and had added another animal to their number. He didn't for a moment believe Una's clumsy lie, but he felt sorry for the girl. Sorry. Shit. What the hell? Was he going soft or something? It was these bloody people. Not his type.

He was actually completely wrong. He was in fact a second cousin to the noble lady whom Caro's father had married. But he didn't know that, even if his mother had.

Shari had shrugged at the news. The lack of sleep the night before and the knowledge that the Ectipain antidote she now carried was insufficient was wearing on her. "So long as he's not going to get worse. I'll give him 'till morning to recover further. I need the rest myself right now."

Tanzo's curiosity about the crown was too intense, however. She hurried off, Sam, looking rather forlorn, in her wake. They were too late. Both the boy and Una were fast asleep, she cradling his head against her thin chest. She looked Madonna-like. There was a tiny smile on her face, for the first time that Tanzo could recall. The two didn't stir as Tanzo tossed Una's blanket over them. Only a pink nose came out and whiffled at the Yak and the Countess.

"She needed someone to mother, even more than she needed mothering, poor child," Tanzo said softly. "Still, it must be nice to have someone care about you."

"I care about you." Sam Teovan. Capo-regime in the Carrenzia-Heiki. One of the most feared men in the Yak underworld. He felt extremely stupid. He didn't know why he'd said it. He just knew that he meant it.

It wasn't the right thing to say, or at least not the right time to say it. Tanzo drew herself up to her full five-foot two. She'd lost weight and gained muscle tone and colour over the last five days. Also, without the thick-rimmed glasses and the misapplied make up, she was a great deal more attractive looking, the Yak thought. But now, she just looked furious. It had obviously been bubbling beneath the surface for some time, and it erupted with unexpected force. "Yes, you care for me. Like Hades! Where were you when I got beaten up trying to stop that child being raped?"

The Yak's face changed. The unfamiliar tender expression fled, and he assumed his usual closed expression. He shook his head. Then he turned on his heel and walked away.

Tanzo found her way to her bed-roll with difficulty. She was so *angry,* so *upset,* so illogically miserable. She lay and tossed and turned, despite her tiredness. Eventually she got up. She tripped over Lila, and found the .22 muzzle pressed to her midriff. She had to explain. Apologize. And for reasons she could not understand she found herself pouring out the whole story, and several other details which she found somehow essential to tell the younger woman.

"But he was just behind Jarian. I was scared my bullet would go right through the little creep and hit the Yak."

Tanzo blinked in the moonlight. "But... he was sitting next to me..."

"He slipped around in the dark, I suppose. It was a lot less stupid than running headlong at the little scumbag with a rock in your hands, if you don't mind my saying so."

"Are you sure..." Tanzo faltered.

"Ask Brettan. Or Mark Albeer. They both saw him."

"My God, what have I done!?" she said guiltily.

Lila shrugged. "He'll get over it. Men always do."

"Where is he sleeping?"

"Just between those rocks. See, that pointy one with the moonlight on it."

Sam Teovan wasn't asleep either. He was wrestling with himself. What a fool he been. What a damned fool. Well, even Sal had let a woman get to him once. He heard somebody stumble in the dark, heading toward him. He pulled the chisel out of his waistband. Heard a quietly placed foot crunch on the gravel he always arranged around his sleeping place. Good. He could use killing someone right now.

He moved like a striking snake. The person he had seized was surprisingly soft and small. Startled, he slackened the arm around the throat of his would-be victim. "Sam. I just came to say... I care about you too," she said, her voice held carefully steady, despite the fright she'd had. "I'll go away, now, if you'll stop pushing that knife against my ribs."

He dropped it. "My God, Locktickler, I nearly killed you!" he said thickly, taking her gently, tenderly into his arms without knowing why he did so, except that it was the right thing to do. Some part of his instinct knew this. Yet another instinct said it could get him killed. But the older instinct, that which has preserved genes over the eons, knew this was more important.

And she in turn clung to him fiercely, like a drowning person.

In the darkness the Dagger of the Goddess heard them, as he heard the other tell-tale sounds of humans in the night. He felt a detached kind of jealousy, but that was not what was troubling him. Why, when he was off-world, sent out on the most far reaching mission that the High-Priest had ever sent him out on, was he faced with the ancient evil instead? And why did the one with the crown have a human face. Was it a hallucination? Was it merely a device of Imperials, a human in a Denaari crown, to force him to reveal himself prematurely? Was it a trick of the evil ones, with demons assuming human form? But why then leave the betraying crown unhidden? Sleep was a long time in coming and it was unnaturally heavy when it came. He was still asleep in the morning when Shari took herself to interview the boy.

"My name is," a sequence of clicks and squeaky noises, "Shut-up. Sorry, that's my other half. I'm Juan Biacasta." Juan still felt pitifully weak, but he'd struggled to his feet to bow respectfully when she came to him. She'd sat him down, firmly. It was difficult to be coherent when you'd just turned sixteen... somewhere in the last few days, and were faced with a living legend. It was more difficult when you were sharing your brain with a set of alien memories. "I'm from Amritsar Station. I... er, stowed away on your ship."

So: that was no way back. It was a disappointment, but she didn't allow it to show. He explained how he'd got onto the barge, where he'd been going, and with his ears burning, why. Then the ejector capsule, and attempting to find them.

"And that?" She touched the crown. It was warm. Much warmer than the early morning air.

"It was in the ejector-seat. !whistle paa!tch, my Denaari half, died there. It's... it's his memories. I've got take it back to the vaults. For his hatchlings."

You could hear both the determination and sadness. The responsibility which had been thrust on him had been hard. But he had accepted it and emerged a man. It gave Shari a moment's pause. "You realize," she said gently, "that it was three thousand years ago? His hatchlings are dead. There isn't a place to take the crown to."

He shook his head. "The vaults are alive. They won't die even if the Denaari themselves are gone. They were grown to survive forever. They've been there for thousands and thousands of years, growing all the time. I must take !whistle paa!tch there, even if I can't bring his body for his children and loved ones to eat." He suddenly realised what he'd said. "It sounds horrid, I know, but !whistle paa!tch believed that was how you," he paused, "went on in the body as well as," he touched the crown, "in the mind."

Tanzo stared at him. She'd arrived possessively holding the bemused looking Sam's hand. "You mean that's a machine for storing Denaari memories?"

"No. It is an animal, not a machine. !whistle paa!tch's people didn't really have any machines. Everything was alive... grown. But yes, it does store memories."

"So..." she said pensively, "You wear that crown and you get all of his memories?"

"Well no. If you were Denaari it would, but it can't give it all to me. I just have seen the visual bits... smelt the smells too. It's... very confusing. Um... part of me seems to have become !whistle paa!tch. He understands... I don't."

"Still, it is a window on an alien life! It's wonderful, isn't it, Sam?"

He nodded, but Shari thought he looked doubtful and... jealous?

"Hmm. I hope you can tell us more about their planet anyway. Do you think you can walk today? We like to travel while it is still cool."

"I think so, Your Highness. My legs still felt a bit wobbly when I stood up, I'm afraid," said Juan.

"Well, if you can't walk, we'll take turns in carrying you again."

"I will try my best," he said, standing up, determined that he would manage somehow rather than make the Princess carry him. He wasn't going to let the slim girl with the short red curls who had talked to him in the pale pre-dawn carry him either. The crown fed him memories, at his recall of her face. She'd cared for him, soothed him, when he was not Juan-human, but !whistle paa!tch trapped in a confused and weak alien body. Then, the crown beast who, after all, had no understanding of the material it recorded, replayed the first time Juan had seen her, and what had transpired. Whoever 'Prince Jarian' was, he Juan, was going to smash his face in. If he was still alive. He'd run off, hadn't he?

Shari smiled at him. "Well, I must see why my other walking-wounded is not up," she said, looking worried. "Eat, not that we've got much, and drink. Then it is up-valley again. It is getting steeper, I'm afraid."

"Er, Your Highness, why up-valley? That's away from the memory-vaults. They're," he pointed at the sheer red wall of the canyon, "over there."

"Water and bits of wood come down this canyon. We hope we'll find the source of them. Perhaps there'll be sources of food there. We don't have very much left, you see. Your memory vaults may prove to be as far off and unreachable as going home is, I'm afraid."

His reply was a strange expression and a series of clicks and whistles. Then "Sorry, I... !whistle paa!tch that is, says there are no plants on this world. Or carbon-animals. Not outside the Bio-zoos."

"Oh. Well, we found a perfectly," she paused slightly, "edible snake."

Juan though of his own encounter. Blenched. Station-food was always aseptically portioned, packaged and anonymous. "You *ate* it!"

"Better than eating your father," said Lila dryly. "Like your Denaari-half did."

"The Denaari weren't cannibals, really. I mean, not like we feel about it. It was love, and, and respect. Um... There was a big Bio-zoo somewhere here. Near the way down."

"Good. Maybe the snake was an escapee."

"But we can go home. That's why I have to the get to memory vaults. They're on the edge of the pupping grounds."

"What!" He had all their attention now. Everybody gathered around him. Even Deo who had woken to sound of Alien speech.

"We can ride a Stardog home. They wait to be... I don't really understand. But the young Stardogs wait there, before they can go to space."

There was a long silence. At last Shari spoke. "That was a long time ago. I doubt if anything would be waiting now... Mind you, Stardogs are very long-lived. But anyway we have no ship to get off-world. And no Stardog barge, even if we could get off-world." It hurt to rob them of their sudden hopes.

"But we could go and look?" a pleading, whining voice. Juan looked. Recognized the face. Stepped over to Jarian, took him by the shirt, and hit him. The highly civilized Stationers frowned on physical combat. Juan had never had a real fight before, and anyway he was as weak as a cat. The Dagger of the Goddess, Martin Brettan and Mark Albeer would have rated the blow about 1.03 on a 1-10 scale.

Jarian had been hit once before in his life. That had been hard enough to frighten and stun him. This was just enough to stir the resentment that bubbled beneath his sullen exterior. This was the idiot who had cost him his power! He hit back, fortunately just as ineffectually. Mark Albeer, who happened to be closest, pulled them apart with negligent ease. "Break it up! Now, what's all this about?"

"You leave me! I'm going to pulverize him for what he wanted to do to Una!" Juan swung furiously and ineffectually.

The stocky bodyguard grinned. "First get your strength back, youth. And then see you come to me for some lessons, at least in how to make a fist. You'll break your thumb like that. Unless you want me to pulp him for you? I'd be glad to oblige."

Juan caught sight of Una. She was cowering away. He felt embarrassed and ashamed. "No. You can let go of me. I won't do anything. But I'm warning him, if he goes near her again I'll... I'll..."

"I'll give you some lessons, son," said Albeer, approvingly. "Now eat and drink. We want to move out in a few minutes."

Five minutes later they began walking, Jarian in the lead, with Shari telling Sam and Lila to swat him if he didn't move fast enough. "I'm using him as a probe, Teovan," she said quietly. "I don't like doing it, but if someone has to get hurt or killed let it be him. Quite honestly, we'd be better off without him, but we may get into a situation where we need every human. Besides, I can't just kill him, or turn him out to starve or die of thirst."

So Jarian moved ahead, thinking dark and murderous thoughts. He had a little list on which the names of Juan, Mark, Shari, Sam and Lila featured prominently, with Una and Martin Brettan as also-rans.

They walked. And climbed. Took too short a siesta for their tired bodies, and then walked and climbed and scrambled some more.

By late afternoon it was obvious they were getting closer to the source of the wood fragments. Now flood-shredded fragments were relatively frequently jammed into head-high cracks in the wall... or even higher. Just before dusk they came on three prizes. A whole dead tree, filigree roots and all, bleached white as snow, and jammed high between the narrow vertical walls, a sand-bar yellow with dry and twisted cirrith stems, stripped of seeds by something, and a bone. A long femur-bone, half-buried in the sand, stippled by little gnawing teeth.

They stopped right there for the night. It was an effort to reach the jammed tree, but the brittle-dry wood burned brightly. They'd climbed steadily from the crash-site. The night here was bitter. The fire was a delight.

The infrared flare of it was clearly visible from above. From the eternally circling satellite-traveler it was noted. It was just another data point added into the weather information that was transmitted down to Ground-Control, while the castaways slept knowing they must be near to a place where there was enough water to grow trees, where there was cirrith which was at least edible, and where big game roamed. Only Tanzo was a little uneasy about that bone, and what sort of animal it might have come from.

888 388

They were up bright and early the next morning, eager to walk on.

"Antidote time." Shari spilled the precious tablets out of their vial and onto her palm. Squinted at them. The Dagger of the Goddess was standing near at hand. She held out her hand to him. "Look. They're two different colours."

"Different batches probably," said Kadar, who was standing ready.

The Dagger looked at the tablets. Carefully he picked up the violet one. Smelt it very cautiously. He put it back in her hand. Then he took one of the other tablets. They were more mauve and far fewer in number. He sniffed these too. "Garlic. These are Ectipain antidote. The others are probably Dormantin, by the colour and complete lack of smell."

Shari's face fell. There were only a comparative few antidote tablets, presumably the ones she'd got from Deo's stock. It put the horror of decision closer. "What's Dormantin?"

"The original Mickey Finn, Princess. Knock-out pills." Martin Brettan's eyes were slit narrow, angrily staring at the ex-prince.

But Jarian too appeared shocked. "I paid nearly a quarter of a million Imperials for it.... Dormantin's cheap! They cheated me! They dared!"

"If we'd had Ectipain... and no antidote, we'd all be dead." Brettan grabbed Jarian by the remains of his fine silk shirt. "I suppose," he said slowly, "that you bought your Ectipain from the same supplier. The bulging eyed Jarian could only nod. The viscount threw him down. "Ectipain starts with the fingers and toes... not the damn stomach. You were had, and so, dammit, were we!"

Shari felt as if a huge weight had been lifted from her shoulders. She also wondered about the roughly labelled ectipain in Deo's bandolier. There had been several empty jars. It was a typical Arunachali trick. She was willing to bet there'd been nothing wrong with Jarian's supplier, just with Jarian's care of that case they'd confiscated from him. It had to have been that first night while Deo's wits had still been with him. But she said nothing of this. Just "Time to move out." Inside, however, her heart was bubbling with light and laughter. How could she have doubted him?

Martin Brettan cursed softly to himself. In his pocket rested Jarian's original vial with the two left-over tablets. A few moments ago they'd been his insurance, and incredibly valuable. He grimaced. Well, perhaps a couple of doses of a knock-out could be useful too.

After about three hours of walking the canyon opened up. Ahead a ridge, a vast mountainous ridge, towered. Already heat shimmered it into a blue-purple vague massif. A plume of smoke could be seen off toward the one edge. This was a young mountain-ridge, and still growing.

"We'll never get over that!"

"The water must come from this side, youngster."

"But the vaults must be on the other side." Juan's other half saw the mountains and flooded Juan with images of a world he loved. A world where Himalayan heights were commonplace, and where flatter areas like the ancient tectonic-plate across which the canyon cut were rare. He was still looking up when he kicked something which clattered. He looked down and screamed.

He couldn't entirely be blamed for this reaction. What he'd kicked were ribs, which had, until his foot struck them, still been attached to the rest of the skeleton. He had looked down straight into the empty eye sockets of the skull.

"A gorrilloid or something." Martin Brettan poked at a long strip of hair with a stick he'd acquired from the dead tree.

"It looks human to me," said Lila dubiously, edging away from it.

"It is too small."

"A child perhaps? Castaways like ourselves?" Shari felt pity.

Tanzo had knelt down, next to the skull, and was examining it. She shook her head. "The teeth are very worn. And I'm no anthropologist but this skull doesn't look right. I'd say ape...

She was interrupted. "Somebody stuck him, Tanzo. Stuck him in the back. Look here." Sam pointed.

A three-quarter inch thick wooden shaft protruded from the lower rib-cage. If you looked past the ribs you could see the beautifully bevelled edges of an obsidian spear blade.

The party was silent, each locked in private thoughts and horrors. Finally Tanzo spoke. "They've been here a long, long time to learn to make spear-points like that."

"And they don't have anything against sticking them into people either," Sam said looking at Shari. "Well, Capo. Now what?"

Shari shrugged. "We go on. What choice do we have? We've food for three more days, even rationing what little we have. We go carefully, that is all. With our weapons ready. We have an edge there."

They walked on up the boulder-scattered valley cautiously, but met or saw nothing human. After an uneasy siesta period and a drink, they walked on. Desert-wise people would have seen signs of life, but the castaways were too busy looking for people with spears. They rounded yet another bend in the valley and saw the great grey-black igneous cliff-wall. From a hundred or so feet up, far from the top of the cliff, a silver-bright thread of a waterfall tumbled to scatter into rainbows before it reached the bottom. And around the base of the fall and a little way into the valley was something they all found fairer than rainbows: stunted *green* bushes.

The waterfall failed to reform into a stream at the base of the cliff. It would have taken skilled mountaineers to scale the spray-damped sheer rock to the top of the waterfall. But half-way up the left-hand slope a wide ledge cut across the cliff to the top of the waterfall.

Even if it was uphill and hot, and there might be savage people with spears waiting, everybody tackled the slope with a will. The sight of green and growing things had lifted their spirits.

The bowl in which the Bio-zoo had stood, so convenient to the Geosynch-line anchor, was worth the climb to see, even had it not been cloaked in greenery. It was a valley indented into the main cliff, being perhaps fifteen miles long by three wide. There was a turquoise lake and, perhaps five miles away, an enormous pyramid-structure of pylons and semi-transparent stuff which reflected the afternoon sun like some vast smoky-yellow diamond. A second look showed that a corner had been sheared away from the huge structure. Pylons stuck jaggedly from it like broken teeth. It explained a great deal to Juan's other half. The organisms should have been self-repairing, but something had gone wrong. The creatures the Bio-zoo had held and nurtured in their artificial Eden had escaped. Some, it appeared, had flourished. It was a numbing and saddening thing for Juan-Denaari. He had somehow hoped, against all logic, that at least some of his kind had survived the Sil plague.

The pyramid was so compelling to the eye that they all failed to notice the patchwork of tiny fields by the lake-side until later.

Only Sam felt the frightened eyes that watched them from the fringe of trees, even if he could not see the watcher. The Dagger of the Goddess, however, heard the movement in the forest as the watcher slipped away.

CHAPTER 18
BETWEEN THE DEEP BLUE LAKE AND THE DEVILS

"Homo sapiens should be sued for fraud under the
trade descriptions act and for contravening
advertising standards in its choice of a name for
itself. It is obvious that Earth is our ancestral land,
from which we were forcibly removed. We want it
back."

**From the speech by Raintree Pig-ear's-daughter to the
UP congress of 2517.**

Events wait upon each other. When *anything* happens it is a result of other, often minor incidents, eventually piling up. Thus, when things finally do start to happen they tend to cascade. The heat output of the fire of the previous night was so atypical of the normal geothermal events recorded by the eternally circling traveler-satellite and sent to Ground Control, that Ground Control eventually referred it to Central.

Central snappily demanded a reply to its earlier communication. Seven point two microseconds later it got it. Then it tied this to the tracking record that sector civil defense biocomputer had pestered it with. The analysis was so stunning that Central actually paused for .038 microseconds to re-analyze. Survivors. Or the ancient enemy or... a remote possibility, something else. It could effectively dismiss the last two possibilities. The probability of other aliens using a Stardog approached zero. It opened long-unused priority transmission frequencies to the sector Delat civil defense biocomputer, to Ground-Control, as well as to several other Command Centers. Depression was forgotten, along with the analysis in microscopic detail of Vault-data. Central had something to live for. Or was it something to die for?

Information from sector Delat civil defense biocomputer came in, without Central even reacting to the snippy 'I-told-you-so-but-you-wouldn't-listen' tone from the unit. For the first time in millennia, Central had to plan a reaction which wasn't pre-programmed.

It did something which no mechanical computing system could have done.

It dithered. Wasted 2.1 microseconds.

●●●●●●

Central wasn't the only being having trouble making up its mind. Shari had focused her effort on getting them all to water and food. She hadn't really thought about what they'd do when they got there. Jarian was in some ways far ahead of her. He'd been stealing things against this moment. He had a head-light, a pipe-soldering blow-torch, Brettan's lighter and a kitchen knife. It was pity he couldn't get a gun, or even his poisons-case. But with what he had he was ready to set himself up as a God-king.

"I suppose we'd better go down to those fields. Try for a peaceful meeting with the locals. If you're right, Sam, they already know we are here." Shari and the others were distracted, with no one chasing the ex-prince to front. He slipped to the back, and then away into the forest they were skirting. It was more than ten minutes before anyone noted his absence.

It was Una who noticed, and who pointed it out to Juan. He in turn pointed it out to Mark. The bodyguard called the rest of the party to a halt.

"Bugger the little snot." Sam was irritated. He hadn't got as much sleep as his body felt it needed the last few nights. If it was up to him Jarian would have been dead after they'd recovered the supposed antidote.

Shari felt much the same way. Still, she felt she had a duty to all of them. "Who saw him last, and where were we?"

"He said he needed to relieve himself, um... I think we'd just passed those tall trees there," volunteered Johannes, the tail-ender.

They went back in a tight group, Johannes Wienan making absolutely sure that he was no longer tail-end Charlie. Lila, with her youthful experience of tracking strayed sheep on the ramshackle-fenced farm of her childhood, had no trouble following Jarian's footsteps in the leaf mould. After a few minutes in the dense forest Shari called a halt. "We might as well go back to walking along the forest edge. This is hellish going, and it is obvious he ran off, and wasn't ambushed or captured. Well, what I say is, if he wants to go, let him."

Everybody agreed, some of them very forcefully.

ᴏᴇᴄᴐᴆᴄ

Jarian found his journey to triumphal rule, even enlivened with graphic plans for the unpleasant demise of the rest of the castaways, harder than he'd imagined. Getting away had been easy. Walking through the forest was not.

The bio-zoo had obviously not held all the species of the visited worlds. This had been but one of fifty-two of these treasure houses. Its focus had been on carbon-based animal life. The plants were incidentals, cage furnishing. But the Denaari were master-ecologists. The cage furnishings had been remarkably complete. When the major quake and flooding had occurred many of the specimens had been killed. Others had had their numbers reduced to such an extent that they became extinct. The cage furniture however... ask any zoo-keeper. Such plants as are chosen for this role are tough. And natural selection had made the survivors even tougher. The jungle resultant from the escapee plant-survivors of fifty-two worlds was the stuff of nightmares. It was still tame compared to some of the beasts that stalked there. The first Denaari expedition to Earth had brought back the most deadly creature that the explorers had ever found. An animal more dangerous than wolverlope or archo-ligers.

These creatures ruled the forest now, with something far more deadly than any claw or fang: Brains.

Jarian's previous experience of heavy forest had been the Imperial gardens. Not creepers laden with thorns, and worse, a creeper that slithered off when he put his hand on it. He was sure the others must have heard that shriek. That gave him impetus to push through the immense tangle of springy fireleaf underbrush.

He of course didn't recognize the nettle-equivalent from Sofala II. He didn't even understand why his hands and face were coming up in burning angry red weals. He just knew it was all going wrong. He was menaced by an arachnodeltid, its upraised fangs dripping toxin, and ran backward straight into a hook-and-stab bush. Scratched, bleeding, burning from the fireleaf, Jarian would happily have rejoined the party he'd planned to abuse, torture and kill... except that he was already lost. Then he stumbled onto a game trail. This was easier to walk along, even if he still didn't know where he was going. He kept it up for ten minutes, getting deeper into the forest.

●●C ϽΘΘ

The three hunters had come to check their traps. They were unaware of what the gasping lookout was panting out to the village matriarchs three miles away. The ledge-access was usually watched for a few weeks after anyone had fled into the desert. Sometimes those exiled tried to come back. Nothing good came out of the desert.

The hunters heard Jarian blundering along the path. The animal must be either sick or wounded to make so much noise. They waited. Meat tonight!

The animal was like none they'd ever seen before. Pasty with lank yellow fur on its head, and the rest of its integument odd.... scales. It must be fine, fine scales on a loose skin. The creature seemed to be in moult, by the ragged bits. But it shambled upright. It walked like one of the people, even if its face was amazingly, monstrously ugly. They watched as it came closer and closer to the trap. And then... it stopped. Moaned piteously. Produced a water bottle and drank.

Silver-tip Wildscallion's son was well known as the bravest of his folk. He could see the animal was perhaps going to get away. "I will taunt it," he said, stepping onto the path, gripping his spear tightly.

●●C ϽΘΘ

Jarian stared, his eyes bulging. It... it couldn't be! How had these crash survivors slipped that far from civilisation... from the human norm? Then he pulled himself together. Well, they'd be glad to have a handsome, wise ruler like himself. And with the smack of firm governance, he could make something even of fur-clad low-browed chinless wonders like this. Perhaps he would keep that Leaguesman who had wielded the whip so well on Brettan. Jarian took out the pipe-soldering torch and the lighter. "I

200

am your new chief, sent to you by the gods from my home in the sky," he announced pompously.

❦❦❦❦❦❦

Silver-tip had been joined by his two fellow hunters. They didn't want Silver-tip to be able to claim all the credit in the boasting. They were puzzled by the creature's noises.

"Do you think it is trying to talk?" whispered Fireleaf to Silver-tip.

They were obviously, thought Jarian, overawed by him. They were probably the descendants of castaways from centuries back. Well, he'd start as he meant to go on. With them respectfully frightened. "I have very strong magic. Watch."

He lit the blow-torch and the three wide-eyed hunters scrambled back. He advanced, laughing. The thin sticks holding up the cover of broad leaves so carefully covered by scattered leaf mould gave way. Jarian's triumphal laughter ended abruptly on the sharpened stakes below.

It had never occurred to him that the hunters might not understand a word he said. But then, the *Homo neanderthalis* brought here by Denaari ships for their Bio-zoo nearly forty thousand years ago didn't speak his language.

❦❦❦❦❦❦

It had taken a long time for the other castaways to skirt the forest, walking along the edge of a hard sill that sub-irrigated the forest with ground water from the mountains. Then they followed the largely dry river bed to the lake-shore, beside which the patchwork fields were scattered. At first they couldn't see anyone.

Then Juan spotted someone darting from one of the huts. Running for cover. But not running away from the castaways. Advancing on them. Otto barked, his fur standing on end.

"We've got to get out of here!" said Sam. He shuddered. "They'll eat us." A vision, a stark *real* vision of being alive but helpless while a cheerful group of Neanderthal women flayed the skin off his Tanzo, washed across him. He knew with absolute certainty that that was what would happen if they failed to run now. "Run!" He said in a fierce undervoice, "Run for those rocks."

"But..."

"Run!" Shari had spotted flankers to their right.

At this point three triumphant hunters, deep in the boasts they planned for the punyatchet this evening, emerged from the forest, at a point about midway between the village and the castaways. On a pole between two of them hung Jarian's limp and bloody body, suspended by the hands and feet. His head, hanging at an odd angle, was half severed.

The hunters dropped their catch and ran to join the rest of the people. Their chagrin was great. All that hard work which had gone into preparing boasts was wasted. None of the girls would be interested in them now.

A hail of stones and a few spears were flung at the castaways. The Viscount was struck on the temple by a stone. He staggered. Then he stopped. Took his pistol out, and stood like a marksman. Fired.

There was a scream, and another ragged shower of spears. "Come on, Martin. You can shoot from cover!"

Instead he waited. The next target presented itself and he fired again. There was no scream this time, but he was sure he'd hit. There were still spears and stones being flung, but there were no visible targets now. He legged it after the rest of them, blood streaming down his face. The cluster of rocks at the lake-side seemed too far.

They made it. It was not the ideal shelter, the rocks being rounded and low and offering next to no shade. But there was a flood-scoured rock-sheet plain in front of them, and the lake at their backs.

"They're no strangers to fighting," said Martin Brettan as Caro dressed his head.

"There seemed to be fields up-valley too. There are probably several villages. They may fight amoungst themselves."

"They're damned good at keeping out of sight," said Mark, peering over a rock, looking for the source of the stone-tipped spear that had shattered against his shelter. Indeed, their attackers moved like ghosts. They were predators, after all. The most deadly predators, winnowed by a natural selection process harsher than any other.

Brettan felt his ribs gingerly. Nodded. "They're skilled hunters. Come nightfall and we'll all be dead meat."

Shari was still stunned by the sight of young Jarian's body. She'd despised him, but... "I'm out of ideas. What do you all think we should do next?"

Tanzo shrugged. "All I can suggest is talking to them. We can shout from here, without getting speared."

"All right," said Shari tiredly. "Try it Tanzo. Tell the monkey-men we mean them no harm. Tell them we're also castaways, just as they are. They must surely at least have stories about it."

Tanzo tried. Unfortunately oral history, while longer-lasting than written history, had not survived 40 000 years. And these weren't castaways, they were captives. Their oral tradition was about the destruction of Eden, and having to flee from its snake, into the wilderness. Anyway, they thought animals crazy enough to run into a herd of snoozing petrovores were probably just baying in their insanity. Neanderthal speech, which was long on sibilants, gutturals and clicks sounded nothing like that. They continued to fling rocks. Sooner or later that would wake the petrovores. The only one who was dissatisfied with this stratagem was Fireleaf. He decided to count coup in a quicker manner. Perhaps he could use some of the boasts he had planned after all.

"Could we swim across? Get away to the other side, perhaps?" asked Juan tentatively.

At this point the lake was not very wide. Perhaps 300 yards of blue separated them from the other bank. "It's an idea," said Shari. "If we slipped into the water in the dusk, and swam across…"

"I can't swim," Lila said regretfully. Water, in that quantity, had never been a feature of her life as a debt-slave or farm-girl from the semi-desert of New Texas.

"Me neither." Sam looked out between the rocks at the azure water.

Tanzo signed to Una. The girl shook her head. "She can't swim, and I couldn't swim that far," Tanzo added.

"Besides, if they spot us, we'll be sitting ducks in the water."

Shari made a wry face. "I suppose the good swimmers could take the non-swimmers across."

Sam had continued staring at the water. "Look. What's that?"

Whatever it was, they were not going to be swimming. All they could see of it was a head with cold reptilian soup-plate sized eyes staring back at them. The head was the size of a dinner-table and the long snout held far too many teeth. Sharp teeth.

For a moment they stared at it. Then, without a ripple, the head disappeared back into the water. They could dimly make out a huge dark shape sliding away into the depths.

There was a collective exhalation. "Next idea, anyone?"

Fireleaf had chosen to sneak closer along the waterline as soon as he saw the Mega-ichthyodile. It was sure to distract the attention of the strange animals. What a coup! How he would brag. He wouldn't be surprised if one of the matriarchs themselves took him. He stepped around the petrovore's bulk, as Shari said 'anyone', his spear ready.

The Dagger of the Goddess had seen the demon in the water. He was wondering at its meaning, when it was abruptly made clear to him. It was a vision. A warning of the evil that stalked within the man he had to kill and become. Amadeo Cerros was no innocent servant. He was a spy and a murderer. A foulness who killed for money and pleasure. The Dagger had been thorough in his research of the man.

When Fireleaf stepped around the rock the Dagger of the Goddess did not see a young Neanderthal with too much testosterone for his own good. He saw a man to whom the Dewa would refuse rebirth. Amadeo Cerros. A man he must kill and become. Fireleaf's chance of boasting his way to in between a matriarch's thighs died, before he could push the spear forward.

Deo began the cleansing, ignoring the dead. Only Shari heard him say, "Tenfold be your damnation in the pit, Amadeo Cerros."

Amadeo Cerros. Shari swallowed. She knew that the next person he had gone to kill had been herself. Her neck felt vulnerable and exposed.

Tanzo stared at the body. Wished desperately she'd paid more interest to anthropology. But it had always seemed so tame compared to the alien Denaari. There was something about the heavy, short-bodied hairy man that she ought to understand.

The close proximity to the killing had horrified Una. She clung to Juan and sobbed. The boy was fairly horrified himself. What was that man in grey? Some kind of robotic-killing machine? He moved his back up against one of the round boulders. It throbbed. A Juan-Denaari memory plucked insistently at him. Rounded rocks. Rounded rocks that throbbed... They weren't rocks! "We've got get away from here. These rocks... they're petrovores! They're alive! They're going to wake up and start feeding. We've got to run!"

"What!?" This was one crisis too many for Shari on top of what Deo had just said.

The young stationer grabbed her hand and pressed it against the rock. She felt it throb. "It is alive! They'll liquify the ground here and start to feed any minute now!"

Sam obviously felt something too. "Yeah. This place is turning bad. We gotta chance it, Princess-Capo. Soon."

One of the Petrovores groaned, and then began to hum and vibrate visibly. Shari looked for a way out. Their foes were mainly hidden in the dead reeds of the flood margin. These were thickest back towards the waterfall. There was only one route that would not force them to run through this. That was up valley, towards the towering golden structure. "The pyramid. It is our only chance."

The broken corner of the Bio-Zoo was at least a mile off. But the ground was flat and open, with little cover for Neanderthal ambushes. Several more of the rounded rocks moved, and groaned. The humming became almost overpowering. The ground began to shiver.

They ran, Shari carrying Otto. Spears and rocks flailed at them. And then they were in the open, running desperately for the broken corner. The Neanderthals ran too. Not after them but towards the forest margin, to cut them off. It never occurred to the locals that any creature would voluntarily run into the Pyramid. When they saw where the party was headed, they were astounded. The snake was still resident in Eden. No animal, no matter how alien, could be stupid enough to run in there, surely? The average Neanderthal outcast would not have hesitated to choose the desert, before venturing into that place. The Neanderthals were the most dangerous creatures outside... but inside, trapped inside by its bulk, was something worse. Far worse.

Panting and exhausted, bleeding and bruised, the little band of castaways reached the huge golden structure with profound relief.

"They've stopped chasing us at least." Tanzo pointed back. "They're all standing back there at the trees."

"They probably regard this place as a holy temple or something." Johannes panted, looking about. This part didn't look very temple-like. Debris outside had plainly blown in and fragments of the shattered pyramid-stuff and pieces of twisted pylon also lay about.

Sam shook his head, trying to clear it. A rock had hit his ear back there. This place didn't feel good.

"Stop shaking your head like that, Sam. You're splattering blood on me." Tanzo held his head still and examined the cut. "You'll live, lover. Here, press this against it." She handed him a folded strip torn from her petticoat.

From outside they heard ululation. "It sounds like they're getting their courage up. We'd better move further in and find a defendable spot."

Cautiously, through shattered chambers between twisted girders, they made their way deeper and deeper into the vast structure. Golden light streamed in and vegetation grew wildly, a mixture of types from various empire worlds. Yet there were no signs of animal life. It was not difficult going though. There were huge, wide smooth trails, twisting and turning but easy to follow through the various chambers. Now, further in, they found that they were on the bottom storey of the vast pyramid. Obviously there were many layers above this. They moved through an impact-shattered piece of wall into yet another chamber.

This was dryland. Scattered ink-berry bushes, fruit laden, and tufts of turpentiny grass. Even the light changed. It was squinting bright in here. The trail in the sand was full of tiny ripples. Lila looked suspiciously at it. This place was agonizingly like home, but she'd never seen a track like that. Could it be that of some kind of alien vehicle? Her grip on the .22 pistol tightened.

They moved into yet another chamber. Now the light was distinctly green and muted. The plants that flourished here were purple-black of foliage. Martin Brettan peered at the odd-shaped frilly leaves, the coiled and twisted fronds. "I've never seen or heard of anything like this. This is no empire world's vegetation, I'll swear."

"I must admit I have never seen anything like it either," said Shari.

Juan's Denaari knowledge drifted upward in a flood of images. "There were other places. Worlds explored but not on Stardog routes… maybe this was from one of those?"

"What gets me is that there aren't any animals. The bushes back there were full of inkberry. Normally the jeroos strip them, even before most of the berries are ripe," said Lila warily. "And what is this track?"

"What strikes me is that this Denaari installation is still functioning. Yes, it is damaged, but it is still functioning. Some of those trees outside must be hundreds of years old. Yet this place still has functioning light and water and nutrient control. The track, I suppose, is for some kind of maintenance vehicle," said Tanzo peering at it.

"But it is so quiet in here. It worries me. Out there you could hear, well, birds and things. This place makes me uncomfortable." Caro looked nervously around.

"Yeah. I don't like this place," said Sam. "What's that noise now?"

It was a clicking, slithering sound, coming from where they'd been. "It must be those damn ape-men getting their courage up and coming after us. Quick. Let's move on."

There is a world orbiting a small reddish sun near Pleides. It is a rich, verdant world. Life is abundant here, and predation is fierce. The dominant predator is the frill-snake hydra. They get quite large, with an arm-length of, say, ninety feet or so. They don't have determinate growth, so, if it was not for a seasonal infestation of blood-parasites they could go on growing forever. The parasites, by clogging arteries, slow blood-flow to the brain of the Hydra. That is not serious in the smaller, shorter-armed beasts. But the bigger ones are seriously slowed down by anoxia. The smaller ones never give anoxia a chance to kill the really big ones. Instead, as soon as the big ones slow down, the littler ones eat them.

Then, as winter comes, the parasites in the poikilothermic hydras become gonad-sacs, then burst and fill the frill-snake hydra's blood with gametes. Fertilization in the sea of gametes is inevitable and the zo-oolites are excreted by the beasts, often onto the low frond-grass favoured by the polykapi, the grazer which are the favored food of the hydras. The parasites have their winter life-stage in the liver-kidney of the polykapi. The polykapi in turn return the parasites to the predators to complete the life cycle.

In summer polykapi don't have parasites. In winter frill-snake Hydras don't. The Denaari collectors had of course stocked the Bio-zoo with both Polykapi and Frill-snake hydra. Only they hadn't collected them in the same hemisphere. The parasite never made it to the Denaari Eden, unfortunately. And the largest of the hydras, having eaten all its smaller compatriots, had just kept right on growing. The Bio-zoo provided living things with essential nutrients. But the hydra preferred live food. It had eaten everything animal in its domain, even the smallest, and most indigestible alien creature.

The barrel body-pod of the hydra was huge now. So big it was effectively jammed between the floor and the ceiling. The body-pod also now occupied most of the controlled environment cage. The hydra could never move from here. Only its forty-eight arm-heads could search the corridors and punch into cages in the Hydra's unending quest for live food. The arm-heads were only seven hundred yards long. As yet there were a few controlled environment cages at the top of the Pyramid which it couldn't get to, but the rest of the pyramid was within reach.

The paths they had followed were the squirm-tracks of the

arm-heads as they slithered endlessly through the ruined bio-zoo, their sense-organ frills spread wide to detect even the faintest prey-sign. The arm-head slithered through what was left of the New Texas environment cage from which the Condor-harpies, diamond-backs and jeroos had escaped to help populate the outside world. It raised itself briefly, twitching the frill. Fourteen lifeforms. It could smell-taste even the rat in Juan's pocket. A nerve-message went back to the body-pod. Other head-arms were pushed out, slithering along different routes to the chamber where the castaways were now.

●●●◌●◌

Otto gave the alarm, making them turn in time to stop somebody being eaten.

"It's a snake! The biggest snake in the world! That's what these tracks are. Hell!" The hydra arm-head that had picked up the scent of their passage in the semi-desert of the New Oz room slithered slowly forward. Herding the prey, toward the other hastening arm-heads which were slithering at top speed toward the green-lit chamber.

The Dagger of the Goddess stared at the eyeless head. At the mouth full of three-pronged teeth. At the enormous flapping frill around it. The mouth must have been fully fifteen feet wide in its gape. What demon thing was this? Mark Albeer stood beside him and fired, straight into the gaping maw.

He might as well have patted the creature, for all the difference it made. The mouth was not a true mouth leading to a gastro-intestinal tract. That was back at the body-pod. The pseudo-mouth merely held prey and crushed them. Many of the hydra's natural prey animals had been armoured with spikes and spines. The pseudo mouth was surrounded with a thick, tough gristle-layer. In a hydra this large that was nearly three feet thick, and there was nothing vital behind that anyway.

Lila's hands shook hopelessly. Her shot hit the frill. And the arm-head writhed and pulled back. Even the body-pod reacted. It had not felt such pain for a thousand years. It sent another three arms slithering along to the body of the injured one to back it up. When the questing head began to come forward again, it was cautiously.

"That frill," shouted Shari. "That must be its eyes." Actually the frill was a great deal more, but it wasn't a bad guess.

The Dagger of the Goddess ran and sprang, as the great maw shot forward. Somehow he managed to get onto the snake-neck, behind the frill. He clung with his legs and stabbed with a long wavy-bladed knife in each hand. The scales were diamond hard, so he slashed at the frill. The arm-head went wild as its senses were slashed away, rearing up and twisting and tossing itself into a furious and desperate arc, trying to reach its attacker. No rodeo rider could have hoped to stay on for more than a few seconds. The man in grey somehow managed to cling for yet another desperate slash, before he was flung away like a piece of spume in a storm-wind. Had he hit anything hard Deo would have died, broken. Instead he landed in masses of dark-purple coils of sponge-fronds. Damage was still enough to drive the nano-surgeon within nearly frantic.

The pseudo-mouth could not scream in agony. But the enraged bellow that erupted from body-pod was so loud that even the ululating Neanderthals, nearly a mile and half away, were stilled. The now sensorially stripped arm-head backed away hastily, the mouth threatening vaguely in the wrong direction.

"Deo!" Shari scrambled through the thick undergrowth, to where he lay. The holy assassin sat up, looking dazed. He put the one knife he still held away, without ceremony, and looked for the other, swaying. Shari saw it. Knowing how sharp it was she carefully picked it up by the hilt and gave it to him. A coin-sized piece was sheared out of the finest folded Damascus steel. The man was horrified. His right forearm was also obviously broken but, by comparison, he seemed unconcerned by this. He allowed Shari to put the arm into a crude sling. She winced, seeing the odd angle of the arm and the limpness of the fingers.

Several of the others had also run to help, and between Shari and Mark Albeer they got Deo back on his feet and back to the wide trail.

"Oh God! There are three more of them!" shouted Kadar, who had been staring down the trail of the retreating head-arm. He was right. Three more 'snakes' were nosing their way forward, one on the trail, and the others cracking their way through the underbrush.

"Come on! The other way!"

They fled. "Up!" shouted Sam. "We must go up!" They hurried through another hydra-punched hole and into a dry savannah landscape, complete with Erzulie's famous porcupine trees. And another 'snake'. Martin Brettan wrenched off one of the long, straight spine-branches, and ran at the open mouthed monster. He didn't try to spear it with the razor tip of the porcupine-tree branch. Instead he belaboured the frill with it.

It reared away and struck at him. He dodged back. Several of the others had grabbed branches by this time, and they joined him beating at the frill. The hydra roared again and pulled back. But they had scant time to celebrate their victory. The three arm-heads from the previous chamber were catching up. They tried assaulting the frills of these ones too, but the three defended each other.

"Hurry!" shouted Caro. "That one that Martin hit is coming back with some others." They fled again, deeper into the pyramid. Dodging the questing frill-snake arms they found a spiral ramp. Up they went, panting, hitting out at the frills of the snaky heads pursuing them, pausing briefly to try to defend a level, beating at the heads of the fifteen arm-heads now after them. Then another 'snake' appeared, already on that level. They were forced upward again.

Frill-Snake Hydras are not very intelligent. But even the stupidest predator could have understood that the prey was heading for the one part of the pyramid it could not quite reach. Arm-heads were sent squiggling up through smashed ceilings to block the cargo-ramp access to the uppermost level. Nineteen of them waited at the up-ramp mouth when the castaways struggled up onto the platform of the second to highest level. They fled into the Prala V equatorial Taiga. The Hydra didn't like this level much. This level was cold-worlds. Thermo-control still worked partially and the cold slowed the arm-heads. But at least here it could hunt down the prey at its leisure.

CHAPTER 19
CONTACT

The view from the top is inevitably of a higher place.
The view from the bottom is inevitably of whoever is
on top, which is all right if you happen to like them.

The Indigo Kama Sutra.

Several hundred yards from the up-ramp in a small clearing dotted with tiny ice-flowers they stopped, more from exhaustion than for any other reason. "Do you think," pant, pant, "we're safe here?" Johannes was not the only one of the party stumbling with exhaustion and hunger, but he was one of the worst off. His laziness, and the unfitness that had resulted from this, were destroying him.

Lila was still too breathless to speak at this stage. She shook her head, and pointed down. The trail they'd run down through the thickets of praspruce trees was plainly a snake's one.

"We're doomed!" Kadar lamented.

"Oh shut up, you fuckin' streak of misery," said Sam. "Look Capo. The only safe place is up."

"How do you know, Yak?" snapped Martin Brettan.

"It's obvious, you idiot," Tanzo replied for him, her steel showing. "Why else do you think the creatures were trying to stop us going up there?"

Caro shivered and leaned against the bodyguard. The bodyguard's stolid brain ticked over as he put an arm around her. "You mean," he said slowly, "the environment up there might be something that the snakes can't deal with?"

"Probably too hot. Or if they're like any other snakes, too cold."

"If it is going to be colder I could use a fire. My feet are freezing," said Caro snuggling closer.

Juan snapped his fingers. He still had Una's arm round his shoulders. He'd staggered, and nearly fallen in one of their closer encounters. She'd rushed in and lifted him. She'd hung on to him. She was used to being scared, but somehow the Prala V environment disturbed her deeply. "That's it! Fire! Um... In a vid I watched... The Revenge of the Mutant Kandrags... the hero fought the monsters off these with burning sticks."

"This isn't exactly a vid-nasty... but it is worth trying. Anything's worth trying at this stage," said Shari grimly. "Come on everybody. Gather some dry stuff. It's no use just standing and waiting for the snakes."

The under branches of Praspruce are sheltered by the conical layers above them. There was an abundant supply of dry twigs and needle-leaves there. Praspruce has a high resin content. It burns easily, with hot and smoky eagerness. Martin wasn't able to light the bonfire pile however, as his lighter was conspicuous by its absence. A search of Mark Albeer's pack revealed that the pipe-soldering torch was missing. It was fairly obvious who had taken them, if too late to do anything more than wish stomach aches on the Neanderthals who ate Jarian. Fortunately, Deo was able to light the pile of twigs when Shari asked him. It apparently had not occurred to him to offer.

The heat-sensors cells in the frill detected the fire from a quarter of a mile off. Excitement as well as predatory hunger flared in the small mind of the hydra. The head-arm didn't pause, or attack with the degree of caution it had previously displayed. Instead it struck with all the eagerness that the super-attractor called for. The fire was gone in a gulp, leaving Mark Albeer immensely relieved that the bunch of twigs he'd been trying to make a torch from had gone out.

The snake-creature did not appear at all distressed by having eaten the fire. It didn't appear damaged either. In fact there was considerable damage, but the lining of the pseudo-mouth had no nerve endings. Instead the frill-snake head calmly slithered back, to go and deposit a pile of burnt sticks in the ground-floor maw of the hydra body-pod.

The party stood stunned, looking at where their fire had been. Tanzo's quick mind was the first to assimilate what had happened and see in it a way to get past the blockade of snakes at the up-ramp. "We'll draw them out with fires. They'd rather attack fires than us. There are about thirty of them... so far. If we make a whole lot of little fires we can make for the ramp."

They'd done it. And it had worked. But if only the Denaari had been less efficient in organizing fire-prevention. They were all soaked to the skin. The other thing, thought Shari, as she shivered, that she could use besides dry clothes, a good meal and a safely anonymous existence on a distant planet, was some ear plugs. The body-pod of the frill-snake hydra was expressing its anger at being fed piles of charred sticks, and its frustration at being unable to reach its prey in terrible howls and bellows. The ramp was blocked solidly with snake-heads, opening and closing mouths full of wicked teeth. There seemed to be some that were burned quite badly. But there were still forty of them. At least they came no further.

Compared to the immense ground floor the top level of the pyramid was tiny, a mere forty thousand square yards. The enviro-cages here were still intact, and populated with creatures from various Denaari-colonized worlds. The transparent walls were obviously some kind of one-way glasslike substance. The animals appeared ignorant of being observed by non-Denaari invaders. As yet they'd found no way into any of the cages. The food they could see contained within was as unreachable as if it had been on the moon.

They eventually found an access to the outside, a huge sliding panel where the flying Denaari must have entered the Bio-zoo. Below them they could see the forest-choked valley, tiny fields, the towering mountains and the distant desert all trailed with the long shadows of evening. Looking up at the distant mountains, Shari saw how the last of the sunlight briefly caught a thin razor-slash line from the red-trimmed mountains up into the purple darkness.

eececeee

Central had settled on using three cargo transports. The animals were rather dim for the job. One was loaded with such medical repair beasts as Central's cold vaults still had in store.

The other two had missiles and energy projectors hastily fitted. All had direct-link auxiliary bio-comp units roughly cobbled onto the huge cargo-lifters' thought-centers. It had been two hours since Central had finally become aware of the castaways. The transmissions from Rat had come from some distance away from the bio-zoo then. Now they appeared to be right inside it.

While the cargo-transports were in their laboriously slow flight across the mountains Central accessed the file-records from the Bio-zoo. Central was not competent to understand why the records made it uncomfortable. It didn't really understand guilt. It determined that when this mess was sorted out the stupid little Bio-zoo could have at least some of the resources it asked for. If the Bio-zoo still existed then: Central was seriously weighing up the proposal from Ground-Control for dropping a nuclear device onto the whole structure.

Nucleonics were one of the things that contact with the Sil had taught the Denaari. But they'd never actually used the devices they'd built. Considering the degree of misunderstanding about the engineering process, that was just as well. But Central didn't know that. Central had decided that if it proved to be alien saboteurs, and the weapons dispatched proved inadequate... well, at the first sign of problems Ground-control had the missiles ready. The bio-zoo was only 48.3 seconds away from nuclear destruction.

Central attempted for the 326th time to establish communication with the Bio-zoo's brain. And was rewarded for its patience. It rapidly began wishing it hadn't been. The points in favour of Ground-control's proposal increased.

Firstly, there was the reality of the situation at the bio-zoo: Only 1.72% of the total environmental display area was still intact and functional. A massive earthquake had sheared off the one corner of the bio-zoo unit and damaged or destroyed 17.9% of the enviro-cages. If that wasn't bad enough, one of the specimens had subsequently destroyed the most of the cages and consumed most of the rest of the specimens. And the stupid Bio-zoo's brain had been too apathetic to do *anything* about it.

Secondly, if Central followed Ground-control's recommendation, it would stop the Bio-zoo's interminable whining about it all being Central's fault. On top of it all, although the Bio-zoo could give Central internal vision on all the envirocages, there were no eyes in the service and observation corridors. That must be where the transmitter signal was coming from, because the

Bio-zoo's cage-eyes showed Central nothing but devastation, an incandescently angry hydra and a few well-kept envirocages on the top level. There'd been a fire on the penultimate level, which the Bio-zoo had successfully dealt with by altering the precipitation regime. Fires sounded like saboteurs, not survivors.

●●●ᗝ●●

"We might as well eat what we have. There must be a way of getting at the food inside those chambers." said Shilo Kadar.

"Eat and sleep," said Martin Brettan with a cracking yawn. "It's been a hellish day. But at least we have found a sanctuary at last. The snakes don't seem to be able to get up here, and those stone-age monkey types can't get past the snakes."

Shari looked at the fast-gathering darkness outside. Already it was dim in the high-roofed corridor. "Let's eat then. But we must still ration what we have. Do you mind organizing that, Martin? I just want to have a look at this arm."

The Dagger of the Goddess was passive as she gently undid the sling. She was not to know that his confused mind was still pondering the symbolism of the breaking of the holy blade. Or that he felt he ought to recognize her. Not as the Dewa... but as someone human, and close to him. Someone beloved and someone he would have to kill.

The arm was straight. Within it the slave-units of the nanomech surgeon had been busy with prodigious engineering feats. Their host did not know this. It astounded Shari. "It was bent..."

"You ought to splint it," said Mark Albeer. "Here, Princess. I've still got a few pieces of straightish stick. It looks as if you've got it nicely in position." So the arm, already plated from within, was splinted and strapped on the outside too.

They ate by the glow of a lumitube. The moons were not yet up, and Shari had vetoed a fire. She hadn't forgotten the sudden wetting that their fires had brought them earlier. Then they were in the dark, with only the stars. There was a squalling howl from below. "Snakes sounding miserable again," said Sam, feeling uneasy.

Then the roof light-strips came on. As Central had intended, when it had told Bio-zoo to do this, the castaways where blinded by the sudden intensity of it. The Bio-zoo opened the sliding portal as the cargo-transporter slid level with it. Two heavy-duty stevedore beasts controlled by brain-auxiliary units disembarked, carrying energy projectors. Central was worried about those energy projectors. The energy projector beasts were old and distinctly cantankerous.

The other cargo-vessel had entered the lower door of the Bio-zoo. It had met a questing head-arm. The hydra, angry with the proceedings of the day had attempted to attack the craft for moving, even if the silicon and metallo-chitin lifeforms on it were unsuitable prey. It had received a sound chastisement... from the Bio-zoo, via the roof of the chamber in which the body-pod reposed. Now two more of the stevedore beasts were approaching from the other end of the corridor. The humans were caught like rats in a trap.

●●●○●●

Otto gave the alarm, before pressing against his mistress's leg. It was indeed something to be alarmed by: The creatures were the size of rhinoceroses. They were bright blue, with at least ten tree-trunk legs and an equal number of thick ropy arms, with huge grab-like hands. These hands held things which could only be guns of some sort. They looked rather like blunderbusses made of green and purple plasticine by a demented epileptic, but something about them said 'deadly'. On top of the spoon-heads of the beasts sat the vermilion hedgehog-helmet brain-auxiliary units, controlling their vast mounts with difficulty. Stevedore-beasts are stupid, and very good at simple routine tasks. They were jittery and uncomfortable in this role. It was all the brain-auxiliary units could do to stop them from placing the energy-projectors on their cargo pallets until it was time to unload them. When it came to actually discharging the projectors the beasts would have to stand still. They didn't handle cargo while they were moving. Rabbits would have had more potential as warriors.

The enormous blue creatures halted. The guns came up slowly. The images transmitted back to Central were not encouraging. The creatures were bipedal and wingless. This compared to the images of the Sil on file. The Sil had been taller and four-armed, and sky blue. Perhaps there were color variations? Perhaps the arms were hidden. Through the mouth of the brain-auxiliary Central addressed the humans with its limited Sil vocabulary.

It was a mistake. The nano-surgeon connected to the Dagger of the Goddess's ear heard the booming command to surrender or die. The Sil response to such a challenge was always aggression. The control circuits damaged when the host had been struck on the head by the pipe had not been fully repaired. The huge network of myriads of nano-hair filaments would still take months to fix completely. The nano-surgeon could manage to force the host to make a few coarse movements. However the degree of fine motor-control that made the host into a deadly killer was out. But there was enough control to make the host do something it was already largely committed to.

The holy assassins kill with their hands. The will of Dewa's dark incarnation is best served by the hands and her holy trinity of the two sacred knives and the strangling- scarf. The assassin should be close enough for the victim to touch. Killing at a distance verges on the sacrilegious, and is a domain reserved for cowards. Yet, as one of many aspects of the training that the assassins receive, they are taught to handle projectile weapons and lasguns.

The laser-unit the Dagger carried was not quite identical to the one with which he had trained. The best the Empire sold were single-shot units, and bulky at that. The one the Temple had provided for him had aspects of engineering about it that had fascinated the Stationer-engineers who had dissected it. The Sil had managed to make a hand weapon which had been capable of three discharges of infinitesimally short duration. After station engineers had finished with it, it could fire five times, before needing to be recharged. However the Dagger did not know that... any more.

The Dagger fired left-handed with precision that would have done the Nano-surgeon proud. There was no reason that he could not use the plated right arm, except that the sling was in the way. Within three point two seconds he had shot three brain-auxiliary units. That was too fast for the lumbering stevedores. A few energy projectors were discharged, balls of incandescent red flying about wildly and ploughing ineffectually into the surrounding, pyramid crystal, filling the passage with smoke. It was still ridiculously slow to Central. Before the third shot was fired the nuclear warheads were on their way.

Juan was unused to things happening so fast. He was still half asleep and the man in the grey had already shot three of the big stevedores... harmless things, and frisbeed a flat pak grenade at the fourth before he had time to sit up, and shout for help in Denaari.

●●●つ●●

"Impact 42.4 seconds, and counting." Along with screeds of trajectory data Ground-control transmitted to Central came the count. Any one of the five warheads would have made a nuclear desert of a fifty-mile radius. The energy released by five... It amounted to using a five hundred megaton asteroid to flatten an ant. You were likely to squash yourself in the process. Central shunted the data to a holding circuit as it focused all of its great brainpower on reconstructing the last moments of transmission from the fourth brain-auxiliary unit.

The visual had been of a Mnemonic crown. And that could have been, just could have been a 'nestling in distress' cry, if the nestling had a severely damaged beak.

"Impact 39.1 seconds and counting."

Central flicked into its data files. Would a nuclear device destroy a Mnemonic crown? The answer was an unequivocal 'yes'. It replayed the audio in real time. Yes. In the midst of that noise that was a 'nestling-in-distress' cry. It activated responses which had been so much part of Central's own Denaari programmer-parents basic instincts that it could not gainsay them. An adult Denaari would kill itself to help a nestling.

"Impact 30.0 seconds and counting."

"ABORT! ABORT! ABORT!"

"Cannot Abort. Missiles on in-fall track. Locked on." Ground-control replied stolidly.

"De-activate the warheads."

"Warhead triggers being withdrawn."

Central had no teeth to grind or it would have ground them. True, the missiles wouldn't go off. But the missiles would strike the bio-zoo pyramid, and dust it with a large volume of refined radio-actives.

❦❦❦❦❦❦

"You idiot!" Juan raged at the Dagger of the Goddess, unaware that he was in great danger. Not because the assassin might take offence. That was extremely unlikely. But wearing a Denaari crown was risky. The Church used them as Demonic symbols. He'd run after the man in grey and now was threatening the most deadly assassin in human space with an unloaded but shaking finger. "They're harmless, groink whistle click, stevedores. Look!" It was true. The surviving three blue beasts had put the energy projectors onto their cargo pallets and were docilely waiting.

The Dagger was somewhat taken aback. Why had he done just what he had done? He had been ready, true. But his hand had moved of its own volition. How had he known that the red hedgehog-helmets were what he ought to shoot? But it was true that the animals now stood like statues. He'd been going to kill them before the boy had got in his way. But it really didn't appear that there was any point in killing them. Also he would have to knock down and possibly kill the boy first. And who was this boy anyway? Then there was the slight girl who had come to back the boy up. He could see in her shrinking attitude that it was not in her nature, but she *would* fight to defend the boy. Something about her said 'rider'. Rider? Why was that word so important, so full of secrets? Like an elusive fish the answer slipped away from him. But it was close. And he had to admire the boy's courage. He would not attack. There was great virtue in such bravery. At least if the boy had to be killed he would be surely be reborn closer to the Dewa. The stocky man too was watching him, edging round for a better angle. Well, he had dealt with multiple attacks before. Attacks? But he was the one who attacked, surely. Why did the role of defender feel so familiar?

●●●○●●

"What other control do you have over the missiles?" demanded Central of Ground-Control.

"None. They are independent, calculating their own drop vectors, so that they cannot be diverted by the enemy once targeted."

"What other inputs do they have?"

"Just the open weather channel, to allow the missile micro-brain to correct for the wind."

"Insert a wind speed of 720 zhat South-west to your weather broadcast."

Ground-control needed a stutter circuit. "But......that's not true!"

"Just do it! NOW!" Central included in the communication string the code sequence of ultimate command which none of the other Bio-computers could gainsay. It realised just what an awful thing it was ordering a fellow brain to do.

"Complying under protest. Impact 29.4 seconds," grumbled Ground-control.

Looking warily into the darkness the castaways did not see the cargo transporters. Central had pulled these back. They did see five streaks of sudden fire off to the north-east. They hit the desert 10.3 miles away with the satisfaction of job well done. Such thought-paths circuits were always bred or gene-spliced into organisms which would be destroyed in their proper function. The

219

Denaari firmly believed that a happy organism performed best.

Central had been obliged to track them through channels which excluded Ground-control. That poor bio-computer was being inundated with demands for more information about the hurricane from half the Control centers across the planet. Central dispatched a team of specialist radioactives seeker-eaters to the area. The creatures would have a feast, and would hopefully recover some of the precious material.

Now to try to establish contact with the source of the distress-cry.

⊖⊕⊂⊃⊖⊖

"We need somewhere to hide. Those were probably meant to hit us. Also there is a patch of sky over there which is dark. It should be full of stars," said Martin Brettan, peering into the night. Shari had intervened in the incipient fire-fight between Deo and Mark Albeer. Deo had responded. Slowly. As if something were nagging at him. Now they were standing on the other side of the remains of the second stevedore, looking out of the now open sliding portal.

"What! Down to the snakes in the dark? Or do you think the lights will be on there too? Besides, two of those things came from down there," said Lila wearily.

"It is a choice of down the inside or down the outside." Shari stuck her hand out. "The stuff is glass smooth. You'd be sliding faster than a bullet before you hit the bottom."

"If only we'd worked out how to get into one of the cages," moaned Johannes. "We could hide or... or pretend we were just some of the animals or something."

"It's worth trying," said Shari. "Would one of those grenades blow a hole for us, Deo? Or what about the laser?"

He realized she was addressing him. Felt the wall. Shrugged. "The laser is discharged, Dewa. It is possible that a grenade may do the task. This material does not feel like glass. The grenade is not a shaped charge. Most of the force would not be directed at the wall. The hole may also be small. I will try."

"Why not just tell the wall to open?" Juan's Denaari side said... in the wrong language for the rest of the castaways to understand. The Bio-zoo wall understood however, despite the atrocious pronunciation his odd shaped mouth forced on the words. It complied, as it had been bred to do.

For a moment they all stared at the open wall section next to them. Then Tanzo realised what had happened. "Quickly. Inside."

They hurried in. Once they were in the alien environment, Shari turned on the boy. "Just what did you do?"

"I.... I told it to open."

"Well, tell it to close, and be quick about it," she said cheerfully.

A few moments later they were in the moonlit dark, shut into the enviro-cage. The Denaari had been master zoo-keepers. If the creatures of the world now known as Mali V had been accustomed to the light of seven moons, they would still see seven moons. Mali V was a Sahel world. A boom-and-bust place, where, because of the vast tides caused by its moons, the weather alternated between torrential downpour and searing drought and heat. The cage was in the just-after-the-rains' growth phase right now. The grass was as high as a Taur-elephant's eye, which is about eight foot. And it was still growing. Everything was growing, breeding and eating with frantic haste. In another two months the cage would be a dying place. In six months the only signs of life would be seeds, eggs, and hibernating Taur-elephants.

The native species of Mali V didn't stop to sleep when things were good.

As a cage to hide in, the grass made it a good place. As a choice of environments to be in, it was terrifying. You couldn't see anything for grass, but the place was full of noise. Bellowing beasts. Things munching to all sides. What could only be predators they could not see making their kills. Hoots from something big, really big, in the distance. And the sound of Mali-grass growing, and starting to seed.

They made their way forward cautiously. On a low mound, actually a Taur-elephant hibernation burrow, they formed a defensive ring. "Well, I suppose we're safer in here than we were out there. At least here we can't be seen."

Sam didn't agree with Tanzo. He had a cold 'you-are-being-watched feeling' in the small of his back.

●●●○○○

At last Central had decent visuals of them. The Bio-zoo's in-cage monitoring system was still in perfect order. The one with the mnemonic-crown was not a Denaari. Central did not understand how to feel heartbreak, but the entire great bio-brain was stilled for a moment.

Then it lurched back to reality. It had been a futile hope, really. But the alien with the crown was definitely not Sil. A hasty search of data files produced a near match, in specimens held in

Bio-zoo units 23 and this one, 48. The match to the specimens in Bio-zoo unit 23 were closer. The ones which had been lost from this unit were related, but had died out by the time the monitoring station had been set up on the planet the castaways called 'Earth'.

They had been considered as a nascent space-travelling species back then. The estimates on their achieving interstellar travel had been approximately 4000 years. It had been the Denaari's intent to withdraw all but the most carefully hidden observers from that region of space well before this time. If, and Central noted from file records that this had been a big *if*, the species had been allowed into space. As the nest-minders had said, it was better to withdraw heat from the egg than the chick. As a result of the conflict with the mechanistic Sil, many of the Denaari had been scared of having any other space-travelling species in their sphere of space.

They must have come with the returning Stardog. Obviously, with the collapse of the Denaari Domain the aliens from Earth must have encountered and learned to use the Stardogs. One of the Stardogs must have begun to die in flight, and come here. The animals' first and most basic safety imprint was to return. The hasty imprint that had gone out to expunge the way home to the Motherworld from the Stardog route-maps when the Sil plague began, could not override such an intrinsic part of the Stardog's core indoctrination.

Now that Central knew what they were, and how they had got here, the great Bio-computer faced yet another dilemma: What should it do with them? The Denaari had regarded the species as potentially dangerous. It looked at the party huddled on the low mound in the Envirocage. They did not appear dangerous, but they had attacked and destroyed the brain-auxiliary units and a harmless stevedore. Attacked and destroyed without pause on being told to surrender. Then a logic circuit clicked in. They had been addressed in Sil. They'd appealed for help in the Denaari tongue. Perhaps these were allies, or at least aliens struggling against a common foe. It was yet another factor to be weighed in Central's deliberations. The Denaari had set a program in motion to solve the nano-plague problem. The answer had come too late for the Denaari, but Central still had crystallised stocks of nano-mech specific viruses in store.

One point in the favor of these aliens was that they had come by Stardog. The Stardogs had always been willing servants of the masters they loved. That, after all was the Denaari way. Stardogs could not be made to do anything if they did not love these aliens too. But the records from the Observation Station back on earth were not encouraging. Certain of the vid-records could only be interpreted as a species which revelled in cruelty. The killings themselves were not intrinsically bad. The Denaari had accepted food chains and the role of the various species in them. Predators were predators, and to kill was part of their nature. But to wish to hurt...!

Central made up its mind. Firstly, it wanted that mnemonic crown. It might help, especially if it had been able to store data about these aliens. Anyway, it could only be one of the missing sixteen, and possibly it could be a vital piece in the jigsaw of Denaari racial history with the Denaari memories it held.

The crown must be recovered. If necessary the aliens would be killed to get it. Central was a Denaari creation itself. Their death would be quick and clean. If it didn't have to kill them, it would assess them further. Possibly they could go to Bio-zoo unit 23, where records indicated that a viable breeding group of the species was held.

CHAPTER 20
CHOICES

*Liberty implies freedom of choice, and personal
responsibility for those choices. Most people prefer
chains, although they spend enormous amounts of
effort swapping sets of chains.*

From the collected sayings of Saint Sugahata the Reviled

The Taur-elephant mowed through the Mali-grass like the dream
of all lawn-owners. The scything tusks moved in twenty foot
sweeps leaving not a blade of grass standing. The long prehensile
upper-lip seized the grass and shoved it into a maw full of grinding
molars. The molars were remarkably effective at shredding the
tough grass. They were just as good at mashing anything else that
came along as incidentals with the grass. Strictly speaking Taur-
elephants were omnivores, although they only harvested grass. If
you were mobile you left fast when the grass fell, otherwise you
got eaten.

They knew the Taur-elephant was approaching because of
the fleeing animals. The mound would be relatively safe, as even
Mali-grass would not grow there, and the huge harvesters
wouldn't go there unless there was food, or time to sleep. Both
Martin Brettan and Shari had been to Mali V, and seen Taur-
elephants, and had some idea of what to expect. There, hunters

followed along the mown trails behind the Taur-elephants. Inevitably game fleeing other members of the herd would run across the open space. Here in the cage the ecosystem had not been disturbed, so instead of hunters the weasel-like Elines prowled behind the Taur-elephants. Elines are weasel-like in all but two respects: They lay eggs, and they're bigger, about eight feet long. Elines are not courageous, and prefer small, weak or wounded prey.

The one which came racing out of the dark from the far edge of the mown of the strip just behind the Taur-elephant therefore streaked straight for Una. It had not seen Otto on the other side of the circle.

Only, as it was about to spring, the roof above them spoke. Startled by the booming voice the creature missed its neck-snapping pounce. It landed in Una's midriff instead, all claws and snapping teeth. Juan, who was, of course, nearest, managed to grab the beast by its long, graceful tail. It turned on him instead, as Central, via the Bio-zoo's mouthpieces, boomed out a message of goodwill in ancient Egyptian. Lila's blow aimed at the weasel-head with a porcupine-tree branch bounced across Juan's face. Teeth met through the meaty part of his hand between the thumb and fingers. Claws raked at his face and chest. There was a resounding thud, and the Eline left, yelping. The yelps ended abruptly as the creature fled into the path of another Taur-elephant in the herd.

Juan looked up at a pale-faced and bloody Una with a rock in her hand. She hugged him fiercely. The boy part of Juan was enormously confused.

"Are you two all right?" Shari asked. Juan nodded.

She continued. "I think this place is just too dangerous. We'd better try another cage. Besides the Taur-elephants have removed the cover between us and outside. By the way, Denaari experts, can you tell us what that loudspeaker announcement was about? Or were you too busy fighting that thing off?

Juan shook his muzzy head. His mouth was still too dry to speak easily. "Not Denaari." he managed in a croak

Shari shrugged. "Well, let's get out of here, anyway."

They walked down the cut path across to the envirocage's crystal wall, avoiding the huge mounds of steaming pungent dung that was already drawing coprophagous snark-beetles. From the inside they could not see out. And no matter how Juan asked, the cage would not open. Central had instructed the Bio-zoo not to respond.

"We're stuck. Stuck in one of the toughest environments of all of the Empire worlds." Already the new-mown Mali-grass was growing. There was a mournful yammering howl. Then an answering howl, closer.

"Stilt-tigers," said Martin Brettan quietly. "They hunt in pairs." There was a cold feeling in the pit of his stomach. The animals had been frightening enough, from the relative safety of a palanquin when his father had taken him on that long-ago safari on Mali V, as guests of the local Grand-Duke. He knew someone was going to die unless they got out of here very smartly.

The roof above spoke. This time it was a stream of whistles and clicks. Juan replied. Central had analyzed the fact that they had not responded to the message to stay put on the Taur-elephant burrow, and that in their attempt to get out, Juan had used several variations of the Denaari word 'open'. It now addressed them in Denaari, which they plainly understood, even if they could not speak it properly.

"Stand close together, everybody."

A minute later the huddle of humans was encased in a sample-cage. Outside the Stilt-tigers howled in frustration. The cage sprouted small gas-jets and drifted upwards and out, the wall opening co-operatively before them. The floor swayed rather a lot and they were obliged to sit down or fall down.

Once again they were subjected to a string of Denaari orders. Juan put his hands protectively over the crown.

"What is it saying?" demanded Martin Brettan, beating the others to the punch.

"It says I am to place the mnemonic crown in that receptacle," Juan pointed, "and then that we will be transported to Bio-zoo unit 23, where we will be safe and comfortable and there are many others of our kind."

"Here we go again. Out of the frying pan and into the fire," said Sam cheerfully. "I wouldn't give it to them if I were you, boy."

"Of course he must!" Johannes was horrified by the idea. "We're prisoners and all hostages. I dare say these aliens will kill us all if he doesn't do what they say."

Juan battered his vocal chords about and whistle-click-chirped at the wall.

"What did you say?" asked several people.

"I said it was my duty to take the crown to the Memory Vaults."

Kadar clicked his tongue in annoyance. He stood up, not without difficulty, as the stevedore beasts were manhandling the sample cage onto the cargo-transport. "You little fool. Do what you're told. Stop endangering all of us, or we'll take it off your head and do it for you."

"Speak for yourself, you slab of misery," said Sam shortly, staring out at the alien craft, trying to *feel* what would be best.

"Do the Denaari lie?" asked Tanzo of Juan.

"I don't think so. Um. It's difficult... I'm only Denaari when I'm not really all me... But the Denaari part of me believes that the Denaari would put us in a safe place, I think. They don't look at killing as lightly as we do."

"So we can join other humans, and be safe if you co-operate. Well, I'll do it for you," said Kadar, making a grab at the crown.

Mark Albeer pulled Kadar's legs out from under him. He fell, and struggled to strike at the thickset bodyguard.

"That's enough!" Shari snapped. "Don't you realize you're being watched? You're making fools of the entire Human race, you idiots. Now stop it. The boy's reply established us as responsible aliens deserving some respect. We want that respect, ladies and gentlemen. I hope they don't put honorable and responsible aliens into their Zoo. I'd rather be free, than caged and safe."

"I'd rather have food and drink," muttered Johannes. But he didn't say it too loudly.

Martin peered out at the stars. "We're going to cross those mountains if we keep going in this direction. Toward where young Mr. Biacasta said those vaults were. It appears as if you may be right, Princess Shari."

Martin Brettan was unaware of the time-bomb his accidental use of the honorific just then had set in motion within the Dagger of the Goddess's head. Brettan's own thoughts were far from the Factotum, who had proved to be such an adroit killer. The alien machinery in this place still seemed to be functioning, after all these years. Surely that meant the Denaari still survived? Nothing could really have lasted 3000 years without maintenance, after all. Could the Denaari be used? The Emperor would not thank him for their return, wishing to reclaim their Empire. However, if the Denaari could be suitably convinced... made allies against the League, well, that would please Turabi. A darker idea came to him. Apparently, there were other humans here, on this world. No need to turn to Turabi the blob at all, perhaps. He could have his own army and own Denaari allies... while they were convenient.

Now that Johannes and Kadar had got over their initial fears, different variations of the same idea were occurring to both of them too. It kept the three from the welcome sleep that the rest of the party had slipped into.

cecoee

The cargo-transport came to a soft landing outside the vaults. The back wall of the sample cage slid open. Juan stared at the high arched doorway of which he had received such clear images. The Denaari would naturally have thought nothing of the door being fifteen feet off the ground. Juan found himself spreading his arms and felt remarkably foolish. The cargo-transport abruptly began to move, edging itself closer to the platform at the foot of arched entrance. Obviously someone or something had been watching and had realized they could not get into the vault.

With the cargo-transport up against the wall, and a leg-up from Mark, Juan was able to pull himself up. He was about to walk on, his momentous task weighing heavily on him when Una called him back. She was reaching her arms up to him, with a trusting, hopeful puppy look. He could no more have left her behind than he could have deserted Rat. She was, he noticed as he pulled her up, heavier than she looked. She didn't let go of his hand as he turned to walk into the open archway.

cecoee

Central knew it was gambling. One of them, even the helmet wearer, could be a saboteur. This was possibly the holiest place on all Denaar. They could damage or even destroy it, although that would take some doing. Yet Central allowed the aliens access and watched them to assess their behavior. Of course it was the sort of gamble which a computer would be prepared to undertake. It couldn't actually lose. The most precious part of the vaults were the memories. Those existed in quintuplicate, with the other copies being kept in four separate distant sites. Everything else could be replaced if need be.

cecoee

Juan knew the others had come behind him. He could feel their presence. It mattered not. In fact it was fitting. He was Juan-Denaari now, come to perform the last and most sacred rite.

The hall was vast, the high arches soft lit and distant. In Juan's mind he saw how it had been once when !whistle paa!tch had come here as a new-fledged to receive his own father and mother's precious memories. The air had been full of winged bodies, and thick with the scent of the nutmeg-and-lemon Theez incense. The air had been full of keening sorrows and deep joys too. Una squeezed his hand. He glanced at the slight alien girl and saw, to his surprise, tears coursing down her thin cheeks. Then he felt that he too was weeping, his alien body responding to the emotion which this place stirred in him.

At the end of the hall were the rows and endless rows of crown receivers, their pedestals blackened with hundreds and hundreds of generations of Theez smoke. Juan-Denaari knew that this was but one of the many halls in the memory vaults, once all suffused with the fragrance of the Denaari myrrh-incense. As he came up to the receivers he must have commented in Denaari about it. Somebody asked what he'd said, and as he walked forward he explained in English.

"Wait. Here." Caro handed him a tiny exquisitely cut crystal bottle. "It's not incense... but it is all I've got."

It was the right thing to do. Juan-Denaari poured the entire contents of a rare and fabulously expensive perfume out onto the pedestal. Then he took the crown from his head and put it in the receiver. The crown slid down and the myriad nerve tendrils of the colonial organism that was the vaults began to share the memories they drew from it. Once these would have been re-imprinted into the crown of descendants. The creature which was the mnemonic crown gave up its memory-store with joy and haste. It had finally returned to the vector. Now it could breed, at long last.

●●●○○○

The Dagger of the Goddess followed ten paces behind the boy. He walked slowly, his head bowed. Confusion stirred within him, threatening to overwhelm him. This was a holy place, a place of love and sadness, full of ghosts. Yet it was a Denaar-filth place. Who could have dared to consecrate and make holy a place of the ancient evil? And was that truly Princess Shari Tamar of the Imperial House walking a few paces before him? Why did he feel that he should have encountered her in a garden, not within what could only be a temple?

His right hand twitched, and then jerked spasmodically. Within him the Nano-surgeon worked frantically. The control-web had to be re-established, even at the risk of killing the host.

The Dagger looked around at the rest of the company, feeling as though he was a man staring through a mist which eddied and swirled, almost, almost allowing him to know who these people were, before obscuring them again. There was the tall, well-built man. A Viscount... he felt he must distrust the man. But who was he? The blond who had provided the scent offering, who was she? How did he know she was trustable but foolish? The stocky, dark man who held her hand as you might a flower, must be watched. The Baroness... how did he know she was a Baroness? She didn't look like one, but he knew that she had become both thinner and infinitely happier, as she walked beside the... thief? The left side of his face twisted in a sudden rictus. He really did not feel well. He would have liked to have a drink of water and to lie down. But this was a holy place... and where were the League-scum? Who were the League-scum, and why were they to be so despised and hated?

The boy placed the crown in the small well in the stone-like pedestal. There was a moment of silence. Then the walls suddenly reverberated with the voice of Central, shocking the Dagger-almost Deo out of his puzzled reverie.

eecɔee

The huge bio-computer that was Central had watched their progress with care. Eight sentient aliens had accompanied the crown-bearer into the Vault-mouth. Nine plus two other life forms. Interesting. The Denaari had often brought other creatures with them too. Yet two of the same species as the crown bearer had not come to honor the passing of the memory. Why had the thinner one restrained the other in the red integument-covering and led him away to a point out of sight of the vault-mouth? The behavior of those within was appropriate, even if they could not follow the ritual flight-pattern dance. The stuff used was unlike Theez, but the gesture was unmistakable. Central was a computing device, but it was self-aware, and those who had made it had attached much to these rituals. Central was impressed. Then the crown-data began to flow into its data analysis and codifying system. Within micro-seconds billions of terabytes of processing ability were at work.

eecɔee

Juan felt both a tremendous satisfaction and vast emptiness, as he stood watching the crown sink away into the pedestal. He knew he would not be two vastly different entities within one body any more. Yet, equally he couldn't just be Juan Biacasta, aged sixteen, (just) of Amritsar Station again. Part of !whistle paa!tch would be with him always, coloring his perceptions in alien shades which his human eyes could not see. !whistle paa!tch must have been the alien equivalent of sixteen once, but he had been much older when he'd been part of that last brave and desperate attempt to negotiate with the Sil. He had brought a huge leap in maturity and understanding to Juan. Not all of it had left with the crown. Juan looked down at the fingers entwined with his. He squeezed her hand gently. The old pre-crown Juan would have blushed and pulled his hand away. But the old pre-crown Juan hadn't really understood how his father had felt about his step-mother-to-be either.

Then Central began speaking to them in English. In Stationer-accented English. With Juan's voice. It was the only source material it had, but Juan found it disconcerting to hear himself calmly greeting them. It continued.

"I am what you would call a computer, however, what you think of is totally different in nature from myself, although we perform the same function. You are, the mnemonic input informs me, under some physiological stress. If you will collect the other members of your party, I will direct you to a small bio-botanical unit, where you may be able to find appropriate food for your species."

It was the first time any of them had noticed that the two leaguesmen were missing. They went in search of them. Juan lagged behind with Una, thinking about what the computer with his voice had said. Somehow it didn't ring true, although he didn't know why. If he'd thought it through he'd have realized that it sounded just like himself, when he was evading a direct lie by skating around the truth.

They found the two leaguesman sitting very innocently on the cargo-transport. If they'd been a few minutes earlier they'd have found Kadar frantically searching for controls.

The Bio-botanical unit was indeed barely a flap or two away to the Denaari, but it took the party a good five minutes to walk to it. It was a smaller version of the pyramid they had encountered the frill-snake hydra in, but this one had no broken corners. A large panel slid aside, and allowed them into the cargo access. Soon they were walking along the immaculate corridors, shepherded along by the Juan-voiced Central. These bio-botanical units were not sealed as the animal cages had been. The party entered a park-like landscape re-creation of the gentle world that humans called Tarsus. The dew-pear trees were full of luscious curved fruit. The place was soft with Sambar-lily scent.

GGCƆ&G

Central faced a dilemma. The complex language, with more exceptions than rules had been, by comparison to the other problems, simple. Of course there were words and whole concepts which didn't translate. The two species saw a different range of wave-length of light for starters. Each had names for colors that the other species could never see. Still, Central could make itself understood.

The aliens' philosophy was something else entirely. Their society, their way of life, was strange... More Sil than Denaari. They considered themselves separate and superior to other living creatures. Yet, the affection felt by the crown-wearer for the small creature known as 'Rat' was deep and genuine. And they could communicate with Stardogs. Yet not all of them could... It imported data from bio-zoo unit 23. The society these specimens had come from was what the crown-wearer would have referred to as 'ancient Egyptian'. There were several thousand years' worth of observation records to analyze.

It would take a long time, by Central's standards, to do so. Central decided to ship them off to the nearby Botanical unit for the fifteen or so minutes of computational time it needed to decide the fate of the castaways. If need be they could be imprisoned there, or should it be necessary, mercifully killed.

Another factor was worrying Central. It understood and approved of Rat's transmitter system. The saboteur that the civil defense unit had tracked was of course harmless. But there was a spectrograph trace of Sil-typical metal alloy inside one of the humans. Could the enemy still survive, and wish to destroy even the memory of the Denaari? Were these humans' stalking-horses for something far more sinister? Or were they innocent victims of the Sil too?

eecɔꝺꝺ

Memories are more frequently triggered by smell than all the other factors put together. Analyzing and associating smells was once the primary function of the brain, and perhaps we haven't evolved as far we think we have. The scent from the hanging curtains of Sambar-lilies filled the Dagger of the Goddess with a terrible feeling of *Deja vu*. Was his life trapped in this cycle, until he did it right? He followed her through the hanging curtains of flowers between the trees.

Shari too had recognized the smell, and decided it was time to stop living with the fear that he would kill her... this time around. It had to be dealt with, like the situation they now found themselves in. She had also seen the implications of a Computer that could learn English in moments. She remembered what Juan had said about going home. She walked away from the others who were enjoying the buttery fruits, and pushed past the hanging curtains of lilies to a small glade where she hid from the rest of the party. She sat and waited, replaying her life. Thinking.

He came, almond eyed and silent.

"I suppose you have come to kill me." There was no fear. That was good. For her whole life there had been some fear. Now there was only sadness. She stroked Otto gently.

He stopped. She was determined to break away from the script, to try and set him free from the cycle. "How are you going to manage a garrote with only one arm?"

He looked at his arms. At the sling he'd shaken off. At the crude splint. "It's broken, Deo. I saw you break it. I strapped it up. That was only yesterday. Nobody heals in that short a time."

"You are Princess Shari Tamar Alstenn-Wienan of the Imperial House and the Duchess of Arunachal?" he asked.

She could lie. He had taught her to lie so that the voice and body did not betray her. But she was damned if she would. "I am. And you are the Dagger of the Goddess. You have assumed the persona of one my servants, Amadeo Cerros, a man you despised and killed. You have come to harvest my soul for the Kali-Dewa for persecuting the holy church."

"How do you know all of these things?" he had looped the garrote around her throat, showing no signs of having trouble with the broken arm.

"Because we have done all this before. Don't you remember Otto?"

The dog thumped his tail at the assassin.

"I did not kill you.... I remember. I remember!"

"No. You didn't kill me. Instead you killed those who had come to murder Otto and me. After that you protected me for eighteen years."

"Which is why I must kill you now. I must do that which is right."

"You did what was right. You aren't a murderer, Deo. They trained you from before you could walk to be a fanatical killer. Yet you are not a murderer."

"I have murdered many men and women."

"You killed them, yes. But a knife is not guilty of murder. The person who holds and directs the blade is guilty. You were a knife, a human knife they conditioned and indoctrinated from earliest childhood. They made you their killer. They could not make you a murderer. They made you kill Sugahata, your only friend, although you tried not to strike. They tried to make you kill Dugra, your lover. But you loved her so much, even if she hated you for killing her brother, Sugahata, that you managed to defeat them, subtly, cleverly so that they did not know you had contrived her escape."

He was silent. The wire was still taut. Tears streamed down his face, but the wire was still taut. "I am the loyal servant of the Dewa. I must do as she commands."

"But the High Priests of the Holy Church of Arunachal are not loyal to the Dewa. They were the ones who ordered Sugahata's death, not the Dewa. They sent you to kill him because they were afraid. But his death did not destroy his teachings. So instead they decided on a show of force. To show that the church was still strong they sent their best assassin to kill the daughter of the Emperor." She knew that what she had said was heresy. She said it with all the conviction she could muster, because what she said, she was *sure* was true. He must read the truth from her words.

"You... you speak the truth." His hands dropped. "But I have sworn to kill you." The wire tightened again. "My head is so full of clouds, my Princess."

Her heart leapt to hear him address her like that again. "Am I to be given a chance to pray?"

"It is honorable to allow the victim a last prayer to cleanse their soul and prepare it for a rebirth closer to the Dewa. But I remember you have nothing to beg forgiveness for. I remember!"

"But I do have something to confess... this time."

He was silent, waiting.

"I confess to having loved you for a long time. I confess that I was never brave enough to tell you."

Deo dropped the garrote.

"Pick it up Deo. You may need it. You see, I may need you to kill me, and all of the others."

He started, nearly dropping the garrote again. "Why... My Princess?" The term itself was a caress. Inside his head the morning sun had come out and was burning away the confusion-mist. There were still gaps, things shadowy and frightening. But he remembered one thing clearly now: his moment of epiphany. She was indeed the Dewa. Or, at least, she was his personal Dewa. He could remember her beside him and leading him through his purgatory, through the demons and trials. He knew now that when the High Priest had called for her death, the priest himself had committed the ultimate heresy.

"Because dearest Deo, if there is a way of getting back to the Empire worlds we may destroy everything millions of people have lived and died for. If we return with a new Stardog, and a new world to colonize, we will give both the League and the Empire the lifeline they need. I can't betray so many people's dreams. I'd stay here or even die to stop that happening.

He nodded gravely. "I am yours to command. My life and theirs are in your hands, My Princess."

She looked at him, long and steadily. "I warn you, if we don't all have to die here, or go on living here forever, I intend to indeed become the scourge of the Holy Church on Arunachal. I will not rest until it is utterly destroyed."

He was shaken yet again. "Why…"

"Call me Sugahata's latest convert, if you like. I'll destroy them for what they did to you. They will never turn a child into a murder weapon again."

CHAPTER 21
OLD ENEMIES

*"Nothing is truly forgotten. Memories may drown in
later events, or grow dim, but given the right
stimulus they will revive, and old hatreds return as
fresh and sharp as vinegar. Thus it is best to bury
your mistakes if you cannot rectify them."*

**Suttulej Subramoney Mercy, high priest of the Holy
Church of Arunachal; His Epistle to the Church at
Brahmasville, where St. Sugahata had taken up his
teaching.**

The leaves parted. Mark Albeer and Martin Brettan came through.
Shari looked carefully at them. How history repeated itself. Two of
her murderous brother's killers. Yet the bodyguard was an
uncertain quantity. He had, she was sure, been party to Selim
Puk's plottings, yet he was very unlike the usual material Selim
recruited.

"Just came to see if you were all right, Princess," said the
bodyguard. He was watching Deo uneasily.

"We found what I presume is a fake stream," said the Viscount. "The water tastes a great deal better than what we've had for a long time, although it's not exactly Chateau Lafitte. I've brought you some."

She felt guilty. They had been tarred with history's brush. She took the cup of water gratefully. "Thank you, Martin. We'll pretend it is wine anyway. We need to drink a celebratory toast. Deo has recovered his memory."

The assassin nodded. "It is still patchy... Viscount Brettan. But my wits are with me again."

"Well, have a drink to them staying with you," said Brettan dryly.

Shari smiled radiantly. "We'll drink to that," she drank, and handed Deo the cup.

A rare smile spread across his face. "I will drink to your courage, my Princess."

They walked back to the others. Shari noted that the two Leaguesmen had also gone off somewhere. Sam was pacing about looking worried. He looked relieved to see her. She found herself answering his greeting with an unstoppable cracking yawn. It was pleasant there among the dew-pear trees, to sit down on the soft grass... the two dormantin tablets that the Viscount had carried and crushed before adding them to the water were singularly effective. She did not see the return of the Leaguesmen with their drawn weapons. A Tarbin mark III machine pistol in Kadar's fist and a nine mm Kessel Flat in Johannes Wienan's. They'd come for Juan, Una and Caro Leyven.

●●C⊃●●

"We need a rider, and the boy to give the computer instructions. He is the only one who speaks Denaari," said Shilo Kadar. "You, Countess, are coming too. Step over that way."

"We'll have the rest of your weapons. You won't be harmed in any other way if you co-operate." Johannes said quietly.

Nobody moved. Deo and the Princess were dead to the world anyway. "Just what are you playing at, you idiots," snapped Tanzo. "We've a real problem. The Princess and Deo are unconscious for some reason."

"They are irrelevant. You are all staying here with them. Now, one by one, your weapons, or I will shoot one of you as an example. You, Baroness, will be that example. You don't show the proper degree of respect." Kadar was ready to kill.

Sam was sure that he *would* kill some of them. But the man

was like a cat. He liked to play with his prey. The Yak stepped forward, deliberately obscuring the leaguesman's line of fire on Tanzo. Slowly he drew the chisel from his waist-band. Dropped it. "What do you plan to do with us?" His instincts said to keep them talking. Perhaps that computer voice would speak or something. Any distraction would do.

"Don't worry. You'll all be fine. There is water, food, safety and shelter here. We're sorry to have to do this, but it is in the interests of peace and stability of the whole human race. Really, we are doing this for the best."

"Doing what?" asked Caro, genuinely puzzled, and not letting go of Mark Albeer's hand.

"Control of the Stardogs must remain with the League, Countess. This computer system must control access to them. So we must take it over, get it to give us the Stardogs. There would be chaos and war otherwise." Johannes did it well. He sounded sincere, plausible.

"Oh. But why can't we go home? I mean, the Princess is sick, and needs a doctor. She doesn't just pass out like that."

"Enough chatter. Come. Weapons or I start making an example. Step out of the way, Yak or it'll be you. Brettan, you next." Kadar lifted the machine pistol.

The Viscount stepped forward slowly, coolly. Carefully he took out his automatic and dropped it next to the chisel that Sam Teovan had patiently turned into a knife. "Why are you doing this, Johannes? The League had your mother and nearly all of her family murdered, you know."

Johannes Wienan nearly dropped the Kessel Flat. "How do you know about...?"

"I'm your uncle. Your mother was my older sister. They killed her. They killed my parents too, all because she brought you with her."

"Shut up, Brettan. Shut up or I'll shoot you," said Kadar, thumbing the machine-pistol off rapid fire to single shot. The Tarbin was notoriously inaccurate on rapid.

Martin Brettan shrugged. "Very well. But the Emperor would reward you well, Shilo Kadar. Very well indeed, for a supply of Stardogs. Kadar, you're not a Wienan. You won't get anywhere in the Wienan League. And Johannes has a place by birth in the Empire."

"Shut up, I said!" snarled Kadar as he drew a bead on him. "Get back with the others. Move!"

He moved. But he was satisfied. Johannes was wavering. Staring at him, gun-pointed at the ground.

Juan was frightened by the guns, by Kadar's barely leashed violence. But it didn't make sense. I wouldn't work. And Una was more frightened than he was. It wasn't right to frighten her, just when she'd been starting to get over all the terrors she'd had. "I have to tell you something," he said, wishing his voice had no tremble to it.

"Shut up, boy. Come over here."

Juan went. Una went too, clinging on to him. "It's important."

"Let's hear what he has to say, Kadar," said Johannes. "He knows about the Denaari."

Kadar did not like Johannes's interference one bit. For a minute it was touch and go as to whether he shot his fellow Leaguesman or not. Then he shrugged. "Be quick."

"Well, Central, or what you are calling the computer system, is not a machine. It is alive. It thinks and decides for itself. You can't make it do anything."

"You made it do something. You spoke to it in its language and it obeyed you. That's why we're taking you along."

"But it speaks English now," burst out Una. "You mustn't take Juan! You can talk to it."

Johannes stared at her. "How come," he said slowly, "you heard what was said?"

"Leave her alone. I'll go with you. Just leave her alone." Juan defended the wide-eyed girl.

"Oh no. She's coming too. Even if we didn't need a rider, I'm going to get to the bottom of this," said Kadar, his gimlet eyes boring hard into her. "The Emperor's spies are behind this, I swear."

His mention of the Emperor darted Johannes's eyes to Martin Brettan. Brettan was equally surprised, but was quicker on the uptake. He nodded, cocked his head briefly at the other Leaguesman. The moment's distraction had also been sufficient to allow the bodyguard to begin to draw his weapon quietly. Mark had slipped himself into a shielding position in front of Caro. Another second…

Then Lila botched it. She attempted to get her weapon out fast. She was a good shot from youthful experience, but not practiced at a quick draw. The front-sight hooked on her waistband. She ripped it clear, but it cost valuable fractions of a second. Kadar's eye was caught. The heavy-caliber bullet knocked her backwards. The .22 fell to the ground. His second shot was aimed at Mark Albeer. The bodyguard was already diving, pushing Caro down beneath him. By pure fluke the shot hit the trigger-guard of the bodyguard's pistol, breaking his finger, and plucking the weapon away.

"You shot her! You shot Lila!" Johannes's voice was high with shock. He pointed a wavering gun at his compatriot. She had served him for five years. Somehow... he'd come to feel that she was a piece of his permanency. She might have treated him with disdain since the hi-jacking, but he didn't want her dead.

"I had to, you fool. She was going to shoot me." The man stood like a marksman, his eyes flaming, and pistol still at the ready. He thumbed it to rapid fire.

"You hated her! You promised you wouldn't kill anyone... I'm going to *kill* you!"

Kadar swung to face to him, bringing his weapon to bear. "You couldn't," he said scornfully. "You Wienan's are bred out. I'm going to take over."

Johannes laughed. It was high pitched and hysterical, but it was still a credible effort. "Half Imperial, half Wienan. And as that, I *order* you to drop that weapon."

It nearly worked. It also distracted the man long enough for Sam to finish wriggling across to his fallen faithful .22. He dropped Kadar with his trademark head shot. It was still not quite quick enough to save Johannes.

●●●Ɔ●●

The pyramidal structures which the Denaari had used for their bio-zoos, and botanical storehouses were complex colonial organisms. Like icebergs only the tip of the organism was visible. The area above the surface was essentially merely the shop-display window. Below lay the endless cryo-chambers, where the vast treasure-hoard of genetic material was stored. Even the frill-snake hydra had only successfully invaded a tiny proportion of the whole bio-zoo, and never penetrated the storage area. This was a smaller unit, but it still had the necessary cryo-units. A surprising volume of carbon-based animal life had turned up with the botanical material over the years.

Central did not entirely understand the drama being enacted above. But it did respond to Juan's muttered appeal for help. The memories from the mnemonic crown, as well as the alien's behavior in returning it, suggested its conduct would have been approved of by the Masters. That was clearer than the reams of data about water-based theocracy coming from Bio-zoo 23 anyway.

"Stop the bleeding."

"I can't. It's pumping out between my fingers."

"My God, she's going to die!"

"So is Johannes Wienan. I don't think there is anything we can do for him."

The first cryo-unit arrived on hissing jets of self-generated steam, closely followed by a second, and a third unit.

"What the hell?"

"Keep it away from her!"

Central's Juan-voice responded. "Stand clear. The cryo-unit will preserve the organism. Several hundred valuable specimens have been successfully repaired and revived."

"Juan. Do we trust it?" demanded Tanzo, still pressing the pad made from the ripped remains of Caro's skirt against the wound.

He nodded, feeling too sick to speak.

"She's dying. We don't have any alternative," Mark Albeer was white-faced with pain. None of Caro's ministrations were going to save that finger.

Tanzo bit her lip and stepped aside. The unit dropped over Lila, who was mercifully unconscious. Johannes wasn't. He managed a brief bubbling scream as the second unit enclosed him. Both units began to rise on their jets again. The third unit picked up the dead Kadar.

"Where are they taking them?"

Central spoke again. "The main cryo-units are below. The mobiles are merely snap-freezers and transporters."

"You... froze them?"

"No. The organisms are still receiving buffering solutions. They will be at -170 o Celsius before they reach the storage units. Should it be impossible to revive them the material will be stored for future gene-splicing. We have considerable reservoirs of genetic material from carbon-based species. Unfortunately the same system is not practicable with silica-based organisms. Material from those can be maintained for cloning and regrowth only for a matter of weeks." It had meant that while the gene-banks held specimens of long-extinct animals from hundreds of worlds, specimens of humans, and even of the Sil, which Central could regrow at will, the Denaari, the beloved masters, were forever lost.

Central continued after the briefest pause. "Had they been wearing mnemonic crowns, we could recreate them. I have dispatched a mobile unit with crown-beasts which have been adapted for your species." Central had utilized part of Juan's memories of lies he'd told himself, and been told, to justify making this false statement. If lying was a human norm, then Central too could lie to these aliens. Had they, as Denaari would have, worn the mnemonic since hatching then the statement would have been the truth. As it was, Central was merely hoping to gather more data. It was heading towards momentous decisions, and it wanted more information about these aliens.

The crowns arrived while they were still strapping-up Mark's finger. A low-bedded sleek relative of the stevedore beasts came bearing nine of them.

"What do we do with these?" Martin Brettan eyed them dubiously.

Juan had already picked one up. He paused. "Put them on, of course!"

"What is it going to do to me?"

"Nothing. These are blanks, aren't they Central? New animals."

The bio-computer replied in his own voice. "Yes. They will have no memories but your own."

"You mean that thing will read my mind?" Martin Brettan said warily.

"It won't read your past memories. But if you think about things the images and information will be stored. With a little experience you can prompt it to give you precise recall."

"So that computer can pick my brains. Not likely!"

"Oh for heaven's sake, Brettan!" Tanzo picked one up and put it on her head without any further ado. She took it off and undid her hair. It descended in a dark waterfall to nearly her waist. Even Sam was stunned. No-one had ever seen Tanzo with her hair down. She put the crown back on. "There. No ill effects. And if the Denaari's computer wants my thoughts it is welcome to them. "

"But you could betray the empire's secrets..."

"Like what? It was their Empire, remember."

"I'm still not going to put that thing onto my head."

Tanzo shrugged. "Suit yourself." Brettan soon found himself the only person not wearing a mnemonic crown. Juan and Una had even put them onto the unconscious Shari and Deo. This didn't worry Martin Brettan. They should stay under for at least eight hours. By then… he'd either see that they would never wake again, or it wouldn't matter.

Central spoke again. "Several of your number have expressed an interest in departing Denaar. The Stardog on which you came has successfully pupped. It will be some time however before those pups are well-grown enough for wormhole surf. There are some other pups from an earlier litter which are ready to mate and imprint."

"An earlier litter… You mean other Stardogs have come here, since the Denaari plague? Not just us? "

"Yes. Only those who began to die in surf, of course. Or those which were off on mapping expeditions. All Stardogs must return to Denaar to pup. Returning to the gravity well is a one-way journey for the creatures, so they only come at the end of their lives. I will guide you to the imprint center, where the young ones are gathering for mating. There is a Geosynchronous-upline there, and Ground Control is sending a space-craft for you."

"What about the Princess and Deo?" asked Caro. "We can't just leave them here."

"I will send a further small-carrier beast for them. And also for yourselves. Analysis of the data from Juan reveals that you would consider it a great distance to walk."

They loaded the Princess and Deo side-by-side onto one of the low-flatbacked creatures similar to that which had brought the crowns. Otto showed no hesitation about leaping up next his mistress. Another two creatures provided transport for the rest of them. The creatures did have legs but it was apparent these were secondary to their flying ability. This was just as well as the imprint-center was half a mountain away at the edge of a vast plain. The mountain itself would have been hell to traverse on foot. Its steep sides had once been neatly terraced, but time and erosion had made the proud crystal fields of yesteryear into a shredded landscape. Seeing it hurt Central. It was time it was all put right again.

They flew towards yet another typical Denaari-place. Endless rows of soaring roost-towers faced the plain. Juan knew that it had once been a much-loved place, a place where Stardog-pups met their Denaari. It was also in Denaari terms a glamorous and above all a sexy place. Streams of new Denaari fives had come here to enjoy the Denaari equivalent of a honeymoon. The Denaari had few hang ups about sex in their relationships, compared to humans. Sex and reproduction were an intrinsic part of a five…

platonic relationships and such polite fictions were for other species. The emotional backwash from Stardog matings made this the most aphrodisiacal place on the planet.

Central wanted to see how the aliens responded to it.

On the third carrier Deo stirred. After the amount of Dormantin Brettan had dosed them with, neither of them should have been capable of any voluntary movement for at least another three hours. The Viscount had disregarded them from his plans for at least that time. However, Martin Brettan did not know that only part of the Princess's manservant was unconscious. The nano-mech surgeon had all its slave-units out working frantically. The host's metabolism was working at nearly double its normal rate.

They landed at what was the Denaari equivalent of the Bali Hilton. This was one of the tallest towers, balanced like a turnip on a chopstick. The same enormous self-repairing crystal windows looked out onto the plain. Long ramps made for easy take-offs of mating fives. At the base of the roost-stalk were the imprint caves. No place could be closer to where the Stardogs would want to mate.

The eggs would hatch somewhere out there, the hatchlings devour the remains of their mother, and begin silica-feeding their way to the breeding-grounds. By the time they got here, they'd be nothing but a huge segmented caterpillar of gametes, emotion and an empty head. A head with a vast potential but quite unusable until they'd stopped being entirely focused on sex. Juan looked out and saw seven of them coming in from the plains. He found them easy to identify with, even if they were alien, virulent green and chartreuse striped, caterpillar-like, and ninety feet long into the bargain. They were still rather like human teenagers.

The males had got there already. They had a serious advantage in that they didn't have to grow very large. They only had to carry gametes to their mates, not passengers across deep-space. They were only a few feet long, but their display colors would have put peacocks to shame. They'd begun their display dances along the plain-edge.

Juan found himself subject to an overpowering urge to rip Una's clothes off and to make passionate love to her. He found himself blushing furiously and holding his own hands to stop them taking independent action. She rubbed against him and traced interesting patterns on the inside of his upper thigh. He began to feel dangerously close to exploding.

Martin Brettan was calmly questioning Central. "So how do

the beasts know where to go?"

"Once the female has male gametes from sufficient males she will enter the caves below. The source-creatures are asteroid dwellers at this stage. They pupate and develop into the mature form, which is space-motile. The masters changed this pattern very slightly. Only the female is space-motile, and because of the gravity-well, the pupae are transported into space. The pupal-brain is fully developed, but sensorially deprived in the cocoon. Map data are rapid flashed with ultraviolet through the cocoon material onto the retina while they are going up to space."

Behind the Viscount, Deo stirred again and half sat up. He collapsed back onto the carrier beast. His mind was beginning to function but his body was still disobedient. The Viscount was pursuing vital information and did not notice. "So where is the launch-pad? How do they get into space? And why haven't more Stardogs arrived at human-worlds?"

"There is a geosynchronous line up from here. What you might term a skyhook. The animals and their passengers ride up on that. What you termed a barge is being readied even now. The Stardogs, since the Sil, have not been given navigational data for the old worlds of the Denaari Dominion. Instead they have route-information about the new worlds. The animals who are going to mate now will have the routes to the old Dominion imprinted as well as it appears the Sil too are extinct."

"You mean... there are more planets?!"

"Another 22 have been mapped which are considered Denaari-optimal worlds. Suitable for your species.... There are many listed with too high a water proportion to be Denaari optimal. Perhaps a further 730 worlds, discovered pre-and post Sil are habitable by your species."

The Viscount closed his jaw with a snap. He turned to the others. "Do you hear that!!!?" But there was no one listening. The others had all left him in a hasty search for some privacy. Even Deo was back in a highly erotic dreamland, his body twisted against that of Shari, who was occupied in a graphic dream of her own. It was a confusing one. Why should the writhing of psychedelic colored worm-like creatures be so compellingly sexy? Only Viscount Brettan, deep in dreams of power, was unaffected by the Emo-telepathic erotica. But then, to Martin Brettan, sex and power had always been facets of the same thing.

He concluded that they had all decided to act before he could. He checked the magazine of Kadar's Tarbin machine-pistol. He was glad he'd appropriated that, as well as having gone through the dead Leaguesman's kit while they were travelling. He'd found two spare magazines.

He looked at the sleeping Princess and her man-servant. God! The two of them looked like they were screwing! She was smiling, a wide happy smile. He nearly killed them both then and there, but decided against it. Dead they would have to be, as would all the rest, except for the rider-girl, but at the moment these two were hostages.

He addressed the computer again. "Central, when will the spacecraft be ready to leave?"

"In your timescale approximately one hour twenty-seven minutes and seven seconds, although it can be delayed."

"And where is it?"

"Approximately 1.8432 of your miles away." Central did feel it was being deceitful in omitting to mention that the way-up was also on the top of a mountain, and that more than half of that distance was a vertical component. The Geosynch line began on the mountain between the Memory Vaults in the breeding grounds. This alien had failed to respond at all to the stimuli that would have had the masters joyfully spiraling all over the sky. It noted that the others of the party were not unreceptive, even if their attempts lacked grace in its Denaari colored mentality. Perhaps this was one from whom the heat should have been withdrawn as an egg? Juan's memories suggested that this was not a normal thing for humans to do. The memories suggested that love was lavished even on callous offspring.

Viscount Martin Brettan was not the sort to sit around waiting. He ordered the flatbed beast to follow him, which it obligingly did, and went looking for the others. Central in collusion with the roost-tower ensured that he did not find them for seventeen minutes. Below the Stardog-larvae had finished mating, and had crawled into the cocooning caves. By the time Martin Brettan did find the others he was good and mad. He didn't expect to find the six others all together looking out over the plain, looking sheepish. And... happy? Especially the ridergirl. She was radiant. As if her life finally had a meaning. Well, it would have in a minute or two.

He raised his hands in an odd sequence of patterns

"Is that some kind of greeting, Martin?" said Tanzo dreamy-eyed, shaking back her long shawl of hair.

"Fudge." It was a six year-old's voice that replied from Una's mouth.

His hands moved, forming the numbers 662.

Sam knew with a sudden and terrible certainty that he had arrived at one of those decisive points, where he could choose between life and death.

οοοΣοο

In the soft shadows behind the Viscount, Deo sat up like a badly controlled marionette.

He was not meant to attempt to move yet. Of this he was utterly certain. Something was using him. Was he possessed by Denaari Demons? What was this thing on his head? He took the crown off with oddly clumsy fingers. And stared in horror at the Denaari crown. He put it down slowly, and wiped his fingers frantically against his trousers. Praying, he closed his eyes and lay down again trying with all his might to will himself back into the arms of Morpheus and the sweet if disturbing dream.

Central's vermilion hedgehog brain-auxiliary wobbled off the carrier-beast's head and across to the discarded crown. It began inputting data.

The brain auxiliary sent the data string directly to Central. And Central began arming weapons, even if it feared to use them here. The ancient enemy had come again. There was one possibility. The virus. A high-speed carrier was sent hurtling towards the breeding-grounds.

CHAPTER 22
OMEGA AND ALPHA

Think of the death of a revolutionary as compost production. The death of one can give rise to many others.

Nicola Para-Machiavelli: Obliterating a Prince

Ideas are somewhat like globe-artichoke seeds. They are difficult to germinate, but the plants are nearly impossible to destroy.

The Upanishad of the Gardener-Dewa Celine

The rider-girl moved like an automaton. A deadly automaton. She had taken the weapon from Martin Brettan as if she had handled one for years. Indeed she had, back then, if not one quite like this. Her eyes were empty, terrifyingly empty.

The Viscount smiled. All teeth and no humor. "In a few minutes we'll be heading off-planet. Myself and Una, or should I say, Celine. The rest of you have had the brief privilege of meeting the man who will control human destiny from now on. And now it is payback time. There are some little scores I have to settle."

Of the five people watching him the most horrified was Juan. A few minutes ago he had been exploring a most intimate world of tenderness with the slim girl. He'd been experiencing things his fantasies had totally misled him about. Sharing them with someone, a gentle loving someone who had only not been terrified... because he was. Now suddenly she was transformed into this... deadly stranger. "What have you done to Una?!" he burst out.

Brettan smiled, cruelly catlike, enjoying the boy-man's distress. "Celine. Una never was. She was just a persona created by our psychologists. Your girl was an Imperial sleeper, a way to penetrate the League's ridercorps. She was a good imitation of a rider. She would have been one if we hadn't got her first. Now that I have woken her, she has forgotten that and become the perfect slave. She'll do exactly what I tell her to. If I told her to, she'd kill you, too. Eh Celine?"

"Yes Master," she agreed unemotionally.

He looked at her, his eyes suddenly narrowing. "Which reminds me. How come you can hear me?"

"I am not to remember that part of my life," she said unemotionally.

"I order you to remember it, but not be influenced by it. I want to know why you haven't been deafened."

The girl stood stock still for a moment. Juan saw a brief spasm of pain wrack her elfin features. "I was deafened, surgically. Stationers provided me with a bone-induction hearing-aid which restored my hearing."

Brettan stared at her and then at Juan. Sam knew that if he dived then he could be out of the room before they could shoot him. He was certain of this. He was equally certain without any resort to his precognitive skills that Tanzo couldn't do it in time. He stayed.

"Stationers! Why?"

"I was told that it was vital to the rebellion that the Princess be protected. The stationers were aware that something was planned for this voyage. I was to gather information by eavesdropping on the Leaguesmen."

You could have knocked Brettan over with a feather, just then. "Well, I'll be damned! This alone would get me at least an earldom from Turabi! Shari plotting right under my damn nose. I've a good mind to take her along and make her suffer for that!"

"Don't you dare touch her," Caro Leyven said, protectively.

"Don't tell me you were involved too? Countess Screw-me Hair-wit! God!"

"I didn't know what she was doing. But I know that she is

brave and... And good. I would have helped her if I could. And I won't let you hurt her. You'll have to shoot me first."

"That is going to be arranged, believe me."

Mark Albeer balled his fists.

The Viscount laughed at him. "Huh. You'd be fool to try it. Believe me, you wouldn't last five minutes."

The bodyguard was not a fast thinker, but he saw the window of opportunity. "I'm not afraid of you! You're a coward who needs to hide behind a gun. Otherwise I'd whip your ass."

For a moment, a long moment, Brettan nearly shot him. Then he looked at his watch. "I've still got more than an hour and this isn't going to take ten seconds. Celine, disarm them. Then I'm going to teach this stupid peasant trash some manners."

"Don't you want me to tie one hand behind my back?" The scorn was palpable. Brettan was unaware that he was being professionally baited.

"Bah! What sort of martial arts skills have you got, cock-of-the-whoop?"

"None. But I don't need them for a wind-bag like you."

As this was being said, Una-Celine was relieving them of weapons. Quietly, professionally and without a word. She did start when her hand found Rat. He recognized a familiar smelling food-provider and gave her a friendly nuzzle. For an instant an expression of bewilderment and despair flighted across her features. Then they froze again, and her eyes became empty once again.

"Take the machine-pistol, Celine. Shoot anyone who attempts to run or interfere. I'm going to kill this peasant-born scum with my hands. Maybe he'll learn his place before he dies."

Mark Albeer shrugged off his jacket. The broken finger was going to be a problem. "At least my mother knew who fathered me." He stepped forward, raising his hands.

Viscount Brettan was a third dan black belt in the reformed Funakoshi School. He was prepared to slaughter this innocent. He was not prepared for an open-handed slap from the bodyguard's still bandaged right hand that left him staggering, tasting blood, with a head full of smoke.

The sweeper kick he aimed was dodged with ease. Mark Albeer was no martial arts expert, trained in an expensive and exclusive dojo. He was, however, the federation amateur middle-weight champion of Carab. The club where he'd learned to box had been anything but exclusive, and somebody losing it and putting in a kick at your balls was par for the course.

Within a minute the Viscount had realized that if anyone was going to be killed in this fight it would be him. The only thing that was keeping him alive was that the bodyguard was using his injured right hand only in defense. And there wasn't much need of that. Albeer stayed close, hitting him trip-hammer style, with that solid left smashing into the bigger man's ribs.

Brettan tried to back off, but Albeer followed closing with him. The Viscount tried to hit the injured hand. Succeeded. Pain slowed the bodyguard. Brettan managed to follow it up with a kick to the man's stomach. Albeer staggered, but he did not fall. The bodyguard knew he had to finish it now. He feinted with his left, and, as the Viscount ducked and blocked, he gave the scion of the nobility's chin his Sunday punch with the injured right. It was agony. But Brettan went down. He sprawled on the floor, eyes half glazed. The bodyguard came in, big hands reaching for the Viscount. Brettan scrabbled backwards. "Celine," he screamed: "Shoot him!"

She did. The Tarbin machine pistol is known for its lightness, its tremendous rate of fire, and its inaccuracy. Even on single shot. It had not been a weapon they'd trained the sleeper with. Which is why she shot him in the shoulder and not the chest. It was enough for Brettan to escape and take the weapon back from her. Caro had run forward to the injured man.

"Back off!" shouted the Viscount, backing off himself. He tripped over the low-bed creature that held the drugged Princess. Otto barked angrily at him.

He stood up, swaying. Furious. He pointed at the barking dog. It epitomized all that had gone wrong. "Celine. Kill it!"

She walked up, pointed the Viscount's own automatic at Otto.

The small hairy animal looked at her. She was a friend. He gave a tentative friendly, what-is-the-matter whine.

"Shoot it, I said!"

Her hands shook. Otto walked forward, and turned his head slightly on one side. Her hands quivered so much it was unlikely that she could have hit a barn door from inside. "No." It was barely a whisper.

"I'll shoot the damned thing then!"

She dropped the automatic and flung herself on the dog, shielding him. With Otto wrapped in her arms she screamed, "No! No! NO!"

"Shit! Don't you try and move towards that weapon, Yak. Back off, all of you. Back off I said!"

"She needs help." Tanzo and Juan were coming forward. Sam hadn't moved. He felt the weight of the moment to be pressing on him. 'Stay still' his instinct clamored. But she would be hurt... He could not hold himself back. He was going to die, but she wasn't! She was NOT!!!

"I'll shoot her..."

"You won't. You can't fly a Stardog without her," Tanzo snapped.

"Then I'll kill *you*." He fired. But Sam was already in front of her, pulling her down beneath him...

There was a silence. She pushed herself up from the floor and picked him up with a strength she never knew she had. Held him against her breast, his lifeblood pumping out onto her.

"I chose..." Sam's voice was barely audible.

Tanzo stared at Martin Brettan, and then at something else behind him. Then, with deep satisfaction, she said a ritual phrase in Ghurkali. It was something she had picked up on her abortive trip to Arunachal. Everyone who had served in the Imperial forces in that hell-spot knew what it meant. She knew Martin Brettan had spent a month there, before his family had used their influence to have him transferred elsewhere. He would know the phrase. It was right he should know what was coming.

Translated it meant 'You are already numbered among the dead.' It was the message given to those whom the holy assassins had been dispatched to kill.

●●●◌●●

Juan was almost unaware of all of this. All of his being was focused on the sobbing girl he held in his arms. She was fortunate in having found the one man on this planet who understood exactly what it meant to have two people sharing one body.

●●●◌●●

The nano-mech surgeon had forcibly roused Deo for another far more cataclysmic purpose. But the ancient words triggered deeply conditioned responses. The Viscount was no match for the Dagger of the Goddess. Even the surgeon-beasts of Denaar, creatures skilled beyond any possible human attainment, could not have put the Viscount Brettan together again. But the assassin didn't even pause for the ritual cleansing. He didn't even retrieve the one knife. Instead he left at a dog-trot. The nano-mech surgeon would have made him move even faster if it had had that bit more control.

252

Descent from the roost-tower was difficult but not impossible. The nano-mech drove the host creature towards the mountain. If it could get to the base of the geosynch line, and get past the inevitable defenses, it could strike a blow against the enemy which would cripple them. The host, and therefore the surgeon, would of course be destroyed but that was a small price to pay.

●●●つ●●

Shari awoke from her sweet dream to chaos. The remains of a man cut into several pieces lay scattered about the roost. Caro had staunched the bleeding and was attempting to bandage Mark's shattered shoulder. Juan was still attempting to comfort the hysterical Celine-Una, and Tanzo.... Tanzo was staring at the Denaari mnemonic helmet she held in her hands. Her own helmet lay discarded on the ground beside her. Of Deo and the little Yak there was no sign.

Tanzo stared at the Princess. "He chose... He chose to get killed for me. If only..."

"Sam?"

Tanzo couldn't speak. She just nodded.

"Where is Deo?" asked Shari.

Central replied. "The other human is some distance away, climbing towards the base of the geosynchronous line. I am unable to locate him precisely. We are still attempting revival of the man called Sam. His heart is too damaged to allow effective infusion with freezer buffering solutions."

"He's dead." Tanzo said it with finality and heartbreak. "He knew he was going to die. He was always right."

"Technically he is in fact dead. Surgeon organisms are keeping the brain supplied with Oxygen in a soluble solution. There is a 17.3 % chance of successful revival."

Shari was wary. Deo... why had he gone? Was it the head injury? Was it to escape this alien... computer? She couldn't think of it as a computer. It was a being in its own right. "Central... Why did the other human leave?"

"Evidence suggests that he may not have done so of his own will. The mnemonic helmet records a belief that he is possessed. Spectrographic analysis of a metal weapon carried by the man are identical to those typical of Sil manufacture. His naive assessment may literally be correct. He may be possessed by a Sil mechanical-organism"

"Where or what is a Sil?"

"They are our ancient enemy. They are the species who

destroyed the masters. In appearance they not unlike your species. The chameleon-wall over there is capable of displaying images. Look at it and you will see the Sil."

Only to the Denaari could the two species be described as similar. They were both bi-pedal and tailless. But the Sil had four arms, a blue skin and impressive fangs.

"The wrath incarnation of the Kali-Dewa." She'd seen the picture many times before. It was on the inside cover of the Arunachali Kaiita, the Holy New Veda-Gospel that Deo had always carried.

"You have encountered this species?" Central had found no such recognition in Juan's mnemonic record.

She explained as best she could. "What could he be trying to do? Or what is whatever is controlling him be trying to do?"

"He appears to be heading for the geosynchronous line. Perhaps he wishes to escape or thinks to damage it."

"What is it?"

"I can best explain it as a cableway to space. You should be familiar with them. Sixteen of them had been grown on planets of the Denaari Dominions, where gravity and planetary dimensions permitted. The carbon-carbon bond was not strong enough to allow us to use the cable elsewhere on larger worlds."

Shari felt sick. Sixteen... Tanzo had told her about sixteen worlds too... the evidence of war, the *only* evidence of war on the formerly Denaari worlds. The destruction must have been horrific. Even after more than 3000 years the scars of those bombardments could still be seen. "Have you been able to associate the names we use with the planets the Denaari colonized?"

"To a large extent. Juan Biacasta has studied celestial navigation, but unfortunately he spent the examination time patching the examining computer into the Space-station web. The data are therefore less extensive than they should be."

"Was the world we call Amritsar one of those which had this cableway?"

"Yes. Juan's memories indicate no knowledge of such a thing. It is virtually impossible that it should be unknown."

"The only other two planets names I can remember are Sarbia and Brandahar. Did they have lines too?"

"The planet you refer to as Brandahar, yes. Sarbia is not in my data-set."

"Amritsar, Bendic, Brandahar, Carab, Gehenna, Intigua II, Jyr,

Kammab, Lingua IV, Nambour, New Tambor, Sarbia, Starkadd, Tibetsi, Verena and Xi. The bombed worlds. Please, how is my Sam doing? Is there any change?" Tanzo had plainly been listening.

"Eleven of those names are those of planets with geosynchronous lines. The other five are not in my data set. The human called Sam is not progressing well. The surgeon animals inform me of considerable success in surgical repair. He should be recovering but the brain-output is still diminishing. It is almost as if the creature is trying to die. The surgeon creatures have resorted to electrical stimuli to try and reactivate it."

"He is dying! He knew he was going to die, so he is. He is a precognitive telepath. My God! Let me get to him! Please!"

"Very well. The risk of operative infection is small compared with the probability of brain-death at this point. Take the door to your right."

Tanzo ran out as fast as her short legs could carry her.

Shari was left thinking, "Could these alien enemies have somehow made this cableway explode?"

"No, the cable-beasts are not capable of explosion. But the cable is 16459 miles long. It hangs balanced between gravity and centrifugal force. Should the cable be somehow severed, the lower part will fall. Several thousand miles of falling superstrong cable will be more cataclysmic than any bomb. It will destroy many organisms in the equatorial zone. I, myself, am made up of many modules, but some of these will undoubtedly be destroyed. Then I will cease to exist as a coherent entity. I am dispatching all motile organisms to stop the Sil-carrier, by any means possible. I have vials of Sil-metal digesting virus on hand, but if need be the man you call Deo must be killed. You are confined here until this is done."

She went cold, but controlled it. The death of a world compared to the death of this one person had become unimportant. She knew it was wrong, but it was still true. She shrugged with a superb imitation of unconcern. "You have what Deo would call a time of grace to make your peace with your Goddess. I suggest you pray, or do whatever you do to prepare for death. Or you get me to the bottom of your cable with some of that virus. That man out there is an Arunachali. The mountains on Arunachal make this hill look like a plain. You'll never find him, let alone catch him. He is also an assassin. The best, I believe, of many thousands. Anything you send to stop him will die."

"This concurs with and explains some of the data from the mnemonic helmet he discarded. Very well. I will transport you to the cable base-station."

Two minutes later she left, clinging to something more like a gigantic arrow than an animal, with an unhappy Otto left behind. Then a surgeon beast now free from its mammoth labors on Sam came and took Mark Albeer off to attempt to repair his shoulder. Caro refused to be parted from him. That left Juan and Una-Celine alone to comfort Otto. Or not quite alone. The Stardog pupa below stirred in its pupal sleep. Felt them there and reached for their love.

●●C⊃●●

The tunnel was both deep and dark. But at the far end was a clear white light. Sam moved towards it, slowly, inexorably, despite all the efforts to drag him back. Then his fleeing mind was flooded with hers. And he knew abruptly that while he'd been certain he would die if he did what he had chosen to do, his vision of the future had included another variable: her actions. She had pulled him down as they had fallen. The shot which should have hit his head had struck him in the chest. And now... she would not let him die just because he believed he had to. She believed he *would* live. His body was being repaired. He *could* live. He received all this from the mnemonic crown that she'd thrust onto his head regardless of the extensive damage she caused in the process. Damage could be repaired. Life could not be brought back.

The clear white light receded and there was only darkness, with just the tiniest of glowing sparks.

Then darkness and one heartbeat. One EEG trace.

And then a second one. After a brief burst of electrical stimulus a second heartbeat too. Weak. Erratic. But beating its way up, up. Out of the darkness.

CHAPTER 23
FINALE

Even the saint may carry an assassin within his heart.

So too can an assassin carry the saint. We are what

we choose to be. Well, most of the time anyway.

From the collected sayings of Saint Sugahata the Reviled.

Deo resisted. Or wished to resist. He was powerless, however. The surgeon had not re-established full control over quite all of the muscles, but having briefly lost control in the roost, it was keeping a careful watch over its host. Still, minor muscles, like those of the face, vocal chords, and the toes of the left foot were uncontrolled.

Unwittingly Shari had lied. For the Denaari's creatures to catch Deo on a mountainside was virtually impossible. For them to catch the nano-mech surgeon and its unwilling host would have been easy. The Surgeon suspected, rightly, that Deo would kill himself rather than assist with the climb. The surgeon had all the skills, in theory, to move the host wherever it wished. In practice, over rough terrain, the Surgeon was slow and clumsy.

On the pupa-transport monorail inside the mountain Shari travelled far faster. The Geosynchronous cable base-station was typically Denaari-unfussy. A 36 inch thick cable, a cargo deck and a flight ramp. No frilly bits for the place from which the Denaari wings had stretched their wingtips to the furthest stars. From here and other equatorial localities seven other cables had taken the Denaari and their genetic engineering genius into space. At other places an equal number of down-cables had brought back the wealth of their vast Dominion. The cables were alive, self-aware and self-repairing.

Shari knew now from Central that if one cable should fall... the others would follow. None of the so-called 'bombed worlds' had had more than one cable. The devastation here would be of an unimaginable scale. It would mean final extinction for a myriad species, not least, the Stardogs. As a trivial aside it would almost certainly mean the death of herself and the other surviving castaways. Shari wasn't worried about that. She knew if she failed, it would be because she was dead. Central was saving its greatest strength for defense of the cable itself. She had been allowed the outer perimeter of the cargo deck and flight ramp. She had a small vial of the viral cocktail. As a standby, and last resort, the stuff was in her too. She'd swallowed a good half pint of it. She hoped that was why she was feeling a little queasy.

●●C⊃●●

The nano-mech surgeon was struggling. The energy demands of the host's body were high. The processing requirements of making the host climb a mountain, even by the easiest route, were high. The mountain was high too. And it still had to spare enough of its processing capacity to re configure its body, and to extract the various necessary elements from the host's body. Part of the host's liver had been redesigned to do just this, but right now the climb's metabolic demands on the host were slowing processing down. The surgeon with its nano-circuit brain was less than a 16th of an inch in total length. It had to climb the cable, it calculated, to at least 7 000 miles. This was going to take it months, using solar power, and patience. It would use those months to analyze the cable composition and develop a catalytic degenerative chemical treatment to cause failure of the cable-bonds. It was, in a way, the reverse of the way it was designed to deal with toxins introduced into the host's body. The nano-surgeon was rather self-satisfied about it all. It would, with a single blow, destroy its creators' enemy, or at least severely damage their home world.

●●C⊃●●

She spotted him. That puzzled her. True, he had taught her

258

as much as he could, but she knew he could move across broken terrain like a ghost. She slipped from her lookout on the launch-pad with the vial in her hand. The stuff was in a dilute acid-base, designed to etch skin. Once it was in the system... it would locate Sil-alloys within minutes, and then feed, using them, and replicate itself. She wished she had thought to loot Caro Leyven's gear for an atomizer. Just breathing it would have been enough, perhaps. She had to get to him, and get to him fast. She knew his chances of living through the last twenty yards to the cable were very small.

The nano-mech surgeon's visual input remotes detected her. The Nano-mech recognized the human. The implications were unpleasant. She had got here before him. How had she known where he was going? Well, the host was a superb killing machine. And if the host was destroyed before it could reach the cable base that would have little effect on the supertough nano-mech. It was not made of the frail flesh and bone of the host. It could survive pressures of up to 25 of these feeble gravities, and withstand immersion, acids and extremes of heat that would instantly turn the host to ash. But it was small. And covering ground-distance would be laborious without the host, now that it had adapted itself for cable climbing. It would take the host as close to cable-base as possible. The first step was to kill this human-woman. Whatever she held in her hand was probably a weapon. First it would destroy that.

The mountaintop was full of wind-sculpted rocks. She dodged among them. If she could get above him and pour the stuff over him... Abruptly they were face to face. If it were not for the croak of warning Deo uttered, she would have lost the hand that held the vial. As it was the knife shattered the vial she had instinctively parried with. The knife's razor edge peeled a long strip from her palm before it skittered along the stationer-fabric of her protective jacket. A few drops of the precious liquid ran down her fingers onto the raw flesh. The acid stung. Desperately she flicked the blood and acid at him. The nano-mech dodged the host back, perceiving some kind of threat. The last of the precious fluid fell onto the bare rock. Now she only had what was within her.

"Tanner." Deo used the out breath to say it, though nano-mech had clenched his teeth. It might as well have been Greek to the nano-mech, but it was a clear message to Shari. It brought tears to cloud her eyes. She blinked them away. She could not afford to cry yet. Garuda Tanner had been a bodyguard, who, when paralyzed in an ambush, had told his diminutive employer to fire at the attackers through his body. Deo was telling her to kill him.

Shari was unarmed, but she still wore her stationer-jacket. It would stop bullets and knife thrusts. It was no use against the laser-weapon. She hoped it wouldn't decide to use that. The nano-mech had in fact decided to save the laser for the final approach. It forced the host's body into a high speed knife attack.

Deo had long since established that he could move the toes of his left foot. He waited for the opportunity to use this tiny advantage best. He knew this strike for neck, so, at the crucial moment, the toes curled down, dragging. He closed his eyes, even though it appeared whatever possessed his body could see even when they were closed. He'd tried to kill himself earlier that way but had failed.

The slight stumble was enough. The blade struck her stationer-jacket protected body instead of her exposed throat. She chopped at the knife-arm, as he had taught her. The nano mech was faster, however. Her blow should have hit the knife-blade, which would have been enough to sever it. But Deo saw that the hand of the Dewa truly protected Shari. Her wrist intersected the knife just at the point where the frill-snake hydra's muscular twitch had taken a piece out of it. Instead of her losing the hand, the nano-mech lost the knife.

And she wrapped her arms around him. She was kissing him. His lips were still his own, and they opened and responded, even as the nano-mech brought his hands up to throttle her. Her mouth was full of blood from where she had bitten her own cheek and tongue. As those terrible hands squeezed, and the world blackened, she bit his lip, before frantically kicking herself free.

The nanomech drove the host forward, coming in for the kill. And one of the remote vision sensors on the host's nose suddenly died. It was only one virus, tinier even that the remote, and it only affected a few molecules of Sil-metal. They just happened to be part of the transmitter. But, finding food, the virus fed, and bred, and stripped more essential molecules out of the Sil-metal. A few other viruses in capillaries were transported elsewhere. A second remote died. The host decided to close its eyes again. And now the vision of the Nano-mech was indeed somewhat impaired. The kick aimed at the woman's head missed. She scrambled away.

The nano-mech decided to bypass her and press on. She'd poisoned the host, it decided. It must use the host while it still could. There were only a hundred yards to go. That was nothing to the host, but a long, long way to a mechanism less than a sixteenth of an inch high.

It forced the host to a run. The heart rate increased, and blood circulated faster. Of course the brain always gets the first and the best of the blood supply. Another vision remote went down. And the host tripped over a stone.

⊖⊖C⊃⊖⊖

She saw him stumble. But he was always as sure-footed as a cat! It must be working. Somehow she ignored her pain and ran after him. She had to slow him down, give the virus time to work, before he reached the kill-zone around the cable-base. But then she saw it was unnecessary. He blundered like a drunk in the darkness, his face wreathed in a broad smile. Then abruptly he collapsed, twitching epileptically. She ran to him. Would it try to kill him in a last act of defiance?

But deep within the Dagger of the Goddess, the last war between the Sil and Denaari had already been fought and lost by the Sil nano-mech. The fate of planets and empires had been sealed with a kiss.

EPILOGUE:

ENDS, ENDS AND BEGINNINGS

*You have failed to recognize that governments
possess a life of their own. They can best be
described as colonial organisms. All organisms have
one primary overriding need: to survive. The
organism you term 'a government' seeks both
immortality and reproductive success, as both of
these are ways of achieving the primary need. The
basic tenets of genetic engineering hold true for
governments too: For society to be served by
(instead of being the servant of) government service
must be intrinsic to the survival of the organism.*

The Denaari Bio-computer Central

At first it was good enough just to have survived. Good enough
to have a future. But eventually they had to decide what to do with
it. What to do with themselves, what to do with Central, and what
to do with several thousand other humans in Denaari-Biozoos.

There were the Neanderthals too. They could not just be left... especially with Central planning to repair the Biozoo. They were at odds with Central about this. The Biocomputer did not accept that a certain level of intelligence made you ineligible to be a zoo-specimen.

They had returned to the Roost-towers on the edge of the Stardog plain for their council. Sam was still too frail to be moved anyway. Una-Celine and Juan had reluctantly agreed to leave their new-hatched Stardog. They'd been on the long cable-ride up to the ballast asteroid at the far end to watch the creature take its first flight. They'd left it and the other four new-hatched Stardogs grazing in a defensive clump around the asteroid. The wild Spacedogs could still endanger small pups. Fortunately an adult who had been off surfing the new worlds had come back and was now guarding them.

For this was the situation. Many Stardogs had returned, their eggs had hatched, and they had mated and returned via the cable to space, cruising between the worlds discovered since the collapse of the Denaari dominion. Exploration continued. And there were many worlds that the Denaari had shunned, that humans would find more pleasant than any Empire world.

Central had reached its decision. There were fifteen crowns outstanding. A wingclaw of Denaari fives might survive somewhere. They might even have bred, and have hatchling upon hatchling. It was its duty to keep Denaar against their return. But the humans were allies and also victims of the Sil. And, although the species lay somewhere between the Sil and Denaari, it had decided that humans tended toward the Denaari viewpoint. It had been grown to serve. Too long now it had been purposeless. It would serve the humans too, given certain conditions.

There were eight of them, sitting, looking out onto the breeding-plain, in a Roost-room so like the one in which Martin Brettan had finally awakened the sleeper-side of her that it still made Una-Celine shiver. The ninth councilor, Central, listened from the walls.

"We can't go back," Shari said determinedly.

"But why not?" Caro asked. "I thought that was what we were trying to do?"

"Don't you see? New Stardogs, new worlds. We're a lifeline to the Empire and the League."

"Without Stardogs the Empire and the League will die, but so will a lot of people. All the stationers for starters. My mother and

father. All the riders. We can't just decide to run out on them."
Juan had grown up. He was no longer afraid to challenge the
Princess, just because of what she was. "With an independent
and unreachable base like this we could provide anti-toxin to all
the Stardogs in months, not years. Besides, I know my father
expected the Empire to start coming apart soon. The social-
scientists on Brandahar-station predicted it should start to happen
any day. If it has already happened, the stations, Stardogs and
riders will need us desperately. And if not... there are bound to be
more sleepers like Una was. The ISPCA work must be discovered
soon."

Shari was surprised at the vehemence of his declaration. But
then she had not shared the story of Una-Celine's life as he had.
She turned to Deo for support. He nodded. Not to her, but to Juan.
"It would be possible to return to Imperial space secretively,
according to Central."

"But Deo..."

"The scourge of the Holy Church must come to Arunachal. It
is not right that my people should be puppets to aliens. Especially
ones such as the Sil." Deo wore a Denaari mnemonic crown now.
Having his body stolen had led the Arunachali assassin to
question deeply the hate-training about the works of the Denaari.
He had studied the information Central had given him long and
with a great deal of thought. He was not a trusting man, but he
would not forgive the aliens for making him and his beliefs into a
pawn in their war. As he had said to Shari, he had been
indoctrinated from infancy to believe the Denaari intrinsically evil.
Had the Sil device merely asked him to destroy Denaar by taking
it to the cable base-station he would have done so. The realization
that the killings which he had taken to be holy compulsions had
been mechanically orchestrated was enough to make him
consider atheism... after revenge.

Central had modified its voice. They had all decided to
contribute mnemonic data to it. Now it was no longer Juan
speaking. It was shades of all of them. It spoke. "The orbiting
watcher reports that a dying Stardog has just come into the
system. It has released a metal object. Ground Control reports
that the object is sending radio messages. Shall I relay them
here?"

There was a silence. Then Shari nodded. They'd all been
there.

"..... Mayday Mayday. Can anybody hear me? Mayday."

"Can we transmit? Can we do anything for them?"

"With the Stardogs at the ballast satellite we can prevent their entering the atmosphere. I will send transmissions on the same frequency. Speak."

"We hear you, ship sending Mayday. Over."

"Station! Thank God. Where the hell am I? The Stardog has dropped us and the rider's flipped, poor bastard. We've got half a dozen badly injured. A bunch of Imperial system craft jumped us. Come and get us... please. Over."

"We'll do our best. What ship is that? Over."

"Free Systems Alliance Starbarge Salimar. Lieutenant Balsam, ranking survivor. I'm a space-marine and know bugger-nothing about spacecraft." There was a longer silence than could be accounted for by the transmission gap. Then a suspicion tinged voice came across the airwaves: "What Station is that? Are you Alliance or Imperial? Who *are* you?"

There was a silence in the roost-tower. Shari took a deep breath. "This is Denaar. There is no Space-Station here, and this is not an Empire world. I am Shari Tamar Alstenn-Wienan. Over"

There was a silence. A long silence. Then, "Did you say Denaar? You mean the Denaari motherworld.... Princess! Princess Shari? But you're supposed to be dead! The whole revolution started because you'd been murdered!"

"They tried, but failed, Lieutenant. And who the hell said you could start the revolution without me?"

●●●〇〇〇

Events shape decisions nine times out of ten. Mark Albeer did not want to return home, because he was a lowly bodyguard, and she was a Countess. Besides, outside of an arena of scarcity, he was sure she wouldn't look twice at him. Caro Leyven didn't want to go because Mark didn't. She didn't give a damn what his rank or station in life was. But if he didn't want to go back, she wouldn't. She'd run rather short of contraceptives, and hadn't yet told him that she was pregnant. Would he want her when she went bulgy? She hoped so, because now that she was pregnant, she found that what she really wanted was a baby.

Sam didn't want to go back... not to the life he'd led before, not with her. And he was not going without her. They had shared too much. Also, he was rather a different man after having died, however briefly. Still, the Yak did not part with their own easily. If he went back, sooner or later the family would find him. Although, by the sounds of it he could be reasonably safe on Arunachal...

Tanzo wasn't leaving Sam, and wasn't leaving Denaar, in that order.

Shari didn't want to return to her old life of fear and deceptions either. Even the hardships of being a castaway had been better. But events had caught up with all of them. And how they dealt with those events is another story.

APPENDIX 1
FUTURE HISTORY

2040: Joan Cheng makes contact with Stardogs. Human Diaspora begins

Hans Wienan forms Space Development and Control League with the blessing of virtually all major powers, with directors drawn from the ruling elite of the G8 families. League moves to contain Joan Cheng and isolate her. Only earthside contact brief meeting in RSPCA office, Knightsbridge, London. Thereafter access denied.

2041-2055: Exploration and contact with other Stardogs established. Hans Wienan personally recruits new pilots. Attempts by G8 to restrict access to space division of colonial rights. The Texas Rebellion is brutally put down. A secret message begging for help is sent to RSPCA official from Joan Cheng.

2055- 2103: The colonial period. With 432 worlds on Stardog routes found, colonial expansion outstrips Earth control. Wealth flows to Earth, little returns. But all flows both ways were taxed by the League. The League only revealed 130 of the less viable worlds to Earth, and colonized the others for a secret powerbase.

2104: The Brandahar rebellion. Stage-managed 'revolt' against Earth taxation. The League is 'forced' to assist rebels until Earthgov came up with better conditions for League, including rider recruitment legislation. Then the rebellion is brutally crushed.

2104-2130: Colonial retreat by Earthgov. Sybaritic life on Earth by rich is pestered by religious fanatics, convicts etc. which are dumped by Earthgov. They are sent off on League transports without Earthgov bothering to find out where they go. These malcontents are the source of the Imperialists future troops.

2131: The Post of Managing Director is declared hereditary. Earthgov protests. The great embargo of earth follows. It is stage-managed to leak just enough to keep Earth dependent on Interstellar trade. From this point the league League's own secret service begins to increasingly become all-powerful.

2135: End of the embargo with the 'Council of planets agreement.' This is a puppet council controlled by the League

2215: The Starkadd Coalition: An attempted and partially successful coup by the once-puppet planetary councilors. League control of planets in the coalition is shattered, although they still have control over Interstellar travel. The League panics. Planets are isolated, and Selim Alsten-Wienan, a rising young thug, is made into a new 'Emperor', and given access to mercenaries on former convict worlds of Carab, Selbourne, Canto and New Tambor.

2215-2393: With the League artfully manipulating supplies, the colony worlds are maintained (the League does not wish to lose its tax base, or labor pool) but militarily crippled while the new 'Empire' picks off worlds one by one.

2393: The fall of Phillipia, the most powerful, populous, mineral rich and verdant of colony worlds. Salman Alsten-Wienan II declared Supreme ruler of human Space.

2412: Last isolated open resistance brutally suppressed on isolated worlds such as Arunachal, and New Texas. Minor guerilla skirmishes continue.

2459: Declining numbers of League children forces the guild to take the step of recruiting new blood, with Managing-directorship and Security only being reserved for pure Wienan's.

2488: Turabi I, having arranged for the assassination of his father, ascends the throne.

2507: Now

APPENDIX 2
GENERAL BACKGOUND INFORMATION

The Denaari: A silica-bat, egg-laying semi-marsupial species. A wingspan of +-25 feet, a bodyweight of +- 30 kg. Bi-lateral species, ie: Two eyes (vision more into uv. spectrum), two ears, (higher frequencies), scent, pressure, and temperature sensors on either wingtip. A single magnetic sensitive barbel. A face like a walrus (with tusks for mineral-mining.) Dexterous toes (three) and wingclaws (3). Therefore they counted in 12's. Food: Able to use solar energy and also farmed crystals, grown in carefully maintained terraced mountain soup-ponds. Society: More structured than human society, with gene-dictated castes: Not warlike, but given to individual combat. These are largely ritual battles. Also practice genocide of 'non-humane' groups. On planet this meant nest-minders (egg-warmers) would withdraw their heat, and destroy gene lines of chicks, this had been extrapolated into passive extermination of non-emotive sentient alien species. They live/d in colonies in rookeries presided over by a senior egg-layer, Egg layers are bigger and higher fliers, (egg-layers are less emotive and more inclined to fight than eggwarmers) sex ratio 4 egg warmers to 1 egg layer. Female carries and lays the egg, the males warm egg, and then pouch-rear the young. The female can lay more eggs than males can rear.

Denaari homeworld: A tectonic hell-hole. A lot of mountains, some impossibly huge. A lot of volcanoes. Relatively little water. Geo-sculpting by wind rather than water erosion. Wind is almost incessant. G: 0.82 earth normal. Temperatures at Equator. 5-20o.

Temperature at poles in winter approx. -170o. Humanly habitable up to +- 30o line. No major seas or lakes. Few streams and small rivers from high altitude precipitation in Subtropical region of stable ancient plate chosen for launch-imprint center. Mountains are old and wind-worn on the plate at the launch center. The area was probably Denaari idea of the pits to live in. Vegetation, pre-dominion breakdown was non-existent. Life forms are numerous but only accidentally inimical. Many are modified ie. rock-burrower miners, Mineral drifters (tiny balloons deflating and burrowing into new mineral sources), solar sheeters which cover hillsides and collect sunlight, and then lay high-energy eggs (harvested by Denaari) before tumbleweeding. In the breakdown, Zoos and several botanical museums lost specimens, which have colonized a few wet bits. There is now a small carbon-based biota, including vicious predators. Now rock-leguvaan, bouncer-hyrax, jagular, and sliver-python, diamond-back pseudosnake, red-mottle thrush and feral peccary occur in the wild. The vegetation is more varied, plainly from a number of sources, occurring wherever there is water.

The Denaari Dominion: 432 worlds settled + homeworld. Ruled by gene-selected, gene modified castes, egg-layers ruled and decided, but egg-warmers controlled succession. A flying species, therefore they had no roads, but had communal rookery type dwellings. A society where gene-tailoring was second nature. Very little was ever made of inanimate material, but they shaped life-forms to their ends. Even a Denaari toothbrush was alive. They had a Buddhist-like life-religion about animal forms. Originally no plants lived on the mother planet. Some of the worlds of the Dominion also had no carbon-based lifeforms, and these were most popular and largest settlements. Early settlers cleared vegetation and altering climates before the vegetation / carbon-animal relationship was understood. Worlds were selected for lower G, colder, drier thinner atmosphere, preferably with abundant mountains for eyries. Numerous humanly habitable worlds (ocean-planets, jungle worlds, hot worlds, higher G worlds) known, but were not colonized or on Dog-routes. Earth only had an observation station, a small one, because of intelligent life there. It was not considered suitable for colonization. Alien societies were assessed and if inhumane: prevented from attaining space travel or destroyed. They were assessing earth, when 'plague' destroyed them in part of a conflict with the Sil.

The Imperium: The first Emperor, Selim Alsten-Wienan, was little more than a figurehead, a front-man for the League's opposition to the Starkadd Coalition of planetary Councilors (which itself had begun life as a league puppet). However some of the worlds he drew his mercenaries from would change the nature of the conquest. He originally styled himself as The Leader of the Peoples' Liberation Struggle for a Democratic Federation of Planets. In the first load of those who had been forcibly settled on Selbourne were a small lunatic fringe of plotters from Earth, almost all of whom could be found in the pages of the now meaningless *Almanac de Gotha*. In a cargo which was otherwise composed of unassociated dregs of Europe they had proved the most cohesive group. Before later ships of convicts had arrived they had assumed total feudal control, which they maintained, destroying new rivals, or, if these were too strong, raising them to the peerage. The bickering fiefdoms and endless postage-stamp duchies had provided a rich supply of younger sons to make skilled officers. Canto, one of the main sources of cannon fodder, also had a strong feudal-type robber-baron system. The officers wanted payment not in money but in hereditary fiefdoms. The League, to whom the form of politico-social system was unimportant, as long as they maintained control, was happy to oblige. Of course their man had to have a higher title, that was all. With the children of Selim intermarrying with the Selbourne peers, the dream of the original Almanac de Gotha rebels of a return to rule by divine right or at least by genetic right was achieved. Names were assumed from the Holy Roman Empire. The aspirations they brought were of course passed on to the future emperors, reaching its peak in the rule of the Emperor Vespasia. The Empire had known nearly a century of relative peace and steady increase in bureaucracy. By the start of the reign of Turabi I, the system was groaning from increasing taxation and the employment of nearly a third of all people in the civil service. The army, once powerful, had become little more than a brutal riot-police for suppressing the increasingly restive populace.

Riders: projective-receptive Telempaths. Possibly an innate human ability, it only tends to be expressed by sensitive, intelligent, emotionally deprived, usually insecure, often unhappy and physically abused people. Their emotional sensitivity is heightened if they have communication problems. The League began with natural cases but very soon resorted to physically imposing conditions including deafening of riders. Selection was vastly refined in 2130 with the discovery of emotional-moss, a

Denaari relic, a species of emotional echoing silicate-animal, little more than a fuzzy patch which changed color when in the presence of empathic-projectives. This stuff remained one of the trade secrets of the League, not even available to the Empire, who thus had to resort to more brutal methods of finding sleepers to infiltrate into the riders. A mechanical device, less effective and sensitive, was devised by the Satellite folk. Armed with this the ISPCA had been attempting to find rider-recruits before the League, and provide shelter for them.

The riders were trained in schools where the conditions to heighten their misery were deliberately engineered. From these conditions they were taken to rider compounds, then into space and introduced to their dogs. Thereafter while the life of a rider on shipboard or in the spartan compounds was no easier there was an end to actual physical abuse. Riders were still held in thrall by the toxin canisters placed in the missile launch tube and linked to the EEG and heart monitor of the League agent who rode with them. On a normal ship League and rider quarters and airlock were wholly separate from the other people onboard. The rider would actually sit, suited, between the Stardog's eyes. Early riders had lost themselves, dog and spacecraft, by running out of air or freezing to death. Now hookah lines pump warm air to them and jumps are restricted to short hops. In space, but out of jump the League operates a cell-system restricting contact.

Sil: Warlike, xenophobic and totally mechanistic culture on world close to Arunachal. Engaged in active aggression against first Denaari explorers, and foresaw rapid conquest of the same. The Denaari genetic engineers tailored copper-devouring bacterium which caused famine and near-total destruction of society, but the Sil turned to the use nylons, plastics, and a new special alloy to build silicate/chitin complex disintegrators which they let loose on starlanes. The Denaari replied with a sterilization plague virus: This gave Sil years to develop own mechanical 'plague' of mutable self-replicating nano-circuit brained microscopic robots and send it out. The only Sil colony was on Arunachal, a Denaari-mapped for colonization world. The Sil colony hid itself successfully from the Denaari, but with mechanical destruction of Sil Homeworld, was isolated and gradually became run down. The Sil colonist numbers declined due to a lack of trace elements. The last survivors did meet Humans before the species became extinct. Intervening in the human conflict they used their appearance to give rise to a new religion, which preached undying hate for Denaari.

Stardogs: originally feral with limited wormhole surfing capacity. Silicate, sheetlike, filamentous, like vast bearskins when feeding or drifting (top- fibre-optic skin for effective light collection, bottom-modified cilia for mineral ingestion). In flight they change their shape to allow optimal micro-rocketry positioning and acceleration or braking. They can build up and lose velocity by minor flatulent rocketry shifting mass with inertia. Often they assume a half-open umbrella-shape. They have vastly complex nerve-nets with endless local nodes and billions of inputs. Their eyes are large and telescope-like, and bifocal. They have brilliant visual imaging and memory. A low intelligence, but a vast memory.

They have huge canine-tusks from their feral pack status-maintaining origins. They ingest small asteroids or leach minerals from larger ones, and use solar energy to feed. They enjoy titbits of certain chemicals. Enjoy filament combing with a food/comb. Only visit worlds of the long dead Denaari Dominion. Because of the Sil plague they may not return to the Denaari Homeworld, which they are genetically imprinted to do to breed. They have long lives, but need males (planet-bound) to mate. Fertilization occurs at the end of the larval (planet-bound) stage, when females are transported into space. Eggs are laid after crash-down. (Original feral species, both sexes flew, but the Denaari, to control numbers, removed flight capability from males. This also assured that females were available for route imprinting. There is a huge imprinting center near breeding grounds. Stardogs can live a maximum of 4000 years, therefore those in service in the Human Empire are nearing the end of their natural lifespan. At the time of this story there are about 2200 Stardogs in human space. Initially there were more than 3700 when humans were first encountered. The number of Stardogs is the main limit to interstellar commerce. Most Stardogs used to live +- 200 years, normally linking their lifespan to a Denaari egg-warmer. At the start of the plague there were about 40 000.

The Wienan League: Hans Wienan had strong political connections, which got him into space. Quick thinking, he saw the potential advantage of Stardog control. Using Joan Cheng's inarticulateness, he claimed credit and sole control for himself, silencing the rest of the crew with bribes of power and wealth, or resorting to outright assassination. He moved rapidly with his powerful political connections to isolate her and to control her, after early attempts, by Wienan and several pet scientists, to communicate with the Stardog had failed. On establishing that Joan Cheng could communicate and take the dog star-hopping and that there were several other 'biological starships' (the name never caught on. Stardogs is what they remained) out there. Wienan then set about working out why she could. Intuitively, he decided it was some kind of emotional bonding, and brought a group of children from an abused children's refuge up to the Stardog. He located immediately another communicator who had remarkably similar psychological characteristics to Joan Cheng. Thus with the collusion of senior government officials the interstellar space development League was formed with a board drawn from the ruling elite, who actively and secretively recruited Stardog riders. These unlucky individuals simply ceased to exist as far as the populace of earth was concerned. Control over them was maintained as the powers that be had no desire to lose potential control of the starlanes to 'mentally unstable individuals'. The League was given *carte blanche* to recruit and control the riders with the political heads of earth's governments thinking that they in turn could control the League. They were wrong. From the first Hans Wienan conspired to obtain total control. Those he could not blackmail, he bribed, the one he could neither blackmail nor bribe he married. The League released information to the G8 about 130 of the 432 of the discovered worlds — The least promising 130. These it opened up to colonization and exploitation at a small price which was steadily and slowly increased. The remaining worlds the League began colonizing and ruling as its private fief.

With sole control and understanding of how the Stardogs were managed the relatively tiny League with some twenty thousand members, agents and sycophants maintained an increasing stranglehold on trade and movement between the stars. Increasingly the organization became two arms, those who rode the dogs with the riders, and those who conspired to maintain the status quo. The formation of the security arm of the agency from fifteen years before the Brandahar rebellion, marks the beginning of the golden period of the League, which ended in the reign of Vespasia (2403- 2416). Thereafter the Empire began actively attempting to succeed from the League, and through sheer enormity had, to some extent, managed

The League, long aware of declining Stardog numbers have a cloning project off New Tambor: Aims: to create a Stardog that

Leaguesmen can control mechanically, a Stardog which is not imprinted with a fixed library of stars.

Yak-Syndicate: Criminal guild controlling crime on most worlds. Run 'smugglers' but are unaware that these are controlled by League. League profits from illicit traffic in drugs, slaves, etc. Hierarchical (based on Mafiosi) with Russian-Mongol underclass, ruled by Chinese-Italian overclass. Loyalty enforced brutally. Upper echelon bought titles etc. Attempted to penetrate the Empire's power core, but resisted by Imperial secret service who uses them. Their use has been too pervasive and the Empire has decided they're getting too much of a share of the lifeblood of society. One parasite does not easily tolerate another.

ABOUT THE AUTHOR

Dave Freer lives on a remote island off the coast of Australia, with his wife Barbara, several dogs, cats, pigs and chickens, in a sort of chaotic experiment into self-sufficiency, supplemented by a hunter-gatherer lifestyle.

He the author or co-author of some 19 novels (hard to keep track) including SLOW TRAIN TO ARCTURUS, which was listed as a Wall Street Journal sf bestseller. Various other books have been on Locus bestseller lists. He is also the author of a large number of shorter works. For a complete list and work will be available nowhere else see the official Dave Freer website, Davefreer.com. For more about his bizarre life and links to other sites, see his Amazon Author's page.

www.ingramcontent.com/pod-product-compliance
Lightning Source LLC
Chambersburg PA
CBHW070853180626
46817CB00003B/759